MASTER

OF

RESTLESS

SHADOWS

BOOK ONE

GINN HALE

MASTER
OF
RESTLESS
SHADOWS

BOOK ONE

GINN HALE

BLIND
EYE
BOOKS

blindeyebooks.com

Master of Restless Shadows
 by Ginn Hale
Copyright © 2019 by Ginn Hale
Published by: **Blind Eye Books** 1141 Grant Street Bellingham, WA. 98225

Edited by Nicole Kimberling
Copyedit by Megan Gendell
Proofreading by Alan Williams

Ebook design by Michael J. DeLuca

Cover Illustration by Zaya Feli
Cieloalta city map by Rhys Davies
Cover Design by Dawn Kimberling
Interior design and typesetting by Dawn Kimberling

This book is a work of fiction and as such all characters and situations are fictional. Any resemblances to actual people or events are coincidental.

First Edition October 2019
ISBN: 978-1-935560-63-0
Library of Congress Control Number: 2019944115

To Nicole who was always on Atreau's side. To A. for loving spiders and to J. for your boundless energy and fearless leaps.

Also huge thanks to Gwen and Zaya for everything!

CONTENTS

CADELEON &
SURROUNDING NATIONS

Usane

Radulf
Lands

Labara

Rauma

Ceiloalta

CADELEON

Anacleto

N

S

Salt Islands

CIELOALTA

SHARD OF HEAVEN

GADO BRIDGE

PERALORO RIVER

MARKET SQUARE

SOUTH GATE

1 CROWN HILL
2 LORD QUEMANOR'S MANSION
3 SAGRADA ROYAL PALACE
4 COUNT ODALIS' HOME
5 DUKE OF GAVADO'S HOUSHOLD
6 ROYAL BISHOP'S HOUSEHOLD
7 RED STALLION

8 GREEN DOOR
9 FAT GOOSE
10 CIRCLE OF WISTERIA
11 KNIFE MARKET
12 LORD NUMES' HOUSE
13 SAVIOR'S CHAPEL

CHAPTER ONE

As Narsi rode through the towering city gates of Cieloalta, a sense of great accomplishment swept over him. Twenty days of road dust caked his body, hair and clothes. His dappled mare's coat looked gray as clay. He wasn't certain which of the two of them smelled worse or felt more relieved to see the renowned beauty of the city's public fountains. After years of study, planning and longing, he'd at last reached the capital.

Merchants in painted carriages rolled past, while herdsmen drove swine, cattle and sheep around the statuary, likely en route to the famous market grounds. Narsi dismounted, rinsed his face and allowed his tired mare to drink. From a column at the center of the fountain rose a stone sculpture of three stallions and a single soaring eagle. The horses Narsi recognized: *Faith*, *Honor* and *Strength*. But he couldn't recall from which sermon the eagle originated. "Heights of Bravery," from the *Book of Trueno*? Or was it "The Rise of Courage," from the *Epistles of Bishop Seferino*?

It hardly mattered, for the sheer beauty of the carvings, coupled with the relief of fresh water, awed him. His sense of wonder only grew as he turned around, taking in the towering, angular Cadeleonian architecture that lined the wide, straight thoroughfare. Even in this modest quarter, building after building boasted blue-washed walls, bright yellow roof tiles and downspouts in the shapes of horses. Far across the river, royal emblems and colors blazed still more brilliantly from the royal palace. There immense lapis-lazuli-inlayed walls supported gilded spires where dozens of indigo flags bearing the stark white form of the Sagrada stallion fluttered. Overhead, flocks of white messenger doves moved like clouds across the bright summer sky.

"It's just as Lord Vediya describes it in his memoirs," Narsi told his horse. "*A royal city made so bright and proud that it would challenge the heavens if only they would listen.*"

Narsi grinned and stroked his mare's jaw. She ignored him and kept drinking.

He felt as if he'd stepped into one of the thrilling epics that he so loved to read. He wondered suddenly if he might be able to find the plaza where the notorious swordsman Elezar Grunito had fought duel after bloody duel before going on to battle monsters in the savage northlands. Or better still, could he hunt through the narrow lanes surrounding the opera houses to find the green door of the kaweh tavern where Lord Vediya had penned so many of his daring, brilliant memoirs?

Or should he head closer to the river where a veritable palace full of exotic and medicinal herbs were maintained by royal decree? The doors opened to anyone bearing the silver signet of a trained physician, and he wore his newly cast ring proudly on his right hand.

Cieloalta was the city where the best and brightest people flocked to find the patronage of princes, dukes, even the king, and where a young man like himself stood a chance of meeting them all.

"Make way, you brown bastard," a sunburned pig herder shouted, and Narsi reflexively stepped aside as the red-faced man and his squealing charges shoved their way past. Narsi's mare snorted and stamped when a sow snuffled too near her legs. The herder paused to eye Narsi with the disgusted expression of a man confronted by a two-headed lamb.

Tall even for a Cadeleonian, Narsi's big hands and broad shoulders made the rest of his slim figure appear all the more gangly and adolescent. And he supposed the streaks of gray road dust and crusts of mud had lent a particularly ashy pallor to his dark skin. Likely, neither the dirt nor sleeping in a bedroll on the roadside for weeks had imbued his curly black hair with any semblance of civility either. All and all, he probably looked like he'd stolen his horse, bags and gray coat from a real physician whom he'd throttled in the woods. But Narsi doubted that this scruffy pig herder was taking exception to his unkempt appearance.

His recent travels had familiarized Narsi with this particular reaction. Still, it was discomforting to be gawked at as if he were freakish beyond imagining. Even rural Cadeleonians living this far north had to have encountered Haldiim—or at least bands of nomadic Irabiim—and they saw one another day in, day out. So Narsi didn't understand why they so often appeared taken aback when laying eyes upon his mixed features. Did they really think it utterly impossible for a Cadeleonian and a Haldiim to fall in love and produce a child? Or was such a union so blasphemous that they could not help but stare at the progeny?

Narsi frowned at the dozens and dozens of Cadeleonians all around him on the street, taking in the uniformity of their stout bodies, pale faces and straight, dark hair. It had been at least a week since he'd sighted anyone as dark-complected or lanky as himself, much less as blond or light-eyed as his mother had been. He didn't want to admit it, but that absence gnawed at his initial excitement and inspired a sudden feeling of unease.

But he couldn't let the sheer number of Cadeleonians surrounding him intimidate him. The swineherd shot him an even more suspicious glance before hurrying his pigs up the road to the butchers' square.

"Better to be a traveler he disdains than the piglet he smiles upon and leads to slaughter," Narsi murmured to himself.

He wondered if the thought was worth jotting down in his shabby little diary.

Likely not.

He'd just swung back up into his saddle and started down the crowded road when he spied a mounted man clad in the black and violet robes of a Cadeleonian priest riding toward him.

"Berto?" For just a moment Narsi hadn't recognized his childhood friend. He looked so distinctly Cadeleonian now, with his formal robes, short-cropped hair and dapper cap. He'd filled out handsomely.

"Narsi, Lord bless me! You've grown even taller!" Berto's broad grin transformed his stern face back into the beaming countenance of the twelve-year-old classmate that Narsi remembered from when they'd both lived in the chapel of the Grunito household.

"You haven't been waiting here for me, have you?" Narsi asked. He'd had no way to send ahead and inform Father Timoteo of when exactly to expect him, and yet it seemed an unlikely piece of luck that Berto should happen by just as he passed through the south gate.

"Father Timoteo asked the duke's couriers to watch for you on the King's Road. We've been kept abreast of your progress every other day or so."

"And here I'd presumed myself traveling alone and unknown across a vast, strange land," Narsi commented and Berto laughed. How like Father Timoteo to find a way to watch over him even across the miles of mountains and wilderness.

"Has the Holy Father kept well?" Narsi asked.

Berto's expression sobered.

"His spirit is stronger than ever, but his body . . ." Sorrow showed so plainly upon Berto's face that it alarmed Narsi.

"Has he kept anything down?" Narsi gripped his mare's reins. There was no time to tarry if Father Timoteo had succumbed to grippe again. "I've brought powdered cloudroot but we may need to brew bluedust—"

"No, no. He's not collapsed again. He's only been restless lately. Not eating or sleeping as he ought to. Nothing new." Berto's long-suffering expression eased a little. "But he'll be better once you're with him. You always know how to convince him to show himself a little kindness."

"That's less my doing than my mother's recipe for velvet soup. I can always tempt him to eat a little more than he thinks he needs." Narsi tried not to let his pleasure in being capable of moving Father Timoteo show. All too often people jumped to the wrong conclusion when they noticed Narsi's resemblance to the priest. The last thing Narsi wanted was to burden Father Timoteo with another bout of cruel rumors of some illicit affair with Narsi's mother.

"So how have you been?" Narsi asked Berto. He noted that his friend's robe still bore the silver insignia of a scholar rather than the violet of a priest. He'd not yet taken the final holy vows of obedience and celibacy. "Is life as a scripture scholar in Cieloalta all you hoped?"

Berto laughed but his expression struck Narsi as bitter.

"I'll tell you all while we ride." Berto cast a wary glance back at one of the uniformed city guards, who slowly strolled from the shadow of the city gates toward them. The guard wore a captain's epaulettes. His hand rested on his sword hilt.

"Of late, the city guards have not been overly fond of men in priestly colors," Berto murmured. "If relations between Prince Sevanyo and the royal bishop worsen we may well witness open brawling in the streets. The bodies of two decapitated priests were found here at the south gate only a week past and a novice nun went missing only two days ago."

Narsi glanced again to the city guard and realized that the man's glower was aimed at Berto. Narsi and Berto quickly reined their horses forward.

Berto led the way down a narrow lane that was refreshingly free of livestock. As they wove between carriages and oxcarts, Narsi inquired about the deteriorating relations between Prince Sevanyo and his brother, the royal bishop, but Berto refused to be drawn out on the subject. Instead, he entertained Narsi with descriptions of the odd and amusing occurrences in his life since he'd followed Father Timoteo to the Duke of Rauma's palatial residence.

"I've actually met the duke several times now, though the first encounter embarrassed me to the core. I somehow mistook him for one of those good-looking grooms that are so fashionable just now," Berto said, grimacing. "I handed him my horse's reins. And then he humored me by actually accepting them! It wasn't until I decided to tip him for seeming so attentive to my mare that he explained that he didn't need my pennies, as he owned all of Rauma."

"I have heard that Lord Quemanor is quite strange in his own way,"

Narsi commented.

"In many ways," Berto responded. "But he and his wife have been very welcoming to Father Timoteo and myself." Berto told him how he'd ingratiated himself with the duke's elegant wife after driving off a mangy black cat that had been stalking Lady Quemanor's parrot. Then he went on to describe his single sighting of Count Radulf's towering, flame-haired sister, who had sailed from the wilds of northern Labara apparently just to horrify the Cadeleonian court with her casual references to her brother's taste in men and her own prowess as a witch.

Even in the Haldiim District of the city of Anacleto, people rarely spoke so blatantly of attractions or practices that transgressed Cadeleonian holy law—certainly never to Cadeleonians.

"Did the royal bishop have her arrested?" Having just read Lord Vediya's scandalous memoir recounting his time in Count Radulf's court, Narsi felt an attachment to the count's young sister. Lord Vediya had brought her to life as proud, vulnerable and so relentlessly loyal to her brother that Narsi couldn't help but think protectively of her.

"He's decried her as a heretic and has dispatched the infamous Captain Yago to throttle her," Berto replied casually, and Narsi supposed it showed how common noble machinations were here in the royal city that the plotted murder of a nineteen-year-old girl didn't alarm his friend. "But Prince Sevanyo's fourth son, Jacinto, is rumored to have been enchanted—perhaps literally—by the girl and is suspected of sheltering her from his uncle's thugs."

"Even a person so lofty as the royal bishop can't really be so rash as to order the murder of a foreign dignitary, can he?"

"Who truly knows?" Berto shrugged. "Courtiers' gossip is half exaggeration and half lies. Most of mine is secondhand on top of that."

As they rode down the narrow street a woman with her hair tucked into a matronly snood dumped a pitcher of murky water from a second-story window, while across the way a little girl gleefully tossed down marigold flowers. Narsi caught one and felt several others fall into the dark curls of his hair. The girl gave a startled squeal and then disappeared back into her house.

"Already charming the ladies," Berto commented dryly.

"It's a wonder I'm still single," Narsi replied. "You know, I had expected that you and Father Timoteo would have been received into the royal bishop's retinue by now."

"Oh, we were invited last fall. Bishop's robes had already been cut, fitted and embroidered for Father Timoteo." Berto scowled out to the shining gold of a distant towering steeple. "But then at supper the royal bishop brought up his plans to suppress the revival of Haldiim religious practices in Anacleto." Berto sighed. "I think he truly expected Father Timoteo to simply agree with his condemnations."

"The royal bishop hadn't encountered Father Timoteo before then, had he?" Narsi met Berto's gaze and they exchanged a smile of sad understanding.

Father Timoteo practiced brutal self-denial and was truly devout, but he also recognized miracles even when they occurred outside the consecrated halls of Cadeleonian chapels. He readily accepted Haldiim and Mirogoths into his household and collected and studied holy texts regardless of their origins. In his own way Father Timoteo could be as much of a radical as his infamous younger brother, Elezar.

Perhaps more so, since Father Timoteo supported his assertions with scripture that not even the royal bishop could condemn.

"They argued and then the royal bishop basically turned us out into the street with nothing," Berto replied. "Thankfully, the Duke of Rauma took us in the very next morning."

"And you immediately mistook him for a groom?" Narsi commented.

"Yes. You have no idea how mortified I still feel about it." Berto drew his mount to a halt at the top of a hill. He pointed beyond the surrounding squares of neat homes and boisterous businesses, past the two huge stone bridges, to vast tracks of ornately planted grounds and what looked to Narsi like dozens of gilded palaces. "There to the west is the Sagrada Palace, and just east of it is the duke's household, where we're bound. And if you look down there you'll see the Peraloro River and the Shard of Heaven."

Narsi followed Berto's direction and was amazed anew. From the middle of the river rose the Shard of Heaven. Four furlongs wide and nearly as long, the bright blue stone rose high above the turbulent waters. Huge seams of shining gold flashed as the afternoon sun caught the angular facets of the massive crystal. Truly it did look as though a piece of blue sky filled with rays of golden sun had fallen from the heavens and turned to stone.

A bridge arched out from each riverbank as if to lash the Shard of Heaven down. The huge chapel squatting atop it would likely have looked resplendent anywhere else, but compared to the effortless grandeur of the stone, all the temple's gilded buttresses, statues and spires struck Narsi as garish.

"*How rare and wise is that man who recognizes the divine without crushing it beneath pulpits and palisades.*" Narsi quoted Lord Vediya, feeling he now understood the author's words.

"Tell me that you aren't still quoting that poxy whoremonger Atreau Vediya day and night." Berto cast him a disappointed glance.

"He's Lord Vediya to you," Narsi corrected, though he felt absurdly pompous the moment the words were out of his mouth.

"Fourth son of a destitute baron and some Labaran trollop." Berto rolled his eyes. "His nobility runs as deep as my foreskin. Even he doesn't call himself anything but Atreau."

Narsi resisted the urge to point out that the man's books were all proudly attributed to Lord Atreau Inerio Vediya.

He and Berto agreed on most subjects, but Lord Vediya remained a glaring exception and had been since eleven years prior when they had both met the man. Berto blamed Lord Vediya for the pregnancy and departure of a maid who'd always secreted him sweets. Narsi wished that he could have assured Berto that Lord Vediya had not been with the maid that night, but to do so Narsi would have had to reveal how he knew.

That would be dangerous for both himself and Lord Vediya. So, Narsi kept the knowledge to himself along with his vivid memory of Lord Vediya's warm lips brushing his own—the scent and taste of the other man melding into the swell of distant music and the deep shadows of the dark garden of the Grunito townhouse in Anacleto.

"You know that he was nearly executed for publishing his latest obscene epic?" Berto asked, but then he went on. "The bishop's men-at-arms and the royal city guards joined forces for the first time in probably a generation just to scour the city for every copy of that filthy book and burn them all."

Again Narsi decided to keep his mouth shut. It would only annoy Berto to know that an entire library of Lord Vediya's works had been translated and published in the Haldiim District of Anacleto. A copy of the contraband tome lay snuggly packed in the top of one of Narsi's saddlebags at this very moment. *Five Hundred Nights in the Court of the Scarlet Wolf*. Like Lord Vediya's previous book, *In the Company of the Lord of the White Hell*, it recounted his part as well as the roles of his friends in historic plots and battles.

The books were also famed for their detailed and rather extensive erotic passages.

Narsi adored them all the more for those, but wasn't so foolish as to say so to Berto.

"Atreau keeps company with gamblers, degenerates and Salt Islanders," Berto grumbled. "And he calls Father Timoteo 'Tim' and refuses to attend chapel regularly, nor is he often sober when he does appear."

"He's still in attendance in the duke's household then?" Narsi asked, as if he'd not known.

"He's laid claim to a suite of rooms, if you can call that attendance." Berto shook his head. "What good he does the duke I couldn't say. He's certainly perverted a number of the pages and servants. And on top of all that I suspect that he gave one of his obscene books to Delfia—"

"Delfia?" Narsi broke in before Berto could work himself up into another rant against Lord Vediya.

"Hadn't I mentioned her?" Berto's expression brightened all at once. "She's the sister of the dance and fencing instructor, Master Ariz. The instructor is plain as a clod of dirt, but his sister . . ." Berto's gaze drifted as he seemed to struggle to find a word that could sum up this Delfia. "Well, she's not young, but not too old. Not exactly a beauty. But when she's speaking and laughing and dancing, she's so alive and vibrant she just lights up a whole room. You'll understand once you meet her."

"I look forward to it," Narsi responded.

They rode on, descending past the shops belonging to woodcarvers, carpenters and smiths of all kinds. Berto pointed out the craftsman who'd made his silver prayer beads and another who'd created Father Timoteo's spectacles. Narsi noted the designs of holy gold stars painted over both doors. Other shops displayed the rampant royal stallion, but none bore both symbols together. The entire city, it seemed, had taken sides in the battle of church against state.

By the time they crossed the bustling Gado Bridge, afternoon shadows had spread and the pale crescent of the moon lit the twilight-blue sky. Narsi's initial surge of excitement at having reached the capital had faded like the sunlight, and now the fatigue of twenty days of travel began to claim him. Berto maintained a pleasant running commentary on the resplendent buildings and spectacular fountains of the wealthy north side of the city. Narsi suppressed a yawn and tried to focus his attention on yet another gilded Cadeleonian mansion.

Just then a figure seemed to break from the cover of the imposing hedges of hawthorn. Narsi squinted into the shadows of the hedge searching after the skulking figure, but now he saw no one.

"Here at last." Berto called his attention to a white pebble drive that led to a massive black gate. Beyond that the imposing silhouette of a vast mansion loomed like a small mountain. Pots burgeoning with yellow roses lined the drive and perfumed the cool air. As they made their way up, a courier wearing the royal colors raced past them and out to the wide streets. Another rider trailed far behind them, looking dour in his orange velvet doublet. Perhaps he resented the heraldry of his ancestors burdening him with colors that lent him an unmistakable resemblance to a ripe pumpkin.

The two men-at-arms standing guard before the broad gates leading into the courtyard wore gold and green liveries and held deadly-looking pikes. But unlike so many others Narsi had seen, they smiled as he and Berto drew near. Their high brows and long noses made Narsi think they were father and son.

He and Berto both dismounted and Berto greeted the guards by name. He introduced Narsi and spent a moment catching up and speculating about the royal courier who had just departed.

"It could be that at last the royal bishop has decided to allow his father, the king, to pass into holy immortality and thus make way for Prince Sevanyo's coronation," Berto suggested.

The importance of that event had just registered in Narsi's mind when a motion across the courtyard caught his attention. A well-built man stepped from the shadows, leading a gray horse toward them. Narsi's heart instantly began to pound in his chest as he recognized Lord Vediya. He was not as Narsi remembered, and yet Narsi knew him without a doubt even through the fading light.

He remained just as tall as Narsi recalled, but over the years his slender body had filled into the solid bulk of a grown man. His pale skin was deeply tanned, and his once soot-black long hair now appeared streaked as wood grain from sun and weather. His rumpled, loose clothes conveyed nonchalance bordering upon sloppiness, but his expression remained bright and alert.

He smiled as he drew near their party and Narsi couldn't keep himself from smiling back, though no sign of recognition lit Lord Vediya's countenance.

Closer up, Narsi could see that a decade of travel, war and debauchery had carved the lines of those experiences into the handsome planes of Lord Vediya's face. He looked older than his thirty years. Wrinkles edged his eyes and mouth, but to Narsi they seemed to convey character. A deep crease clearly marked his habit of arching one brow, while another etched the curve of his crooked smile.

Berto glanced up just as Lord Vediya drew alongside them. His condemning glare provoked a lewd grin from Lord Vediya, who lazily traced the sign of the holy star over his silver belt buckle by way of greeting. The two guards simply nodded to Lord Vediya, neither of them bothering to acknowledge his rank with a bow.

Lord Vediya appeared utterly unconcerned with any of them. He narrowed his eyes, focusing on something in the distance, or perhaps simply in contemplation of his evening's journey. His hand gripped his mount's rein. In a moment he'd ride away, just as he had eleven years earlier. And Narsi would be left behind again because he lacked the courage to simply speak.

Narsi's pulse raced and his hands felt clammy. Berto was going to be so disappointed in him, but he had to act, had to say something.

"Lord Vediya," Narsi called, and to his relief the other man stopped.

Narsi quickly dug into his saddlebag and drew out the book he'd pored over throughout his travels. Flowing Haldiim script curled in an elegant arch over the wolf embossed into the red leather cover.

Narsi didn't look to see Berto's expression or those of the guards. He rushed five paces to Lord Vediya's side.

"I've been reading your memoir and very much enjoyed the writing—I felt almost as if I was there with you when the demon lord awoke. The way you captured the chill and darkness of the city as that gigantic, fiery serpent rose up over the rooftops—it was beautiful and terrible all at once . . ." Even as the breathless words rushed out of him, Narsi felt like an utter fool. He hadn't sounded this flustered and ebullient when he'd been an awestruck twelve-year-old. "I was hoping that you would do me the honor of signing my copy for me?"

He had no doubt that behind him Berto cringed in embarrassment, but he thrust the tome at Lord Vediya, who took the book and smiled warmly.

"I'd not seen the Haldiim translation yet. It looks beautifully made." He studied the cover for a moment, then glanced to Narsi. "Have you a graphite stylus?"

"Yes. Of course!" Narsi silently cursed himself for not thinking of that before requesting to have the book signed. As he rifled through his saddlebag for one, he felt incredibly aware of everyone—possibly even the horses—watching him fumble. The bags weren't huge, and yet it felt as if hours passed while he groped around medicinal jars and reams of notes and maps.

He heard another rider closing the distance between them. Then he at last found the stubby little remnant of a stylus and returned with it to Lord Vediya's side. Out of the corner of his eye Narsi recognized the orange velvet doublet of the Dour Pumpkin. Armor clattered as the guards behind them straightened, but Lord Vediya didn't acknowledge the rider or his roan stallion.

"I take it from the ring you wear that you're a physician?" Lord Vediya asked Narsi.

"Yes. Master Physician Narsi Lif-Tahm," Narsi supplied, hoping that his name might rouse some memory for Lord Vediya. It did not seem to.

"Have you much experience treating men kicked by horses?" Lord Vediya asked, at last casting a glance at the new arrival.

"Some." Before Narsi could inquire as to why Lord Vediya should ask, the man in the orange doublet swung down from his stallion and drew his sword. Instinctively, Narsi stepped back. Lord Vediya remained where he stood but let his horse's reins fall from his hand. His gray stallion trotted ahead, but only to sample a display of yellow potted roses.

"Atreau, you degenerate screw-worm!" The man in orange strode past the potted flowers and gray stallion, intent upon Lord Vediya. "You will return my fiancée at once or I will kill you right here!"

The guards started forward, but Lord Vediya waved them back. He smiled crookedly at the furious man in orange. He didn't draw his sword; instead he simply held Narsi's book in one hand and shook his head at the man stalking toward him.

"Suelita is not yours, Ladislo," Lord Vediya said. "No more than she is mine to take or give."

Ladislo responded with a sweep of his sword, which Lord Vediya eluded in a quick step. Narsi's hand went instantly to his hunting knife. He would not simply stand by and see Lord Vediya murdered. To his shock, he felt a hand grip his arm and jerk him back. He spun to see Berto holding him.

"This isn't a matter you want to become entangled in, Narsi," Berto whispered to him.

"He's going to kill Lord Vediya!"

"Trust me, that reprobate can look after himself—" The rest of Berto's words broke off as Narsi elbowed him and jerked free of his hold.

As he did so, Lord Vediya let loose with a piercing whistle. Suddenly his stallion slammed one of its hind legs into Ladislo and sent him sprawling across the pebbled drive. Then Lord Vediya sprang forward and easily launched himself into his saddle. An instant later he and his stallion were gone from sight. For a moment Narsi stood stunned and staring at the haze of dust that drifted over the drive in Lord Vediya's absence. Then his attention snapped immediately to where Ladislo lay sprawled on the ground.

Narsi stepped over Ladislo's fallen sword and knelt down beside him. Ladislo swore and wept at the same time, his face flushed nearly as red as the bleeding scrapes along the side of his head. At least one of his ribs was likely broken.

"I'll bring you duera for the pain, and then we can get you inside and tend to your—"

"Burn in the Black Hell, you Haldiim whore!" Ladislo lashed out to strike Narsi across the face. Narsi caught his hand and Ladislo screamed, "Don't touch me, you heathen shit!"

Narsi released the man's hand and stood. Cursing and spitting blood from his split lip, Ladislo staggered up to his feet and then stumbled to his horse. After two attempts he managed to climb into his saddle. Then he rode away, leaving his sword behind.

"I told you that Atreau could manage for himself," Berto said.

Narsi nodded, still feeling stunned. He'd only been in Lord Vediya's presence for minutes before the man had yet again ridden away. And Narsi belatedly realized Lord Vediya had taken his book with him.

CHAPTER TWO

Inside the smoky confines of the Fat Goose, surrounded by boisterous drunks, gamblers and cold-eyed cardsharps, Atreau's attention strayed from his cards to the wonderful book on the table before him. The leather cover looked supple and already well-worn as a favorite glove. He could see where fingers had cradled the spine and bent the cover, leafing through the pages again and again.

Placed in my callous hands, a testament of devotion, unspoken, and yet laid bare as a naked breast.

Atreau snorted at his own conceited turn of thought.

Still, the simple fact of the book's existence pleased him.

He'd not seen the Haldiim translation and had half suspected that the publisher had forgone printing after the Cadeleonian volumes had been transformed into so much ash and smoke.

For a moment he pictured the dark young man who'd handed him the tome. How striking he'd appeared amidst so many Cadeleonians, and yet something about him—his angular jaw? Perhaps his long, lean build? Or it might have been his sharp brows and dark lashes?—Atreau didn't know but something about the Haldiim physician had filled Atreau with a sense of familiarity. Absently, Atreau wondered if the young man had known that marigold petals clung to his dark curls like drops of gold.

"Stare at the cards all you want. The winning hand is still mine."

Across the table from him Sabella Calies tapped the four cards she'd laid down and then took up her beer mug. Tall and weathered as a warhorse, Sabella was as much a fixture of the capital's unseemly side as was her uncle's Red Stallion sword house, where people gambled fortunes and lives on the speed of their blades. Over the course of her forty-odd years Sabella had taken both from a good number of men. But here at the Fat Goose the stakes were very different, as was the game. Here the kingdom stood to be lost to the church. Or won for Prince Sevanyo.

Atreau's cards came very near winning but missed by only a point. He had indulged himself in the drama of making it appear a close match. Sabella played along, since the money would be hers no matter what cards he dealt. This game, like almost every other hand of cards he played, served as a pretext for Atreau to dole out Fedeles Quemanor's payments to his informants and agents across the city.

Atreau pushed a plain coin purse to Sabella. She opened it and then pulled the drawstring closed again and dropped it into an inner pocket of her leather coat.

Between her lanky build, plain face and close-shorn brown hair Sabella nearly passed for a man. Certainly the heavy doublet and thick riding trousers she sported added to the impression, though they did not create a perfect illusion. Nor did she need them to. She'd patronized the Fat Goose for more than twenty years and all but the most callow of youths knew better than to cause her trouble.

She drew a sheaf of papers from her doublet and pushed them to Atreau. He skimmed the content quickly. It seemed that the royal bishop was collecting ancient scriptures, most having something to do with the Holy Savior's final battle and the Shard of Heaven. Likely the bishop believed the holy blessings that had destroyed the demon hordes so long ago were desperately needed again now to combat a new threat to Cadeleon.

Five years ago Atreau would have found the entire matter amusing or perhaps thought the royal bishop deluded. But since then he'd seen both the wonders and horrors that ancient spells unleashed. He understood why previous generations of wiser men and women had attempted to hide them away.

"We need to know when and exactly what he intends to do with this," Atreau said. "Actual places and dates would be good."

"You don't ask much, do you?"

"I don't pay so little that I should," Atreau replied.

"Suelita is working on decrypting the third letter, but it's not like the others," Sabella informed him. "She thinks it was encoded using a key."

Atreau frowned. Captain Ciceron had been certain that the value of the letters justified the execution of two priests and a young nun. If they couldn't be decoded then those hapless couriers had died for nothing.

"There's a good chance that the key to the third letter is still at the Sacred Heart Hostel, where the nun was staying," Sabella said softly. "I've procured a habit and I think I may be able to slip in to search the place."

"If you can, then by all means do. I'll see to it that you're rewarded for the trouble. Though," Atreau couldn't help amending, "I should be charging you for the annoyances I've endured from Ladislo Bayezar hounding me day and night over your lady-love."

Sabella laughed.

"He still thinks it was you who helped Suelita escape her father's house?" She shook her head and then drank more beer. "Well, it's not as though the rumor could degrade your reputation."

"No, but the man wastes my time and I'd feel a little contrite if I were forced kill him."

"If it comes to that, I'll happily shoulder your guilt and see he floats out with the rest of the turds in the river. Just give me the word." Though Sabella spoke offhandedly, Atreau knew that she made the offer in earnest. Her ease with murder rivaled a cat's facility for killing rats. In that she re-sembled every other duelist Atreau had come to know in this beautiful, degenerate city.

But if he could, he wished to spare Ladislo. He'd schooled with the man and at one time had thought that the abuse they'd both endured might have allowed them to become friends—but of course Ladislo had felt no interest in being associated with an impoverished reprobate like himself. Still Atreau's sympathy for the other man lingered.

"He's a fool for falling in love, but not so much of a clodpoll that he deserves to die," Atreau replied.

"He tries to take her back by force and he won't be a fool any longer," Sabella stated. "He'll be dead."

"I think I've slowed him down for the time being," Atreau assured her. "Hopefully a little time in a sickbed will give him a chance to realize that he should turn his attention to a lady who is desiring of his devotion."

They both quieted as a serving woman in a drab gray smock and stained apron approached their table. Atreau folded the papers away and picked up his deck of cards while Sabella ordered another round of drinks for them both. Atreau shuffled his cards and then dealt two meaningless hands. The serving woman sauntered back to the bar, where the slim owner of the establishment—the Salt Island Spider, as he was calling himself now—made some mark on Atreau's tab before pouring out the libations.

"Do you still want me to watch over Jacinto, as well?" Sabella asked.

Atreau nodded and Sabella made a face as sour as a lemon.

Prince Sevanyo's fourth son took great pleasure in slumming through the Theater District, but preferred to travel unaccompanied by bodyguards. He felt they made him stand out in the crowds, as if his silken clothes, costly rings and high-handed manner were utterly commonplace. Thus, Jacinto's protection fell to the small group of eccentrics that the prince patronized and whom Fedeles secretly subsidized.

"He's a pain in my ass, you know." Sabella lowered her voice as she added, "And this latest escapade of his, keeping Lady Hylanya housed across the way at the Green Door, is going to get us all killed if someone doesn't move her damn soon."

"I know," Atreau assured her.

Someone at a distant table crowed with delight and several men cheered a lucky throw of dice. Atreau looked the pretty-faced loser over. From the leers of the sailors surrounding the youth, Atreau guessed that the tanned man with the dice in his hand would see his winnings paid out in sloppy lip service in the alley. Such arrangements between men weren't legal, but in the Theater District they were far from uncommon.

Very briefly, Atreau pondered whether he would throw to win or to lose were he to gamble against such a rough, brawny sailor. There was something about the man's thick beard and broad shoulders that reminded him ever so slightly of Elezar.

"Is the lady still . . . ill?" Sabella's question drew his attention back to his own business.

"I wouldn't describe her as being in any condition to travel across the city," Atreau answered.

"What we need is a real physician. Not one of those quacks that hang around the bawdyhouses. Someone who could fix her up and keep his trap shut. Why can't your master retain a single . . ." She trailed off as the serving woman returned their cups to them, Atreau's filled with a red wine so watered down that it couldn't have intoxicated a fly and Sabella's a third full of dregs. Atreau cast a quizzical glance back at Spider and received a teasing grin.

Then a moment later the wiry man himself brought them their real drinks and sent the serving woman away to bestow the pink water and dregs upon the sad sacks at the bar who'd come to beg off paying their gambling debts.

"Well met, little brother." Spider greeted Atreau with a slap across his shoulder. He nodded curtly to Sabella and then pulled up a chair and seated himself. "Thought you might be interested in something I happened to overhear last night."

"Always delighted to hear any wisdom you deign to share," Atreau replied. He dealt four cards to the Spider. Two were grinning jesters.

"There was a man who's been coming here for a while now. Loses a great deal but doesn't seem to care." Spider tossed aside the two jesters and drew different cards from the deck. "He wears Duke Quemanor's colors. A guard, from the look of him and his blade. His debts are under the name Dommian and I got the impression that he's not been in the city long. In any case he drank himself nearly legless last night and then when I was throwing him out at closing he started to blubber about not wanting to kill the kiddies, or something like that."

"Kiddies?" Atreau asked casually. He discarded a grim-faced queen and drew a hazel-eyed page from the deck.

"That's what he said." Spider shrugged. "I thought I'd pass that along just in case it means something."

"Thank you." Atreau and Spider hadn't always been on amiable terms. There'd been a decade when they'd not exchanged a single word or even known whether the other was alive or dead. But after surviving the war in Labara, Atreau had been gripped with the need to find Spider and try to salvage something from the wreckage of the childhood they'd shared.

"You wouldn't happen to know of a discreet physician, would you?" Sabella asked Spider.

"You've gotten Atreau with child, have you?" Spider grinned at Sabella. "I always knew he had the makings of a fine little wife. If he could just meet the right man."

Sabella rolled her eyes and then lay down four kings. Spider folded and glanced to the door. A group of Haldiim performers entered and approached the bar with a youthful excitement that spoke of something done on a dare. Atreau recognized one of the bright-eyed actresses from the Candioro Theater. She was called Yara and possessed the sort of sharp memory that Atreau had found useful on previous occasions. Now he simply offered her a friendly smile and she waved in return. The woman at the bar directed the group to a small table.

Atreau returned his attention to Sabella and Spider.

"Inissa's not joining you?" Spider asked.

Atreau shook his head and pretended not to notice Spider's disappointment. He understood the excitement and pleasure that Inissa inspired. But the fact of the matter was that even if Inissa hadn't been tasked with watching over Lady Hylanya, her safety and livelihood relied entirely upon Prince Jacinto's favor. She couldn't risk an affair, not even with a man as caring as Spider.

"*She'll not roam where she wishes. For she is owned by another man's riches.*" Atreau sang the couplet he'd penned long ago for *The Rogue's Folly.*

Sabella shook her head, while Spider stood and left them without further comment. Atreau didn't take offense. That was simply Spider's manner.

"None of my business, but you might have put that more subtly," Sabella commented.

"He doesn't deserve to have his heart broken." Atreau tasted his wine. Dry and sharp as a rose thorn. "I know too well how poorly a romance with Inissa ends—"

"For you," Sabella replied.

"For everyone." Atreau set his wine aside. "Inissa's survival depends upon Jacinto's affection. She can't afford to indulge a lover's passion or jealousy. It's not a happy notion, but it's a truth I've learned. If the choice is mine then I'd save Spider the pain of learning the same lesson."

"Ah." Sabella smirked at him and then quoted from an old poem of Atreau's own writing: "*Remember this my dear boy. Were there more kindness in my cruelty you'd bleed to death of joy.*"

Atreau raised his glass to her in return.

All around them conversations rumbled and dice clattered across tabletops. Elusive as a shadow, luck toyed with men's fortunes and fled at the turn of a card. Atreau considered his own hand. A hazel-eyed page gazed out from the field of scarlet hearts with a coy smile, while a dour king behind him held his sword high. Atreau folded the hand and returned the cards to the deck.

Then his attention returned to the Haldiim translation of his memoir and he fell into ruminating over the tall, dark young man who'd offered it to him. Atreau wondered if it had been his imagination or if the other man truly had held his gaze a moment too long to be a stranger. And then he remembered the silver ring that had adorned the man's right hand.

They needed a physician, and now fortune favored them with one. Was that too much of a coincidence to trust or too perfect of an opportunity to miss? Atreau shuffled his deck of cards twice and then drew from the bottom. The page smiled at him and Atreau decided on his answer.

"What on earth are you so pleased about all of a sudden?" Sabella asked.

"Nothing yet." Atreau drank a little more of his wine. He would need to charm the physician and get Fedeles's imprimatur—but it could work. "Perhaps the beginning of something, soon."

 CHAPTER
THREE

The fountains at the south gate splashed and spit geysers into the twilight sky. Shadows leapt and danced, giving form to the moonlight's play over the water. Ariz Plunado waited, dull and motionless as a stone. Two city guards, just off duty but still in uniform, strode within arm's length of where he crouched in the shadow of the stone stallions.

The guards shared a joke and laughed harder than it merited. But Ariz let them have that happiness. Then they each tossed a penny into the fountain for luck. Ariz allowed the first guard's coin to drop into the water. But the captain's he caught.

As the guards started down Market Street, Ariz rose and followed. People passed him but took no note, for there was nothing about him to notice. He cultivated plainness, from his lank, walnut-stained brown hair and dull gray gaze to his shapeless clothes and dusty brown boots. He forced his right arm to hang slack while he carefully held his left as if hooking his thumb absently on the leather of his sword belt.

He plodded behind the guards wearing the vaguely bored expression of a man untouched by any inspiration or imagination beyond the contemplation of his evening meal.

Another group of two men and three women passed him—revelers, these five, and already flushed and merry from wine. They sang together, missing notes and confusing lyrics and laughing all the more for it.

Ariz neither met their gazes nor darted his glances away guiltily. He bowed his head as if contemplating the road beneath his feet. All the while he rolled his eyes beneath the shadow of his lashes, tracking the guardsmen. Mastering such an averted gaze had required years of practice, but then so had nearly every aspect of his unremarkable air.

Most men could not have trailed Captain Ciceron of the south gate guards home night after night without once being noticed. Certainly not while carrying an unsheathed blade. But the long dagger Ariz gripped in his left hand appeared as sheathed as his short sword. The flat of the blade had been etched and browned to appear dull as leather and Ariz held it against his sword belt as if resting his hand there. Only a glint of moonlight along the dagger's razor edge might have betrayed the naked blade, but no one looked long or closely at Ariz, much less at the silhouette of his hip.

Captain Ciceron and his lieutenant slowed, then stopped beneath the painted sign of their preferred alehouse and Ariz continued walking with a feeling of relief. As he closed in, he willed the captain to enter the light and boisterous company of the crowd already gathered inside the tavern. Ariz would not follow him in among witnesses. The captain could live another day.

But as Ariz neared, the captain shook his head at his companion's invitation and set off in the direction of his home, where his pretty wife and their three young children waited. Ariz swore silently, resisting what he knew must be done. The old scar that disfigured the flesh over Ariz's heart flared, sending burning warnings across Ariz's chest. He clenched his jaw against the pain but didn't resist further.

He stopped thinking of ways in which the captain might elude him for another night and crossed the street. While the captain hummed the melody from a popular opera to himself, Ariz outpaced him and turned into the narrow lane that the captain always took on his way home. Two raised walkways arched over the lane like miniature bridges. Night-blooming jasmine cascaded from flower boxes lining the walkways and lent a perfume of elegance and romance to the place.

For an instant Ariz held out a hope that a prostitute might be working her trade in the shadows. Twice the presence of such women had won Captain Ciceron reprieves. Tonight only a cat occupied the lane and she fled with the body of a dead rat clamped between her jaws the moment Ariz neared.

He could find no further excuses and contemplating them set the brand searing into him as if it were once again a white-hot iron burning into his chest.

A cold sweat rose at the back of Ariz's neck and he shuddered with the waves of remembered shock. He'd nearly died that morning, kneeling on the chapel floor; he wasn't sure if he considered himself fortunate or unfortunate to have survived.

Certainly it was to the captain's bad luck that Ariz hadn't died.

Ciceron paced along the lane, and beams of moonlight illuminated him as he grinned at the white jasmine blossoms and pulled a few free to carry home with him. Then he stepped into the shadow where Ariz awaited him.

Ariz lunged forward and rammed his dagger to the hilt into the captain's chest. The captain started to cry out and his right hand went to his sword hilt, but Ariz caught the captain's throat in his own right hand and slammed the man's head hard against the stone support of the walkway. The captain lurched but Ariz held him like a spider punching poison into a dying fly. Three more times he smashed the captain's skull up against the stone. By the third blow the man was already dead. In truth he had been doomed the moment Ariz shoved a dagger into his heart, but Ariz paid him the respect of letting him fight hard and go down like a soldier. Assassination afforded Ariz little honor, but at least he hadn't simply landed the fatal strike and then darted away to watch the man bleed out like a slaughtered sow.

Ariz lowered the body to the ground, easing the captain so that his lolling head and chest lay in the moonlight. Had it been his choice Ariz would have taken his dagger and been done with all of this. But his orders were not so simple. He drew his sword, took careful aim and sliced through the captain's muscular neck in a single blow. A sluggish wash of blood spilled out from the gaping wound. The cloying smell of it coiled around Ariz, like a cologne. That too-familiar musk of iron and allspice blossoms.

Ariz gripped the captain's forelock and, as cleanly as he could, rolled the severed head into an oilskin sack. Then he jerked his dagger free of the decapitated corpse and wiped both his blades clean across the captain's dun jacket.

He sheathed his sword and his dagger and then hefted the sack up under his right arm. It felt warm and slack. For the first time in weeks the brand over Ariz's heart ceased to burn.

∾ ∾ ∾

Two hours later, as night bells sounded through the darkness, Ariz arrived at another fountain and again waited. The noise of the river and the gurgle of the fountain created a haze of sound that made Ariz uneasy. He could just pick out the whisper of robes and soft footsteps, but the noise echoed and distorted through the long corridors of the towering chapel behind him. He narrowed his eyes, trying to pick out a man's figure through the gloom. Veils of perfumed smoke drifted across the grounds, further hindering Ariz's senses.

For all the beauty of its sky-blue stone and seams of gold, Ariz hated stepping foot upon the Shard of Heaven. Tonight the way the moonlight lit the stone to sapphire blue seemed sinister: the royal color shining up at him like an omen. Priests inside the white walls of the holiest of chapels intoned the last of their evening prayers, singing the souls of the Hallowed Kings of Cadeleon to their nightly rest. This was a place too near the next world. Here the dead could not be depended upon to remain silent.

Ariz shifted the weight of the oilskin sack.

Hierro knew that he hated this place; no doubt that was why he wanted him here. It certainly wasn't subtle. Even before he could briefly savor a spiteful fantasy of gouging Hierro's eyes out, Ariz's brand seared to life. The pain brought tears to his eyes. He forced himself to contemplate the ground and listen to the splashing water—distancing himself from his anger—until the pain relented.

Best not to even think of Hierro at all, for rebellion and rage inevitably followed and those only brought him suffering.

Instead he let his mind drift. He remembered the spark of pride he'd felt last afternoon when Prince Sevanyo had visited the Quemanor household and the duke's five-year-old son, Sparanzo, danced for the prince's entertainment just as Ariz had taught him. The boy had moved with a grace that had been far harder won than anyone but Ariz had known. He'd wanted to crow with joy for Sparanzo when the prince had applauded him and gifted him with a jewel-studded toy horse. But of course he hadn't made a sound, just slunk quickly away before anyone noticed him spying.

And then he focused on this morning and the strange thrill of at last winning a laugh from Lord Quemanor during his fencing session. Not that the duke was a reticent man—between his exuberant displays of emotion, lean build and often tousled black hair he presented an almost boyish figure of disarming frankness. Rather it was painfully rare for Ariz to amuse anyone, much less such a vibrant fellow as Fedeles Quemanor. Normally only affable, eloquent men like Captain Ciceron captured the duke's attention.

Ariz scowled down at the sack in his hand. He hadn't noticed before, but at some point Captain Ciceron had raked three deep gouges across his right forearm. He should have felt them earlier but the agonizing pain of the brand had become so constant that he often failed to notice lesser hurts.

Still, it wasn't like him to allow a target to touch him, much less do him harm. He should have punched the dagger in and then leapt out of reach, waiting for the few minutes it took for the captain's heart to stop. But he hadn't wanted to, and thinking on that, Ariz felt that familiar chill. A part of him had wanted to be hurt, had even hoped that the captain would kill him.

All at once he remembered the first time that desire had risen up. He'd been sixteen, still at school and still a recognized nobleman, but he'd already been worn down by two years of bearing a Brand of Obedience. He'd thought himself Hierro Fueres's creature completely—as broken as the man's horse. Then at the yearly sword tournament Hierro had ordered him to humiliate and bleed the one Haldiim boy who had dared to school at the Sagrada Academy. But Ariz had felt deeply moved, seeing

the Haldiim youth battling with all his heart despite the jeers of his opponents and classmates. He recognized and understood the pride and
anguish in the slim Haldiim's struggles all too well. Something in Ariz
cracked just enough to free a splinter of rebellion.

He'd not outrightly disobeyed Hierro—the pain would have been far
too much for him—but he'd made mistakes inside the dueling ring. He'd
not struck with all his strength and he'd allowed the duel to drag on long
enough for the Haldiim youth to recognize and exploit his attacks.

After losing that duel he'd suffered hours of agony at Hierro's hands,
but he'd also felt a kind of triumph, because his defeat had also been
Hierro's.

Ariz had seen a Haldiim youth again today—not the same man—this
fellow had been much taller and his hair so dark that the marigold petals
caught in his curls looked like shining embers. But of all the courtiers
and couriers on the street only that one Haldiim youth had seemed to
notice Ariz stalking through the shadows. The man had looked straight
at him and for an instant Ariz had felt as if he gazed back at the omen of
his destruction.

The idea filled Ariz with a cold dread but also a glimmer of hope.
Perhaps he might end this all at last.

The sound of footsteps on the cobblestone path interrupted Ariz's
contemplation. He rolled his eyes to the left and picked out the handsome
form he knew so well and hated utterly. Hierro moved quietly, particularly for a man of his stature, but his vanity undid his stealth. The gold
spurs adorning the heels of his costly boots produced a distinct jingle
that reverberated like an alarm bell in Ariz's awareness. Dozens of golden
embroidered swans glinted as moonlight fell across his dove-gray velvet
doublet.

"The trophy you requested, Lord Fueres." Ariz hurled the oilskin
sack at Hierro, who caught it easily.

Even in through the gloom, Hierro's close relation to the royal Sagradas as well as Fedeles Quemanor showed. All of them tended toward
tall, lean builds, exceptionally pale complexions, black hair and eyes like
polished jet. Hierro's strength and grace rivaled his physical beauty, and
yet the sight of him never failed to sicken Ariz to the core.

"Clara will be delighted." Hierro stopped just short of Ariz at the
edge of the fountain. "But where have your manners gone, Ariz?"

Hierro extended his hand. The instant Ariz considered slapping that
hand away, the brand seared to life. To stop it, Ariz kissed Hierro's signet
ring and then knelt on the cobblestones. Hierro laughed.

"So you do remember how to greet your master. I had feared that so
much time in Fedeles Quemanor's household had made you forgetful."

Hierro ran his hand over Ariz's hair as if he were stroking a dog, then he cuffed the side of Ariz's head hard. Ariz rocked but didn't fall from the blow. He'd expected it.

"It is done." Ariz didn't lift his face. "Am I free to go?"

"No, pet, you are not," Hierro replied. He turned and started toward the inlayed doors of the chapel. "Come."

Ariz rose and obeyed.

 CHAPTER FOUR

Night had fallen by the time Berto unlocked the double doors that led from the overgrown garden into Narsi's new rooms. He bestowed the key on Narsi with a little flourish.

Thankfully someone had made a fire in the small hearth and now the low flames offered just enough illumination for them to find two oil lamps to light. To Narsi's delight he found the exam room was huge with large windows, though randomly littered with an eclectic assortment of shabby furniture. The different designs of the chairs and the mismatched quality of the three medical cabinets and two long examination tables indicated to Narsi that these rooms had been occupied and then evacuated by numerous physicians before him. From the obscene denouncements of the duke slashed into one of the cabinet panels he surmised that not all—if any—of the departures had been happy ones.

Narsi had heard rumors of Fedeles Quemanor's immense distrust of physicians. People said that he often dismissed one from his service the moment he laid eyes upon him. Once he'd supposedly fired a man even sooner by sending a courier riding directly behind the courier that his wife had dispatched to offer the position. There were so many tales surrounding the duke that it was difficult to know which to believe, but this one sounded as if it might be valid. But Narsi would be in Father Timoteo's service and not directly answerable to the duke. Otherwise his stay at court might be quite short.

A door, directly opposite the garden doors, opened out into a dimly lit hallway. Narsi thought he heard voices, but they sounded far away, in distant chambers.

He stepped back into the exam room to investigate the two other adjoining rooms.

"I had a maid in yesterday to air the room and dress the bed for you."
Berto frowned down at one of the two examination tables that stood a
few feet from the desk. With a look of disgust he nudged the stiff body of
a dead rat.

"It seems the cat you mentioned has arranged a welcome for me as
well," Narsi commented. "Does the creature have a name or an owner?"

"Neither. The thing is a vagrant sack of fleas." Berto's expression suddenly turned stern. "I know you have a soft spot for scoundrels, but that
one is a beyond redemption, you realize."

"You know me too well." Narsi leaned into the chamber adjoining the
exam room on the east side, hoping to find a bath. Instead he discovered
a huge space—a surgery, perhaps—furnished with only one stool and
the remains of another dead rat. He tried the other doorway and found
an even larger room, furnished with a tidy bed, a side table and a simple
wooden wardrobe. The large, round window let in enough moonlight for
Narsi to pick out the corpse of a third rat.

Narsi collected the stiff rodents and took them outside and dumped
them in a weedy plant bed of the neglected physic garden. Then as he
closed the garden doors behind him a thought came to him. "If the
rooms have been locked up all this time, how do you suppose the cat has
managed to get in and out?"

"Supposedly there are secret corridors," Berto replied. "Before Fedeles Quemanor inherited this place it belonged to the Tornesal family,
and apparently they couldn't get enough of creeping around behind the
walls."

"Really?" Narsi regarded the bare wood walls with a newfound excitement.

"Well, if you believe gossip. I've seen no sign of any myself," Berto
replied. "I expect that the animal has just managed to slip in and out
behind the house maids."

"You're probably right. Still it could be fun to search the walls, on the
off chance of finding something."

Berto smiled in the indulgent manner of a man who knew better
than to waste his breath arguing against a flight of fancy.

As Narsi gazed around him he couldn't help but wonder exactly where Lord Vediya's rooms were in this vast mansion. If they were
near then perhaps the two of them might see each other in one of the
many gardens? Perhaps then he might reclaim his book or rekindle their
fleeting acquaintance. Narsi stopped his train of thought before it could
wander any further into some besotted fantasy.

Lord Vediya had not recognized him or remembered his name, and he knew that his own imaginings were to blame for his disappointment. Indulging in new fancies would only worsen his discontent.

"I need a bath," Narsi realized.

"I'll see if I can't secure you a washtub and water. It won't be warm, but . . ."

"Better than nothing." Narsi said. "Thank you."

Berto left through the door that opened into the mansion. As he went Narsi glimpsed two footmen out in the hall, lighting candles in the two nearest candelabras hanging from the high ceiling. From somewhere not too far away the strains of music drifted down. Narsi had to resist the urge to wander out to introduce himself and explore. He could indulge in that after he'd bathed. In the meanwhile he ought to unpack.

He'd not been greatly weighed down by possessions, so it didn't take long to disgorge his saddlebags, however he did take a little care in arranging his two prized sketches—presented to him by Lady Riossa Grunito herself—and his medical books. His towel and white prayer clothes he set on a chair in preparation for his bath. Last he laid out his tattered diary. He considered writing something to mark the occasion but only ended up scratching out *Have arrived in the duke's household. Don't know what to expect as of yet.*

He left the diary open on the desk to dry and took up the sealed letter that his mother had entrusted to him. He turned it over, fighting with his curiosity as he did every time he saw the thing, then at last he set it aside. Whatever last wishes his mother had needed to convey to Father Timoteo, she had not wanted them shared.

He suspected that his mother had kept the contents of this letter from him for good reason. Still he picked it up a second time and briefly held it up in front of the lamp flame. The rag paper lit up and shadows of Cadeleonian script appeared in a tangle. She'd folded the pages within. As he had a dozen times before, he sought out the small corner where he could almost convince himself that he saw the words "husband and father" written.

Her husband? His father? The mystery that he'd been warned away from as long as he could remember?

"He was the best of men murdered by the worst," his mother had told him the one time he'd found her in the Cadeleonian chapel weeping. Beyond that, he'd learned precious little from her or from Father Timoteo. As a child he'd been persistent—and was warned more than once that curiosity killed more than cats—but as he grew older he'd become warier of learning the truth. He now understood what the word "murdered" truly meant; he'd seen bodies on autopsy tables. He also knew that the sort of men whose murders inspired relatives to go into hiding, instead of seeking justice, were most often the worst kinds of criminals. Was he prepared to learn that he was a slaver's son? Or the child of an assassin?

All those childhood fantasies of the brave, stalwart man he'd imagined his father to be would die. Then what would he do with his desire to somehow make "the best of men" proud up there in his Cadeleonian paradise?

Narsi set the letter aside again. Only then did he notice a black cat, lounging on one of his exam tables. It regarded him for a moment, then hefted a scrawny hind leg and got to work licking its ass. Narsi laughed and felt pleased to let go of his maudlin contemplations. They didn't suit him, really. He unpacked the last of his medical supplies.

When a loud knock sounded, the cat startled and slunk into the bedroom. Narsi answered the door. A footman carried in a wooden tub that might have been big enough to serve as a hip bath for a dainty girl. Another footman followed with a pitcher and a scrub brush that looked fit for a horse.

"Is the master physician here?" the footman asked Narsi.

"I am indeed," Narsi replied.

A brief silence followed and, oddly, the footman holding the pitcher paled.

"The duke sends his regards." The footman holding the wooden tub dropped it on the floor and turned around to leave; the second footman, however, paused.

"It's not because you're one of them Haldiim. I don't care how unnatural you are. That's your business." He eyed Narsi as if he feared for his soul. He footman set the pitcher and brush down on the exam table. "The duke just hates physicians, is all. So we had to bring these to you. You aren't gonna put a curse on us, are you?"

Narsi laughed and the footman backed away from him nervously.

"I assure you I'm not going to curse you." Narsi quickly lifted up the pendent of his necklace, showing the footman the holy Cadeleonian star embossed in the silver. "My father was Cadeleonian and I was blessed in a chapel after my birth. I served Holy Father Timoteo before I attended my medical studies, and he has sent for me to attend him now as his physician."

The footman's expression changed completely at the mention of Father Timoteo. Suddenly he grinned at Narsi as if they'd been fast friends for years.

"The father was saying that he'd send for a physician for the household. We've been without forever . . . I just didn't realize—he didn't say anything about you being—I mean you're . . . so brown . . ." The footman snatched up the scrub brush and then lowered his voice. "Don't you worry about this. I'll have the girls bring you a proper tub in two flicks of a tail. And I'll get the word around. Otherwise you'll be having potato peels and raw ox ears for your supper."

"Truly?"

The footman glanced quickly from side to side as if he feared someone might be lurking in a corner of the room, then he whispered, "The duke truly hates physicians."

Then the man raced off and Narsi closed the door behind him.

Only a little time later six sturdy Cadeleonian women arrived with an actual hip bath, a sable wash brush and several pails of steaming water. The youngest of the women made the Cadeleonian holy symbol at Narsi and he returned the gesture, which seemed to reassure her, though Narsi wasn't sure why. It wasn't as if the motion would actually ward off any form of sorcery—not if Lord Vediya's book was to be believed.

A gray-haired and particularly plump woman looked him over as she poured the last pail of water into the tub, then commented, "You're a quite a towering youth, aren't you?"

"My father was a Cadeleonian," Narsi replied.

"A Cadeleonian what? Oak tree?" The woman's expression struck Narsi as genuinely friendly and he returned her smile. While the other women hurried out of the room, she lingered surveying what few belongings he'd brought.

"No solstice lamp?" she asked.

That took Narsi off guard. Outside of Anacleto, few if any Cadeleonians knew anything of actual Haldiim traditions. Those within Anacleto were often careful not to seem too knowledgeable to avoid accusations of secretly worshiping at the White Tree.

"I left it with my aunt. I was afraid that it would break, being carted around on horseback," Narsi replied.

"I'll lend you one of mine, then," the woman said.

Narsi gaped at her and she burst into laughter.

"Don't look so shocked, my boy. You aren't the first soul to have made the journey from Anacleto, you know. I and my husband—bless his soul in his next life—tended the gardens for a Haldiim potter there. She gifted us with any number of pretty lamps over the years." The woman's expression turned slightly wistful. "I was there when the White Tree lit up the whole sky with Bahiim blessings. Even caught one in my hand."

She held out her thick, callused right hand. Narsi resisted the urge to place his palm against hers. Wearing a symbol of the Holy Cadeleonian Church wasn't going to get him far if he gave himself away as a heathen by pressing palms to share a blessing.

To his surprise the woman reached out and drew his palm to her own. Her fingers felt tough from hard work but also warm and strong, like his mother's had been before she fell ill.

"That's for good luck," she told him, and then she whispered in flawless Haldiim, "You aren't as alone as you might think, child."

Narsi stared at her, at a loss, and she laughed again.

"I'm Querra—Querra Kir-Naham—mistress of the kitchen gardens." The woman slipped back into Cadeleonian. "If you need anything to bring these medical gardens back, come to me."

"I will, thank you." Narsi replied, now feeling stunned.

Among Haldiim physicians, the Kir-Naham family was famous for extensively stocked pharmacies, their encyclopedic medical knowledge and their intolerance toward non-Haldiim. Never would Narsi have expected to find the name attached to anyone who appeared so Cadeleonian. Then Narsi chided himself for his closed mind. If anyone ought to know that love and marriages crossed cultures—regardless of disapproving relatives—he should. He wondered if Querra, like his own mother, had been shunned as *heram* and been forced to find work among Cadeleonians. Or had she gladly left Anacleto after her spouse's death?

Curious as he was, he knew better than to ask, so instead he simply stood there looking dazed. Querra offered him a smile.

"Well, I can see that you're tired from your long journey," Querra said. "I'll let you relax with your bath while the water's still hot." Then she slipped out the door.

Low bells rang out from far across the city, and from somewhere much closer a dog howled. Narsi washed the dust and grime from his body. To his surprise he found several marigold blossoms clinging to his hair. He plucked them out, hoping that he'd not made too strange of an impression wandering around with flowers strewn through his hair. He wrapped his towel around himself and dumped the filthy water out into one of the dry plant beds outside his window.

Still wearing only his towel wrapped around his waist, he dropped into the chair nearest the hearth. He let the low flames warm and dry him, luxuriating in both the freedom from dirt and the knowledge that he wouldn't have to wake at dawn tomorrow and ride.

A knock sounded at his door, but having at last sat down, he didn't want to rise.

"Come! It's not locked," Narsi called out.

Berto leaned in and frowned as Narsi's sprawled figure. "What if I had been a lady and I saw you like this?"

"I would instantly have offered to marry you and thus have salvaged your maidenly honor," Narsi replied. Then he spied the tray in Berto's hands. He caught the scent of beef and onions and felt all at once ravenous. Oddly Berto glanced down at the tray with a guilty expression. He handed it to Narsi, who managed to thank him before tearing into the small roll of warm bread and then slurping up several mouthfuls of the beef and onion soup.

"Delfia had this made for you," Berto commented as he pulled up a chair beside Narsi's. "It seems the duke . . ."

"Let me guess. He arranged for my plate at the master's table to be heaped with potato peelings and topped by a hairy ox ear?"

"How did you know?" Berto asked.

"One of my many mystical Haldiim powers—hadn't I mentioned it before?" Narsi finished off the roll. With a rich, warm meal in front of him, Narsi could easily afford to see the humor of the situation.

"Don't even joke about that around here." Berto lightly cuffed the side of his head. "People in the north take the accusation of witchcraft seriously. Two women were hanged only a month ago."

That deflated Narsi's mood a little. He ate his soup quietly. Across from him Berto frowned at the fire.

"Father Timoteo wants to personally introduce you to the duke tomorrow evening," Berto said. "After you've had time to rest and feel your best."

"Should I dress and go speak to the father about it now?" The sooner he handed over his mother's letter the less likely he was to do something stupid like break his promise and read it.

"No. He's already retired to bed."

"You're certain that he isn't ill?"

"Certain. He's just had a very long day." Berto must have read something in Narsi's expression because he suddenly added, "He's not avoiding you."

Narsi sighed. Considering how tired he felt, it probably wasn't a bad idea to save his reunion with Father Timoteo for tomorrow, particularly if it was to be followed by an interview with a duke who already hated him.

   CHAPTER
          FIVE

On the previous occasions that Hierro had summoned him to the
Shard of Heaven, Ariz hadn't been allowed beyond the fountain garden.
Now a round-faced young acolyte dressed in simple black robes held
open a small side door for him. The interior of the ancient chapel was
nothing like Ariz would have imagined. Instead of pews, the long nave
was filled with exquisitely carved sculptures of men, women and monstrous creatures.

Normally depictions of the Savior's holy battles against demonic
hordes decorated the walls and altars of a chapel. But here, Ariz felt as
though he had stepped onto one of those ancient battlefields. So many
figures, tangled in combat, populated the space that Ariz had to walk a
winding, confused path to make his way around them—though several
times Ariz paused in amazement at the incredible detail of the carvings. In
all his life he'd never seen so many perfectly lifelike statues. Some forgotten
artisans seemed to have reproduced every hair of a giant wolf's body, every
bristle on the back of a huge boar. Old Gods cast in stone surrounded Ariz
on all sides, as did the human champions who battled them. All of the
hundreds and hundreds of statues appeared as carefully formed as living
creatures. Among the human figures, details as minute as cracked fingernails and split knuckles astounded him.

The flickering light of the lamps hanging high above threw jittery
shadows across the stone giants, making them seem almost to breathe.
But the light also illuminated a particularly horrific detail. The head of
every single statue—human and monster—had been chiseled off and
stacked on the shining blue floor to form a magnificently grotesque altar.

On that stood a huge, gilded pulpit, which supported three towering
crystal tanks filled with a murky green liquid. Something in one of the
tanks moved. Ariz frowned and wondered why anyone would keep fish
on a holy pulpit. Then he saw a pink tongue writhe out from the murk
to lap against the tank's glassy surface. Human teeth jutting from bare
jawbones closed around the tongue and then sank back into the green
murk and out of sight.

Ariz stared in horror.

Hierro glanced over his shoulder at Ariz and laughed.

"How like you not to recognize the highest and most holy when you see them," Hierro chided him. "You should feel honored. Few men outside the attendant priests and the children of royal bloodlines are ever allowed into the presence of the Hallowed Kings."

"Those are the kings . . ." Ariz hadn't felt this sickened by a mere sight since the first time he'd butchered a girl on Hierro's command. The few times that he had thought of the Hallowed Kings, he'd imagined the sorts of relics that so many chapels housed. Dead, dry bones or teeth, laid out on satin and enclosed by golden casks. Even Bishop Seferino's sainted heart was just a dry husk housed in an ornate red and gold vase. He knew that the Three Hallowed Kings chose not to ascend into heaven immediately for the sake of the kingdom and the benefit of their heirs, but he'd somehow thought that their souls simply lingered, benign and invisible until the next king was allowed to pass and the eldest of his Hallowed ancestors was released to paradise.

This struck Ariz as more of a torture than an honored rest.

"Do they suffer?" Ariz asked.

"Of course not." Hierro smiled and then struck Ariz's cheek. "You need flesh to suffer."

As if objecting, the tongue in the third tank again slapped at the crystal panes restraining it. It moved, Ariz thought, like an eel flailing in a bucket.

A young priest appeared from the shadows of two decapitated statues and rushed quickly up the blue stone stairs to the pulpit. He dropped to his knees and at once began to sing a low, soft lullaby. His voice reverberated through the vaulted apse, creating harmonies from its own echo. The liquid in the third tank stilled and once again the skull closed its gaping mouth around the flapping tongue and drifted from sight.

"Come," Hierro commanded. "Before you disturb old King Gachello any further."

He led Ariz around the altar of glowering stone heads and back to a staircase carved into the brilliant blue stone. They descended some fifteen feet, and then the stairs opened into a huge golden chamber. Lamplight reflected off countless golden inlayed prayers decorating the walls and filled the chamber with brilliance completely at odds with the darkness above them.

Ariz recognized both of the men lounging at the white marble table. Hierro's father, the Duke of Gavado, pushed a dish of cherries to Remes Sagrada, who was both Prince Sevanyo's second son and also the royal bishop's heir. The slender, dark-haired woman at the table had never been formally introduced to Ariz, but he knew her from his boyhood visits to the Fueres holdings: Hierro's thrice-wed sister, Clara Odalis. Currently, she held the title of countess, but Ariz had no doubt that if the opportunity arose her current husband could meet an untimely end to free her to build her father a more powerful alliance.

At the sight of Hierro, his sister leapt from her place at the table and hurried to his side. Hierro gazed at her with a smile that did not seem affectionate or brotherly.

"Is it done?" Clara asked.

"Captain Ciceron will never rob or murder another nun." Hierro held the oilskin sack out to his sister. "He has seen the error of his ways."

Clara took the sack and smiled quite beautifully at Hierro.

Of course, it was not hard for any of them to seem lovely; they were all well-made and dressed in the finest silks and velvets. The Fueres siblings, their silver-haired father and their royal cousin, all of them possessed beauty that Ariz felt reflected nothing of their true characters.

Clara opened the sack and peered into it, then laughed and took it to her father and Remes. The prince slid Captain Ciceron's bloody head onto an empty gold platter, as if it were a centerpiece.

Clara glanced to Ariz and he averted his gaze to the floor.

"Hierro, let us have a look at your varlet!" Clara called to her brother.

"Go, bow for them," Hierro ordered and Ariz obeyed, feeling relieved that his expression remained blank, so that none of them read his revulsion. He did not meet their smug gazes but simply sank to the floor in a deep bow.

Hierro joined his family at the table. They took their supper, gossiping and laughing, while Ariz remained, bent low, studying their feet beneath the table. Only Hierro's boots betrayed the scuffs and dust of walking a public road.

Ariz listened as they picked up their conversation concerning the royal bishop's growing concern over the Grunito family's Labaran and Haldiim alliances.

"But he keeps getting distracted, by some nonsense about ancient wards. He's become fanatical about reclaiming all the relics mentioned in the Battle of the Shard of Heaven Even having ancient texts dug up and sending our best agents out to try and locate some moldering old relics," Remes said. "Who knows what for."

"Perhaps he too believes that a second holy war is upon us. We might have need of those relics that once saved our kingdom. Though few remain with us in this corrupt age," Clara said quietly, almost whispering to herself. "The demon Meztli raised his shield on Crown Hill, but it was shattered. Trueno's wings are thought to have been lost during the first Mirogoth invasion. The horns of the Summer Doe were said to have been thrown into the sea along with Bhadia's locket."

"Well, that's obviously a lost cause, and it's a distraction to what we need him doing," Remes said, then added, "I've encouraged him to openly move against the Grunitos, but he's a sly old man."

"He'll come around soon enough. Once he does, we all know who will rush to Nestor Grunito's rescue," Hierro commented. "People already whisper of the rift between the Duke of Rauma and the royal bishop. When the time comes they'll know who to blame."

"I'd be happier if we had the Grunitos in a more vulnerable position and had secured better insurance against the Labarans. My uncle isn't entirely wrong about the danger the two present. I don't know why he won't see the intelligence of taking Lady Hylanya hostage. But the doddering old fool insists on having her exiled or executed," Remes replied.

"We need to find her before his men do." Duke Gavado scowled at his plate.

"Or before that whoremonger Atreau Vediya manages to slip her out of the city and back to her brother," Remes agreed.

"Oh, I'm sure she'll turn up." Hierro speared a carrot and ate it.

Ariz fixed his gaze on the floor tiles. He couldn't afford to have Hierro realize how much he knew about the part Hierro had played in Lady Hylanya's disappearance. Likely the only place anyone would find her now was deep in the ground. No doubt her ability to see his spells and implicate him as a witch had threatened him, though Ariz guessed that it had been her unbowed strength and pride that had driven Hierro to have her poisoned.

"A wastrel like Atreau makes no difference," Hierro stated. "It's his benefactor, Fedeles Quemanor, who represents our real challenge, particularly now. You wouldn't think a half-mad inbred idiot would be so hard to ferry into the next world. If only he'd fall off one of his damn horses and break his neck—"

"Some other accident might befall him." Remes sounded so smug that Ariz looked up at him. "Tonight, for example, he might find himself run through—"

"Tonight is too soon," the Duke of Gavado objected. "He must survive long enough to take the blame for the others."

"There will be no end of Hellion scapegoats available to us," Remes answered. "And anyway, my father is far too fond of him. The old man is already jabbering about changing his choice of successor. I wouldn't be surprised if he named Fedeles just to spite us all."

"That's exactly why we can't afford to openly attack him. Prince Sevanyo will suspect us and—" the duke began, but Prince Remes cut him off.

"It will appear to be an accident. A sword stroke gone wide in the midst of a duel," Remes replied. "I want him removed."

"It is not so easily done as it may seem," Clara said softly. "Every failed attack against Fedeles Quemanor only awakens more of the abomination within him. He's recently taken to riding out to Crown Hill, and I fear that his mere shadow may corrupt the place."

"Fear not, pretty, I will take the utmost care," Remes replied, and he offered Clara an indulgent smirk.

Ariz suppressed all response to the thought of Fedeles Quemanor being murdered, though it tore at him. And it did not stop there, as the Duke of Gavado could not seem to resist going on to defame Oasia, his estranged eldest daughter, as well as the son she'd born Fedeles.

"There was a time when midwives had the good sense to smother children born crippled."

At least Clara spoke up in in the boy's defense, saying, "Papa, Sparanzo is only a child and your grandson. He cannot be blamed for the deeds of his parents. He should be spared. I would gladly take him as my own."

Again, Ariz suppressed any reaction at the implications of her words, though his brand began to prickle.

"Does not the *Book of Obedience* teach us to guard against pity, for it is too easily made a devil's weapon?" Remes chided Clara.

"Certainly, but I do not speak from mere pity," Clara replied. "The boy is an innocent in all of this, and as Bishop Seferino wrote, 'Those who sacrifice the innocent claiming it serves a greater good have already left the path of righteousness and stepped onto the cobbles of the Black Hell.'"

Clara did know her theology, and Remes acknowledged her with a nod of his head.

"Even so, I don't like the thought of allowing Fedeles Quemanor's whelp to survive his father," Remes replied. "Not only would he inherit the duchy of Rauma, but he shares my royal blood through his great-grandmother and grandmother. He could contest my claim to the throne."

"That's quite correct." Hierro looked to Remes, and something in his expression made Ariz feel certain that Hierro found Remes's anxiety amusing. "Fedeles Quemanor too claims royal blood, as obviously does Oasia. There's no doubt that, when the time comes, we must eradicate that entire bloodline. Otherwise your rule will never be secure."

"Exactly." Remes drained his wine and then poured himself another glass. "I won't be safe so long as any of them draw breath."

Sweat beaded the back of Ariz's neck as the brand seared through him, and still he couldn't stop his rising fury at the thought of anyone harming Fedeles or Sparanzo.

"Give the boy to me as a wedding gift and I promise you that I will ask for nothing else from you," Clara said softly. "Please, Remes."

Ariz rolled his gaze up at her. Could it be that some shred of kindness persisted in her? Might she harbor the same strain of rebellion that had led her sister, Oasia, to flee her brother's control and wed Fedeles Quemanor?

Clara stared intently at Remes while Hierro and his father, Paulino, frowned at them. At last Remes shrugged.

"Very well. *If* he survives the purge, then the boy will be yours. But when you are my queen I will hold you to your promise. You must ask for *nothing* else." Remes grinned as if he'd laid down a clever hand playing hearts and cups.

Ariz dropped his gaze quickly before any of them could catch his brief expression of shock. As a second son, Prince Remes was not his father's heir but his uncle's, and no royal bishop took a wife, much less made a queen of her. This was wildly dangerous ambition.

"There is no point in extracting promises from your future wife before she's been made a widow," Hierro said, then he raised his voice just a little. "Ariz, come and pour my wine, as you used to do in our academy days"

Ariz stood and served Hierro from a glass decanter etched with a motif of swans. He concentrated on the way the golden lamplight refracted through the glass and cast small pools of color across the white marble tabletop. Anything to distance himself from his distaste for Hierro's proximity. It seemed almost impossible now to believe that once he'd imagined himself in love with the man.

"It seems that a fortune-teller has predicted that Count Zacarrio Odalis will meet with his end very soon," Hierro told him.

"And will the fortune-teller be wanting the count's head on a platter as well?" Ariz asked.

Surprisingly, Clara laughed. But Hierro shot Ariz a threatening glower.

"No," Hierro stated. "But he will need to be dealt with before the masquerades begin. Do you understand?"

"Yes," Ariz replied.

"And you will do as I order, will you not?" Hierro added, and Ariz realized exactly why he'd been brought here. He was being shown off to Prince Remes like a particularly well-trained dog.

"I will," Ariz replied, though having the words forced out of his mouth made him want to smash the wine decanter across Hierro's face.

That fantasy provoked a powerful flare of burning pain and Ariz had to exert all of his will to keep from crying out or dropping the decanter.

"He really must obey any order you give him?" Remes straightened in his chair, looking excited but not quite convinced.

"Yes. He can say nothing of what I want kept secret and must obey my every whim. Simply knowing that I wish something done, he must do it. Shall I demonstrate?" Hierro and his father exchanged an amused glance, but Clara dropped her gaze to her plate. Then Hierro drew his dagger.

"Hold out your arm for me, Ariz," Hierro commanded.

Ariz set aside the decanter and held out his right arm. He knew what Hierro intended. He'd endured the razor edges of Hierro's knives throughout his youth. Hundreds of fine scars lay across his arms and back like strands of cobweb. Once Ariz had feared that every inch of his skin would be slowly flayed away, but even Hierro had grown bored with Ariz's silent obedience after six years. And when Hierro's sister Oasia had requested Ariz as a retainer, Hierro had sent him away with so little remark that Ariz had briefly hoped he'd escaped the man forever. But now that he'd won a position so near the Duke of Rauma, Hierro had rediscovered his pleasure in using him.

He should have expected Hierro's knives sooner and been better prepared not to respond.

As it was, Ariz struggled to suppress his rage. Immediately the brand engulfed his body as if he were in flames. He felt the blood draining from his lips and his hands shook from the pain. In comparison, he hardly noticed Hierro drag the dagger across the three wounds left by Captain Ciceron. Blood welled up and spilled across the marble tabletop.

"You see, Your Highness," Hierro told Remes. "He cannot even draw his own hand back if I do not wish it. He is my creature completely. Of course, I would be honored to use him in your service."

Desperately, Ariz tried to shift his awareness from Hierro. If only he could blot out the man's gleeful expression as he sliced a second track across Ariz's arm.

"It delights me to no end to accept your offer, Hierro." Remes lifted his glass as if toasting the sight of them and drank.

Ariz stared past Hierro's shoulder to the gold prayers covering the far wall. He'd not studied much of the old holy script but he recognized a few of the words.

. . . in that moment, at the height of battle when all seemed lost, the Savior unfurled the Shroud of Stone. Winds died, waters stilled. Armies stood unmoving. All was as stone . . .

If only *he* could be turned to stone, or better yet be struck dead. But no, he couldn't abandon Delfia and her children to Hierro. He had no doubt that Hierro's recent threat hadn't been idle, nor was his claim on the children unfounded. As their father, Hierro had a legal right to them—regardless of their illegitimate birth. Ariz clenched his teeth in pain and frustration.

"Enough, Hierro," Clara spoke up, though softly, more entreating than commanding. "Such a loyal servant deserves your mercy, dear brother."

Hierro's lips quirked and he cast Ariz an amused look, as though they shared a joke, both of them knowing just how little mercy Hierro possessed.

"If you send him back into Lord Quemanor's household cut to ribbons, people will ask questions. Oasia will certainly suspect. Too much depends upon Ariz's proximity to the duke and his friends for us to risk that, don't you think?"

"She's right," Remes said, though his gaze rested on Clara's bodice.

"Anything for Your Highness." Hierro lifted his dagger and made a flourish of wiping it clean of Ariz's blood with a table linen.

And though he did not despise Hierro any less, the desire to murder him faded enough for the brand to ease its torture. Ariz stepped back from the table, but Clara's hand on his elbow stopped him before he could withdraw as far as he would have liked.

She handed him a kerchief, emblazoned with swans.

"For your injury," she told him.

"Thank you, my lady." The silk square was far too small to stop his bleeding, but it was the greatest kindness he was likely to receive here, so he accepted it.

CHAPTER
SIX

A rap at his door sent Narsi leaping from his seat and nearly straight into the glowing coals of his fireplace. He staggered back, still only half awake. A second knock sounded, this time much more quietly. Anxiety lingering from his disturbed dreams made Narsi suddenly fear that his first patient in the duke's household could be dying in the hall—the knock growing weaker as lifeblood drained away.

Narsi bounded to the door and pulled it open, fully prepared to discover some bloodied page boy, a trampled groom or a maid in labor. Instead Lord Vediya stood before him, tousled and looking in perfect health. He held up Narsi's book.

"I noticed lamplight . . . ," Lord Vediya began but then drew back a step. "I didn't mean to wake you."

"You didn't," Narsi replied, if only to keep Lord Vediya from vanishing once again.

"Didn't I?" Lord Vediya arched his brow as he took Narsi in. "Should I be flattered by your lack of modesty in greeting me, then? Or simply awed in the presence of such magnificent endowment?"

Suddenly it occurred to Narsi that he stood in the doorway stark naked. His towel lay in a crumpled heap at the foot of his chair. He flushed with mortification.

"I meant that I was only napping—"

"I assure you I would be the last man to judge," Lord Vediya said. "But perhaps I should come in or go away, instead of keeping you here in the open hallway."

"By all means, come in." Narsi stepped back, then hurried to the examination table where he'd left his thin, white prayer clothes. "I'm afraid I haven't any refreshments to offer yet," he called over his shoulder as he tugged on the cotton pants.

Lord Vediya stepped in and pulled the door closed behind him, all the while looking around the room with an expression of quiet interest.

"I've not had time to put everything in order," Narsi told him. "But in a week or so . . ."

Lord Vediya nodded and then picked up one of Narsi's two small, framed pictures. He studied it intently.

"This is the Grunito townhouse in Anacleto."

"Yes." Narsi couldn't help but smile at the drawing. Small as it was, he could just make out several of the dogs and the stringy figure of himself as a twelve-year-old boy. "Lady Riossa Grunito drew this one and the other and gifted them to me when I left for my medical studies." As much as he adored the picture of the grand house, Narsi loved the other drawing far better, because it consisted of quick little studies of nearly all the Grunito family. Sometimes when he looked very closely he imagined that he could recognize his own profile peering out from Father Timoteo's shadow.

"Whyever would you leave Anacleto for the capital?" Lord Vediya asked.

"Father Timoteo requested that I come, and—" Narsi thought better of mentioning the promise he'd made eleven years before. It embarrassed him to even think of it, much less discuss it. "And where else could I have hoped to encounter so many fascinating new people?"

"A great number of whom will treat you poorly on sight," Lord Vediya commented.

"Then that's their loss," Narsi replied as lightly as he could. "But it seems unkind not to even allow them the opportunity to meet me."

Lord Vediya laughed and then set the framed picture aside. He held up Narsi's book.

"Speaking of opportunities," he said. "I was hoping you would give me your full name again. I pray you won't be too offended if I confess to being a little distracted when you first introduced yourself."

"Because a man was attempting to murder you, you mean?" Narsi replied. "I'm not offended; in fact I'm a little surprised that you didn't drop my book when you made your escape."

"Actually the marigold blossoms in your hair fascinated me far more than Ladislo's sad attempt."

Narsi felt his cheeks warming but didn't mistake Lord Vediya's offhanded flirting for anything of substance. The man had confessed in more than one publication to flirting compulsively when uneasy—also when bored, maudlin, drunk or hungry.

"I'm Narsi Lif-Tahm." Narsi pulled back a chair for Lord Vediya.

"Atreau," Lord Vediya supplied before flopping into the chair. "Just call me Atreau. Everyone does."

Narsi scowled at that. He couldn't help himself and Lord Vediya arched a black brow questioningly.

"Are you opposed to such familiarity?"

"Myself, no. There are few titles among Haldiim and nothing like Cadeleonian nobility." Narsi sat down across from Lord Vediya. "But once, years ago, I met a young nobleman—a fourth son of a minor lord—who confessed to insisting that everyone around him call him by his given name so that those who wished to insult him in their address would have nothing to take from him."

Lord Vediya's smile looked almost frozen on his face. For a moment he stared hard at Narsi and Narsi felt certain that he would remember their night together. But if he did he gave nothing away and only offered a light—if slightly forced—laugh.

"That sounds like the thinking of a sensitive young fool."

"I didn't think so, but I admit that at the time of the conversation I was hardly at the height of intellect myself." Narsi shrugged. "Still, his words did make me think quite a bit about the respect implied in addressing a Cadeleonian by his title and how it should not be stripped from him."

"I suppose I can see your point." Lord Vediya opened the book but then let it fall closed again. He studied Narsi, then leaned forward. "But here in the capital there are so many petty bullies who throw minor titles around that it grows tiresome and ridiculous. Particularly when all one desires is to engage in an honest conversation. Men known to each other by their given names can say what they like and tell one another when their thinking is right and when it's utter bullshit. But give one of the two the title of prince and the other the rank of footman and all that is lost."

"Yours is an interesting argument, Lord Vediya, but one inherently flawed by your lordly perspective. In the case of your footman and his prince I would suspect that honest conversation would be whatever the prince decided it is, regardless of how the footman addresses him. It's a conceit of the prince's that his footman would be so easily fooled into forgetting which of the two of them can have the other hanged for his familiarity."

Lord Vediya's expression turned playful and he leaned even closer in toward Narsi. The very faint perfume of rose oil drifted from him.

"I will concede that point. But let us suppose," Lord Vediya suggested, "that the prince has arrived disguised as a common man and struck up a conversation with a footman in a tavern."

"Then the prince has already engaged in deceit and once again there is not an honest exchange by both parties." Narsi leaned in as well.

"What then if the prince has lived in exile as a common man for a decade?"

"Then I would say that he's gone to a great deal of trouble just to chat up a footman," Narsi replied.

"Ha! As witty as you are winsome, aren't you?" Lord Vediya eyed him with a much too overt expression of appreciation. And Narsi knew at once that no desire lay behind it, only the wish to fluster him.

"Befuddling me with flattery still won't win you the argument, my lord."

Lord Vediya laughed again, but this time it wasn't the practiced display of a courtier. A genuine snort escaped Lord Vediya. Narsi felt relieved knowing at least that had not been stripped from Lord Vediya over the years.

"Very well, I concede the debate. However, I still insist that you call me Atreau." Lord Vediya raised a finger, cutting off Narsi's protest. "If only because there are four other Vediya lords at court and if I'm the one who you are calling out a warning to, I'd prefer to know at once."

"A warning?" Narsi asked and he thought of Ladislo.

"Atreau, watch out for that falling chamber pot. Atreau, your creditors are on their way to seize your belongings. Atreau, that dog is a wolf." Lord Vediya shrugged. "You know, the common sorts of things a man of my character must be wary of."

"But surely the dog is simply poor-mannered and maligned, not a wolf." Narsi felt certain that Lord Vediya was having a private joke about the current Cadeleonian terror of Count Radulf, the "Scarlet Wolf." "As anyone would know if they'd read your latest book instead of burning it."

This brought a genuine grin to Lord Vediya's handsome face.

"I'm heartened to know that at least one person has managed to read and understand it." Lord Vediya opened the book again, and this time he drew a slim graphite stylus from his pocket and wrote quickly on the title page. Narsi thought he recognized the flourish of a signature but couldn't read the rest of the faint gray words.

"I couldn't help but notice that you've made a number of notes on many of the pages." Lord Vediya flipped through until he came to a section where the margins were filled with Narsi's Haldiim script. "Corrections of the translations, or are these arguments against the ideas I've published?"

"They're notes," Narsi admitted, though he had to speak around a yawn. "Information about Labaran laws and customs. My thoughts about the medicine they practice and their surgical tools. I was fascinated by your description of treating the wounded during the night battle."

In fact Narsi had wept while reading the graphic, heartbreaking descriptions of the struggle to save overwhelming numbers of wounded men while surrounded by the chaos of a raging battle. Lord Vediya's expression sobered as he frowned down at the page of notes. Narsi realized that the horror of that night remained with the man and decided to quickly shift the subject.

"And of course I've made all kinds of guesses about what exactly it is that the Labaran sister-physicians do to make their condoms so much better than any others you've encountered."

That won him a smile.

"And what have you surmised?" Lord Vediya inquired.

"Well, they are fantastically thin, so obviously not sewn from balm-soaked linen like those you find in common night markets. And since the Labarans are famous for both their sausages and leatherwork, I'd bet that their condoms are made of animal skin or intestine, but that still doesn't explain how they keep them as supple as you describe."

"I do have a precious box of six still in my possession," Lord Vediya commented. "Perhaps when you're more rested we might try a few?"

"I . . ."

"There's a pretty woman of my acquaintance," Lord Vediya added. "She'd be happy to accommodate us—"

Lord Vediya went silent and looked to the door. Narsi wasn't certain if he was relieved or disappointed by Lord Vediya's sudden cessation of speech.

An instant later Narsi, too, heard voices in the hall. A woman and a man argued in whispers as they drew closer. Narsi thought he heard the woman say, " . . . see the physician . . . ," but he wasn't certain of the man's low reply.

Lord Vediya stood and started for the garden doors.

"It will not do your reputation any good if it's known that I was here with you at this hour," he said.

He was correct, Narsi knew that, but he also had no intention of joining the great number of men and women who privately enjoyed Lord Vediya's company while publicly disavowing him. Far too many of the fair-skinned Cadeleonians whom Narsi had grown up with in the Grunito household had done the same to him out on the city streets and in public taverns.

"Stay," Narsi said firmly. "I wouldn't deserve a good reputation if I turned my guests out into the dark night like unwanted cats. Anyway I might need a man who's seen the worst of surgery and kept his stomach."

Narsi turned away quickly to open the door, though he didn't miss the odd expression that flickered across Lord Vediya's face.

As he stepped out into the dim hall, Narsi caught sight of a tall, chestnut-haired woman, clothed in a yellow silk dressing gown and tugging at the belt of a man who leaned back into the shadows as if trying to melt away.

"Can I be of assistance?" Narsi asked.

The woman looked to Narsi with an expression of flattering and profound relief.

"Master Physician! My brother is injured and I think that he needs your attention." Then she scowled at the lank-haired, plain-faced man with her and hissed, "Just let him look at your arm. Or so help me I will start wailing to wake the entire household."

The man relented at once and sloped behind his sister while gripping a wad of blood-soaked cloth to his right forearm.

As Narsi turned and closed the door behind the siblings, he saw that Lord Vediya had left his seat by the fire and settled on the farther of the exam tables.

"Master Ariz, Mistress Delfia, greetings." Lord Vediya offered them both a half bow from the exam table and then made a little show of fastening his belt buckle. "I pray that it's not too much to ask that I and my merrypox visiting the physician not be shared with the entire household."

"Your discretion ensures ours, Lord Vediya," Delfia said. "Certainly my brother does not want it known that he tripped while showing off a sword dance to me and gashed his own arm open."

Mistress Delfia—Narsi remembered that she was the woman who had captured Berto's interest and who had also sent a warm meal. That would make her brother the sword and dance instructor whom Berto had described as plain as a clod of dirt. And perhaps he was to Berto's eye, but Narsi found him fascinatingly difficult to read.

Master Ariz allowed Narsi to lead him to a chair beside the examination table. He sat and Narsi frowned at the massive wad of cloth that Master Ariz held against his right forearm. Blood had soaked most of it through and seemed to still be pouring out. Yet he betrayed neither pain nor alarm.

"Can you raise your right arm above your head?" Narsi asked.

Master Ariz wordlessly complied.

"Help him keep his arm lifted, will you?" Narsi asked Delfia. She reached out and supported her brother's elbow while Narsi went to his medical satchel and then took a bottle of distilled coinflower from the cabinet shelf. He glanced over his shoulder to Lord Vediya.

"I could use those bandages from the shelf behind you."

"I live to serve." Lord Vediya swung off the exam table and gathered up the rolls of bandages. Narsi hoped they would be enough. If they weren't he'd have to strip the sheets from his fresh bed and use those.

Narsi directed Master Ariz to lower his arm just enough that it rested on the table. Then he carefully pulled away the wad of kerchiefs and rags covering the wound. He knew at once that these deep gashes had not resulted from a mere accident. The strokes were too clean and perfectly spaced. They also overlaid three shallow but much more ragged gouges.

Narsi noted that although Master Ariz said nothing and gave no sign of pain, the man was watching him from beneath his dark lashes. Narsi pulled the last of the cloth free and poured the coinflower distillate into the open wounds. Normally reflex at least made a person tense when the stinging fluid washed over a cut, but Master Ariz didn't flinch—didn't even blink.

He reminded Narsi of a fresh corpse that he'd dissected during his studies.

"You'll need stitches," Narsi told him. "Remove your doublet and shirt—"

"No." Master Ariz's voice was deep and chillingly emotionless.

"You can let your sister help you remove them or I can cut them off you with surgical scissors," Narsi told him. "But they're filthy and they must come off."

Master Ariz started to rise and Narsi realized that the man meant to walk out. Lord Vediya stepped forward to block him but Mistress Delfia caught him first.

"Ariz." She only said his name, but her expression was that of a strict mother commanding a rebellious child—an expression Narsi knew well. Master Ariz returned his sister's stare with his own dead-eyed gaze, then with the slightest sigh relented and dropped back down into his seat.

He allowed Narsi and his sister to quickly strip him. As they worked Narsi was happily surprised to see Lord Vediya had begun to unpack the surgical needles and silk from his satchel and then use the cleansing dish to soak both in coinflower distillate.

Narsi would have thanked him but he was distracted when he at last lifted away Master Ariz's doublet and almost dropped it due to its immense weight. Chain links of some kind lined the entirety of the ugly brown garment. Narsi could feel them through the cloth.

"Please let me take that for you, Master Physician." Mistress Delfia reached out and snatched it out of his arms. The fact that she gave no sign of the immense weight told Narsi that she expected it and made him think that she was at pains to hide it. Perhaps her brother wore the heavy doublet as a penance for some wrong that she didn't want Narsi speculating upon. Narsi made no comment and hoped that his silence would put her at ease. He wanted to treat her brother, not collect gossip.

Master Ariz's shirt he deemed too torn and bloody to waste time salvaging and simply cut it away. The body revealed beneath was shocking in its perfect muscular definition. Narsi didn't think he'd ever seen such a powerful back, toned chest or corded arms, except perhaps carved from marble in a chapel. But unlike the flawless statues of the Holy Savior, Master Ariz's fine skin was crisscrossed with hundreds of long, thin scars.

Did Master Ariz number among the zealot penitents who scourged themselves during the week of Our Savior's Misery? Had he been flailed, or somehow dragged across a field of razors? Certainly the pain and extent of injury these scars testified to would make the gashes in his forearm seem a lesser trouble. The thick circular burn scar on his chest alone bespoke torturous agony.

Narsi did his best not to stare. Instead, he focused his attention on applying duera drops to the wounds to slow the bleeding and ease Master Ariz's pain—even if he gave no sign of feeling any. Narsi rinsed his hands and then took the prepared needle and silk from Lord Vediya and carefully stitched the wounds closed. When he had tied the last knot and cut the silk, Lord Vediya passed him a washcloth to wipe the blood from his hands. Then he handed over a roll of bandages.

"Thank you," Narsi said, and he meant it. Lord Vediya's assistance made the entire procedure fast and simple. A few moments later Narsi finished wrapping Master Ariz's brawny forearm and tied the bandage off with a suture knot.

Master Ariz's expression remained one of bland disinterest, but his sister thanked Narsi graciously and listened attentively as he prepared a weak tincture of duera and explained what signs to watch for when the bandages were changed.

It was only after the two of them departed and Narsi collapsed down into his seat by the fire that he realized he'd neglected to secure any sort of payment.

Lord Vediya stood frowning at Narsi's door.

"Master Ariz and his sister have served in the duke's household nearly five years, but before now I would never have suspected him of being anything but drab beneath his clothes. Certainly not . . ."

"Such a beautiful ruin?" Narsi said as the image of all those scars filled his mind again. What sort of person inflicted such wounds upon such a perfect body? He couldn't imagine, or perhaps he didn't want to. Instead he stared at the gold seams of the embers burning low in the fireplace and his tired mind drifted. His eyes fell closed. He heard the rustle of clothes near him and the creak of a floorboard.

Narsi cracked his eyes open to see Lord Vediya leaning over his chair. For the first time Narsi noticed the lock of gray in his hair.

"Shall I help you to bed?" Lord Vediya asked.

"Mine or yours?" Narsi chuckled. His eyes fell closed, but then he shook his head. No, that was too dangerous and too foolish to even joke about. He forced himself up to his feet. "No, that doesn't deserve an answer. I shall take myself."

Lord Vediya nodded indulgently and then took his leave.

In the bedroom, Narsi found a freshly killed rat on the floor and the lanky black cat already asleep on his blankets.

CHAPTER
SEVEN

"You have a feeling about Timoteo's new physician?" Fedeles cast Atreau a skeptical glance. Then, realizing that the glow of all the surrounding blessings did not illuminate the gloom for his friend, he added, "It isn't simply the flush of too much wine?"

"Were my warmth inspired by wine, I'd tell you that his naked body is a wanton dream and his eyes are wonders of copper and emeralds. No. He's striking, but it's more his character that I found fascinating."

"His character? Next you'll be telling me you've fallen in love with a girl's skill at needlework," Fedeles replied, and he was only half teasing. He reached out to press his palm to Atreau's brow. "Are you fevered perhaps?"

"You'll understand when you meet him." Atreau shrugged off his hand. "He's exceptionally genial. Though that doesn't quite describe the quality . . ."

"When words fail you," Fedeles said, "then I know I've had you working too long on my account. You need to rest, I think."

"Yes. I do. But not as much as I need a physician for . . . her." Atreau said softly.

Fedeles couldn't stop the sound of disgust that escaped him.

Just the sight of a physician's silver signet made Fedeles shudder in horror. When he'd been a student a physician had taken possession of him. For three years the man locked Fedeles's mind in a prison of gibbering madness while secreting a murderous shadow curse in the very blood and bones of his body. Even after the possession was broken, a vicious remnant of the curse lingered in Fedeles. Every year it seemed to grow and Fedeles's loathing of physicians grew with it.

Everything about them revolted and terrified him. A whiff of coinflower, the clink of medical instruments, or a glimpse of an exam table could set his body shaking and his heart hammering with panic. And always, his terror roused the shadow within him—ready to lash like a murderous demon. Indiscriminate and fatal.

"He's friendly with the Grunito family and of Haldiim descent, so I very much doubt that Bishop Nugalo claims his allegiance," Atreau added. "And if he is one of theirs, he's gone out of his way to make himself familiar with the most obscene of my works."

"How? Can he read ashes?" Fedeles asked. Even as a duke he'd been hard-pressed—and heavily fined—to protect his private collection of Atreau's written works. He couldn't imagine how a mere physician could have done the same.

"Apparently the royal bishop thinks so little of the Haldiim people in Anacleto that he failed to consider that they have their own publishers. One of which has printed a rather lovely volume of my latest book."

The happiness in Atreau's voice surprised Fedeles. That warm, musical tone had grown so rare of late; he'd nearly forgotten Atreau could sound joyful. Fedeles knew much of that was his doing, but it could not be helped. He'd come to rely upon Atreau more than he would ever have imagined back in their school days.

"I shall write Nestor and request that he procure a copy of the book for my collection." It didn't matter to Fedeles that he wouldn't be able to read the Haldiim script. Atreau's work—and the history it recorded—needed to be preserved. Fedeles owed Atreau that much at the very least. A letter to Nestor could also serve as a foil to pass along a message to Alizadeh in Anacleto.

Not for the first time, Fedeles wondered what it was that Alizadeh could have done that had caused the Bahiim in the capital to bar him from entering the city. Perhaps the man was as contemptuous of Haldiim holy law as his student, Javier, had been of the Cadeleonian church.

Beside him, Atreau lifted his face to contemplate the stars overhead.

Fedeles could hardly see them or the dark heavens. Too much light radiated from blessings and charms decorating the wide promenade that surrounded the palace grounds. Prismatic color flared. Magic of different kinds shone—flecks of wild, raw power glinted like veins of gold through the granite flagstones at his feet, while blue, red, green and violet hues cloaked the multitude of statues in spells.

He narrowed eyes against the brilliance flashing at him from a lion statue, which had been seized generations before from the kingdom of Usane. Then, as they passed a burbling fountain, Fedeles gazed at the exotic collection of wan blessings glowing from so many foreign coins scattered beneath the waters. Fedeles couldn't read any of the illuminated symbols, but he felt their intentions. His shadow curled toward them with lazy interest but didn't rouse to any threat.

The most recent wards lining the promenade were no mystery to Fedeles. Over the past five years his wife, Oasia, had strung hundreds of delicate cerulean protections across the grounds of the royal palace. They gleamed like fine cobwebs shining with dew. No doubt Oasia could have created much more powerful spells, but she, like Fedeles, had to tread very carefully when it came to magic.

Any number of Labaran witches and Haldiim Bahiim spoke freely of how spells and places of power shone like constellations for them. Fedeles's exiled cousin, Javier Tornesal, had once demonstrated his sensitivity to magic by reading a text using only the magical light thrown off by a small talisman of a piglet. But in Cadeleon, admitting to seeing such things, much less manipulating them, was to confess to practicing witchcraft and committing heresy.

Lady Hylanya Radulf had learned that the very worst way.

She'd arrived in the capital as a potential bride for Prince Jacinto Sagrada, though privately she'd confessed to Fedeles that the true purpose of her tour of the city had been to investigate the aging wards that had once banished demons from the world—spells forged during the Battle of Heaven's Shard and maintained by the Hallowed Kings to this day. Fedeles had put Atreau at her service, tasking him with watching over her.

But Hylanya had discovered far worse than aging wards. Many of the protective spells had been torn asunder, and where the light of those spells failed, she'd been able to peer deep into the Shard of Heaven and perceived the ancient, deadly magic at its heart.

She'd not recognized it or known how to combat it. But she'd felt its power and malevolence like a desolate wind that had left her shuddering. Since then more wards had dimmed, and now Fedeles, too, caught glimpses of the roiling mass stirring within Heaven's Shard. His shadow prickled whenever he went near the place.

Did a furious Old God like the grimma smolder within the Shard of Heaven? Or could another demon lord like Zi'sai slumber inside? Or did the Hallowed Kings protect them all from something even more relentless and killing—a vast, unrestrained shadow curse, like the one that lived within Fedeles? Was that why his shadow had grown so much more restless of late? Did it sense a malevolent power like itself?

That possibility ate at Fedeles, filling his dreams with burning skies, crumbling houses and the crushing knowledge that *he* had caused countless deaths. It hadn't been so long ago that he'd been used to terrorize and murder his friends. Then, he'd tried to end his own life, but the shadow within him wouldn't allow him to escape.

Now, Fedeles could barely bring himself to think of the matter for too long. Instead he tried to entrust it to other people—better people—than himself.

He'd sent messages to Javier and Alizadeh, but neither could offer him much reassurance. The Battle of Heaven's Shard had left few survivors and almost no reliable records. Even most relics remaining from those days had been lost or hidden away by the secretive clergy of the Holy Cadeleonian Church.

All that was certain was that if the wards maintained by the Hallowed Kings failed, then whatever magic lurked within the Shard of Heaven would break free. Learning its true nature could cost them the entire kingdom.

Hylanya's attempts to repair the ancient wards should have pleased the royal bishop. At the very least her undertaking would have ensured his survival along with that of thousands of other Cadeleonians. It would have served him to ignore her. Instead he'd condemned Hylanya, ordered his priests to exorcise all of the protective wards she'd built around the Hallowed Kings and dispatched an assassin to poison her.

While the royal bishop's guardsman had hunted Hylanya, seemingly blank pages of tattered paper began to arrive for Fedeles. Letters written in shining white light that few people other than Fedeles could see.

When Hylanya had been poisoned, both Javier and his Bahiim master Alizadeh entreated—then ordered—Fedeles to claim the ruins of Crown Hill. There, beyond the royal bishop's grasp, lay the derelict remains of primitive wards—broken and scattered like a shattered shield. Moldering and long abandoned, they had been raised before Cadeleon stood as a unified nation. They had fallen to neglect when Cieloalta was only a muddy harbor town. But if the Hallowed Kings failed, they might offer the only protection to be found for all the people of the city. So Fedeles had ridden up into the ruins.

Yet the way the shadow curse within Fedeles roused as he walked over the heights of Crown Hill alarmed him. And the way the old wards responded to his shadow made him fear his own corrupting influence. For a time he'd held out hope that Hylanya might recover and take on the work in his place. But now he recognized that he could wait no longer. Hylanya needed to escape to Labara and he had to find the self-control to rebuild the shield of Crown Hill without setting his own curse loose.

A party of royal guards dressed in dun-yellow uniforms marched past them, drawing Fedeles back to his present surroundings.

He'd grown fond of the sight of those uniforms. One of the guards paused and exchanged a few comments with Atreau; the guard had been moved by one of his poems and wanted to tell him as much.

While they spoke, and Atreau gleaned belowstairs gossip, Fedeles glanced to his favorite sculpture on the promenade. Something about the naked, crouched figure reminded him of Captain Ciceron. Probably the bulging muscles of the bowed back. Or maybe it was the sly glance over his shoulder.

Weeks, even months often passed between the captain's visits, but the nights Ciceron did spend with Fedeles were delightful. He possessed a beautiful body and could be surprisingly affectionate, especially when drunk. Many soldiers grew violent after too much wine, but Ciceron turned cheerfully lusty, bidding Fedeles to enjoy him as neither his wife nor mistress could.

Ciceron never failed to distract him from his worries, even if only for a few hours. Though recently Fedeles had begun to want someone who would remain at his side in the morning—a lover he could hold in his arms even when they were both sober. Even as the thought occurred to him Fedeles shook his head. How spoiled had he grown that he, who deserved no one's affection, should long for more from a man who already indulged him?

Beside Fedeles, Atreau bid the guard a good night.

"Honestly, I can't exactly describe what it is about him," Atreau murmured. "He's familiar, but I don't know how . . ."

For an instant Fedeles thought it was Ciceron whom Atreau meant, but then their conversation returned to him. Timoteo's physician, and the need to move Hylanya before the royal bishop discovered her.

"Is there a ship ready?" Fedeles asked as they continued their walk.

"Our friends on the *Red Witch* are willing, but they can't delay much longer. The harbor master is already growing suspicious."

"You will need more funds, I imagine." Fedeles always tried to offer so that Atreau wouldn't be forced to ask.

Atreau nodded, then added, "And a physician. This one is already on hand in your household."

Just thinking of a physician in his home churned Fedeles's stomach. He'd planned on personally dismissing the man when he returned home tonight. Regardless of the late hour.

But it had been so long since Atreau had shown interest in or appeared to take pleasure from time spent with anyone that it seemed a shame to send him away. And they couldn't maintain Hylanya in her current condition much longer. If she died, there was no question of the hell that her brother would bring down upon them.

"All right, put this Narsi to work for us." Fedeles sighed.

The physician wasn't his servant to dismiss anyway, he supposed. And so long as he could keep the man and the horrifying implements of his trade away from himself, everyone would be safe.

"You will need to find a way to draw him off without attracting undue attention," Fedeles decided. "If he's as young and . . . genial as you say, then we should take a little care to protect his reputation. I care not so long as he comes nowhere near me."

"Of course. I'll do my utmost to keep him away," Atreau agreed. Then he added, "Thank you."

Already the voices of courtiers carried to them.

The rest of the city's populace might have snuffed their candles, put out their lamps and gone to their beds, but denizens of the Sagrada Palace rarely slept before midnight.

Two guards, both looking sallow beneath the yellow garden lamps, watched them approach and allowed them past without a word. Fedeles wondered if they'd recognized him or if they'd simply grown too tired of challenging every actress and poet that Jacinto Sagrada invited to his private rooms to bother stopping anyone.

At last they reached the marble steps that led up into the Royal Star Garden. A maze of perfumed hedges and blossom-strewn bowers divided the huge circular garden into quarters. Only the wide, pebbled walk before them presented a direct path and unobstructed view straight to the heart of the garden. There, Prince Sevanyo—silver-haired and hollowed by decades of rivalry with his brother—reclined upon silk pillows. Dozens of courtiers, advisers and consorts lingered around him, like little worlds in the pull of the sun.

Notable by their absence were all four Labaran ambassadors. Fedeles recognized only one of the kingdom of Usane's dignitaries, and she appeared to be saying her goodbyes to a circle of older courtiers. Of the twenty flamboyant Yuanese emissaries who normally attended Cadeleonian court and brightened the gatherings with their brilliant feathered robes and wigs, only two had not returned to their homeland. The younger of the two appeared ill at ease, while the elder studied the sky above them with a languid indifference that only vast quantities of black poppy smoke could inspire.

The six Haldiim scholars who for years had been fixtures of the royal court and who had designed this very garden were nowhere to be seen. Which of them had fled back to Anacleto and which ones had been abducted to the royal bishop's inquisition dungeons, no one knew.

No one spoke of it, but it seemed obvious to Fedeles that the royal bishop's actions were those of a man intent on purging the court of any dissenting voices. His call for Hylanya Radulf's execution for violation of Cadeleonian holy law—despite the fact that she was not a Cadeleonian citizen—betrayed just how blind he was to the repercussions of rousing Count Radulf's fury. He hardly seemed to care that his actions put all of their nation's allies on edge. No foreigners could feel safe now, knowing that they might be prosecuted for failure to subscribe to the dictates of the Cadeleonian church. Nor would any allied kingdoms wish to find themselves pitted against Count Radulf and his army of monstrous beasts.

Loud peals of laughter sounded over the quaint melody some distant musician plucked from a lute.

Seemingly unaware of all worldly turmoil, a group of noble Cadeleonian youths sporting slashed blue sleeves took turns peering through the immense golden mechanism of the royal star-glass. Several beautiful young women posed upon bronze astronomical models, which rose all around the garden like a miniature universe. One lady clung to a planetary sphere and swung with it on the circular track of its orbit over a bed of moonflowers.

The Duke of Gavado's spies and the royal bishop's informants numbered among the lovely boys and girls, but then so did several minor nobles in Fedeles's employment. Young courtiers unwilling to serve a powerful lord rarely won the offices or incomes required to enter the company of so illustrious a man as Prince Sevanyo. Despite their carefree demeanors, every one of the beautiful young people gathered here answered to a master. And if they weren't in Fedeles's pay then he had no doubt that they served someone else.

"Cousin!" Prince Sevanyo beckoned Fedeles to him.

He went. Atreau hung back among the astronomical models to keep watch from amidst the quiet figures lurking among the deep shadows that ringed the prince's resplendent gathering. Atreau possessed a knack for charming information out of even his enemies.

Reaching Sevanyo, Fedeles knelt in a deep bow. The prince gently touched the crown of his head.

"Rise, dear cousin, and sit with me, won't you?"

"It would be my honor." Fedeles seated himself on a cushion near the aged prince. An attendant immediately presented a silver platter of spiced cordials and ripe fruit. Fedeles took a glass and a cluster of black grapes, but he neither ate nor drank.

"According to the Yuanese, the stars that mark a man's birth guide his destiny throughout all his life," Prince Sevanyo said. Fedeles suspected that comment was directed more toward the winsome youth leaning up against the star-glass than himself.

A pretty young woman settled opposite Fedeles and proffered Prince Sevanyo a dish of candied berries. The prince favored her with a smile and accepted a sweet before going on.

"I've been told that I was born under an unlucky star, which has fated me to immense hardship for all of my life." Sevanyo paused to cast Fedeles a wry smile. "Can you imagine how spoiled a man born under a prosperous star must be?"

Fedeles laughed and Prince Sevanyo grinned.

"Certainly hardship and indulgence do come in a multitude of forms," Fedeles commented. "But I don't have it in me to expect the stars to decide either for me, I'm afraid."

"Nor do I, though I wish I could." Sevanyo sighed and then stole a grape from the bunch in Fedeles's hand. "It would offer me some comfort to think I could simply look up into the heavens and see the Lord's intentions for my sons written across the sky in starlight. Now that you have a child you know what I mean, don't you, Fedeles?"

"I do."

He'd wed Oasia and claimed her unborn child as his own for purely pragmatic reasons. He'd needed a wife and heir to strengthen his hold on the duchy of Rauma. He'd never imagined that he would grow to genuinely adore his wife or love the boy he'd called his son. Nor had he imagined how that love would change him.

Sparanzo's mere existence made him think about a future far beyond his own life and had taught him greater courage than he'd thought himself capable of. When he rode to Crown Hill and fought against his shadow, it was for Sparanzo's sake more than anyone else's. He understood Prince Sevanyo's desire to protect even his most wayward child.

"We want such greatness for them and see so much potential in them when they're young." Sevanyo scowled. An attendant immediately approached the prince, proffering a silver platter brimming with the dark tar of black poppies and a pipe. Sevanyo waved it away and then gently dismissed the young woman seated beside Fedeles, sending her to join her friends playing on a model of the moon.

"With four sons you'd think I'd have one half as faithful as you, Fedeles." Sevanyo looked tired and not quite well in the flickering yellow light of the surrounding lamps. "Xalvadar, my *heir*, can't be bothered to leave his mistress to visit his wife, much less me. Remes has become my brother's creature. I can see him fantasizing about my demise every time he offers me one of those God-awful smiles of his. He was the one who encouraged his little brother, Gael, to run off to the navy, I'm sure of it. Now Gael is drowned and lost beneath the waves. I won't even have his body to bury beside his mother. And then Jacinto . . ." Sevanyo simply made an exasperated noise in the back of his throat then gulped down his drink.

"I should've had a daughter," Sevanyo murmured. "A devoted girl to sit beside me and tell me all about the gossip in the city and what daring affairs are being undertaken by whom. She'd be here to whisper in my ear when my advisers lied to me and she'd chide me when I indulged in too much smoke and wine. She'd make me a better man. And on my death-bed, I'd scandalize the entire kingdom by making her my heir." Sevanyo laughed and plucked another grape from Fedeles's handful. "I'd do it too. I would." The idea of such an immense defiance of Cadeleonian hierarchy and tradition seemed to invigorate Sevanyo. He tossed the grape in the air and caught it in his mouth. "You should have a daughter, Fedeles. It's not too late for you."

Fedeles offered the prince a smile but knew better than to promise the man any such thing, even in jest. He would never hear the end of it. He kept quiet and a moment later Sevanyo's smile faded.

"Is he well?" Sevanyo asked. "My young wastrel?"

"Jacinto is fine, if a little bored with himself. We are doing all we can to ensure that he stays that way," Fedeles assured him. "The royal bishop has no cause to harm him, I promise you that."

"The red-haired woman that he's so taken with . . . ," the prince whispered.

"Her good work has been destroyed," Fedeles informed him. "I don't know that any of us can rebuild it."

"Then it is in the hands of God." Sevanyo shrugged.

Fedeles knew Sevanyo wasn't completely blind to the multitude of spells that cloaked the city. Once when they'd been in private he'd pointed out the light twinkling from love charms dropped in a wishing fountain, and after making an intense study Sevanyo had been delighted to see them as well. But as a rule, Sevanyo made a point of never looking too hard or long; he left that to holy men like his brother the royal bishop. As far as the Shard of Heaven was concerned, Fedeles knew the prince wasn't entirely convinced of the need for Hylanya's intervention. After all, the ancient wards had lasted for hundreds of years. If their own priests had no concern over the wards, why should they invite a foreign witch of uncertain motive to meddle?

And the royal bishop had given Sevanyo additional incentive to disregard Hylanya's warnings.

Two days past the bishop had suggested that he would at last bless Sevanyo's ascent to the throne, but only so long as Lady Hylanya had been removed from Cadeleon beforehand. Sevanyo had readily agreed. Fedeles hadn't liked it—particularly not the royal bishop's implication that Hylanya's fate should be left to whoever found her first—but he understood how exhausted Sevanyo was of fighting his brother. How badly he needed a little peace, so that he could mourn Gael's death.

"The issue of her stay will be happily resolved by this time tomorrow." Fedeles took Sevanyo's hand in his, offering him the reassurance that he didn't dare to voice. Sevanyo's skin felt paper-thin but also comfortingly warm. "A ship already waits to carry her back to her brother. Please leave it in my hands. My agents have some expertise in these matters."

Sevanyo's gaze flickered to Atreau, who leaned back against a globe. He sang out a pretty melody, though the words were likely to be filthy. A trio of young men grinned at him appreciatively while seven or eight young women gazed at him with besotted expressions.

Sevanyo nodded, then remarked, "Ladislo Bayezar would say you have too much expertise in spiriting women away. He wants to lay a formal charge of abduction. I'm surprised he's not here pressing his case now."

"I heard that a horse kicked him. He may not be able to attend court for a week at least." Fedeles tried not to let a note of guilt creep into his tone. It wasn't his fault that Ladislo mistook himself for a cuckold. "In any case, Suelita Estaban was not abducted. Not by Atreau or anyone else."

"But you do know where she is?" Sevanyo asked.

"I know she's happy and well. And I know we still need her. She has a gift for puzzles."

Sevanyo gave another thoughtful nod. "The Bayezars are firm supporters of mine. If Ladislo lays a charge against Atreau, he will have to appear for trial."

"I'll do all I can to ensure that it doesn't come to that," Fedeles assured him.

"I suppose I can't ask for more." Sevanyo smiled and Fedeles laughed, because they both knew he could ask for anything he desired and generally expect to see it delivered to him. He took another of Fedeles's grapes and bowed his head nearer to Fedeles. "Now that we've struck our bargain, is my brother still perturbed?"

"I'm hardly privy to his private thoughts, but he seems more convinced than ever that there's a plot to overthrow the church and that the Grunito brothers have forged an alliance between Anacleto and Radulf County to return us to an age of Old Gods." Fedeles lowered his voice. "Letters we've intercepted make it very clear that his agents in the north are actively searching for a means to destroy Count Radulf, while in the south he's attempting to wrest control of Anacleto from the Grunitos and suppress the growing Bahiim religion."

"God. How unoriginal he is." Prince Sevanyo rolled his eyes. "He's not made any inroads, has he? In the north or the south?"

"Javier assures me that he has removed all three of Nugalo's assassins in Labara and destroyed their orders before Count Radulf's men could trace them back to the Cadeleonian royal family." Fedeles felt his agitation growing, as it always did when he spoke of his exiled cousin to Sevanyo.

Javier's audacity—so much like Hylanya's—continued to make him an outcast. If only Javier could manage to live quietly, allowing memories of his transgressions to fade, then Fedeles could secure a reprieve for him and bring him home. But instead Javier proudly proclaimed himself a member the holy order of Bahiim; he charged through Labara dressed in flowing orange robes, with his hair hanging to his waist, battling monsters, banishing ghosts and destroying curses. He was becoming famous, which hardly allowed the Holy Cadeleonian Church to overlook his heresy.

Twice now Fedeles had been forced to bring all the wealth and military might of Rauma to bear just to block the royal bishop from issuing a warrant for Javier's death. Every year the possibility of bringing him home seemed to grow more and more remote.

Atreau hardly spoke of him anymore, and even Sevanyo's deep affection seemed to have waned.

"He remains loyal to you and only awaits your permission to return and serve you as he has always wished to." Fedeles squeezed Sevanyo's hands in his own. "You know that his conversion does not make him a traitor regardless—"

"Calm yourself, Fedeles. I know you want your cousin home." He offered Fedeles a doting smile that radiated all the affection that Fedeles had never known from his own parents. "I miss him too. After my coronation I should be able to grant you this favor—though you understand that he will never be a nobleman again. You must remain the Duke of Rauma."

"I know." Fedeles stared down at his own shadow. The edge roiled in the flickering firelight of the surrounding torches. No one comparing Javier's radiant brilliance to Fedeles's failings would have chosen him, but he knew better than to argue the point now. After Javier returned, the better man would be obvious. "So long as I'm needed, I won't abandon my responsibilities to Rauma or to you."

"I don't doubt it. Of all my daring favorites, you have proven the most steadfast." Sevanyo gazed at him as if realizing for the first time how very much older Fedeles had grown in the twelve years since he'd become duke of Rauma. "More loyal to me than even my own sons."

Fedeles felt a flush rising across his cheeks.

Prince Sevanyo laughed, though not unkindly; then he whispered, "Now tell me, what of Nugalo's actions in the south?"

"The royal bishop's spies in Anacleto suspect Nestor Grunito of converting to the Bahiim faith, but they haven't yet obtained conclusive proof—"

"Yet?" Sevanyo asked in a whisper.

Fedeles shrugged.

"I see." Sevanyo fell silent. He gazed out at the garden maze. "Nugalo's up to something . . . He wouldn't have agreed to give me the throne or allow Papa to have his respite if it didn't serve him somehow. Nugalo is always up to something."

"True," Fedeles agreed. As long as Fedeles had been alive, the royal bishop had been engaged in a power struggle against Sevanyo. "But it's difficult to know what. Recently, he's appointed several unusual nuns and priests to his personal staff. They all share an expertise in the history of the Shard of Heaven. And letters have surfaced which seem to indicate that he might be tampering with the same wards that he condemned Lady Hylanya for tinkering with."

"He's not harmed the Hallowed Kings though?" Just a hint of alarm crept into Sevanyo's expression. Not only did Sevanyo's ascent to the throne require that his father take the place of the eldest of the Hallowed Kings, but ultimately, Sevanyo too would join their trinity. Fedeles found the thought disturbing; the sight of the immense rings of spells that held the old kings' souls captive had terrified him when, as a child, he'd been taken to the Shard of Heaven for a New Year vigil. And he still found the sight distressing. Sevanyo, however, looked upon the Hallowed Kings in a much more joyous and protective manner. It seemed to comfort him to think that in death, he would join with his father and grandfather to protect the nation that each of them had ruled in their lives.

"I can't say with certainty. However, it's clear from his letters that he is investigating how the wards and the Hallowed Kings could be weakened—even destroyed. But to what end, we don't know. Right now all we have are implications. Not proof. A third letter is being deciphered even as we speak. Chances are good that it will reveal a great deal more."

"And Remes?" Sevanyo looked almost afraid to hear Fedeles's response.

"As far as my agents have been able to discover, your son is not directly involved in the royal bishop's actions."

"Thank God. I know it's weak of me, but I don't have it in my heart to harm the boy. Not even now," Sevanyo whispered.

Fedeles nodded, thinking of his own son, Sparanzo; he'd rather be struck dead than hurt his child. And yet Remes was no wide-eyed five-year-old.

"After the coronation, I'll reach out to him. We should be a family." Sevanyo's gaze drifted from Fedeles out to the young people all around him. Two jocular young men drew the aged prince's attention. They resembled each other in the way of siblings and seemed delighted in their own company. In that, they reminded Fedeles of the affectionate, boisterous Grunitos, though neither of these two possessed the powerful statures that marked the Grunito bloodline. Prince Sevanyo studied them wistfully. Perhaps he wondered why his own sons could not enjoy one another as these two did.

Fedeles, however, turned his attention to a trio of figures hunching beneath a rose bower. Amid so many tipsy, languid courtiers, these three stood out to Fedeles for their quiet, poised intensity. He didn't recognize either of the two young men, but seeing how easily their hands rested on the hilts of their dueling swords, he suspected them of being professional swordsmen. The woman with them handed over a coin purse and then turned and slipped back into the dark maze surrounding them.

"How do brothers come to this?" Prince Sevanyo wondered. "We should love each other, but our tradition of sacrificing second-born sons to the church only estranges them from their families. Worse, it rouses jealousy in those thousands of second sons that have been disinherited from their family titles and wealth and who feel no calling to serve the Lord. Can they help but resent their elder brothers, or covet their good fortunes?"

"Not all brothers are bitter rivals," Fedeles replied, but without much certainty. His own older brother had tried to have him declared insane and unfit. The accusation had cost him his life.

However, the Grunito brothers seemed to be shining exceptions. When the heir, Isandro died, Timoteo had refused to leave the church and instead undertaken a pilgrimage of prayer for his brother's safe passage into paradise. Elezar, the next in line, possessed both the physical courage and tactical brilliance of a natural leader, and yet he, too, had chosen to abdicate his title so that he could become the consort of Count Radulf. The fourth son, Nestor, also seemed to dismiss ambition in favor of devotion, in that he not only failed to denounce Elezar but also refused to have his simpleminded father declared unfit. Instead, Nestor and his mother protected and supported the damaged old earl when most other nobles would've seized power.

Perhaps it was that quality of selfless love that made the royal bishop so suspicious and resentful of the Grunito family as a whole.

"If only our papa had recognized the harm he did Nugalo by sending him from the family, . . ." Prince Sevanyo murmured. "If only I'd seen the hurt I caused Remes when I gave him over to Nugalo . . ."

An uneasy shiver rolled up Fedeles's spine. The quiet swordsmen he'd noted earlier had padded much closer. One man stepped through the edge of Fedeles's long shadow and it bristled like an angry guard dog. They drew closer still.

Now the nearby circle lamplight illuminated them clearly. The taller of the two called out loudly, as if taking offense at his companion's remarks. The shorter man shouted back, while moving steadily nearer to Prince Sevanyo. He moved too calmly for a man truly infuriated, and the hint of a smile flickered across the lips of his companion.

"So much needs to change, but who among us possesses the courage to dismantle the very traditions that have put us in power?"

Fedeles hardly registered the prince's words.

"I'll have your head for that!" the taller of the swordsmen roared as the shorter man edged still closer to Sevanyo. The taller swordsman drew his blade and charged. The shorter tore his own sword from its scabbard. The two of them clashed, spun and advanced. Fedeles recognized that mere chance and momentum hadn't carried them and their naked blades so close to the prince.

Sevanyo's guards weren't near enough, Fedeles realized with horror.

"Stop!" Fedeles bounded up, blocking the swordsmen's path to Sevanyo. The taller of the two grinned at Fedeles as if he were a hare flushed from hiding. He thrust his shining blade in to drive through Fedeles's chest.

Fedeles barely sidestepped the thrust. The blade whispered through the air as the swordsman thrust again. Instantly the murderous shadow curse that lurked within Fedeles broke free. Black talons surged up from Fedeles's shadow. A flutter of darkness gripped the swordsmen, looking like little more than the flicker of lamplight. Then a bloody gash tore across the shorter man's throat. The other swordsman's body split open from groin to collar. Hot blood spattered across Fedeles's outstretched palm.

Both men collapsed to the ground. Dark streams pooled around their bodies, turning the walkway pebbles slick.

Fedeles immediately jerked the murderous darkness back to the confines of his own body. He felt its rage thrashing and snapping against his will. His heart pounded with his own horror and his shadow's fury. Fedeles clenched his fists, imaging himself crushing the life from the murderous creature within him. The shadow curse quieted, then slowly stilled as Fedeles drew in a deep, steadying breath. At last his shadow lay flat and featureless, while Fedeles stood drenched in cold sweat and shivering as if he were naked.

Hardly a yard from him, one of the swordsmen groped haplessly at the gaping chasm of his chest with a look of terror. Then his hand dropped and he lay as still and silent as his companion. All around them servants and courtiers stared in shock and confusion. Several stole frightened glances to Fedeles but averted their eyes the moment they met his gaze. Fedeles looked up into the bright sky just to avoid their stares. Shame and horror filled him. After all these years he still couldn't control the shadow curse; he was still helpless before its fury.

The black silhouette of a crow winged overhead. Fedeles wished he too could simply fly away from all of this.

"Good Lord!" Atreau swung down from a bronze globe stamped with constellations. "I don't think I've ever witnessed two men cut each other down so quickly. I hardly saw the taller fellow strike back as he was laid open. He must have been one of the finest swordsmen in the city. A pity he drew against his equal."

Then all at once the rest of the courtiers took up the conversation, a few claiming they'd witnessed each stroke of the blindingly quick duel between the two men. Others bemoaned the violent times that they lived in.

Fedeles stepped back, sinking down beside Prince Sevanyo. He clasped his hands, pressing them against his thigh to still his trembling fingers.

He'd gone nearly three years without letting the murderous thing free; he'd nearly convinced himself that he could be trusted. But now two corpses lay where hale young men had stood only minutes ago. Assassins, surely. But still it shook him to the core that he'd so completely lost all hold over the shadow curse.

"I only wanted to push them back," he whispered. Sickness rose through him and he fought for several moments not to vomit.

"Ever my guardian," the prince whispered. Very gently he placed his arm around Fedeles's shoulders. Then Sevanyo gestured to a servant and moments later a group of tired-looking groundsmen arrived and set about the gory work of removing the bodies, spilled bowels and bloodstained pebbles. Soon enough the clusters of courtiers returned to their frivolity, many assisted by the abundant platters of liqueurs and black poppy pipes.

"It troubles you, doesn't it?" Prince Sevanyo asked, but then he nodded to himself. "Of course it does."

Sevanyo had known Fedeles during the terrible years when he'd seemed mad—and he had been half out of his mind. Against his will, Fedeles had slain a dear friend and destroyed the lives of all those who'd been brave enough to fight to free him from Donamillo's grasp.

Afterward, Prince Sevanyo and Father Timoteo had conspired to make it seem that those years had left no mark upon him. But they all knew that the razor-edged shadow curse lingered within Fedeles. He could not escape it.

"You are too good of a man," Prince Sevanyo went on quietly. "If Hierro Fueres carried such a burden as you do, believe me, he wouldn't suffer even a pang of guilt for the terror he would unleash with it. The very fact that it troubles you reassures me that you will not misuse it."

"Thank you," Fedeles replied. He wouldn't argue with his prince, but he didn't share Sevanyo's certainty. Nor did he wish to linger on the subject—too much thought directed at the shadow curse only seemed to stir it, give it more power and solidity. "Would you forgive me if I took my leave, Your Highness?"

"Of course, dear boy. You are good to indulge me for as long as you have," Sevanyo said. "Go with my blessing."

Fedeles withdrew, taking care not to step on the few pebbles still glistening with blood.

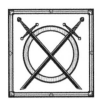

CHAPTER EIGHT

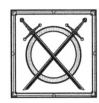

The morning following Captain Ciceron's murder, Ariz returned to his usual practice in the sword hall. Sunlight poured through the long windows and gleamed across the polished floorboards. The mirrors on the far wall threw pools of light across the sword racks and illuminated a pair of miniature paintings that hung between the marble columns that ringed the dueling floor.

Ariz lunged and returned to position while on the far wall his shadow distorted and twisted as if lampooning him. He lunged again and pivoted to slash the air with his blunt-tipped practice blade. His pallid reflection split across the panes of the nearest window.

Outside, two gardeners clipped sprays of scarlet blossoms from the camellia hedges. Soon the flowers would replace the fragrant jasmine that filled vases throughout the great house. After last night, Ariz would be glad of that.

He turned through each of the eight parries with his left arm first and then attempted the same with his right. His stitches pulled and fatigue slowed his motions to the sort of pretense of battle exhibited in so many stage plays and operas. For a moment he even considered singing the sentimental chorus of *The Rogues' Folly.*

Scoundrel born of hate and strife
Loyal to none, cruel to all
Now gladly lays down his life
Redeemed by true love's call

Absolution came so easily in theater. A few lyrics and a murderer transformed into a dashing hero.

Ariz stopped at the fifth position. He could feel blood seeping up from the seams of his stitches. He returned to leading with his left. He ought to have taken Delfia's advice and made an excuse to cancel his morning practice with Lord Quemanor. But he didn't want to lurk alone in his room, nor would it have been wise for him to chaperone his sister and her mistress, the duchess, as Delfia had suggested.

"You know I can't be trusted to keep what secrets I overhear," Ariz had been forced to admit. "It's better that I hear and see nothing."

Delfia hadn't argued. Instead she'd helped him endure the pain while he struggled to confess all he could of what he'd done and witnessed in Hierro's company. At some point he'd lost consciousness. Mercifully, Delfia hadn't continued her gentle, agonizing interrogation after that. She had pressed a kiss to his brow and then gone to report to the duchess.

Third bell rang out and Ariz ceased his practice. Casually he stepped into the shadow of a marble column and gazed out the west-facing window. Mounds of creeping thyme and moss roses carpeted the low, rolling hills leading up from the wooded grounds where Lord Quemanor rode every morning. Lord Quemanor appeared soon after, striding between the potted roses lining the white pebble path.

His resemblance to his cousin Hierro was remarkable, both of them possessing long graceful builds, black hair and dark eyes. But where Hierro cultivated a rarefied pale complexion, Fedeles Quemanor's face was freckled and his arms tanned as any of his grooms'. Today his son, Sparanzo, rode on his shoulders and both of them laughed at something—perhaps simply at the pleasure of each other's company. Ariz observed them with the fascination that he knew other men would have reserved for majestic paintings or sublime music.

But neither art nor melodies meant much to Ariz. Hierro sang beautifully and his sister, Clara, possessed a fine hand for painting portraits and landscapes. Such artistry beautified the world to the same extent that perfume masked the stinking sores of merrypox. It was smiling prettily before spilling poison into a glass of wine. Superficial deceit that altered nothing of the ugliness it disguised.

Genuine kindness, on the other hand, could make even terrible pain more bearable. Just witnessing the affection of father and son, Ariz felt somehow lifted out of himself. But as they drew near he turned away, resuming his lunges. It would not do for Lord Quemanor to suspect how closely Ariz observed him. Instead Ariz studied their approach in the long mirrors lining the far wall. Lord Quemanor swung his son down from his shoulders as they approached and the boy darted ahead.

"Master Ariz!" Sparanzo came through the doors, dashing slightly off-balance ahead of his father and waving a sapphire studded toy horse. "See what His Grace Prince Sevanyo gave me!"

Ariz turned feigning surprise and then immediately leapt forward to catch the boy as his left foot caught on his right. He nearly collided with Lord Quemanor, who reached for his son at the same moment. But even in exhaustion Ariz's reflexes served him well. He caught Sparanzo and then ducked under Lord Quemanor's chin to step clear. Momentum carried him two more steps, then he stopped and propped Sparanzo back on his feet. The boy released his tight grip on Ariz's right arm.

"Careful, young master," Ariz said. "You wouldn't want to break the prince's gift."

Sparanzo stared at him for a moment and Ariz thought he could clearly see Oasia Quemanor's features in the five-year-old's wide, round eyes and delicate brows.

"I tripped on the bad foot," Sparanzo said quietly and frowned down at his left leg, as if its disobedience might merit a stern lecture. Ariz nearly smiled. Though Sparanzo didn't bear a striking resemblance to his father, many of his expressions were perfect mirrors of Lord Quemanor's.

Out of the corner of his eye Ariz watched Lord Quemanor. He waited near the sword rack, giving his often-shy son time to share his news.

"I named him Wind." Sparanzo held out the toy horse. Its jointed wooden legs swung smoothly.

"Very handsome," Ariz commented, then he stood. "You must have performed very well indeed to have impressed the prince."

Sparanzo's expression brightened, and after glancing quickly over his shoulder to his father, he straightened and performed the vine step and kick that he'd practiced with Ariz. Then he dropped down into a kneeling bow.

"Perfect, young master." Ariz clapped lightly and Sparanzo sprang upright, grinning.

"The prince liked it so much that he picked me to bear the flower chalice in his coronation procession."

"Did he?" An uneasy feeling moved through Ariz as he remembered Prince Remes's casual mention of making Clara Odalis his queen.

"You don't think the procession steps will be too difficult, do you?" Sparanzo asked.

"Certainly not," Ariz replied quickly. "We can practice them along with the quaressa dance steps this afternoon if your noble father does not object."

"His father does not," Lord Quemanor called. "But for now it's time you returned to your mother, Sparanzo." Lord Quemanor smiled at his son, then went to the double doors that opened into a long interior corridor.

"It's not far to Mother's chambers. I could go alone." Sparanzo sighed. "I know the way."

"You could, but not today," Lord Quemanor replied. Then he summoned two of his retainers from the hallway and tasked the brawny men with escorting Sparanzo through the great house to Lady Quemanor's apartments. The men bowed and winked indulgently at Sparanzo. Most of the household staff considered Lord Quemanor overprotective of his wife and his son. Ariz, however, worried that the duke couldn't go far enough to ensure their safety or his own.

Both the retainers escorting Sparanzo were experienced soldiers and strong men, but also easygoing and prone to allowing pretty maids to distract them—particularly while inside the Quemanor house. The first landing of the narrow back staircase would be the perfect place to dispatch them. Two sword strokes, then there would be no one to save Sparanzo.

Ariz turned away to the windows, despising himself for his repellant turn of mind. Ruddy gardeners continued pruning the camellia trees. He attempted to take consolation in the certainty that if Hierro attempted to use him against the Quemanor family, the duchess, Oasia Quemanor, would not hesitate to have him put down.

Likely she would employ Delfia. Ariz had already sworn to his sister that he would not resist if ever that time came. In return Delfia had embraced him and promised him as painless a release as she could provide. Her poison needles worked fast.

The sound of Lord Quemanor's footsteps drew his attention back to matters at hand. Ariz turned to see Lord Quemanor strip off his dusty green jerkin and toss it over a stool. Morning light shone through his white shirt, outlining his lean form. His skin looked flushed from exercise and sun. He offered Ariz a friendly smile as he laid aside his sword and took up one of the blunt-tipped practice weapons from the rack.

"A good ride this morning, my lord?" Ariz inquired.

"Quite pleasant." Lord Quemanor stretched and rolled his shoulders. "The view from the top of Crown Hill is superb, with all the wildflowers in bloom and the foals playing in the pastures below. Have you ventured there?"

"I made the attempt a week past, but I wasn't sure of the way and didn't want trespass onto Count Odalis's property . . ." Ariz hoped that his words didn't seem as obviously leading as they felt to him.

"A hundred years of weeds and weather have left very little to recognize of the path." Lord Quemanor took his stance in front of Ariz, then added. "If you're truly interested you should join me tomorrow morning. I'll show you the way."

Ariz's heart seemed to jerk in his chest like a hooked trout. He forced himself not to answer too quickly or betray his pleasure. "A kind offer, my lord. I would be honored to ride with you."

Lord Quemanor raised his blade and Ariz lifted his own to meet it. Then, wordlessly, their match began. Lord Quemanor maintained a tight defense and used his superior reach to hold Ariz at bay. And for a little time Ariz allowed himself to simply enjoy the give and take of their thrusts and parries. Lord Quemanor's vigor rang through his blade as he met Ariz's quick attacks. But Ariz didn't like how easily Lord Quemanor backed off or his restraint when pressed.

"You should not allow me to push you into a corner, my lord," Ariz chided him.

"You think I'm allowing it?"

"I think you are dancing, when you should be fighting."

"Well, I do enjoy dancing quite a bit more," Lord Quemanor said.

"Whether or not you like it, you must learn to fight, my lord. At least to defend yourself and those who rely on you." Ariz jabbed in at the duke's left arm and the duke sidestepped him, but this time Ariz didn't permit his escape. He struck hard with the flat of his blade.

Lord Quemanor grimaced but blocked Ariz's blade the second time he struck.

"Good," Ariz told him. "But don't just block me. Press your advantage."

"I don't want to hurt you." Lord Quemanor's friendly expression faltered. He looked almost stricken.

Ariz drove in fast. Lord Quemanor parried but failed to notice the sweep of Ariz's left foot. He hooked Lord Quemanor's ankle and jerked his leg out from under him. The duke toppled onto his ass.

"With respect, you'll have to learn a lot more before you'll be able to even challenge me, my lord," Ariz replied.

"Yes, I can see that," Lord Quemanor commented as he regained his feet.

Still, Ariz had to knock Lord Quemanor down twice more before the duke struck back with all his strength. Then he moved marvelously and with enough speed to land a few glancing blows. Ariz hardly noticed; the dull practice blades raised welts but rarely broke skin. Instead he delighted in matching Lord Quemanor's attacks and testing his defenses. As his heart hammered and sweat beaded his body, his spirit lifted.

He could not rely on himself to defend Lord Quemanor, but he could train the duke to match him, perhaps even better him.

Their blades rang and scraped. Lord Quemanor charged and Ariz blocked. He feigned to the left, but Lord Quemanor parried his thrust and they continued to circle and strike at such speed that at last Ariz no longer felt the presence of the brand burning into his chest. He fought as he had when he'd trained under his uncle, taking exuberant delight in equaling his partner's prowess.

Suddenly, without warning Lord Quemanor bolted back and held up his hands.

At once Ariz lowered his weapon.

"Are you hurt?" Ariz asked. It horrified him to think that he might have struck too hard and drawn Lord Quemanor's blood.

"No, you are." Lord Quemanor gestured to Ariz's right arm, his expression drawn. For the first time Ariz noticed the vivid red splotch spreading across his gray shirtsleeve. "Did I—" Lord Quemanor began, but Ariz cut him off.

"No. An accident last night. It's nothing," Ariz assured him.

"It bleeds quite a bit for nothing." Lord Quemanor dropped his practice blade and came quickly to Ariz's side. When he reached to take his right hand Ariz sidestepped out of reflex.

"It's been seen to already," Ariz said, hoping that explained his unwillingness to allow Lord Quemanor to see his injury.

"Has it?"

"Yes." Ariz seized upon a sure source of distraction. "And I owe you my thanks for providing us with a new physician. I hope this one will outlast the previous."

"That . . ." Predictably Lord Quemanor's expression soured. And why wouldn't it? The man had spent three years being insidiously tortured and possessed by a physician called Donamillo. Ariz's own cousin, Genimo, had assisted in the crime. And despite Lord Quemanor's gentle manner, many people still whispered about his mania and madness and claimed that traces of that murderous possession lingered in the duke's long black shadow.

Now that shadow fell across Ariz, but he didn't fear it, not even when he noted how it seemed to coil around him. He knew what corrupting sorcery felt like when it crawled over him. Lord Quemanor's shadow didn't sicken him, nor did it oppress his thoughts; if anything it felt calming. Years ago he'd discovered the refuge that the duke's shadow offered while fencing with the man. Now he sought it out almost unconsciously. Some days the fall of the duke's shadow had been the only respite Ariz could win from weeks of scorching agony. Ariz supposed it was no wonder that he'd grown so attached to Lord Quemanor.

"Father Timoteo has retained him, actually." Lord Quemanor frowned down at Ariz's injury. "I've not yet met the man. How did he strike you?"

"He seemed assured in his manner and capable in his practice." The Haldiim physician had stitched his wounds better than most of the barbers and charlatans who'd patched him up over the years. More importantly, Hierro would never employ a Haldiim, not even as an assassin. This new physician might at last be a man who could be trusted to attend to the duke and duchess and perhaps even treat Sparanzo's leg with something other than quackery and malice.

"Yes, but would you trust him? Perhaps choose him as a friend?"

"I . . ." Ariz could not fathom how to answer that question. He hadn't had a friend since he was fourteen years old. "I haven't spent enough time with him to find out if we have anything in common. But I think that he could be a great boon to your household, my lord."

"Really? Then show me his handiwork," Lord Quemanor demanded.

Reluctantly, Ariz extended his right arm and then pulled back his shirtsleeve. He should have kept his bandages on, but he'd not wanted their bulk to give him away and the wounds had seemed scabbed closed well enough when he'd woken this morning. None of the silk stitches had torn out, but blood seeped up from the tender seams of his wounds.

Lord Quemanor scowled. To Ariz the injuries looked quite healthy. Neither pus nor any fierce red inflammations showed.

"The stitches are quite straight and clean," Ariz commented. "And the flesh is hardly swollen—"

"For God's sake, your arm is a bloody mess. We will not be fencing any further this morning," Lord Quemanor stated flatly.

Ariz's spirits sank. These morning practice sessions were the only time he could ever hope to have alone with Lord Quemanor. In fact, Ariz already heard the duke's personal retainers greeting courtiers as they gathered in the hall outside. Soon some page or courier would wheedle his way in and then a sea of men and women would wash through the doors and carry Lord Quemanor off to wittier and lovelier company than Ariz could hope to offer.

But there would be tomorrow, he reminded himself. The promise of the morning ride lifted his spirit.

"As you wish, my lord." Ariz bowed and then turned and replaced his practice sword on the rack. Lord Quemanor went to retrieve his discarded blade.

"There is still a little time left," Lord Quemanor commented.

Ariz waited, watching Lord Quemanor's reflection in the mirror. The duke gazed out one of the windows, his expression distant but untroubled.

"Sparanzo demonstrated a Labaran dance for his mother and me last week. He said you taught it to him."

"Yes, the estanfai." Ariz hoped he hadn't overstepped by introducing a Labaran custom when relations between the Cadeleonian court and the Labaran Count Radulf were was so contentious. Mastering the intricate footwork had seemed to help Sparanzo's confidence. "It's normally a sword dance, but I thought it best to teach him the steps before involving any weapons."

"Probably wise," Lord Quemanor agreed. "Can you teach it to me?"

"Yes. With pleasure." Ariz felt certain that his grin gave him away, but when he caught his reflection he realized that his plain face remained as expressionless as ever. He made a concerted effort and the corners of his mouth lifted, offering Lord Quemanor's reflection a brief, faltering smile.

"Lead on then," Lord Quemanor said.

Ariz demonstrated the steps, once slowly, then at speed. The momentum of an opening spin allowed him to seamlessly shift his weight from foot to foot and from heel to toe, gliding forward and back across the floor as if he were skating over ice. He indulged himself in a backflip before he at last he spun to a halt and bowed low before Lord Quemanor.

"You do possess a magnificent grace, Master Ariz," Lord Quemanor commented. "I doubt I could ever hope to equal that."

"It's just a matter of practice, my lord." Again Ariz tried to return Lord Quemanor's flattering smile, but his reflection showed him a stony, dead expression.

"Certainly there is some joy in it as well?" Lord Quemanor asked as he emulated Ariz's footwork with slow careful steps.

"As you lead with your right leg you will want to shift the weight on your left foot back to your heel," Ariz informed him quickly, and Lord Quemanor nodded and corrected himself. Then he cocked his head as if contemplating Ariz.

"You haven't answered my question, you know."

"I know," Ariz responded. "I'm thinking about it."

"Is joy so strange a thing to you that you must ponder it so deeply?" Lord Quemanor's tone was warm and teasing.

"You missed your backstep," Ariz informed him. Lord Quemanor offered him facetious salute before beginning again.

"When I'm dancing or fencing at my very best . . . it's not exactly joy I feel," Ariz admitted. "More that I lose myself and become pure motion. I imagine it's how a hawk feels as it dives. Speeding so near disaster that nothing else can matter."

Lord Quemanor paused midturn. He met Ariz's gaze with a curiosity that Ariz knew he should take as a warning.

"You are so unlike your cousin," Lord Quemanor said. "And yet every now and then I think that I can almost hear his voice in your words."

Ariz felt the blood draining from his face. There was no need to wonder which of his cousins Lord Quemanor referred to. Only one member of the Plunado clan had schooled with the duke. He'd betrayed Lord Quemanor and his treachery had cost the family everything. Ariz bowed his head.

"I'm sorry, my lord. I meant no offense—"

"No, I worded that poorly." Lord Quemanor frowned past Ariz and pinned his own reflection with an intense glower. "Genimo wasn't devoid of insight or charm. How else could he have wormed his way so deep into my family's trust?"

But what he'd done with that trust had been terrible, and in the end it had not just cost Genimo his life but had also stripped the entire Plunado family of their titles, lands and nobility. All they had once possessed had been surrendered to Fedeles Quemanor by royal decree.

Ariz had no idea how to respond. In all the time he'd served Lord Quemanor's household he'd never used his family name, nor had Lord Quemanor ever remarked upon his relationship to Genimo.

"At one time he was my dearest friend. I suppose that's why I was so furious when he betrayed me." Lord Quemanor sighed heavily, then he turned to Ariz. "My suit against your family must have seemed out of all proportion to the injury done to me. To you and yours, I mean."

Ariz could hardly tell him that he understood what it was to be possessed and used like a mere instrument. He understood the horror of having his own will overwhelmed and feeling his body become a prison.

"Our ruin was not your doing, my lord," Ariz replied, though it pained him to think of all that his family had endured and lost. But the king's ruling had been far from the worst dishonor Ariz or his sister had suffered. They had both already been under the Fueres family's power for years by then. "Genimo was to blame. No one else."

"Yes." Lord Quemanor abandoned all pretense of dancing to pace between the marble columns and scowl at the gold-framed miniatures of swordsmen at practice. "That's what begins to trouble me now that I've had a decade to reflect. Neither you nor anyone but Genimo wronged me, and yet I have taken so much from you."

"What is done is done. I can't imagine the king rescinding his decree." Ariz shrugged.

"Not the current king, but perhaps—"

"Lord Quemanor!" A man's voice rose from the hallway and then the door swung open. A scrawny courier dressed in royal blue and gold pelted into the room at such speed that he slid several feet across the polished floor before he could drop into a formal bow. Sweat plastered the young man's brown hair to his flushed face. Several courtiers peered in through the open door. Of all of them, only Atreau Vediya looked at Ariz.

"Your Grace." The courier paused, attempting to catch his breath. "News from the south gate. Captain Ciceron has been murdered. Beheaded, sometime in the night."

Lord Quemanor did not attempt to hide the horror and sorrow on his face but instead he turned his back to the courier and the pack of gawking courtiers. He strode to the doors opening out onto the grounds and, throwing them open, he let loose a furious, inarticulate shout.

It was no secret that Captain Ciceron was among the duke's favorites. Ciceron's advancement from night warden of the dreary city jail to the prized south gate posting had been Lord Quemanor's doing. Further, the captain had accompanied the duke to the opera on numerous occasions and afterward taken his rest in the duke's rooms. Ciceron had been exactly the sort of brash, vivacious, handsome man whose company Lord Quemanor most enjoyed.

As courtiers edged into the large chamber, Ariz backed to the weapon racks. He stilled in the shadows, abandoning any pretense of animation. He let dead numbness enfold him, preferring it to the guilt of watching Lord Quemanor's back shudder as he slumped forward, convulsed with racking sobs.

At last Atreau broke from the circle of courtiers and went to comfort Lord Quemanor with a brotherly embrace. However pox-riddled and licentious Atreau might be, Ariz was glad that he was here now. He whispered something that won a choked laugh from Lord Quemanor.

After a few minutes the two of them turned back and Lord Quemanor questioned the courier for the few certain details surrounding Captain Ciceron's death. There was little doubt that he'd been murdered by a practiced assassin, likely more than one considering the captain's strength and skill. He'd not been robbed and his head had not yet been discovered.

"His widow and children may need your support," Atreau told the duke. "But there is the other matter as well."

"Yes, you're right," Lord Quemanor said.

Other nobles closed in around the two of them—their conversations ranging from how large a bounty to offer for the assassins to how best to aid the widow as well as what monies might be given to Ciceron's pregnant mistress without causing a scandal. Then there was the matter of the captain's final rites. Already a rumor had sprung up that the royal bishop would refuse to bless the man.

"Timoteo will bless him if you ask," Atreau assured the duke. They drifted out through the garden doors. The duke's attendants and retainers trailed after, leaving Ariz with only his own dead-eyed reflection watching him.

CHAPTER NINE

Narsi had forgotten how unbearably early Berto rose, but the recollection returned to him quickly when he found himself pulling on his clothes in predawn light. Berto paced the exam room while excitedly informing him that the rumors that the dying King Juleo had been sanctioned to become a Hallowed King had proven true. Once the old king's passed, Prince Sevanyo could at last be crowned the new king. And, in a bold gesture of solidarity with the Grunito family, he'd chosen Father Timoteo to preside over the coronation.

"Which means that the royal bishop will have to make Father Timoteo a bishop after all!" Berto all but skipped around the exam room in his glee; then he stopped suddenly. "I'll have to work like mad to have all of his sermons in order if they're to be published in the coronation year. Perhaps it would be wisest to print several separate smaller books. That way some, if not all, of the Holy Father's ideas will be known by the time of the coronation."

Narsi managed a few groggy responses before he awoke enough to realize why his gray physician's coat was proving so difficult to button.

"You could have mentioned that I was putting the thing on inside out," Narsi commented.

"Who am I to judge how you choose to dress?" Berto replied.

Narsi pinned Berto with an accusatory glower, but the other man hardly noticed. He continued to speculate on possible future publications and what new income the Holy Father might expect, which, in turn, could mean increases in his and Narsi's allowances.

At last, properly clothed, Narsi followed Berto across the grounds to the steps overlooking the kitchen gardens. There, Berto wheedled two bowls of barley water from the bakers. Then the two of them ate on the steps. Narsi recognized Querra out with the several groundsmen tending the trellises of ripening red solanum fruit. When she glanced his way they exchanged a friendly wave.

"How can you have already charmed a woman?" Berto commented. "You haven't even been here a day."

"You have your holy studies and I have my interests to pursue." Narsi drained the last of his barley water and stared hungrily at the beds of fat, red strawberries only a few feet from him. "I have to get an early start if I'm ever to entice the Cadeleonian maidens here to allow me the pleasure of their precious bounty."

Berto frowned at him and Narsi rolled his eyes.

"Oh, don't scowl at me like that," Narsi chided his friend. "I'm not speaking euphemistically. I'm far too tired and too hungry to have designs on anything more than strawberries and the eggs that fat hen is clucking on about over in the cabbage patches."

Narsi pointed to where a plump black hen settled herself down amongst the rows of red and green cabbages. Spying the maids collecting eggs from the large coops, Narsi couldn't help but feel a little affection for this one determined bird, which had escaped the henhouse to lay in secret.

Berto chuckled, but then called to one of the passing kitchen maids. The dark-haired young woman clutched her egg basket close to the folds of her yellow skirt and eyed the two of them suspiciously before informing them that the cook would decide if any eggs could be spared for the lunch at the master's tables. But, in her opinion, all that she'd collected should be used to make splendid meringues and custards to grace the table of the duke and duchess.

"Don't lose heart." Berto grinned at Narsi. "All you need do is charm your way to the duke's table. How difficult could that be for a physician?"

"I suspect that will be a fine day in all three hells," Narsi replied gamely. "I'd better save a few pennies to buy my own little hen."

They made their way to the chapel.

The Duke of Rauma's household was a little city in itself. Gardens and acres of carefully maintained woods, as well as a large pond and an ornamental stream, camouflaged the fortresslike quality of the surrounding walls and provided produce, game and even fish for the duke's table. Beyond the three-hundred-room mansion of the duke's private residence lay dozens of workshops where smiths, brewers, carvers and leatherworkers—to name just a few of the craftsmen Narsi greeted in passing—all plied their trades at the duke's behest. The sculleries and henhouses, pigpens and milking sheds employed scores of women, while the armory and guardhouses appeared populated by an equal number of men.

The chapel and its enclosed grounds lay opposite the stables, and Narsi wasn't certain which was grander.

"The duke's horses live better than some bishops," Berto informed Narsi, and he could almost believe it was true. The spacious, tidy stall provided for his mare would certainly have been the envy of most novice monks.

Second bell rang out as Narsi and Berto slipped into chapel. Moments later two teenage acolytes in unlined black robes closed the doors behind them.

Narsi paused an instant after stepping out of the light to allow his eyes to adjust to the dark interior, only to find himself paralyzed by instinctual fear at the sight of an immense wolf snarling down at him. Then, realizing that he was cringing beneath a statue, he took in the rest of the building. The Grunito chapel had not boasted less goldwork or fewer jewels studding the walls, but the carvings of serpents and demons arching up over the heroic figures of the Savior and his saints had not possessed nearly so much detail as these. Somehow despite being motionless, the wolf's body conveyed a snarling, flexing vitality.

All at once he recollected a section of Lord Vediya's memoir, *Five Hundred Nights in the Court of the Scarlet Wolf.* He'd been riveted by the description of Count Radulf awakening stone trolls and other carvings of mythic creatures. They'd burst to life from ancient pillars, walls and even the supports of bridges to battle the invading witch queens. Now it seemed all too easy to imagine the monstrous creatures that formed the chapel's stone walls shaking off their slumber and snapping up the parishioners.

There was something to inspire a few prayers heavenward, Narsi thought.

Though the people gathered in the pews ahead of his seemed to pay the carvings no particular mind.

"I'm afraid I must abandon you for the moment. I've taken up the daily duty of proffering Father Timoteo an inoffensive sermon so that he can disregard it after the first sentence." Berto smiled despite his complaint. "Though . . . would you like me to make introductions for you?" He shifted his gaze out to the parishioners filling the pews ahead of them. Narsi studied the crowd as well.

The majority of them wore the Quemanor colors but cut in the modest design of servants' garb. They seemed largely occupied with their own thoughts and prayers, paying him little mind at all.

"Don't let me keep you from Father Timoteo. I'll be fine."

While Berto strode ahead to the vestry, Narsi continued studying the chapel and its occupants. He felt most comfortable here in the shadows at the back of the building, where he could look on without his presence drawing too much attention.

The finely upholstered pews at the very front of the chapel stood empty, reserved for members of nobility, but those a little farther back from the gilded pulpit accommodated a group of men whom Narsi guessed numbered among the astrologers, mechanists, musicians and more-learned tutors whom the duke retained. Narsi supposed that his proper place should have been among them, but for the time being he preferred to sit back among the cooks, maids, grooms and gardeners to observe his colleagues. He seated himself near a fellow who looked like an undergardener and smelled like camellia flowers.

The fencing instructor, Master Ariz, was not present. Narsi wondered if that was due to his injury or if he counted among the growing number of educated men and women who chose to attend chapel only on the highest of holy days, if ever. None of the other masters appeared to expect him and Narsi didn't hear his name whispered through the quiet of the chapel, so he guessed that Master Ariz wasn't a religious fellow.

Odd. Most swordsmen were inclined toward prayer, in Narsi's experience. Maybe the fellow possessed more the character of a dance instructor. Or, recalling the mess of scars that marred the man's body, perhaps he simply preferred to take his exuberant penance in private.

As the acolytes stepped up before the pulpit, Narsi abandoned his contemplation. The two boys sang out the first notes of Consecration. Narsi stood and raised his voice along with them and the rest of the congregation. While they lifted the notes up to the heights of the azure ceiling, Berto appeared, escorting Father Timoteo out from the vestry and up the steps of the golden pulpit.

Taking in the Holy Father's emaciated figure, Narsi forgot the song, his heart sinking like a stone to the pit of his stomach.

The Holy Father towered over Berto, but his immense height only emphasized his terrible thinness. His long, broad bones—suited to the frame of a giant—jutted from beneath the slack folds of his black and violet robes, lending him the appearance of a spindly marionette. His large hands appeared skeletal, and between his hooked Grunito nose and the deep hollows of his cheekbones his face resembled a death mask more than a living countenance. The man was only thirty-eight, but already his close-cropped hair had gone white and he moved with the slow deliberateness of a man in his sixties.

After the last notes of Consecration faded into soft echoes, Father Timoteo spread his hands and the congregation sat. Then the Holy Father raised his voice in sermon and the sound rang deep and rich as the notes of any great bells. Narsi always marveled that so powerful a voice could arise from an emaciated husk of a body. Faith resounded through him as he spoke of the countless forms of the sacred found in common acts of compassion, forgiveness and courage. Though Narsi didn't consider himself a devout man, he never failed to feel moved by Father Timoteo's words.

Unlike most other priests or Bahiim, Father Timoteo didn't drag his sermons out just for the seeming pleasure of hearing his own voice. He spoke his piece and then offered up blessings for all those who had gathered to hear him. Then his six young acolytes led the congregation in the Song of Six Blessings. After which, Narsi expected that they would all be sent on their ways, but instead Father Timoteo addressed those gathered in the pews once more.

"Some of you may know that I had sent for a physician to minister to the physical well-being of this great household. The good man has arrived and I would introduce you all to him." Father Timoteo indicated for him to stand with a gesture of his bony hand. Narsi rose, feeling quite self-conscious as the rest of the congregation turned in their seats to peer at him. Some gawked, and in the echoing chamber of the chapel Narsi could clearly hear the whispers of "Haldiim."

"This is master physician Narsi Lif-Tahm." Father Timoteo's words rolled through the chapel like thunder, dissipating all other sound. "He is not only a member of my household but a very dear friend. I hope that you all will welcome him as warmly as you have welcomed me." Then the Holy Father bid them all to go forth with blessings in their hearts.

The Holy Father's words silenced the disparaging comments but placed Narsi in the awkward position of having everyone filing out of the chapel pause and attempt to offer him some form of greeting. One of the kitchen women seriously inquired if his people could eat natural food. Narsi nearly asked her what she meant by "natural," but seeing how flustered she looked, he assured her that he could eat just about anything after a breakfast of only barley water. She looked relieved, laughed nervously and then hurried away. Several grooms commented on Narsi's size, deeming him "a big one for one of your breed," "half horse" and "taller than the Savior."

At least two of the maids took in his features and then stole scandalized glances back at Father Timoteo. Narsi supposed there would be no stopping the speculation and gossip, given the resemblance. Still, he appreciated that the Holy Father had spoken up for him. Overall he met mostly friendly expressions and felt welcomed. The slim, brown-haired music instructor even walked out of the chapel alongside Narsi, quite intent upon voicing his dissatisfaction with common cures for piles.

"I've already been fingered by far too many quacks." Master Leadro sniffed. "One begins to suspect they take some perverse pleasure in it."

"Have any prescribed split-pea and lentil gruel?" Narsi asked.

"No," Master Leadro admitted, though he didn't look at all happy about the prospect. "In place of which meals would you say I should have this gruel?"

"Not in place of them, Lord forbid!" Narsi assured him. There was the problem with so much Cadeleonian doctoring, prescribing penances in place of medicines. "Fasting will only make the matter worse. It's far better to take a cup of gruel along with your luncheon and supper."

"Really?" Master Leadro stopped alongside Narsi on the chapel steps. "That sounds far too reasonable. Are you certain you're a physician?"

"I have the ring to prove it," Narsi replied. "Though if it would make you feel more certain of my skill at quackery, I could sell you a few elixirs of questionable origin."

The music master laughed at that and assured Narsi that the gruel would do for now. Then he departed and left Narsi to await Father Timoteo. From what he could remember, the Holy Father usually took a stroll after his morning sermon. Today proved no exception. Just as the bells high in the chapel steeple rang out four clear notes, Father Timoteo emerged with Berto at his elbow. Narsi went to him and bowed his respect.

"Narsi." Father Timoteo reached out, drawing Narsi upright, and then clasped him in a welcoming embrace. "My dear, dear child, you've grown so tall and handsome!"

When Narsi hugged the Holy Father, he felt Father Timoteo's ribs and vertebrae through the light cloth of his monastic robes. The man had starved himself down to bone.

"How have you been?" Father Timoteo drew back a little, though he kept one arm draped over Narsi's shoulder. Narsi leaned into him, taking as much of Father Timoteo's weight as the Holy Father would allow. Berto braced the Holy Father's left side.

"I've been well," Narsi said. "I'm not quite settled in my rooms, but I think I should be before the end of the week. I'm hoping you'll allow me to test one of my soups on you." Narsi wondered how much cream and butter he could introduce to Father Timoteo's meals. Perhaps he should speak to someone in charge of the kitchen.

"Anything I can do to help you settle in here. I have no doubt that once the duke meets you, he'll be charmed. You're so like your mother I can't imagine anyone failing to be delighted by you." Timoteo nodded, then his happy expression faded. Narsi noticed the Holy Father's dark brown eyes taking on a glassy gleam. Berto cast Narsi a concerned glance, but Narsi didn't know what to say.

"She was such a beautiful soul. I miss her and her correspondences terribly," Father Timoteo said before either of them could utter a distracting comment. "I must have her letters organized and published someday. They were so edifying, and so filled with compassion."

Narsi almost said that he had one final letter, but somehow this didn't seem the right time to mention it. After all, he didn't have it with him, and though he and Berto were friends, he didn't know that he wanted anyone but Father Timoteo to know about his mother's final correspondence.

"Shall we have a stroll through the water gardens before we make for the masters' tables for a solid meal?" Berto inquired.

Father Timoteo nodded but then frowned into the distance. Both Narsi and Berto followed his gaze to see a vast party of richly clothed men and women hurrying toward them through the arches of rose trellises. Narsi recognized Lord Vediya second in the group, looking quite serious as he spoke to the striking, dark-haired man at the lead.

Father Timoteo drew himself to his full gaunt height and pulled a step ahead of Narsi. He shot the man at Lord Vediya's side a cold glower. Berto's expression lit with alarm and he glanced Narsi's way.

Narsi raised his brows in question and Berto mouthed, "The duke."

Dread gripped Narsi. He'd been warned that the duke disliked physicians and that his presence wasn't all that welcome, but he couldn't have imagined that he could inspire such a stark expression of rage and hurt in a man he'd never even met. Beside him Lord Vediya looked like a man attempting to soothe an agitated stallion. And in fact the duke did look half wild: wearing neither doublet nor vest, his glossy black hair long and loose, and his pale skin flushed and gleaming with sweat.

Narsi stole a glance back at the men and women following the two of them. He read degrees of expectation and worry in their expressions. Some appeared genuinely anxious, but several looked too excited, as if they were anticipating a thrilling performance. Narsi drew in a deep breath, willing his racing heart to calm. No matter what, he promised himself, he would not allow a Cadeleonian—no matter how powerful— to strip his dignity from him.

As the party drew close, Lord Vediya's words carried. "I'll see that it's done myself—"

All at once Father Timoteo sprang forward in three long strides, stepping directly into the duke's path.

"Fedeles," Father Timoteo began quite firmly, but then to Narsi's surprise the duke threw his arms around Father Timoteo, embracing him for several moments before sinking to his knees still clasping Father Timoteo's hands. Narsi could now see that tears streaked the duke's face.

"Tim, you must promise me that you'll give Batteo Ciceron final rites." The duke's tone wasn't commanding but entreating and broken by the obvious struggle to suppress a sob. "He had his enemies in the holy orders, I know. He wasn't without his failings, but in his heart he was a good man. His soul deserves the respite of paradise."

"As do all souls," Father Timoteo stated as he always did when the matter arose, but then his expression turned uncertain. "But what has befallen the captain? He was hale and healthy last time we argued philosophy."

"Assassins." The duke looked sickened. "They murdered him as he was returning home to his wife and children. They took his head."

Narsi looked quickly to Berto to make certain that his own horror at the news wasn't the naïve behavior of a man unused to the capital. Berto's disturbed expression assured Narsi that despite its reputation, the city had not grown so jaded that assassinations and beheadings were actually commonplace. Though hadn't Berto just yesterday mentioned the city guards in connection with the beheadings of several priests?

Now was not the time to inquire if this murder could be connected to the others, obviously. But it did give Narsi pause, and for no reason that he cared to admit to, Narsi glanced to Lord Vediya. Surprisingly he found that Lord Vediya watched him in return. When their gazes met Lord Vediya offered him a very brief smile. Flustered to be caught out, Narsi quickly averted his gaze to his medical satchel.

He missed some of the exchange between the duke and Father Timoteo as the latter coaxed the former back onto his feet, but quickly surmised that they were making arrangements for a quick, discreet burial to take place here at the duke's chapel. Narsi wondered if he'd be called upon to prepare the body. He'd need to purchase white spirits and camphor for embalming, unless a casket could be made, the grave dug and ground consecrated within the day. Doubtless the warm weather was already turning the remains foul. Narsi wondered how the body would be transported and if he might be granted access to an icehouse, if the duke maintained one.

The duke's manner seemed to calm greatly once Father Timoteo assured him that Captain Ciceron would receive the blessings necessary to assure his eventual entry into the Cadeleonian paradise. Had he been Haldiim, then a Bahiim might have been hired to invoke blessings to ensure the safe conduct of his soul into his next life. And though the captain's loved ones would have mourned his death, they could have taken some comfort in knowing that he would be born again. At least, that was the comfort that Narsi took after his mother's passing. She was gone from him for a little time, but someday he might well see her smile again in the face of a child.

" . . . I hope it won't be too great an imposition, but Master Ariz has spoken highly of him and Atreau feels that a physician may be needed." The duke's words drifted over Narsi, without fully drawing his attention.

He was wondering if his mother would be glad to be reborn or if she would have preferred to have received Cadeleonian blessings and joined her husband. A little guilt still gnawed at Narsi for not arguing the matter with his aunt. But with Father Timoteo gone, it would have been a struggle to find a Cadeleonian priest willing to consecrate a Haldiim soul. And there had also been the terrible thought that he stood to lose not just one, but both his parents behind the great ivory walls of the Cadeleonian paradise for all the ages to come.

"Narsi would surely welcome the opportunity to visit the city." Father Timoteo cast an encouraging glance back to Narsi.

"Yes," Narsi responded immediately, while his mind raced back over the details of the half-heard conversation.

Poppy drops and duera had been mentioned in regard to what might assist the young widow in her grief. Narsi hadn't noticed either to do much good for those who were truly heartbroken. Though perhaps the drops would help the widow sleep.

The duke took a step in Narsi's direction and for the first time, seemed to actually take in his presence. He stared, which was a response Narsi was growing to expect of Cadeleonians here in the north. But the duke's expression wasn't disconcerted so much as filled with recognition. A slight smile curved his lips.

"You were raised in the Grunito house?" the duke inquired. His eyes were blacker than any Narsi had ever seen before. His gaze seemed to bore in as he looked Narsi up and down. Narsi realized that most likely the duke was attempting to work out who among the army of Grunito men had fathered Narsi.

Good luck to you, my lord; if you figure it out be sure and tell me.

"I was, my lord," Narsi responded. Beside him Berto and Timoteo nodded.

"You are younger than I had imagined," the duke said, then he turned to Lord Vediya. "You should accompany him, Atreau. You know the way."

"I do. Though with the festivities planned for this evening, we may be delayed on our way home." Lord Vediya stepped forward.

"I'd forgotten about Jacinto's parade. Yes, take the whole day if you must," the duke allowed. Then he returned his attention to Narsi. "Master Physician, it would seem you have an opportunity to redeem my opinion of your profession. Don't allow Atreau to distract you too greatly, while the two of you are together on your errand."

"I won't, my lord," Narsi replied.

"You know me too well, Fedeles," Lord Vediya told the duke, and in return he received an long-suffering nod.

Before Narsi could manage to concoct a comment or question to verify the exact nature of his errand, a page boy came sprinting up to their party, lugging a sword nearly as long as himself and with a dark green jerkin folded beneath one arm.

"My lord," the plump page boy called. "Master Ariz has sent me with your belongings! He did not want you to be without your sword."

The duke's expression lit slightly.

"I can depend upon my sword master not to let me wander my own home unarmed, it seems." The duke turned his attention to the page, though not before exchanging an odd glance with Lord Vediya. As the gathered courtiers and onlookers watched the duke buckle on his sword belt and make light conversation with the flushed page boy, Lord Vediya nudged Narsi's ankle.

"We must go now," Lord Vediya whispered. "Before any of the courtly lampreys try to latch on. Come quickly."

And with that he set off for the stables, leaving Narsi to offer a hasty goodbye to Berto and Father Timoteo and then race after him.

In the stable Narsi found Lord Vediya already mounted. A groom led Narsi's mare to him, though Narsi found it suspicious that he could have saddled her so quickly. Unless Lord Vediya or the duke had already planned for Narsi's departure before ever speaking to Father Timoteo.

"All that about the widow and poppy drops?" Narsi asked after the groom had left.

"A necessary prevarication," Lord Vediya said. "We'll come to the truth once we're away from here."

He nudged his gray stallion ahead and Narsi urged his mare to keep pace, as they rode from the duke's household out toward the tangled city streets.

CHAPTER
TEN

Delfia moved fast and light as a falcon, parrying Ariz's thrust and then darting in with her short blade to strike for his heart. Retreat would have kept her safer, but neither she nor Ariz had been trained in swordplay for the sake of personal safety.

The tip of her dagger scraped Ariz's doublet. He shifted only a fraction from the blade and brought his fist down across Delfia's slim back, knocking her to the floor. She rolled with the force and regained her feet in an instant. Sweat beaded her face and damp locks of her auburn hair hung in disarray. Still, she grinned at Ariz from just beyond his reach and held both her blades ready for another bout. Then she turned to her dark-haired twin daughters.

"You see the importance of a quick recovery?" Delfia asked them. "Particularly when you're facing a very strong opponent like your uncle. No matter how badly you're hurt you absolutely *must* regain your footing and keep him from cornering you."

Celina returned her mother's grin and nodded. Beside her, Marisol looked far less happy but also nodded. At seven years old they were both still delicate and light enough for Ariz to scoop up, toss high into the air and easily catch again. Marisol always laughed, while Celina usually demanded to be launched still higher. Neither of them feared falling.

Ariz didn't think he had been so brave at the same age, but then perhaps they had inherited a little of their father's natural assurance along with his proud features. Certainly neither of them resembled Ariz or Delfia as much as they did their cousin Sparanzo. In Celina, that resemblance had been heightened by cropping her hair and dressing her in the green breeches and ochre shirt of a courtly boy. Marisol, on the other hand, wore a full honey-yellow skirt and a green bodice over her yellow blouse. Her black maiden braids hung nearly to her waist.

"You two try the maneuver now," Delfia instructed the girls.

They hefted up their blunt-tipped blades and took turns attacking, defending and rolling back up into a ready stance. Celina had a distinct advantage; dressed in the clothes of a boy and with her hair cropped short, she wasn't as easily tangled by petticoats or long tresses. Still, Marisol mastered the maneuvers after only a few more rounds with her sister. Her wig only came loose once, and to her credit Marisol quickly improvised the defense of hurling it at Celina.

Delfia laughed, then swooped in to keep the costly wig from being trampled. Neither Celina nor Marisol cared that much about the condition of the hairpiece, but the few times Sparanzo had practiced wearing it—as well as one of Marisol's dresses—he'd been very concerned that he appeared as perfectly coifed as his mother.

After the girls completed the round, Ariz clapped their slim shoulders.

"Very well done, both of you," Ariz said. The girls beamed at him, despite his dull expression. "Sparanzo will be coming for his dance lessons soon, so I think we should end our sword practice here for today."

Delfia pinned the wig back into place on Marisol's head, hiding her short black hair, and then kissed her daughter's forehead.

Celina strode to the weapon rack and set aside her practice blade, then she took up her sword belt and buckled it tight around her waist. She glanced briefly at her reflection in the nearest mirror and brushed her hair back from her face, in the same manner that Sparanzo wore his.

Ariz tried not to think on that too much, but he couldn't help feeling pained. He and Delfia never discussed it; he didn't think Delfia would forgive him if he forced her to voice the exact terms she'd arranged with the duchess. But it ate at him to think that Oasia Quemanor had agreed to shelter him and Delfia only to secure decoys to pass for her son. He tried to remind himself that if they had not been taken in by the duchess then all of them would have been homeless and destitute. Neither Celina nor Marisol would have had access to the food, shelter or education that the duchess provided. They thrived while the rest of the Plunado family filled paupers' graves.

"Are we to learn the promenade along with Sparanzo?" Marisol asked.

"Yes, my sweet," Delfia replied. "If his leg is hurting him or if he falls ill, then one of you might have to take his place in the royal coronation. That would be exciting, don't you think?"

Marisol tilted her head considering the idea, while Delfia adjusted the hairpins that secured the girl's wig.

"It would be me," Celina declared. "I'm a better boy."

"But I'm a better dancer," Marisol responded.

Both girls looked to their mother.

"Don't get too full of yourselves, my darlings," Delfia told them. "Who knows, maybe your uncle Ariz will squeeze himself into one of your little doublets and go skipping in front of Prince Sevanyo himself."

That image won several giddy laughs.

For the next few minutes Ariz demonstrated the processional steps and then the girls practiced, and Delfia allowed them to school her as if she hadn't mastered the entire thing years before. Long beams of morning light struck the surrounding mirrors and lit the room with golden warmth.

When the girls demanded that Ariz join them, he played the clown, performing the procession steps backward and then while standing on his hands. The Brand of Obedience stripped him of the ability to smile for his nieces, but he could at least inspire their grins.

By the time Sparanzo arrived, escorted by the duchess and her cluster of ladies-in-waiting, both Marisol and Celina had perfected the processional steps and turned them into a race around the room. Delfia settled on a stool, her troubled gaze shifting back and forth between her daughters and the gardens outside. Ariz drifted back to the weapon racks and kept his head bowed. Out of habit he assessed the four retainers who'd escorted the duchess and now stood guard at the door. The younger two were easygoing men hired by the duke, but the slightly older pair had recently come from the Fueres house, and Ariz felt certain that one of the two served as a spy for Hierro.

The duchess swept into the center of the room, her gold and green gown shimmering around her like a cascade of glittering scales. Gold and emerald combs held her silky black hair up in a crown of curls and braids. Delfia and Ariz immediately bowed.

Marisol stopped in her tracks and Celina nearly collided with her. Then Marisol dropped into a deep curtsy while Celina performed the show of leg that had become popular among ardent noblemen intent upon stirring the attention of young and excitable maidens. Executed, even expertly, by a scrawny seven-year-old, the bow won Celina several good laughs. Sparanzo rushed to his playmate to learn the maneuver that had so amused his mother and her pretty ladies-in-waiting.

"What is it called, Celino?" Sparanzo asked. Despite being two years younger, he already stood as tall as Celina.

"The buck's bow," Celina replied. She took a few swaggering steps and then executed the bow again. Sparanzo emulated her with an expression of worship. Marisol joined them and declared the bow much easier than a proper lady's curtsy, which led the three of them to attempt a variety of bows and curtsies, before settling down on the floor to play with Celina's dice.

Ariz glanced into the nearest mirror to watch the duchess as she observed her son and Delfia's daughters. The duchess could have been a porcelain statue. Flawlessly beautiful and so outwardly serene that composure seemed to encase her like ice. But a slight smile briefly curved her lips as her gaze followed her son. Without question she adored the boy. And more and more Ariz thought he saw hints of affection when she looked upon Celina and Marisol. She liked them.

Though Ariz wasn't foolish enough to imagine that her feeling went beyond that. The duchess was a Fueres, regardless of what husband's name she took. The fact that she felt anything resembling love or loyalty toward anyone was a miracle in Ariz's opinion. Her tender mercies were certainly not to be counted upon.

"Celino, my dear boy," the duchess called out sweetly. "Come here, I have a gift for you."

Ariz saw Delfia's head come up, her expression a tight mask of happiness. He continued to watch in the mirror as Celina strutted to the duchess, gamely bowed and kissed her proffered hand. The girl had been studying of Atreau, Ariz suspected. But the duchess found it all amusing, as did her ladies-in-waiting.

"I've had a doublet made for you to match Sparanzo's." The duchess gestured at her youngest lady-in-waiting, her nineteen-year-old cousin, Elenna. The young woman held out an emerald silk doublet. Gold threads glinted all across its surface, flashing from ornate patterns of hawks and bowers of entwined ivy. Not even before the family had been stripped of their land and titles could a Plunado have expected to own so beautiful and costly a garment. It was clearly intended for the coronation.

"Thank you, Your Grace," Celina stared at the doublet wide-eyed and then reached out and pulled it to her chest like a treasure. Marisol looked on with an expression of covetous yearning, while Sparanzo continued to play with the dice. Gifts of silk and gold were commonplace for him.

"I hope that you don't think I'm spoiling your son, my dear Delfia?" The duchess commented.

Though Delfia had gone pale, she still managed to smile brightly.

"You are too kind, Your Grace."

"Perhaps but you *must* indulge me," the duchess replied, and what threat the words might have carried was lost in the sweetness of her tone. She turned her attention to Marisol. "Oh, my dear, did you think that I had forgotten you?"

Marisol frowned but shook her head.

"I haven't, dear thing. Come to me." The duchess extended a long white hand and Marisol walked to her, though not so quickly or carelessly as Celina. Marisol couldn't possibly understand the gravity of their situation, but Ariz knew she was an observant child and quite sensitive to the expressions and silent tension of the adults surrounding her.

"You mustn't be shy of me, my dear," the duchess told her. She drew an emerald-studded comb from her own lustrous black hair and placed it in Marisol's small hands. "Isn't that pretty?"

"Yes, Your Grace. Thank you." Marisol gripped the comb and curtsied, then she rushed back to her mother's side. Delfia took the comb and artfully slid its golden teeth into Marisol's wig. Afterward Delfia gazed down at her daughter's head with a distant expression. Ariz felt certain his sister was working out just what she might be able to trade for the costly bauble. Passage aboard a Labaran ship? Room and board in the Salt Islands? Forged papers to trade in the kingdom of Usane?

Bit by bit, Delfia had pinched and saved a small treasury over the years. Someday—very soon, Ariz hoped—she and her daughters would simply slip away to somewhere far from the grasp of the Fueres family and the shame of the Plunado name.

"Well, shall we leave the boys to their practices?" the duchess asked, as if it weren't an order. Then she turned and glided from the room. Delfia caught Marisol's hand and hurried to follow the ladies-in-waiting and handmaids attending the duchess as they trailed from the room. One of the retainers from the Fueres house lingered just a moment too long. Ariz knew the man was called Dommian and that household gossips felt he drank hard and gambled poorly but kept himself to himself. Dommian scowled at Celina as she and Sparanzo laughed and fenced their shadows.

The man was definitely a spy, Ariz decided.

Then he noticed the slight tremor of the man's hand toward his knife and the way his face paled for an instant. Ariz knew that reaction far too well: Hierro's brand flooding his body with murderous impulse and the shocking pain of suppressing it. Dommian was no mere spy, but an assassin.

From the way he watched the children, Ariz guessed that he'd been dispatched to remove the Quemanor heir and his bastard cousins.

Hierro had indeed moved quickly to obliterate any heir who might challenge Remes—and likely he wanted his own bastard daughters removed from any possible claim of inheritance as well. Or perhaps he simply wished to punish Delfia for failing to produce Lady Hylanya's corpse as he'd commanded. Who could say with Hierro?

Ariz dropped his hand to his knife hilt as sweat began to rise across the stocky retainer's brow. The man was fighting the brand he bore, and no doubt enduring agony for his struggle. Ariz felt sympathy and repulsion, because they were standing in broad daylight surrounded by dozens of witnesses and still the retainer could barely suppress his need to attack the children.

"Good day to you," Ariz said, and it seemed to startle Dommian to his senses.

"Master Ariz! I hadn't seen you there . . ." Dommian's voice trailed off and Ariz wondered if the man might not be a little drunk already. "Good day!"

Dommian jerked away from the door, turned on his heel and marched after the duchess and her retainers. Ariz watched him go.

Dommian would have to be dealt with soon, but not this instant or here.

Ariz called the children to attention. For now the menace and malice of a bare blades would hide in youthful play.

   CHAPTER
ELEVEN

Lord Vediya rode swiftly through the wide lanes surrounding the sprawling houses of noble families. Narsi urged his mare into a gallop to keep pace as they veered between gilded carriages and numerous delivery wagons. A man in an oxcart shouted obscenities at Narsi, to which

Narsi responded with an equivalent Haldiim gesture. The streets had not been so congested the evening before, but now everyone appeared to be out making preparations or gossiping about Prince Sevanyo's forthcoming coronation. Abruptly Lord Vediya turned onto a winding backstreet. There common folk brought deliveries of expensive goods and carted away great heaps of waste.

Narsi stole a quick glance over his shoulder, wondering if perhaps the man who'd accosted Lord Vediya the day before—Ladislo Bayezar— or someone of his ilk might be following them. Narsi recognized no one. But several men dressed in the violet coats of the royal bishop's guards seemed to always catch his eye, a little distance behind him. Then at a busy intersection where a convoy of wagons loaded with rich fabrics tangled with several gilded carriages Lord Vediya urged his stallion into the confusion and Narsi followed. Coachmen and cart drivers swore and shouted, but Narsi kept his attention fixed upon Lord Vediya's back. A whip cracked far too close for Narsi comfort, but his mare carried him quickly clear of the infuriated coachman.

Moments later, when they emerged from the crowds of couriers, pages and carriages, the royal bishop's men were nowhere to be seen. Narsi had been so intent on keeping his seat and staying with Lord Vediya that he hadn't realized that they'd actually doubled back to an empty alleyway. Lord Vediya glanced over his shoulder and offered Narsi a game smile, then he lit out again, this time turning his gray stallion toward the Gado Bridge.

There, at last, Lord Vediya slowed and Narsi drew alongside him.

"You were being followed, weren't you?" Narsi asked.

"For the sake of my vanity I always assume so." Lord Vediya offered him a charmingly insincere smile but then stole another glance over his shoulder.

"Was it to do with that man from yesterday?" Narsi asked. Certainly as a noble, the man could have made a moral complaint and demand that Lord Vediya be brought in before the royal bishop. "Lord Bayezar?"

"Ladislo?" For a moment Lord Vediya appeared to have somehow forgotten, but then he gave a dry laugh. "I imagine Ladislo is still in his sickbed. No. He's a trouble that will hopefully pass when his passion cools and he realizes that the world is still full of pretty girls."

Narsi recalled the man demanding the Lord Vediya return his fiancée. Suelita—that had been her name. Narsi supposed she wasn't the first woman to throw over a would-be husband for Lord Vediya's company. His own small pang of jealousy struck him as childish and Narsi ignored it. If this Suelita made Lord Vediya happy then that would be for the best.

Flocks of white messenger doves winged overhead. Narsi wondered how many secret and clandestine affairs fluttered above him.

"This little mission of mercy of ours," Lord Vediya said. "It isn't a matter I or you will want spread around, so I'm taking some care."

"Is it anything to do with the assassination of Captain Ciceron?"

"No," Lord Vediya said, but his tone wasn't certain. "Hunting down his assassins will have to keep for this morning, at least."

It surprised Narsi a little that Lord Vediya's thoughts turned immediately to stalking assassins. It seemed utterly out of character for a man who so readily professed himself to be a coward and wastrel.

Narsi and Lord Vediya both drew to a halt at the apex of the bridge, where a crowd of simply dressed Cadeleonians gathered around a street performer. The singer wore long sleeves and a theatrical mask. He belted out a pleasant melody, and most of the people gathered around him joined in singing the refrain.

"So what are we doing then?" Narsi inquired.

Instead of answering him, Lord Vediya swung down from his horse. Narsi did the same. As they led their mounts around the crowd, Lord Vediya sang along. His voice had grown deeper than Narsi remembered, but he'd lost none of his musicality.

"True love costs a fellow dear
His life's blood or very near
But for a joyful dally
Three coppers in an alley
And still coin enough for beer!"

"Excellently performed," Narsi commented. "And while I commend your discretion on my behalf, perhaps now you could tell me what it is that I'm actually supposed to be doing."

"How familiar are you with muerate poison?" Lord Vediya asked in a whisper.

That took Narsi aback, but only for a moment.

"I know a fair bit about it," Narsi admitted. The deadly black poison was the most famous derivative of the four "profane" herbs condemned by the Holy Cadeleonian Church. Legally they could be grown in only in Royal Physic Garden, and physicians in need of the herbs were expected to petition the church for dispensations of dried leaves, ground roots or flowers.

In practice Narsi, like most physicians, employed more direct means of acquiring the herbs. The abortifacient widow's weed grew readily in ditches and alongside riverbanks, and duera flowers were easily hidden in amongst beds of violets and petunias. With just what he carried in his medical satchel Narsi could have brewed a small dose of the poison, thought he certainly wasn't going to admit as much.

"Have you ever treated someone who has been poisoned?" Lord Vediya asked.

"Once. A fellow student who got the stuff in a cut."

"And?" Lord Vediya asked.

"He lived, but we had to amputate his right hand." Narsi tapped his own forearm just below the wrist. It had been the first surgery he'd assisted, and they'd only saved the man's life because they'd acted so quickly. "How long ago did this poisoning take place?"

"A week ago," Lord Vediya replied.

"A week? That's not possible." Narsi shook his head. "Muerate acts quickly. It either kills or it doesn't, but it doesn't linger in the body. The longest I can recall anyone lasting after a fatal dose was two days. If the person has lived a week, then the poison will have already done its worst and have been purged from the body."

"It's an unusual situation."

The two of them skirted another crowd—this group gathered around two jugglers—and descended into the southern section of the city. Lord Vediya drew to a halt in the shadow of a carver's shop, where the sound of wood hammers nearly drowned out his voice.

"What do you know of witches?" Lord Vediya leaned in as he spoke, and Narsi tried not to find his closeness distracting. That faint perfume of roses drifted from him, as did the stronger scents of leather and sweat.

"One of my mentors was married to a Bahiim, but I don't think they're really the same as witches." Narsi grasped at what little he could recall hearing or reading on the subject. Witches were supposed to be common among the Mirogoths and in Northern Labara, but they weren't unified in their power or practices the way holy Bahiim or Cadeleonian nuns and priests were. "I suppose the only thing I really know about them is what I've read from your account of your time in Count Radulf's court. Are we discussing Lady Hylanya?"

"You certainly add things up quickly, don't you? Lord Vediya gazed at Narsi with an odd expression. "For the sake of conversation, let us say that I am discussing her. Would you be willing to help her?"

"My vows as a physician come before all else," Narsi replied. "I'll do all I can to treat her."

"Yes, but I'm asking a little more of you than just medical service," Lord Vediya said. "I need your assurance that you'll keep this, all of it, to yourself. Not a word even to Brother Berto or Tim. Can you swear to that?"

Narsi didn't like the thought of concealing anything from Father Timoteo, but at the same time he couldn't imagine how knowing about any of this would do the Holy Father, or Berto, any good. Or when it would ever come up.

"You have my word," Narsi replied. How could he do otherwise? Not only was it his duty, but what sort of timid frail would he have to be to refuse to join a man like Lord Vediya in one of his exploits? "The duke will see that I'm served nothing but ox ears if I don't, I imagine."

Lord Vediya smiled briefly, but then his expression went serious as he turned and surveyed the river, where dozens of moored merchant ships bobbed on the rolling waters.

"I've arranged transport to carry her back to her brother's lands, but the ship won't sail until the tide comes in this evening. Before then I'll need you to find something that will allow us to move her without causing a scene."

"Is she in very much pain?" Narsi wondered if duera might help her, though he felt uneasy about employing it if the lady was somehow still suffering from muerate.

"Not exactly—" Lord Vediya frowned and Narsi followed his gaze to the bridge. A man dressed in the royal bishop's colors glowered at the jugglers blocking his mount.

"We should go," Narsi said.

"My thought as well. But not so fast as to attract attention." Lord Vediya easily swung up into his saddle. Narsi mounted his mare with only a little less grace. He'd made a point of practicing his horsemanship after he'd met Lord Vediya and seen him and his friends race magnificently through the streets of Anacleto twelve years before.

"Where are we bound for?" Narsi asked quietly.

"The Green Door," Lord Vediya said.

Narsi felt a kind of thrill. The infamous kaweh house where Lord Vediya and so many other authors gathered to write and debate. He wondered how much it resembled the dank, unsavory kaweh houses of Anacleto, where so many criminals gathered. The thought worried him, but he didn't want to say as much and seem like a coward.

Riding side by side, they turned down an alley and then followed a narrow winding lane that led them east to a weathered wooden bridge. As they crossed over, Narsi's gaze fell on a section of wall across the street. The vitreous tiles covering the wall's surface were dulled by street dust and many appeared to be cracked, but even so Narsi instantly recognized them as part of a Haldiim mosaic. The midnight-blue silhouette of tree branches stretched out in sinuous lines. Brilliant green, gold and red leaves clustered around the branches, each one bearing a white holy symbol. Hundreds of Bahiim blessings spread across the short section of wall before it ended abruptly at the mouth of an alley.

A little farther along the street he noted that another section of the same mosaic peered out from between two ochre-yellow brick walls. Red doves winged across a night sky studded with fiery stars, and the holy Bahiim symbol of peace gleamed white from inside the gold circle of a full moon. Narsi recognized the scene. It and hundreds of mosaics like it decorated public walls and private homes throughout the Haldiim District of Anacleto. Even his aunt's modest house had been surrounded by the same designs of suns, stars and moons.

"That's Haldiim, isn't it?" Narsi asked.

Lord Vediya paused and for a moment he studied the wall that Narsi pointed to as if he'd never seen it before. Then he gave a slow nod and Narsi could see him searching other walls lining the street. He craned his head back as he took in the section of Haldiim mosaic that had first captured Narsi's attention.

"You're right. I can't believe I never noticed them before," Lord Vediya said. "They're beautiful, aren't they?" He nudged his mount and they rode a little nearer the walls as they continued along the street.

"They are. Though I'm surprised to see them here in the north." Narsi still hadn't sighted a person he recognized as Haldiim, though he knew that some had to live here. Several of his instructors and classmates had spoken of relatives living in the capital, and Narsi couldn't imagine them failing to find one another and keep close. So there had to be a Haldiim District somewhere in the city. But it seemed expertly hidden away.

"I suppose the walls are evidence of the vastness of the Haldiim communities that filled the city three hundred years back. I read somewhere that the Haldiim population in Cieloalta was the largest in the nation before King Nazaro's reign." Lord Vediya's expression turned a little melancholy and Narsi felt a sudden pang of sorrow.

He'd grown up well aware of King Nazaro's horrific purges against his people, but in Anacleto the stories had been triumphant ones of Haldiim archers defending their walled district against wave after wave of the murderous king's forces. They had held their city and broken the royal army, sending the king's soldiers back in defeat. The entire population of Anacleto commemorated their victory every year with late-summer games and feasts.

But now the reality of what had happened in the north—the tens of thousands of people who'd been murdered by royal decree—truly sank into him. Sorrow and anger welled up in Narsi, and he had no idea what to do with it. The men who'd tortured and murdered so many of his people had been dead nearly three hundred years. And yet the harm they'd done remained evident in these neglected mosaics and the absence of the thousands of Haldiim who would have populated these streets—whose descendants ought to have surrounded Narsi now. He felt suddenly very alone and isolated, despite the bustle of Cadeleonians all around him.

"The new Haldiim District is to the west. It borders the Theater District." Lord Vediya's expression seemed fond. "The heart of the original sacred grove stands near the Shell Fountain. It's not as large or wild as the sacred grove in Anacleto, but the wisteria trees that make up the inner circle are the largest and most beautiful I've ever seen in my life."

"Really?" Narsi had never been overly devout, but just now he felt a pang of longing to go and walk barefoot under the sheltering limbs of a sacred grove. Or maybe he was just feeling homesick for Haldiim faces and voices.

"Truly. The cascades of violet flowers catch the slightest breezes, to swirl and sway like they're dancing. We should go sometime," Lord Vediya commented. Though he made the suggestion rather offhandedly, it delighted Narsi.

As they rode on he continued to notice little traces of flowing Haldiim script decorating the eaves of old houses. Designs of suns, stars and moons glinted from stone foundations of shops now housing tailors, drapers, haberdashers and a startling variety of mask makers.

Very soon his attention was captured by the noise of drums and horns coming from several large buildings ahead of them. He noticed men and women in odd costumes—some sporting extravagant wigs and masks—lingering at the backs of the establishments. Some sang to themselves, others practiced harmonies. Many of them waved to Lord Vediya and he returned the friendly gestures. Narsi wasn't certain, but he thought that at least two of the masked figures possessed the slender builds of Haldiim.

"The Candioro Theater Troupe," Lord Vediya said. "They and six other companies have been hired by Prince Jacinto to perform in a parade this evening. It's to be in honor of Prince Sevanyo's imminent coronation. If we haven't been apprehended and hanged by the royal bishop's men, perhaps we'll have a chance to watch it."

"I'd be delighted to," Narsi replied. "So long as I haven't been hanged."

Lord Vediya nodded as if both the invitation and threat of hanging were commonplace. And perhaps they were to him.

As the wind shifted, the strong scent of roasting kaweh and rich spices rolled over Narsi. He knew that perfume so well that he could almost picture the walls of the Haldiim District in Anacleto. Anticipation built in him when they turned off the narrow lane into a busy street, and he felt absurdly heartened when he caught sight of two Haldiim women dressed in brightly embroidered vests and full scarlet pants striding across the street.

Brilliantly painted theater facades loomed up over the dusty raised walkways, where Cadeleonian girls with baskets of herbs and oranges took refuge from the bright sun, chatting in the shadows. Between the gaudy scrollwork of opera buildings and theaters, the painted shop signs jutted out over the street. Most of the taverns appeared to only just be opening their doors for business, while the cookeries looked full of satiated patrons. The smells of toasted bread, roast game and fruit pies lent a distinctly Cadeleonian scent to the strong perfume of Haldiim kaweh.

Lord Vediya pointed ahead of them to a broad two-story building boasting bright red and yellow roof tiles and cascades of flowers hanging from the second-story window boxes. Beneath the flowers hung a carved wooden sign depicting a brass kaweh pot with decorative plumes of steam rising from it in large blue curls. The viridian door beneath stood ajar.

"The Green Door," Narsi said. He'd read so many books and poems from authors who frequented the place. He did his best not to appear too excited when Lord Vediya glanced his way. Many of the texts he'd read had heaped particular scorn upon the naïve gaspers who from time to time threw themselves upon the poets, authors and adventurers who'd made the place famous, as if any of them had a responsibility to entertain, initiate and seduce dullards who'd tired of their unsullied states. "You mentioned it in one of your books, I think."

"A few books. Pepylla insists that she get advertising out of me since I so rarely clear all of my bills. Though this last month Fedeles has been rather generous, so you needn't fear being set upon with a boiling pot for merely appearing at the door with me."

They left their horses in the stable of the Fat Goose Traveler's Inn across the way. Lord Vediya apparently knew the owner—whom he referred to as "Spider"—and rented a room from the man. A dull little domicile where he took himself off to write without the sorts of constant interruptions that the life he led inspired, or so Lord Vediya informed Narsi.

The interior of the Green Door was unlike any Haldiim kaweh house in Anacleto, which came as a relief. He was homesick, but not for the dark, smoky little rooms where he'd most often been summoned to stitch up smoke-addled street snakes after knife fights.

Here light poured in through the windows and the large wooden tables were crowded with boisterous Cadeleonians. On the north wall where an open fire would have smoldered beneath blackened racks of simmering pots in a Haldiim kaweh house, a staircase rose up to the second floor. A few smaller tables stood in the shadow of the stairs and several wan-looking men lounged there, sighing and scribbling down notes of some kind. One stocky fellow glanced to Lord Vediya and looked like he might stand to greet him. Lord Vediya gave a shake of his head.

"Later, Ollivar," Lord Vediya whispered as they passed, and the young man bowed his head back over the pages before him.

Men appeared to make up the majority of the clientele, though not all. Several women sat with the men, though none fit the descriptions Narsi had read of Hylanya Radulf.

The two serving women, dressed in modest interpretations of sleeveless Haldiim vests and full red skirts, brought out trays laden with silver kaweh pots, oversize cups and—oddly—jugs of cream. They wore their hair in ringlets, which Narsi imagined were meant to evoke natural Haldiim curls.

The older of the two offered Lord Vediya a casual nod in lieu of a greeting. Then she hurried to serve drinks to a large round table where a haughty-looking man wearing a suit of silk patchwork loudly debated with an angular woman dressed in the black robes of a nun, though no wimple covered her cropped brown hair. The people in the seats surrounding them looked on and from time to time clapped or groaned at one or the other. The woman jabbed a finger at the a man and snapped something about "who bears the burden of love unfettered by obligation," while the man's response rumbled too soft and low to make out.

If they'd been the only people speaking in the establishment, Narsi guessed that he would have caught more of their argument, but dozens of other conversations boomed through the place, as did calls for more drinks, cream and smoking embers. Steam condensed on the warped glass panes of the windows, throwing tiny rainbows across the white plaster walls, and the smell of tabbaq smoke rolled up from the few waterpipes being used at the far tables.

Oddly, Narsi didn't catch even the faintest whiff of poppy smoke, which normally prevailed in Haldiim kaweh houses. Nor did the customers, for all their flamboyant clothing and heated arguments, appear to be knife fighters or gamblers. On the whole they struck Narsi as rather theatrical intellectuals.

"Atreau!" The man in patchwork called out, and everyone at that table and many others looked up, with excited if not delighted expressions. Even the sharp-featured nun broke into a broad grin, though her expression shifted to curiosity as she took in Narsi. Others stared openly at him. He pretended not to notice.

"I've a little indulgence to enjoy abovestairs, but we'll be down shortly," Lord Vediya called back to those seated at the table, and then despite the people still calling to him—several demanding to know who he'd brought with him—Lord Vediya bounded up the stairs. Narsi followed. As they went up, the stairway became so dark that Narsi had to strain to see Lord Vediya. They reached the hall at the top of the stairs then walked past three narrow doors before stopping at the fourth.

"Inissa." Lord Vediya hardly raised his voice, and Narsi didn't imagine that his words carried far over the racket that arose from below them. Someone out on the street blew out series of bright notes from a trumpet.

"I've brought a physician, my darling." If anything Lord Vediya lowered his voice, and yet the door opened immediately.

Narsi wondered if the tousled woman who leaned out had been pressed against the door the entire time. Dark hair hung around her pretty pale face in disarray and her wrinkled blue dress gave the impression of having been slept in. A small mole lay just below the far corner of her right eye, like a dark tear. She threw her arms around Lord Vediya and he embraced her. Just behind her, Narsi noted a brawny blond man, whose long braided hair and rumpled clothes whipped around him as if caught in a gusting storm.

As the woman, Inissa, drew back from Lord Vediya, several pages of paper fluttered past her head and Narsi felt a breeze rush over him. Inissa wordlessly stepped aside to allow the two of them in.

A round window admitted only a single shaft of light into the small room, still Narsi absorbed a sense of the space immediately from the drawing table and multitude of small, framed paintings covering the walls so closely and completely that they gave the impression of ornate tiles. Narsi wasn't certain in the dim light, but he thought he recognized Lord Vediya's face and naked body in several of the miniature paintings.

A large four-poster bed stood near the one window, as did a dressing table and bookshelf, but Narsi hardly noticed them as his gaze fell upon the towering, red-haired woman floating above the bedding with her long arms outstretched and her head bowed as if in sleep. Papers, a silken scarf and what appeared to be a pillow sham whirled around her, caught in the wild wind that encircled her.

"Master Narsi," Lord Vediya said. "May I present your patient, Lady Hylanya Radulf."

Narsi couldn't keep from gaping at the handsome, rawboned woman. He'd read about great wonders of magic, shining white hells, huge demon lords and armies of enchanted beasts. But reading, he realized, in no way prepared him to actually witness the impossible occurring before his own eyes.

Inissa shoved the door closed and the blond man sank down to a stool beside the bed.

"This is Kili"—she indicated the brawny, blond man and then extended her hand—"and I'm Inissa."

"Narsi." He took her hand and bowed his head over her fingers; he'd learned long ago not to actually kiss the fingers of a Cadeleonian woman. Though he did note the flecks of ink and paint that stained the fingernails of her right hand. Likely the art decorating this room and the drawing table was her creation.

Then he turned his attention back to the unbelievable.

"How long has she been . . ." No official medical term describing an unconscious, floating patient came to Narsi's mind. ". . . like this?"

"Seven days and six nights," Kili replied, though his strong Labaran accent gave Narsi a moment's pause.

Seven days, Narsi thought as he stared at the lady. Her red hair whirled and twisted like vibrant kelp drifting on sea swells. The long strings of jewels around her neck were also aloft. Amidst what looked like a treasury of rubies, a single dull green stone glinted. Unlike her hair and the folds of her crimson brocaded dress, the stones didn't shift in their positions. They, like the pale young woman herself, seemed as fixed in the air as stars.

"So did this . . . state occur directly after she was poisoned?" Narsi asked. Then, catching sight of the black-scabbed cut across the back of her hand, he added. "And are you certain the poison was muerate?"

"I'm sure it was." Kili tapped the tip of his crooked nose. "I know the acrid smell of it, and Hylanya recognized it as well. The instant she realized, she withdrew and cast wards to protect herself."

The breeze whipping around the room caught up a kerchief from a bookshelf and sent it too swirling into orbit around Lady Hylanya. Narsi stepped closer to the woman to examine her hand. At once the wind buffeted his head and tossed the debris of papers, scarves and the red pillow sham into his face. He knocked several pages aside. Kili reached out, plucking the pillow sham and then a yellow scarf from the air.

Narsi took another step closer. The wind seemed to intensify, pulling the breath from his lungs and twisting around his throat like a strangling grip. He gasped as the force whirling around his body constricted, nearly crushing the air out of him. Narsi lurched back a half step and the pressure eased enough to let him breathe, though not without some difficulty.

"Are you all right?" Lord Vediya asked.

Narsi didn't look at him; he didn't want Lord Vediya to see his flushed face or watering eyes and think him an idiot. Instead he simply nodded, then he turned his attention to the half-healed wound bisecting the lady's left hand. The famous blue-black stain left by muerate poison stood out along the perimeter of the scab.

Definitely muerate, not some exotic disease or some similar, but slower, poison. So it should have been out of her system—or have killed her—within two days. Though that was assuming that her body had purged the toxin in some manner. With the lady floating and seemingly lost in a deep sleep, he couldn't be certain. Finding out would require a rather indelicate line of questioning.

Narsi glanced back to where Kili hunched mournfully on the undersized stool and then to Inissa.

"Has she . . . passed anything in the last week?" he asked.

Kili appeared confused and asked, "Passed?"

"He means, has she shit," Inissa said. "And the answer is no. She's neither pissed nor shit, nor eaten anything since she floated up off the bed."

Narsi frowned at this.

"She was sick once, but that was before we reached the Green Door." Kili's expression turned pained. "She brought up blood and blackness, like tar. A great deal of it."

"Very acrid smelling?" Narsi asked.

"It stank of muerate poison." Kili nodded.

Narsi had never heard of anyone being able to draw poison from a wound and vomit it out of their body, but he'd also never seen a patient summon a protective whirlwind either, so he took Kili's assessment at face value.

Narsi shivered as the breeze swept over him. It smelled like summer flowers. And standing so close, he thought that he could just glimpse tiny red streams flickering to life as they swirled all around him. When he closed his eyes, the afterimage of a whirling helix seemed to blaze up behind his eyelids.

"I'm not certain that I should interfere with her," Narsi admitted. He looked back to the other three occupants of the room.

Lord Vediya studied him silently from where he leaned against the doorframe. Inissa scowled and batted a lock of her dark hair back from her face. Kili simply bowed his face down into his hands.

"I should have stayed closer to her—"

"You aren't to blame, Kili," Lord Vediya said. "You couldn't be everywhere in the middle of a market. That assassin was faster than any of us could have expected."

"He was a fucking shadow," Inissa said, but then she planted her hands on her hips and scowled at Narsi. "You've got to do something. We certainly can't move her discreetly like this."

"Oh, I don't know." Lord Vediya offered Narsi a quick smile. "Maybe we could tie a rope around her ankle, let her float up to the rooftops, and then fly her like a Yuanese kite out to the dockside and reel her down to the ship."

"You will do no such thing!" Kili sprang to his feet, knocking the stool to the floor. He looked ready to draw his sword against Lord Vediya.

"Of course we won't." Inissa held up her hands and stepped in front of Kili. "Atreau is making a jest."

"I do not find it funny."

"A thousand apologies for my lapse of taste," Lord Vediya said. "I only meant to point out the absurdity of attempting to move Lady Hylanya while she is still in this state."

"Then we won't move her." Kili righted his stool and sat back down. "We will wait until she wakes of her own accord."

"The royal bishop's men are getting too close," Inissa said softly, as if she feared that somehow her words would call them to the room. "They've been here once already. Pepylla put them off, but they'll be back with a warrant to search my rooms anytime now."

"And the *Red Witch* has to sail tonight. They've already stayed in dock waiting too long. People are growing suspicious," Lord Vediya added.

"Then let them sail," Kili replied. He didn't look away from the lady's floating figure. "We have our own ship."

Exasperated expressions passed silently between Inissa and Lord Vediya, then Inissa stepped up to Kili's side.

"You know that would amount to throwing her to the royal bishop. He expects you to take her to her brother's ship. That's where most of the royal bishop's men are lying in wait."

"Then we will cut them down to a man." He looked to Lord Vediya, and for the first time Narsi noticed how red-rimmed Kili's eyes were. "It will be a glorious battle, like the night our Elezar rode against the grimma's armies."

"Except that we'd be starting a war instead of ending one," Lord Vediya replied. "That wasn't why Hylanya came here. You would destroy all the inroads she made with Prince Sevanyo and all hope of a marriage between her and Prince Jacinto."

"A man worthy of her would be with her now, not cowering from his uncle," Kili muttered.

"That's for her to say," Lord Vediya replied.

Kili glowered at Lord Vediya and Inissa. He looked like he might bound to his feet again. His big fist curled around the hilt of his sword.

"There might be one thing I could try," Narsi announced before the conversation could become any tenser. Lord Vediya, Inissa and Kili looked to him as if startled to remember his presence in their midst. "I just have to know a few things before I can say for certain."

"What things?" Kili demanded.

"I need to understand exactly what this wind is that's encircling her. You mentioned wards? Is it some sort of spell that she activated and that just goes on its own, or is it something that she controls with her . . . powers?" Narsi wasn't even certain he was wording his question clearly.

"It is her soul," Kili stated. "Her witchflame, which she has unfurled from her body to form a ward around her."

Narsi took a moment to think about that. Her soul unfurled around her was whipping over him, at this very moment. Was he breathing it in, or was that just the air that her soul moved?

He didn't allow himself to ponder either too deeply.

What was important was establishing that the strength of this swirling cyclone reflected Lady Hylanya's health and wasn't some mere device like a waterwheel that would turn on and on without need of its creator.

If she was healthy enough to maintain this storm for days and nights on end, then Narsi suspected that she could stand to be awakened, if a bit abruptly. He retreated back to his medical satchel.

"What do you intend to do?" Kili demanded.

"I want to try nightleaf distillate to wake her." Narsi withdrew a silk pouch and held the small jar of white powder up. "It stimulates the body more than kaweh but isn't dangerous in small doses."

"How are you going to get her to take it?" Lord Vediya asked.

"It's most often inhaled," Narsi replied. "That's why I picked it. But the real trick will be the dosage . . . and of course how much of it will be flying around in this room to be inhaled by those of us standing here."

Narsi walked to the window and pulled the wooden shutters closed. Thin rays of light seeped in between the slats; still, that was better than leaving it wide open. He picked his way through the gloom back to his medical satchel.

"I think that the three of you should wait on the other side of the door," Narsi said, and then, before Kili could object to leaving Lady Hylanya, he added, "The fewer other people who breathe in her medicine, the more there will be for Lady Hylanya."

That seemed to do the trick.

Kili allowed Inissa to lead him out of the room. Lord Vediya paused a moment in the door and Narsi thought he might ask a question, but then he seemed to think better of it and stepped out, drawing the door closed behind him.

Left alone with his decision, Narsi took a moment to consider the possibility of poisoning himself in the attempt to get enough powder into the air to affect Lady Hylanya. The tiny jar held in his hand carried far more than a lethal dose. He snatched up the scarf that Kili had tossed aside earlier and wound it around his nose and mouth. The nightleaf would still get into his eyes but at least he wouldn't be sucking in such great clouds of the stuff that his heart would give out in a fit of convulsions.

At least he hoped not.

He edged back into the whirling grip of Lady Hylanya's witchflame. For a moment he stood there, reminding himself that this was the calling he'd sworn himself to and that he'd come to the capital for the express purpose of aiding Lord Vediya in his ventures.

He pulled the cork out of the bottle and carefully shook a little of the white powder out into the whirling wind. It whipped away from him but an instant later he felt a sprinkling of the powder wash over his eyes. At once the faint light streaming into the room flared. The shadowy form Lady Hylanya had presented lit up, as did the white haze of nightleaf powder twisting and curling up around her. It swirled around her head like a thin cloud.

Narsi waited, but the lady gave no reaction.

He shook a little more powder into the air. An instant later his heartbeat quickened and despite the chill of the breeze, his body warmed. Moments later, Lady Hylanya's eyes fluttered and she gave a listless nod. A third dash of nightleaf set Narsi's pulse pounding and his ears ringing, and then Lady Hylanya lifted her head and peered at him through the gloom.

He'd done it! A giddy delight rushed through Narsi and he felt certain that only half of it arose from the nightleaf. He quickly corked the bottle.

"Who are you?" Lady Hylanya's thick Labaran accent swept over him with the breeze.

Narsi pulled the scarf down from his nose and mouth. "I'm master physician Narsi Lif-Tahm. Lord Vediya brought me to treat you after you were poisoned."

"You are Atreau's man?"

Narsi wasn't certain if she meant "man" in the Labaran sense or the far less romantic Cadeleonian context of a servant. He didn't suppose it mattered at the moment.

"Yes," Narsi assured her. "He, Inissa and Kili are waiting just outside the door. Shall I fetch them for you?"

All at once the wind wheeling through the room stilled. Particles of nightleaf drifted to the floor and Lady Hylanya dropped down onto the mattress. She swung her legs off the bed and stood.

Narsi briefly marveled at her height. She stood eye to eye with him and possessed shoulders nearly as broad as his own. The young woman returned his curious gaze with pale, dilated eyes.

"I know your face," she said.

"I don't believe we've met before." Narsi knew they hadn't but was at pains not to take an argumentative tone while still under the influence of nightleaf.

"Not that you know of, Master Physician, but witches can see through many eyes." She lifted her right hand and made an odd gesture, as if toying with the air as she spoke. "I liked the look of you from the start. Your bones, the line of your jaw, the curve of your nose. You are a Grunito, born of the same bloodline as our Elezar."

Narsi's suppressed the urge to deny it. But what would be the point, here in a dark room far from Father Timoteo and the Grunito family?

"Please feel free to just call me Narsi," he said instead.

"Narsi." She took particular care in the pronunciation. "Tell me, how long have I been in this place?"

"A week, I believe. You were poisoned, by person or persons unknown, in the city market. Knowing the lethality of muerate, I'd say that it's a miracle that you've survived, though considering that you're a witch I suppose that wouldn't be the correct term. . ." Narsi staunchly resisted the urge to go on talking. Nightleaf always made him far too chatty and he knew it.

Lady Hylanya smiled at him, but then her expression turned grave. She spun from him and went to the shuttered window. She lifted one of the strings of red jewels from her breast and held them up to the tiny rays of light filtering through. Narsi heard the door open behind him and glanced back to see Kili, Inissa and Lord Vediya slip into the room. Lady Hylanya continued to study the scarlet stones glinting between her hands.

"Lady Hylanya?" Kili asked.

She offered a murmur of acknowledgment but didn't turn.

"There are assassins on the streets," she said. "I can feel the spells that hold them in thrall. Many more have lit up since I slept. They are becoming an army . . ."

"You mean outside this building right now?" Inissa asked in a whisper, and Kili drew his long sword. Narsi stared at the huge bare blade.

His heart tripped into a frantic rhythm at the thought of being caught up in an actual battle. He knew next to nothing of combat and, aside from his scalpels, carried only a short belt knife.

"Not here. I feel them scattered across the city and all blazing with the fury of their commands. Their master is plotting something and he means to act soon." Lady Hylanya's voice softened. "There are so many of them. Most are broken creatures. But a few still thrash against the thrall laid over their flesh."

Narsi vaguely recalled descriptions of Mirogoth and Labaran witches casting thralls over common folk and forcing them into obedience, but he couldn't imagine anything like that happening in Cadeleon.

"Could another witch have tried to have you killed? Perhaps someone from the southern counties of Labara, hoping to pit your brother against the Cadeleonian crown?" Normally Narsi would have kept such conjecture to himself, but the nightleaf was definitely making him more impulsive.

"No. This is not the work of a Labaran witch." Lady Hylanya at last released the necklace and turned to face the rest of them. "These thralls are Cadeleonian magic. You can see it in their designs. They're drawn very much in the style of the old, dying spells that surrounds your Shard of Heaven."

"I didn't notice anything that looked like a spell." Narsi's words came out before he had time to consider them. "Though now that I think of it, how on earth would I know the first thing about the form a spell might take? I've read so much that I have these images in my head of what all the magic and conjuring must look like, but really it's purely my imagination. So, whatever do they actually look like?"

Out of the corner of his eye Narsi noted that Lord Vediya and Inissa exchanged a curious look. Kili sniffed the air, then scowled. Lady Hylanya gave a laugh that made her sound very young, then she bounded across the room and caught Narsi's empty left hand.

"I will show you." She traced a circle over his palm and a luminous red line followed her finger. Inside the circle she drew the four-pointed star of the Holy Cadeleonian Church and then a second smaller cross at an angle from the first. Last she pressed her finger down hard. Heat radiated across Narsi's palm.

Both Lord Vediya and Inissa moved closer to study the design on Narsi's hand. Kili sheathed his sword but didn't appear interested in the spell. Or perhaps he already knew about it.

Narsi stared at the shining red symbol.

"I think I've seen this somewhere." Narsi again lost control of his tongue. "I mean I've never been one of those youths who collected fortune cards or bought sacred signs from Bahiim, but I have seen this . . . or something that looked very similar."

"Yes, I had the same thought." Lord Vediya frowned. "But I can't place it."

"Brothel, gaming house, the underside of some bed, tattooed on a sailor's buttock?" Inissa suggested under her breath, and Lord Vediya laughed.

Narsi guessed that Inissa knew Lord Vediya well. They did make a handsome couple, both of them so naturally beautiful that their disheveled clothes and hair only lent them a charm.

His attention returned to the glowing red symbol in his palm as it rose up from his skin like dried paste being peeled away. It floated for a moment, then the flat lines began filling out. The circle became a translucent sphere, not unlike a soap bubble. Inside the sphere, the other forms coiled together into a dark shadow. It twitched and shivered.

Lady Hylanya flicked the thin membrane of the sphere and it burst. For just a moment a shining red form hovered above Narsi's hand. It looked like a leggy tick. It thrashed at the air and produced a tiny, high-pitched hiss. Then it was gone and Narsi stood staring at his empty hand, feeling thrilled and amazed.

"That was the spell laid upon those held in thrall here. It's a strange thing. Most thralls are made so that those in their grasp feel sympathy with their master's wishes and desires. This is made so that those enthralled know that they are being forced to action against their wills. The one crafting these spells enjoys their agony and glories in overpowering them." Lady Hylanya scowled and then spat on the floor as if her distaste for the spell and its creator were a physically foul sensation.

"The spell placed upon the Shard of Heaven shares that Cadeleonian style." Lady Hylanya again traced a circle in the air and the cross of the four-pointed star. "But it is older and less spiteful. Like the spells that created the grimma's sanctums, it serves to restrain an immense force. It feeds upon the souls of your kings, but there is little left of them or the spell anymore."

Lord Vediya's frown deepened at this, but Narsi couldn't help feeling a weird mix of fear and excitement—like those late nights of his boyhood when he'd clutched his blanket close and begged his mother to tell him another ghost story.

"I've read about the Labaran sanctum in Lord Vediya's memoir," Narsi offered. "Your brother destroyed it, freeing trolls and Old Gods that had been captured there."

"Yes. It terrified me at the time, but since then I've come to know both weathra-steeds, frogwives and even a wild troll as friends." Lady

Hylanya smiled and looked to Kili. "Though we still give most trolls and mordwolves a wide breadth when traveling."

"It looked very like a deer through the trees," Kili responded, and Lady Hylanya laughed.

"The assassin who tried to poison you," Lord Vediya said in a tone not far from that of a schoolmaster returning a distracted pupil to the subject at hand. "Was he one of those enthralled, and if so, do you think that these assassins are under the royal bishop's command?"

"If we could prove the royal bishop's involvement we'd have him for heresy and witchcraft." Inissa's pretty face lit with delight and she leaned into Lord Vediya. He gave her a warm smile in return.

"They aren't in the royal bishop's thrall. That old prune's malevolent soul is rooted deep in his mean flesh. He's never cast a spell in his life. I can hardly credit that he's a cousin to such a magical creature as our luminous Javier. He relies upon relics and the remains of other people's power to exert his will." Lady Hylanya shook her head then looked to Lord Vediya. "But I've been thinking on my attack while I slept. I've seen it now many times through the eyes of the cats on the rooftops and stalking the market streets. I realized that the one who poisoned me wasn't the man you and Kili chased through the crowd. It was a woman standing near the wool stall who grazed me with a sharpened lace needle."

"But he fled," Kili objected.

"Perhaps he was a cutpurse who ran because you gave chase," Inissa wondered.

"Maybe," Lady Hylanya replied, though Narsi noticed a troubled furrow form between her red brows.

"You think not?" Narsi asked.

"I think—no, I *felt* the turmoil of his struggle against the thrall binding him," Lady Hylanya's expression turned even more uncertain. "It doesn't make sense, but I felt that he raced to the market to stop the woman who poisoned me. He was terrified for her safety . . . and even for mine."

"Why would he worry for you both?" Inissa commented.

"That I can't say." Again Lady Hylanya knit her brow, though this time Narsi thought she didn't appear troubled so much as concentrating on something far away that only she could see. "I only know that I felt his desire to save us both. He all but shone with it. And when he realized he arrived too late, he ran to draw you away from the woman. I'm certain of that."

"Was she . . . enthralled too?" Narsi asked.

"No," Lady Hylanya replied, then she scowled and bowed her head to sniff her own armpit. Her sour expression almost made Narsi laugh.

"I need new clothes," LadyHylanya announced.

"Ollivar secured a change of wardrobe for you yesterday," Lord Vediya assured her. "Something that might allow us to cross the city without attracting too much attention."

"Ollivar?" Lady Hylanya glanced to Kili. "He's the stocky one who writes long poems, yes?"

Narsi remembered the broad-boned young man downstairs.

"Indeed he is," Lord Vediya replied with an amused smile.

"It's hard to keep track of all your friends, Atreau," Lady Hylanya replied. "I'm surprised that even you don't get confused."

"The trick, my dear, is to recollect only those who can remember me when I'm out of favor with the court," Lord Vediya replied lightly. "It's an extraordinarily small circle of comrades then."

"And we all weep for your suffering." Inissa rolled her eyes and won a laugh from Lady Hylanya. "Now, all of you men, out, so that Hylanya and I can clean up and change clothes."

Narsi snatched up his medical satchel and started for the door while Lord Vediya offered a series of absurdly leggy bows to Lady Hylanya and Inissa, then he backed to the door. Kili, however, remained where he stood, looking uneasy.

"I shouldn't leave Hyla—" Kili began, but Inissa cut him off.

"If you don't want to go downstairs and refresh yourself, you're welcome to stand guard on the other side of the door, Kili. Just out with you. We haven't all day before the bishop's men return."

Kili nodded and followed Narsi and Lord Vediya out into the dim hallway.

"When you come down with Hylanya, take the table near the door," Lord Vediya instructed Kili. "Morisio should be arriving, along with Majdi and Hakarl, anytime now, and that's where they'll be expecting to find you."

Kili nodded.

Narsi had no idea who Hakarl might be, but he recalled Morisio from Lord Vediya's memoir. And the name Majdi was not so common of a Haldiim name. He found himself wondering if this might be his opportunity to meet the famous captain Majdi Kir-Zaki, with whom Lord Vediya had briefly sailed. Lord Vediya had mentioned his ship, the *Red Witch*, so chances seemed very good.

"Quite the spring in your step," Lord Vediya commented as they descended the stairs. "How much of that nightleaf did you end up taking yourself?"

"Not too much." Narsi self-consciously slowed his pace. "It will wear off within the hour . . . I think."

"That's a shame," Lord Vediya replied with a teasing smile. "I'm rather enjoying this more forthcoming aspect of you."

"I am ever forthcoming and honest." Narsi gazed up the steps at Lord Vediya with an expression of wide-eyed and utterly contrived innocence. "I schooled as a chapel boy after all."

CHAPTER
TWELVE

A moment later Narsi flinched back as the blaze of sun streaming through the windows seared into his nightleaf-dilated eyes. Narsi clenched his eyes closed and cursed himself for forgetting how long the effect of the medicine could last. He wasn't blind, but getting through the crowded shop might prove quite difficult.

"Too bright, I take it?" Lord Vediya whispered. Then he threw his arm around Narsi's shoulder and, to Narsi's astonishment, pulled him against his chest. Again that faint perfume of roses and leather drifted over Narsi. Lord Vediya's arm felt hot and the weight of his embrace reminded Narsi of the carefree intimacies he'd left behind in Anacleto.

"Indulge me in this, will you? I think it will serve us both," Lord Vediya whispered into Narsi's ear; then he staggered forward, pulling Narsi with him.

"I'm not so drunk as I can't walk on my own . . . ," Lord Vediya slurred in the too-loud tone of a truly inebriated man. Narsi felt, more than saw, the attention of the surrounding patrons light upon him and Lord Vediya, and then fall away in a multitude of resigned sighs and disparaging murmurs.

"And there's Atreau legless again," a sallow fellow sniffed to his companions.

"Some things never change," came a reply, but Narsi couldn't make out the speaker for the flares of light reflecting off his silver kaweh pot.

Narsi had no idea what Lord Vediya was doing or how he was going to cross the room with his eyes so blinded. Then Lord Vediya clutched him closer and staggered forward, pulling Narsi alongside him. He swayed and stumbled in an amazingly accurate imitation of a stiff-legged drunk, all the while guiding Narsi between crowded tables and past the busy serving women.

"I told you . . . I'm walking . . . my own." Lord Vediya lurched to the left, drawing Narsi past a table and around a serving woman. Narsi felt her full skirt brush the back of his calf.

"Very nearly there, Lord Vediya," Narsi improvised. "Though I dare say it's a little early to already be staggering about."

"You are mop my mother," Lord Vediya replied.

"I should certainly hope not," Narsi sniffed. He felt the shudder of a suppressed laugh pass through Lord Vediya's body and yet his expression gave nothing away. Narsi thought he'd never seen such a skilled actor. Though all of this seemed a bit extreme just to hide the fact that Narsi couldn't see in this brilliant light, but still it pleased Narsi to be made part of the deception.

Then the two of them collapsed down onto a high-backed wooden bench. The other occupants quickly made room for them at the large circular table. Happily, Narsi found that a deep shadow, cast by the sign outside, fell across the seat. As he leaned back slightly closer to Lord Vediya, he managed to survey his surroundings. The angular woman wearing a nun's habit sat on the other side of him, while the proud-featured fellow dressed in blue, red and green silk patchwork occupied the carved chair directly opposite Narsi. A pretty young woman and several men shared the table with them as well, but before Narsi could make any study of them, he noticed that Kili had taken a seat at the empty table below the staircase and near the door.

A long limbed, red-haired boy hunched in the chair next to him. The youth turned only slightly. Then Narsi realized that he was looking at Lady Hylanya turned out in the wide trousers and leather vest of a Mirogoth sailor. With her long hair pulled back in the same simple braid that Kili wore, her strong jaw stood out as distinctly masculine.

She and Kili must have stolen down the stairs and taken their seats while Lord Vediya's theatrics had drawn the attention of all the surrounding patrons. So it hadn't been a mere amusement for Narsi's sake at all, and the subterfuge was far from over, Narsi realized.

He immediately averted his gaze from Kili and Lady Hylanya. He glanced down at the table just in time to notice the angular woman beside him twist and curl her long fingers into a quick series of signs before she picked up her cup and took a swig of kaweh.

The slim man wearing the silk patchwork leaned forward slightly. This close Narsi noted that silver and gold thread decorated his green sleeves and pearls served as the buttons for his doublet. His features and coloring strongly reminded Narsi of the Duke of Rauma's, though he appeared a little older than the duke and much friendlier. He met Narsi's shy gaze with the confidence of a man quite aware of the striking effect of onyx-black eyes and an attractive smile.

"Has Inissa gotten you drunk again, Atreau? A man who cannot refuse his harlot's whims all too soon finds himself serving her pleasures while his own go unslaked," the man in patchwork opined. Then he turned his imperious gaze on Narsi. "I'm Jacinto, by the way. You are?"

"Narsi," Lord Vediya supplied, then he listed to the right, nearly falling into Narsi's lap. "Mystery physician." Then, to Narsi's shock, Lord Vediya lay his head on Narsi's thigh and closed his eyes as if he'd drifted off to sleep. He curled one hand around Narsi's knee and Narsi felt the warmth of his fingers radiating through his thin gray stocking.

The woman in nun's garb raised a brow at Atreau, but there was something about her expression that struck Narsi as less condemning than amused.

"Sabella Calies." She extended a tanned hand to Narsi. He took her fingers, noting how rough and callused they felt. Several thick scars marked the back of her hand and the knuckle of her third finger had obviously been badly broken at one point.

Her name sounded familiar. Had Lord Vediya mentioned her in one of his memoirs? Then he noted the hilt of a sword jutting from her belt and it came to him. Yes, Lord Vediya had mentioned meeting the infamous swordswoman when he'd first lived in the capital eleven years ago, but that wasn't why Narsi recognized her name.

Several printshops in the Haldiim District sold rather romanticized portraits of her, and her exploits had inspired at least two stage plays he'd attended. She'd first gained notoriety at nineteen when she'd taken up her father's sword and avenged his murder in a dueling ring. Since then she'd fought both for honor and sport, and her courage was said to have won her the patronage of one of the royal heirs. At the very least it had granted her a special license to wear a sword in public despite her sex.

"The Sabella Calies?" Narsi asked, and Lord Vediya gave a quiet snort against his leg. Narsi ignored him, though it wasn't easy.

The woman nodded.

"You're famous throughout Anacleto—even in the Haldiim section of the city. It's truly an honor to meet you."

Sabella grinned at him, displaying several chipped teeth.

Narsi guessed that she, like Lord Vediya, was younger than the hardship of her life made her appear. Perhaps forty-five. The age when many folks found themselves reflecting upon the greater purpose of their lives, according to Father Timoteo. So perhaps that nun's habit wasn't so strange a thing. Though Narsi couldn't recollect ever seeing a nun traveling alone, and the habit's breast didn't bear the emblem of any order.

"Are you considering which order to offer your vows to?" Narsi asked.

All seven of the other people at the table laughed at the suggestion, including Lord Vediya and Sabella herself. The bearded man to Jacinto's right seemed to take a particular pleasure in sneering at Narsi as he guffawed. Narsi frowned, feeling embarrassed that his ignorance inspired so much amusement. This was why he so often kept his mouth shut. Damn that nightleaf.

"Fear not, young Master Narsi. I'm not about to burden a convent with my redemption," Sabella replied, and her expression softened as she met his gaze. "Jacinto has saddled me with a role in his wretched play. I'm breaking this costume in before I have to leap across a stage in it. Beware or you may soon find yourself trapped in his idiotic productions as well."

"I've not saddled her with the part so much as she has overwhelmed me with the inspiration," Jacinto interrupted, and he smiled with particular warmth at Narsi, though Narsi couldn't see why. "If anyone was born to play the role of a deviant Holy Mother, battling lusty demons for the attentions of her succulent charges, it would be Sabella, I promise you."

The bearded man to Jacinto's left cast an oddly appraising look toward the fetching girl seated to Sabella's right. Several other men at the table laughed, but not too kindly. Lord Vediya sighed, sounding almost bored, but didn't bother to raise his head up off Narsi's lap.

"Ignore Procopio. He's only recently been allowed to sit at the table with adults." Sabella made a dismissive gesture at the bearded man and then leaned back a little so that Narsi had a clearer view of the young woman at Sabella's side. "This is Suelita."

So this was the girl who'd inspired Ladislo's attack on Lord Vediya. Even more than Inissa she seemed to possess all the traits of an ideal Cadeleonian beauty: curvaceous figure, long silky dark hair and pale skin that gave way to a flush all too easily. She nodded to Narsi but didn't meet his gaze. Instead she remained close to Sabella and scribbled something down in a little blue silk-bound diary.

"Cocuyo." Sabella pointed to a well-built fellow seated in a chair to Suelita's right. His left cheekbone looked just slightly crooked—likely broken at some point—but a smile seemed to come easily to the man's face. His bushy brown hair reminded Narsi a little of old Lord Grunito back home in Anacleto. He, like Sabella and all of the other men at the table, wore a sword.

Sabella then pointed to the wan young man sporting a neatly trimmed mustache and seated on Jacinto's right. "That is Enevir, who will no doubt have you doctoring any number of sickly orphans and kittens if you give him too much of your time."

"My most recent crusade is for a law to allow converted Irabiim to earn ownership of property if they can make it arable." The man eyed Narsi as if he might just have a spot in his campaign for him. He resembled Cocuyo too closely to be anything but a twin, however where Cocuyo appeared rippling with sleek muscle Enevir was gaunt. A sturdy cane leaned against his chair.

"In a rational society we must recognize that randomly persecuting caravans of heathen nomads is both cruel and pointless." Enevir gazed into Narsi's face with a far too intent stare.

"Sorry." Jacinto cut him off with a wide dramatic yawn. "I stopped listening somewhere around 'rational.' Anyway, I'm sure Master Narsi isn't the least bit interested in Cadeleonian church edicts, property law or"—he gave a loose wave of his hand, and this time Narsi noted the large gold and sapphire ring adorning his third finger—"whatnot. He's already putting up with Atreau using him as a pillow for his greasy head."

"I—" Narsi began but Jacinto cut him off.

"It's boring. And nothing is worse than finding yourself trapped in the company of dullards." Jacinto sighed.

"I heard an amusing joke the other day," Cocuyo offered.

But before he could tell it the serving woman returned with a huge silver tray.

She lowered it carefully to the table and spread out an astounding assortment of cups, dishes and tableware. The tall kettle of steaming kaweh, Narsi recognized at once. The aroma rising off it filled him with nostalgia. The cups, too, were familiar, if larger than any that would have been used in the Haldiim District. However the dishes of honey, salt, cream and raw egg yolks baffled Narsi. As did the small glasses of dark gold fluid. He lifted one and caught a powerful whiff of spiced liquor. Then he noticed Jacinto watching him with an amused expression.

No doubt he hoped Narsi's fumbling would entertain him, but Narsi wasn't in a mood to oblige.

"The kaweh is served," Narsi informed Lord Vediya. In response he nuzzled his head against Narsi's leg; the sensation felt far too pleasant for this public place. Narsi caught hold of Lord Vediya's ear and gave him a hard pinch as he repeated, "Your kaweh has been served, my lord."

Lord Vediya pulled upright and rubbed his ear. He blinked at the other people seated at the table and swayed just slightly, so that he took in the view past Jacinto where Hylanya and Kili sat. Then he produced a loud belch and snatched up the glass of liquor. Narsi half expected him to toss it back, but instead he poured it over the egg yolk.

"Egg . . . is duck," Lord Vediya muttered as he picked up a small silver whisk and proceeded to whip the yolk, adding in first a drizzle of honey and then pouring in a fair portion of the cream. In seconds the yolk transformed into a frothy mass.

Lord Vediya paused a moment, as if he'd somehow forgotten what he was doing. Then he took in Narsi and gave a small start. He appeared so convincingly drunk that Narsi had to remind himself that he knew Lord Vediya to be stone sober.

Lord Vediya held up a finger to him and waggled it loosely.

"Don't pinched . . . my ear," Lord Vediya murmured. "Is sensi . . . sensitive."

Then he returned to the kaweh service, pouring the aromatic black kaweh into a cup as he slowly added in the whipped egg as well. While he swayed and lurched the entire time, he didn't spill a single drop. At last he pushed the mixture to Narsi.

"Salt? No . . ." Lord Vediya leaned so close that his nose almost touched Narsi's. "No. Because . . . you . . . are sweet."

Then he flopped against the wooden back of the bench and slid slowly down it until he again returned his head to Narsi's lap.

Across the table Jacinto beamed with delight.

"You see, that is why I shall never allow my uncle to have you hanged, Atreau," Jacinto announced. "You are ever entertaining, even when hopelessly inebriated."

In response Lord Vediya raised a hand and offered Jacinto a salute. Then Jacinto turned his attention back to Narsi.

"Go on, try it." He nodded to the frothy drink.

Narsi's desire to try something new briefly warred with his unwillingness to simply acquiesce to Jacinto. But his curiosity won out. He lifted the cup and took a sip of the rich, sweet concoction. He felt the warming effect of alcohol in the pit of his stomach more than he tasted it. Had he eaten anything but barley water before this he likely wouldn't have noticed it at all.

"What do you think?' Jacinto asked.

"It's nothing like Haldiim kaweh, but it's quite good, thank you," Narsi replied, because it would have been bad manners not to.

He took another longer drink and felt better for it. As he set the cup down he noticed Lord Vediya watching him with a relaxed, half-lidded expression. His streaked hair fell back from his face and lay across Narsi's thigh like a spill of ink. He met Narsi's gaze and then made the slightest motion of his hand toward the windows.

Lifting the cup again, Narsi surveyed the view out the window and caught sight of the violet uniforms of several mounted men, charging down from an alley. Next to him, Sabella made another series of small hand gestures. Jacinto yawned and stretched, turning just enough to look out the wide window behind him. Narsi felt suddenly aware of all of them at the table taking pains not to look to where Lady Hylanya sat drinking with Kili and Atreau's stocky friend, Ollivar.

"Suelita, my dear," Sabella said. "Would you mind trading me places on this bench? I might want to stretch my legs a little."

"Of course." Suelita sprang to her feet and Sabella uncoiled from her seat. Standing, she made a particularly striking and strange figure among even all these flamboyantly dressed Cadeleonians. The stark black of her habit cast the lines of her belt, sword hilt and dueling knife in strong relief, while her cropped hair and riding boots lent a decidedly masculine counterpoint to the slight curves of her spare figure. Smiling nervously, Suelita slid quickly across the bench to take Sabella's place beside Narsi. She went to great care not to elbow him as she slipped her little book away into a small silk satchel. Sabella sank down to the edge of the bench like a cat crouching before it pounced on an unsuspecting mouse.

"Kaweh," Lord Vediya murmured. He pulled himself upright and let his legs sprawl into a position not unlike Sabella's, though Lord Vediya maintained the appearance of languid sloth. Briefly he placed his hand on Narsi's leg and patted him as if offering reassurance, then he took a swig of milky kaweh from Narsi's cup. As he swayed back Narsi noted the fine gold chain and polished gray-green pendant that Lord Vediya had dropped directly between Narsi's legs. It looked like Lady Hylanya's necklace, but Narsi couldn't remember her ever passing it to Lord Vediya. Not unless he'd taken the necklace when he'd been making his extravagant exit.

"Medical satchel . . . ," Lord Vediya said. "Some magic treasure . . . hidden there . . . for my head?"

"I'll see what I have." Narsi picked up his satchel and did his best to smoothly slip the necklace inside while taking out a jar of salt tablets. He handed Lord Vediya the tablet and felt almost certain that Lord Vediya palmed it rather than swallowing it with a second gulp of Narsi's kaweh.

The royal bishop's men strode past the rippled glass of the window, their forms twisting and distorting. Then the big, blunt-faced man in the lead shoved the green door open. He strode in and his men followed, making a racket with the heavy tread of their polished black riding boots. The ten of them created an intimidating wall of black leather armor, slashed violet cloaks, swords and long halberds.

Everyone seated in the kaweh house turned to stare in silence. Out of the corner of his eye Narsi noticed a serving woman quietly retreat into the kitchen. A gray-haired woman emerged to take her place. Fortunately, watching their exchange delayed Narsi from looking to where Kili and Lady Hylanya had turned to face the royal bishop's men. He managed not to gape when he realized that it wasn't just a man's dress that disguised Lady Hylanya, but that she now also sported a very convincing red mustache.

Jacinto took in the armed men and then, with a bored sigh, returned to his drink.

The man at the front of the group, wearing the gold insignia of a captain around his neck, made a gesture and two rangy boys seated at different tables rose and came to him.

"Dirty snitches," a freckled woman at a nearby table hissed. The man across from her shook his head. The two informants spoke in hushed voices to the captain. One pointed to the stairs and then to Lord Vediya, who in return splayed his legs farther apart and offered the man a lurid grin. The captain handed each of the informants a coin and they left the kaweh house with their heads low.

Then the captain drew a scroll of paper from his dark violet doublet. It rolled open in his hand. A florid script of indigo ink filled the top third of the page, while gold and indigo seals studded the rest.

"By order of the royal bishop and his highness Prince Remes, the upper floor of this building is to be searched for the confessed practitioner of witchcraft Hylanya Radulf." He thrust the warrant out at the gray-haired serving woman like a man who felt he'd at last thrown down a winning hand against a particularly challenging opponent. To Narsi's surprise the woman didn't simply move aside to let the men pass, but instead very deliberately set aside the platter she'd been holding and studied the warrant.

"You seem to have gotten the impression that I am the owner of this property, sir," she responded. "But in truth I simply rent the building for my business, and only the ground floor—"

"Do not test me, woman!" the captain ground out.

Narsi noticed Lord Vediya's hand drop from the tabletop to his sword belt.

"I mean you no offense, Captain Yago," the woman replied coolly. "But the keys to the upper floor aren't mine to be had. I think you will need to show your warrant to the owner of the property."

Watching the captain's face flush with anger, Narsi felt his heart beginning to pound with fear for the gray-haired woman. She looked nothing like his own mother, but something about her stubborn calm reminded Narsi of her. He started to stand, but Lord Vediya caught his arm and jerked him back down. At the same moment Jacinto swung around and stood.

"Quite right, Pepylla," Jacinto called to the serving woman. "This matter is my business, not yours, my dear."

Jacinto strode to the captain and frowned at the warrant.

"Captain Yago, is it?" Jacinto inquired.

The captain looked like he might strike Jacinto for his impertinence, but then Jacinto extended his right hand and the captain's gaze fixed upon the gaudy gold ring Jacinto wore. The color drained from the captain's ruddy face, leaving him with a complexion like oat gruel.

"Your highness." The captain bowed low and his men hurried to follow suit, though the narrow entryway of the kaweh house made their motions clumsy.

Narsi stole a curious glance to Lord Vediya. He might have mentioned that Jacinto was actually *Prince* Jacinto—the fourth son of the royal heir, Prince Sevanyo.

Lord Vediya shrugged.

The captain straightened with a grim expression. "The royal bishop's warrant must still be served, Your Highness. I cannot—"

"Oh, my dear man." Jacinto cut him off with a broad smile. "I wouldn't dream of intruding upon my doddering old uncle's whims any more than I would consider having you beheaded. Your men may, of course, search the apartments upstairs. But do order them to behave with some delicacy. I, and a number of noblemen, are very fond of the lady who lives there. I shouldn't be at all amused were she to be mishandled by anyone not paying an extravagant sum for the privilege."

"We will of course treat her gently, Your Highness." Captain Yago gave a stern glance over his shoulder to the men behind him, then indicated for them to take the stairs.

"While they occupy themselves"—Jacinto caught Captain Yago's arm—"you certainly must join me at my table."

"It would be an honor," the captain ground out with such obvious unhappiness that Narsi almost laughed. "But I really should take part in the search."

"Nonsense," Jacinto stated flatly and with a surprisingly commanding tone. "Certainly you ought to remain down here to ensure that no one slips down the stairs past your men. I insist that you join me."

Moments later Captain Yago hunched in the chair Enevir had vacated with a cup of frothy kaweh in front of him and a pinched, miserable expression on his face. He had to crane his head to observe the stairs and when he looked ahead of him, his gaze settled on Suelita, who regarded him with an expression of prim disapproval.

Enevir didn't take much room, but his addition to the bench inspired Lord Vediya to slump his head onto Narsi's shoulder.

Jacinto questioned them all in turns about their favored entertainments, preferred breeds of horses and thoughts concerning the latest popular opera: *The Rogues' Folly*. Most of Suelita's shy whispers didn't even carry to Narsi. But what did intrigued him. He'd not taken her for the kind of girl who'd voice—even very quietly—such strong opinions as ". . . most theater seems a trite glorification of masculine aggrandizement, a fantasy written by men for men . . ."

Lord Vediya slurred something about horses being terrible opera singers—even his own glorious stallion, Nube. For a few moments after that Lord Vediya managed to actually draw Captain Yago into a disjointed but passionate conversation over the weaknesses of the local, dish-nosed breed of horses. Captain Yago agreed with Lord Vediya. Apparently he too rode a northern-bred stallion, but Procopio came to the defense of the local horses and Sabella seconded him, though it obviously pained her to do so.

If there was a Cadeleonian who didn't hold passionate beliefs about horses, Narsi had yet to meet one. Very quickly voices began to rise and Procopio smacked the table with his fist to make his point.

Narsi wasn't certain if he ought to break in before it got out of hand, but then was rescued when Jacinto began announcing his own opinions, over the voices of everyone. The debate immediately quieted and Jacinto returned to the subject of the theater. Happily, the prince's tone and turns of phrase culminated in a monologue amusing enough to distract and entertain.

Partway through Jacinto's description of the ideal heroine, Narsi noticed three very tan men dressed in sailor's garb come through the door and take seats under the stairs beside Lady Hylanya and Kili. One of the men sported hair as curly as Narsi's, but the blond coloring marked him as full-blooded Haldiim. The other two men wore wide-brimmed hats, though when one of them removed his he revealed a shock of sun-bleached red hair. He dropped the hat down on Lady Hylanya's head.

A commotion on the stairs drew Narsi's attention. He wasn't alone; seemingly everyone in the kaweh house looked to the stairs as Inissa's voice rose in shrill protest. She came stamping down with two of the royal bishop's men close behind her. Narsi didn't think for a moment that it was a coincidence that she wore a scarlet dress very like the one Lady Hylanya had worn earlier, as well as an ornately braided wig of bright red hair. One of the men attempted to catch the slashed sleeve of her dress, but she spun on him.

"Lay a hand on me and Prince Jacinto Sagrada will have you gelded and present your tanned ball sack to me as a coin purse!" Inissa lifted her chin and continued down the stairs, then marched to Jacinto's table. The two men trailed her like wary bloodhounds.

"These idiots think that you've been housing Lady Hylanya in my rooms!" Inissa pulled the wig off her head and slammed it into a half-empty kaweh pot. Sugar dishes, cream pots and salt bowls went tumbling. One pot crashed over, spilling dark liquid across the tabletop. Captain Yago shoved his chair back from the table as hot kaweh poured toward him. Narsi reached out and kept his own pot from overturning and Lord Vediya pulled a kerchief from his pocket to mop sloppily at the spill.

"If this is what's going to happen," Inissa went on, "I won't wear this costume even a minute longer. You can take your stupid play straight to the three hells!"

"Well said," Sabella replied. "Believe me, I know your pain. Look how he's having me parade around."

"My darlings," Jacinto said before either the captain or his men could get a word in. "If the clothes aren't broken in, then you won't look natural wearing them on stage—"

"I don't care what I might look like on stage if a bunch of ruffians come beating down my door—"

"Wait!" Lord Vediya bolted upright, drawing all gazes to him. He swayed a moment, then went on. "I have . . . a solution . . . Naked! No costumes. Just . . . naked." He pointed meaningfully at Jacinto and then leaned back on the bench with a crooked grin on his face.

Jacinto pursed his lips thoughtfully.

"Atreau, you might just have something—"

"Absolutely not!" Inissa shot Lord Vediya a murderous glare.

Captain Yago stared at the group of them with the expression of long suffering, then turned his attention to the two men who'd trailed Inissa downstairs. At the same time Narsi stole a glance farther back to see that Lady Hylanya, Kili and the three sailors had slipped out. Now only the brawny young Ollivar occupied a seat below the stairs.

Delight bloomed through Narsi's chest and he forced himself to frown down at his kaweh cup to hide his face. Beside him Suelita gave a soft sigh and for just a moment he and she shared a quick smile.

"Did you find anything?" Captain Yago demanded of his men.

"Only this . . . woman," the taller of the two replied.

"Do you seriously think that I am a Labaran noble?" Inissa turned her furious glower on the royal bishop's men. "Did your mothers drop you on your heads as infants? Perhaps on a daily basis?" Then she spun on her heel back to round on Jacinto. "You had better sort this out!"

"Well, my dear, I don't know what I can do," Jacinto replied. "If you won't wear a costume then all that's left is to perform naked—"

"I mean that you should do something about these ruffians ransacking my rooms and accusing me of heresy and practicing witchcraft."

"Oh, well, that's obviously just foolishness." Jacinto waved his right hand, beckoning the captain up from his seat and over to his side while he continued to smile at Inissa. "I'm certain that the good Captain Yago will offer you a most humble apology before he and his men take their leave."

Inissa and the captain glowered at one another in silence, then Captain Yago performed a stiff bow and grumbled a low "My apologies for your inconvenience . . . madam."

"You see. All is well." Jacinto prodded the sprawling mass of red hair spilled across the table. "Well, nearly everything. I fear I may need to purchase a new hairpiece. But perhaps it's for the best. I wasn't all that impressed with this one. Not quite dramatic enough."

Captain Yago stood there at the prince's side while Jacinto paid him not the slightest attention and went on musing over what represented the best wigs for theater as opposed to those a prince might wear to disguise his identity while wooing a milkmaid. At last, Captain Yago made an awkward bow to the prince, then backed away.

The captain withdrew with his men and Narsi watched them mount their horses and ride away with a growing feeling of triumph. He wanted to crow in glee, or at least congratulate Lord Vediya and Inissa on their spectacular acting. But then he realized that he could do neither. For his own sake and those of all the people involved, he couldn't say a word about this exploit. Not to anyone. Ever.

All at once, he wondered how many other escapades and ventures Lord Vediya had undertaken but never written or spoken of.

"Master Narsi needs . . . paid," Lord Vediya stated, then he patted his own crotch. "Merrypox is gone but so's my cash . . . Jacinto . . ." He pointed at the prince and then slumped back against the back of the bench.

"Yes, yes." Jacinto in turn looked to Enevir, who quickly drew a coin purse from his pocket and counted out several gold coins, each nearly as thick as Narsi's smallest finger. Two stallions stood rampant over the fine relief of the Sagrada crest. Enevir pushed the money past Lord Vediya to Narsi. He'd seen a coin of royal favor before but never laid his hands upon one, much less a stack of ten.

"We appreciate all you've done and thank you for your company and discretion." Jacinto smiled at him. "But certainly I can't keep you from your duties. Go with my thanks, dear Narsi."

He was being dismissed.

Narsi collected the coins and hid them away in his medical satchel, alongside Lady Hylanya's necklace. He guessed that he'd need to turn the necklace over later, but not in so public a space. Sabella and Suelita rose to let him leave the bench. For an instant Narsi wondered if Lord Vediya would come with him, or if he should invite him, but when he looked in Lord Vediya's direction the man wouldn't meet Narsi's gaze.

Clearly, he was to be allowed into Lord Vediya's social circle only while he provided a service. That stung a little. He rose from the table and offered his most formal bow to the prince before departing.

CHAPTER
THIRTEEN

Late in the afternoon, four of the city guards under Ciceron's command brought the captain's decapitated body to the chapel. A flag emblazoned with the white stallion of the Sagrada kings served as his shroud and large brass censers rested on either side of his corpse, swathing his remains in veils of powerful incense. A midwife had already cleaned his flesh and rinsed him with wine and perfume.

While Fedeles and the guards looked on, Timoteo absolved Ciceron's soul of earthly sins. Two youthful acolytes knelt, offering their prayers as protection for his journey through the Sorrowlands and into paradise. Little golden spells flickered throughout the chapel like the flutters of sparrows' wings, but not one altered the captain's death nor eased Fedeles's sorrow. The shining blue rings of radiant blessings that hung over the pulpit might as well have been motes of dust for all the good they did.

Anger and sorrow churned through Fedeles as he silently cursed the monsters who'd harmed Ciceron and then recriminated himself for failing to protect the captain. An hour passed, bells rang out. The snarling stone beasts glaring down from the walls seemed to shift restlessly as shadows stretched through the chapel.

At the end of the ceremony, all of them marched in silence to the cold vault of the mansion's private crypt. There the body would remain until Fedeles's groundskeepers finished digging Ciceron's grave. Dazed and exhausted, Fedeles took in the faces of the four city guards. He had seen them all numerous times before, but he could recall little about them at this moment. Two of them struggled to hold back their tears and the other two looked sick and miserable. Despite Timoteo's pained expression, all of them swore on God's balls that they would avenge their captain.

Fedeles thanked them each for their loyalty to their captain and gifted them with gold coins as they took their leave. The acolytes fled behind them. Timoteo returned to murmuring prayers into the clouds of intoxicatingly fragrant incense. Gaunt and white-haired and mouthing words into the air, he struck Fedeles as looking almost as much like a madman as a holy martyr.

Fedeles gazed down at the still body hidden beneath the silk shroud and then lay his hand on Ciceron's chest as he'd done so many times before. Stripped of all his charm and swagger, he felt cold and stiff as a side of venison. All that now remained with Fedeles was a mere husk.

Ciceron's wife had entrusted his remains to Fedeles's care in return for the horses and carriages she'd required to pack up her children and household and flee for the security of her family home in the southern countryside. Ciceron's latest mistress had accepted the endowment Fedeles settled upon her but had preferred not to see what indignities Ciceron's handsome body had suffered at the hands of his killers.

Fedeles didn't want to see either, and yet he found himself drawing back the shroud to touch Ciceron's bare skin one last time. Fedeles didn't delude himself into believing that their friendship had been anything approaching a romance, but he had cared for Ciceron. They'd made each other smile and done no one any harm in those moments.

Tears filled Fedeles's eyes as he recalled the last time he'd caressed Ciceron's back and felt the heat of the other man's lips on him. They'd attended the opera that night and both laughed at the hapless lovers prancing and crooning across the stage. He couldn't remember which opera it had been, nor did he recall what exactly Ciceron had said. Only that Ciceron had been a little drunk and hadn't bothered to stifle his raucous laughter. Fedeles had felt awed by Ciceron's confidence in his own nature and actions. He never seemed to question his own impulses or inclinations, the way Fedeles so constantly restrained himself. He'd been a free spirit and it had been a joy simply to watch him.

Fedeles thought suddenly that he should have cherished those moments instead of taking them for granted. Now he couldn't clearly recall the eye color of the man he mourned. Nor did he recollect if it was black ale or red that Ciceron most enjoyed. He'd slept on his left side, hadn't he?

Fedeles clutched Ciceron's slack breast, trying to remember the sensation of Ciceron's heart hammering beneath his fingers. He yearned so desperately to feel just a hint of that warmth once more. Something stirred deep within Fedeles. The skin beneath his hand seemed suddenly warmer. A feeling very like that of a faint pulse kicked against his palm. Fedeles spread his fingers, reaching out to capture more of that sensation of a living body.

"Fedeles!" Oasia's voice broke him from his reverie. "Come away from him!"

All at once Fedeles realized that his shadow rolled out from his hands and wrapped itself around Ciceron's corpse. A strange, half-formed curve of misty darkness curled beneath the shroud, where Ciceron's head should have been. The cloth shuddered as if ragged breath fluttered up from beneath the folds.

Horror and revulsion flooded Fedeles. He jerked his hand back from Ciceron and commanded the shadow curse back to him. The shroud fell slack and Ciceron's dead chest stilled.

Had he nearly allowed the monstrosity within him to infiltrate and corrupt Ciceron's corpse?

Father Timoteo stood only a few feet away, wearing an expression that struck Fedeles as not nearly alarmed enough. Oasia strode toward him through the dark crypt. A curl of her black hair had come loose from the crown of braids and gold combs atop her head. Her green silk gown whispered against the flagstones as she sped to Fedeles's side. Faint sparks of blue light lit her hands. Fedeles turned to her and allowed her to ring him in her arms and in a circle of restraining spells. The shadow in him twisted and writhed like a great worm wriggling through his guts, but then it grew sluggish and at last quieted.

Fedeles slumped a little in Oasia's embrace.

"Never fear," Oasia murmured. "I have you now."

"Thank you," he whispered.

"Oh, I'm just happy to think that after six long years you still find me enchanting, my dearest husband."

Fedeles managed a tired laugh.

Oasia was a cousin to him, and like most members of her family, she could have ruled over a coven of witches if she'd been born Labaran. She would have been celebrated, Fedeles thought.

But in Cadeleon, her survival required secrecy and guile. Her innate skill was condemned by the church and her sex made her a mere property. As a girl she'd only escaped her father's grasp through marriage. When her first husband had threatened to annul their union—he'd not been able to share her bed, much less give her a child—she'd used his lover, Atreau, to become pregnant. That had not gone as she would have liked—not for her nor for her first husband or even Atreau—but her perilous situation had offered Fedeles an opportunity to secure his own position.

Oasia had not been all that happy about the arrangement at the beginning.

In fact the first night of their marriage she'd ensnared Fedeles in a web of blazing cerulean spells. She'd very nearly crushed the life from him when his murderous shadow burst out, coming only seconds from slitting Oasia's throat. Oasia had released Fedeles at once to raise a shield of blue spells over herself. Haloed on wild blue magic and glaring at him, she had looked like some ancient goddess, and Fedeles had felt awed by her despite himself. He'd known then that the last thing he wanted was to destroy her.

Restraining his accursed shadow had left him shaking and sweating, but he'd eventually drawn it back across their bed. Even now he could remember Oasia's confused expression when she realized that he would not harm her.

That night, in the midst of torn coverlets, spell-scorched pillows and drifting feathers, they'd reached their first of many understandings. Fedeles swore that he would never make an advance upon Oasia's body. She in turn agreed not to practice magic against him. Then side by side they'd set to work returning the nuptial bed to some semblance of normalcy. What had begun as a cold truce had flourished over the years into a companionable marriage and something approaching friendship.

More than either Javier or Alizadeh, it was Oasia who had helped Fedeles to win a degree of control over the shadow curse. And she shared his adoration and fear for Sparanzo, as no other person could. She took no offense to men like Ciceron with whom Fedeles kept company from time to time. He in return only wished her happiness in her own affairs.

Now, Oasia squeezed his hand reassuringly. Fedeles kissed her forehead in return. Lilac perfume drifted from her dark hair.

"You can control the darkness, my dear," Oasia whispered. "It's yours and you are its master."

It wasn't the first time Oasia had tried to convince him of his inherent connection to the shadow curse, but Fedeles shook his head. He didn't want that thing to be part of him—an extension of his soul, as Hylanya Radulf had insisted.

"I can't—" Fedeles began, but he went silent as a figure darted into the crypt.

"My lady?" Oasia's handmaid, Delfia, stepped into the dim chamber. The light from outside cast long shadows of Oasia's other attendants, who waited just out of sight. "My lord!" Delfia curtsied the moment she met Fedeles's gaze.

"What is it, my dear?" Oasia asked. Her expression remained impassive, but Fedeles recognized the annoyance in her voice. No doubt she had instructed her retinue not to interrupt them in the crypt. Fedeles felt glad for that. The fewer people who witnessed what he'd nearly done to Ciceron's body the better. Fedeles stole a glance to Timoteo, but he remained absorbed in his prayers and rituals, freeing Ciceron's soul from any lingering attachment to his flesh.

Delfia was one of the few people Oasia trusted, so Fedeles felt certain that even if she witnessed the shadow curse creep back into his body, she would tell no one. From her demeanor he guessed that she hadn't seen anything. She seemed very like her calm, self-contained brother in her quiet manner as well as her natural poise. Fedeles found it pleasing to watch both of them—though recently observing Ariz had begun to rouse a restless longing in him that he'd thought long dead.

Fedeles suspected that even now some perverse corner of his heart still fluttered with the thrill of first love when he looked upon the even features and effortless grace that appeared to run in the Plunado family. Genimo, too, had possessed those traits, as well as a wicked sense of humor and tireless desire. Fedeles had loved and trusted him so completely that he'd had no defense against Genimo's betrayal. There was a warning in that, Fedeles knew. Still he found his thoughts returning again and again to Master Ariz.

"Please forgive the intrusion, but a missive has arrived from Lady Elenna Ortez concerning that errand you just sent her on." Delfia kept her head bowed as she approached Oasia. "You wanted them brought to you directly."

"Yes. Thank you for remembering, Delfia." Oasia extended her hand and Delfia passed her the letter. Oasia opened it, glancing over the delicate script quickly. In passing Fedeles noted the mention of a man and doves. Oasia folded the letter closed, then hid it away within the folds of her green silk dress. "My dear cousin is forever confiding court gossip, but this, I think, will require me to advise her immediately."

Fedeles nodded. Pretty and just nineteen, Elenna was only one of numerous women whom his wife had assisted in delicate, private matters and who in return kept her informed. Atreau also maintained the same kinds of relationships—more than acquaintances but never just friends—though with an entirely different class of people. Neither Oasia nor Atreau would have thanked Fedeles for thinking them so similar, but he couldn't help noting it. Despite their first disastrous encounter, the two of them were remarkably alike in character, if not bearing. Both masked their true capacities behind charm and flattery, and both could act with ruthless detachment. They were nearly identical in their estrangements from their families, they both wore perfumes that reminded them of the mothers they'd lost, and both seemed drawn to physical strength and heartfelt sincerity in their lovers.

At times it was almost funny that they could be so alike and yet detest one another so greatly. Though just now nothing struck Fedeles as all that amusing. Plumes of funerary incense drifted over him.

Neither of Oasia nor Atreau had been particularly fond of Ciceron. Oasia had chided Fedeles that he deserved a more faithful companion, while Atreau had disliked the captain's capacity for violence. To Fedeles it seemed pointless to dissect a person into good and bad traits. To him the best and worst of Ciceron's character had been aspects of the whole man: brutal to his enemies but lavish in his affection for his loved ones. Fedeles glanced to the shrouded body and felt sorrow coil around him.

"I had come to ask if you would like to walk with me. But . . ." Oasia paused and her dark eyes moved over him thoughtfully. "Will you be . . . comfortable, here alone?"

Fedeles opened his mouth to offer some reassurance, but then wasn't certain of the truth in such a reply. Could he be trusted to maintain his control of the shadow curse and his grief at the same time? The shining blue spells that held him felt reassuring. He could let himself mourn Ciceron without fearing that the shadow curse would break free of his control. But he knew it wasn't right to expect Oasia to exhaust herself just because his raw emotions were arduous to restrain.

"I'll be fine," Fedeles said.

"And he will not be alone." Timoteo sprinkled a last vial of holy oil over the body and then walked to Fedeles's side. His angular features cast harsh shadows across his face, but his voice and smile conveyed only affection. "And I would very much appreciate someone to walk with me through the gardens. The flowers are so beautiful this time of year."

"Of course," Fedeles responded automatically. He reached out and allowed the frail Holy Father to take his arm and lean on him. Oasia's spells dimmed and then died away, but the shadow curse didn't rise in their absence. Timoteo's tender hold on his arm soothed Fedeles and allayed his anxiety.

Years earlier Timoteo had come to his aid and protected him from suspicions of "spiritual corruption" when his own parents and sister had feared to even touch him. Before then, Fedeles had only known Timo-teo as the elder brother of his cousin's best friend—little more than a stranger—so he'd been truly surprised and then touched by the man's compassion. He'd sheltered Fedeles and sat with him for hours while Fedeles had still been literally terrified of his own shadow. When Javier had fled and the royal bishop attempted to seize Fedeles, it had been Timoteo who'd rebuffed the man and then summoned Prince Sevanyo.

To this day Fedeles didn't understand why Timoteo had risked so much to defend him, but he was glad to do what he could to repay the Holy Father's kindness.

"I would be happy for the company, Tim," Fedeles decided.

Oasia took her leave. Her handmaid followed her in graceful silence. Fedeles gazed after them as their shadows retreated, leaving only golden light streaming in through the open door of the crypt.

"Come," Timoteo prompted. "We should walk in the light while we still can."

They left the crypt arm in arm and strolled through the winding camellia hedges. Three of Fedeles's personal guards trailed them at a distance. For a minute both Fedeles and Timoteo watched as a brilliant, iridescent hummingbird flitted between the blossoms, flashing and spar-kling like some incandescent incantation. Then a sinuous feline shape crept from the bushes and the bird fled into the bright blue sky. The black cat slunk away. Fedeles watched it go. For all that he would rather have imagined himself as that stunningly lovely bird, he felt a strange sympathy with the sinister creeping cat.

"Berto suspects that Narsi harbors a great fondness for that cat al-ready," Timoteo commented.

"Narsi?" Belatedly Fedeles recalled the young Haldiim physician whom he'd sent off with Atreau. The news of Ciceron's murder had made his earlier plans as well as the intrusion of a physician into his household seem distant concerns. "Well, so long as he keeps the beast from bothering my wife's parrot, it shouldn't be a problem."

Timoteo bobbed his head, but his expression remained troubled. "He possesses a good soul. I believe he's just what your household needs."

"The cat?" Fedeles asked with a slight smile.

Timoteo laughed, but then that thoughtful expression of his re-turned.

"I don't think it's my place to judge the morality of a cat. I can only recognize that they, like most creatures, are true to their natures and likely at peace with their own souls." Timoteo stilled at a break in the hedge and turned to gaze along the pebble walk that wound past a miniature orchard to the household garrison.

"I know that it isn't easy for you to accept a physician in your home. But what Donamillo and Genimo did to you wasn't the result of their interests. Their characters, not their callings, were at fault—"

"I do know that," Fedeles admitted. Knowing was easy, but feeling it was another matter.

"Oh good!" Timoteo's smile turned amused. "How foolish I must seem to have worried that you would offer my dear friend Narsi a less than warm welcome just because he's a physician."

Fedeles frowned down at his own hands. No doubt Timoteo knew about the ox ears he'd sent to the physician for his supper. Despite that, the young man had looked well rested and even a little excited when Fedeles saw him this morning. Though more than anything it had been the physician's physical resemblance to Elezar and Timoteo that had made the greatest impression upon Fedeles. He might be a Haldiim, but he was also obviously bred from Grunito stock. Fedeles cast a sidelong glance at Timoteo. Could he be the father? No. Fedeles couldn't credit the notion. In all the time he'd known Timoteo, never once had he observed the Holy Father to betray any interest in worldly pleasures of any kind. He was a man who hardly partook of necessary sustenance. Fedeles just couldn't imagine him succumbing to infatuation, much less indulging in an illicit affair. Probably a cousin's bastard then. Anacleto was well stocked with men of Grunito blood. It would be like Timoteo to shelter a young relative, regardless of his of mixed race.

"Atreau says you've known him a long while," Fedeles prompted. They walked out under the neat rows of snowplums and pear trees. Despite the darkening sky, bees still hummed through the branches. Small blessings and charms scattered across the grounds grew more visible as the sun sank. Oasia's blue and green blessings flickered around the chapel like waking fireflies, and far in the distance a faint golden glow emanated from the peak of Crown Hill.

"Yes. Since he was only an infant." Timoteo sounded both nostalgic and sad. "His father died before Narsi could really know him. Wadi, his mother, she was just brilliant in her grasp of ethics. She taught me so much and was never afraid to challenge my assumptions . . ." Timoteo stopped and to Fedeles's surprise he appeared to struggle to keep tears from his eyes. "She died last year, and that has left Narsi in a rather poor position."

"How so?" Fedeles asked.

"His father's family doesn't recognize him—"

"Could they?" Fedeles asked.

Timoteo nodded.

"He's legitimate?" Fedeles hadn't expected that and belatedly recognized the unconscious bigotry that had led him to assume a child of mixed heritage resulted from an assault or an affair. Kiram would have been embarrassed of him. Fedeles's face warmed with an ashamed flush. "Forgive me, I didn't mean to imply that his mother was—"

Father Timoteo's laugh cut him off short.

"Wadi wouldn't have given a fig about our prudish Cadeleonian expectations of women. She only bothered with a Cadeleonian marriage because she knew how important it was to her husband." Timoteo's smile faded. "But she would have wanted the best for her child, and I gave her my word that I would do all I could for him."

"Are you hoping that I could pressure Narsi's father's family to recognize him?" Fedeles asked. He wasn't certain how well that would go, particularly if that family was some branch of the vast, stubborn Grunito clan. "For an inheritance I presume?"

"No! Nothing of the sort." Timoteo responded almost too quickly. "I simply thought that he would do well here, under your protection. He's a charming young man. Clever, kindhearted and most pleasant company, I think. He possesses all the attributes that I believe could make him a good friend to you. Perhaps one day even a *companion*, as Captain Ciceron was."

The comparison to Ciceron brought Fedeles up short. He studied the earnest intensity of Timoteo's expression.

"You feel Master Narsi might desire to become an *intimate* of mine?" Fedeles chose the words carefully, not quite sure if he actually understood Timoteo's meaning or if he'd wildly misconstrued. He'd never spoken of his physical desires to the Holy Father—why would he?—but neither did he take great pains to hide his inclination from those in his inner circle. He couldn't really. His face betrayed him always. If he loved a man, he looked in love. His dislike was equally appreciable by all who cared to notice. Sevanyo had once told him that honesty was one of his best traits and should be cherished. Though he had been quite inebriated at the time, and had even proclaimed his intention to adopt Fedeles as his own.

But for the Holy Father to attempt to . . . what? Make him a match of his Haldiim foster child? It defied belief.

"Oh no . . . Narsi isn't so calculating as to consider who he should befriend or what power his companions might wield." Timoteo gazed up at the green branches overhead. Then he returned his attention to Fedeles. "This is my wish for him. It's one of the reasons I asked him to come here. His mother was very concerned that after she passed on, Narsi's aunt would attempt to marry him off to a rather unsuitable person. And though Narsi has resisted such a marriage, he is still so young and prone to youthful attachments. He's inclined to feel sympathy for rascals and ne'er-do-well sorts whom I fear would embroil him in trouble but be nowhere to be found should he need them."

"You've put a great deal of thought into this young man's future." Fedeles couldn't help the remark.

"Narsi deserves a good life," Timoteo announced as they passed beneath the snowplums. "A safe life. His father's death robbed him of that, and now without his mother . . . I fear that there's no one but me who truly loves him or wishes to protect him."

"You think he needs protection? He struck me as a rather strapping young man." Fedeles hadn't noticed the lives of physicians as being particularly filled with misadventure or close brushes with the jaws of peril.

Although that was exactly where Fedeles had sent him just this morning. The veil of shame that had settled over him at the price Ciceron had paid for being of use to him and all those who supported Prince Sevanyo reasserted its weight. The young physician had been in his household only a day and already Fedeles had delivered Narsi into the hands of his spymaster with hardly a thought to the physician's safety.

Although to be fair, Master Narsi had struck him as excited for the excuse to ride off with Atreau. Perhaps that eagerness was what actually worried Timoteo, or maybe it was the physician's sympathy for rascals, as the Holy Father called them. Atreau had mentioned that Master Narsi had read his books, hadn't he? And enjoyed them? So, yes, perhaps Timoteo really did just hope that Fedeles would provide the young man with safe, tedious company.

Timoteo sighed heavily, like a greatly burdened packhorse. Fedeles couldn't help but reach out to pat his bony back.

"The royal bishop's latest edicts worry me greatly," Timoteo stated. "His intolerance toward Haldiim beliefs and people must be challenged."

"Yes, I know," Fedeles agreed. But how best to do that, Fedeles wasn't certain.

"I cannot fight him, if I am the only protector whom Narsi can rely upon," Timoteo said.

Fedeles nearly missed his step on the pebble path. He caught himself and tried not to gape at Timoteo. The Holy Father's gaze remained fixed out upon the distant camellia hedges.

"We in the holy orders are responsible first and foremost to ensure that the grace of God is never misused to inflict harm. It falls to each and every one of us within the church to resist him. My position allows me to publicly engage the royal bishop in debate and, if necessary, demand that he be deposed." Timoteo's voice shook with the intensity of his emotion and, belatedly, Fedeles realized that his eyes were glassy as he lifted his gaze heavenward. "He must *not* be allowed to instigate another purge of the Haldiim people. Such evil has no right to hide behind a guise of piety. If I do not act soon then the harm he does—the lives he destroys—all that blood will be on my hands as much as his."

"You can't take responsibility for the royal bishop's actions."

"No. But I am fully responsible for my own inaction. I must oppose him. I feel the certainty of that as if our Savior has placed his hand upon mine and stands beside me urging me to decry the royal bishop." Timoteo made a slight motion of his hand and Fedeles wondered if perhaps the Holy Father wasn't speaking at all metaphorically. "I'm ashamed of myself for hesitating, but I'm afraid. I couldn't bear it if anything I did harmed Narsi . . . or Berto, if it came to that. I need to know that they have a protector."

Timoteo turned his wide-eyed gaze on Fedeles. Despite his white hair and hollowed features, there was a childlike quality to his silent entreaty.

"I have witnessed immense power and compassion within you," Timoteo said quietly. "If I had your word that no ill would befall Narsi, then I could gladly face the flames of—"

"Before we prick our thumbs and promise blood oaths or plan our fiery demises," Fedeles interrupted, "will you give me a little time to see if Prince Sevanyo and I can't bring the royal bishop to heel? Once Sevanyo is king he will be better positioned to restrain the royal bishop, as will you."

"But will Sevanyo intercede on the behalf of Haldiim citizens?" Timoteo asked.

"Of course he will," Fedeles replied with complete certainty.

Timoteo looked like he might argue, but then he simply bowed his head and continued to walk in silence. Fedeles strode alongside him into the maze of camellia hedges. Somehow Timoteo's quiet undermined Fedeles's certainty more than any argument might have.

He loved Sevanyo and believed him to genuinely hold egalitarian ideals. But he also knew that Sevanyo was not absolute in his power. Even as king he would choose to make some sacrifices to maintain a peace, if not with his brother then with his son Remes. The Fueres family too controlled vast incomes as well as powerful alliances. Sevanyo couldn't afford to alienate them before his reign was secure.

Timoteo's fear wasn't unfounded.

"If you choose to oppose the royal bishop"—Fedeles took Timoteo's large, frail hands in his—"on my honor and before the Savior, I swear to you that I will shield you and those who look to you for protection. Even your physician, Master Narsi."

Timoteo's somber expression brightened into guileless delight.

"Thank you."

Fedeles simply nodded.

When Brother Berto found them, he offered his condolences and made amiable conversation. Neither Atreau nor the physician, Narsi, had yet returned, it seemed. But there had been no news of Hylanya being discovered either, so Fedeles did not let himself worry. There was plenty in the city to keep both Atreau and anyone else occupied. At last Brother Berto managed to convince Timoteo to join him for supper. Fedeles wished them both a good evening.

He studied the night closing in around him. In the soft glow of the blessings ringing the chapel, he could just make out the silhouettes of groundsmen lowering Ciceron's corpse into his fresh grave. A glossy black crow alighted in a tree near Fedeles and seemed to consider him. Fedeles felt the shadow within his body flutter. Very purposefully, Fedeles turned away from both the grave and the crow. He'd already had too much of both death and magic this day.

CHAPTER FOURTEEN

Atreau watched Narsi's straight, broad back as the master physician departed the Green Door. He'd obviously been offended by his offhanded dismissal—who wouldn't have been after risking so much and succeeding so well—but he'd not drawn attention to the slight. Instead he took his leave with the cool dignity one would expect of a physician. Several experienced agents in Fedeles's service still didn't possess that level of restraint.

Atreau considered that for a moment. As a Haldiim raised in a Cadeleonian household, Narsi had likely cultivated self-discipline early on.

Atreau had noticed that even broad-minded Cadeleonians often griped about lack of decorum among Haldiim—even when they behaved twice as poorly themselves. The same kind of bias inspired many Labaran poets, authors, and playwrights to hone their writing to elegant perfection to compensate for their supposed national character as uncultured vulgarians.

Atreau didn't bother; publishers and readers alike expected to be scandalized and offended by his writings. It was what they paid him for.

Though, from the notes he'd written and his comments, Narsi seemed to have appreciated far more than just the passages detailing ecstasy in varying forms and positions.

Curiosity roused in him as he wondered what Narsi would think of the city and its people. Under different circumstances Atreau would have happily followed Narsi out onto the street and offered to oblige as his guide. What might he have told Atreau about the Haldiim District, and what might they have discovered together if they ventured into the secret little shops where pearl-drop sellers traded in pornography and sedition?

"Oh, unknown. How tempting your distant figure. The allure of mystery: all the promise of shadows and whispers," Atreau murmured to himself.

Suelita cast him a curious glance, then asked in a hushed voice, "Do you wish to join the master physician?"

"And abandon my current company? Never, my dear!" Atreau replied. He poured himself another cup of kaweh and drained the bitter drink. Far too much hinged upon Yago and his spies dismissing Narsi as some anonymous Haldiim of no importance beyond treating merrypox. His exit needed to pass without remark or any sign of regard.

At the table, Enevir made a comment about Narsi's height and Jacinto offered an approving reply; then he turned the conversation back to casting his play. Sabella informed him flatly that she'd not scamper across the boards like some puppet. Inissa on the other hand agreed to accept a role if it would please Jacinto, but she pointed out that her skills in other areas might serve the prince's pleasure far more. Atreau glanced away from her, thinking of Spider.

Fortunately, Atreau's supposed drunkenness offered him an excuse not to supply a rejoinder.

He pretended to hold his dizzy head and continued to think on the master physician. Allowing Narsi to walk out of the Green Door with a stone of passage was a gamble. If Narsi was taken now, not only would the stone of passage fall into the royal bishop's hands, but Hylanya's whereabouts would be quickly tortured out of him.

However, Narsi was the one person whom Yago could not have known or even suspected would have been here at the Green Door. None of Yago's agents would know to watch for him or follow him. Nor would Oasia's informants have learned of him yet.

At least Atreau hoped they didn't.

Narsi's lean image stretched and flickered through the warped windowpanes as he crossed the street. Atreau tensed, waiting to see who, if anyone, set out in pursuit. If it was one of Yago's agents then Atreau would be forced to act. He dropped his hand to his knife hilt. Only Sabella took note, but she said nothing, though she did shift a little, as if preparing to charge out behind Atreau.

No one followed after Narsi and Atreau relaxed.

Though a moment later he frowned. From his view through the window, Atreau could see that the master physician was not heading back in the direction of the Fat Goose, where his horse was stabled. Instead he strode off in the opposite direction. Clearly he might have been miffed at being dismissed from Jacinto's table, but that hadn't sent him scampering back to the security of Father Timoteo. No, apparently Narsi had decided to wander and explore the city all on his own. Taking Atreau's stone of passage with him. And at the moment there was precious little Atreau could do about it.

Atreau slumped back in his seat.

"Well, let's be on our way then, shall we?" Jacinto bounded to his feet.

Belatedly Atreau realized that his companions had decided to visit the theater, while he had been lost in his own thoughts.

As he traipsed alongside Jacinto and his motley entourage to the gilded Candioro Theater, Atreau noted three men shadowing them. Unlike Yago's snitches, these three stood out from the crowd of orange sellers, street performers and herb girls. Not that they appeared strikingly different from other Cadeleonians in build or complexion, nor even their manner of dress; they'd all three donned the unremarkable garb of middling merchants. One even went so far as to leave behind his long dueling sword and arm himself with only a pair of daggers.

But their brusque, authoritarian demeanors betrayed them instantly as men used to shoving bystanders aside and intimidating onlookers with the mere sight of their uniforms. They walked the street as if they owned it, surveying the lively, colorful populace like impediments. If frustrated, they would resort to simply beating information out of a man, Atreau felt certain.

The men drew to a halt at the stairs leading up to the gold-painted doors of the theater. The way one of them leaned back against the wall of the building assured Atreau that they weren't simply going to wander off of their own accord.

Inside, Jacinto lounged across his favorite divan center stage and declared it amusing to hoodwink Captain Yago but not so entertaining as the adventure Atreau had provided for him in a riverside brothel.

"The owner is half Labaran, like Atreau. So obviously he put absolutely every sensual delicacy on the menu, as it were." Jacinto wrapped his arm around Inissa's waist and pulled her down beside him. "It's only good manners to sample everything offered by one's host—at least once. I had no choice but to indulge . . ."

Sabella and Inissa exchanged a bored glance while Jacinto went on describing buggery, bondage and bestiality as if he were the first Cadeleonian ever to witness such acts.

Procopio listened with the rapt attention of a burgeoning blackmailer while Suelita, Enevir and Cocuyo all stared at Jacinto with expressions of profound shock, which only encouraged Jacinto to embellish his tale with more and more absurdly lurid flights of fantasy. Atreau was hard-pressed to suppress his laughter when Jacinto launched into a description of being utterly ravished by a squawking flock of no less than twelve wanton parrots.

Necessity had forced Atreau to involve Jacinto in Hylanya's escape, but just listening to the prince freely confess to—and even fabricate—encounters that would have gotten a man of lesser nobility imprisoned, he felt relieved that he wouldn't need to involve Jacinto in any further intrigues. Jacinto loved telling tales too much to ever be entrusted with other people's secrets. Though he did possess a wonderful sense of drama and humor. And he wasn't afraid to make himself the butt of his own jokes, which Atreau appreciated.

Atreau lingered, listening and laughing, until actors and actresses began arriving in preparation for the evening's parade. Then Atreau sauntered away from Jacinto and his companions, claiming an inspiration for further casting of the prince's play. He beckoned the Haldiim actress, Yara Nur-Aud, to join him beside the long blue stage curtains. Always lovely, she looked particularly strikingly today, garbed in silk and peacock feathers. The tight curls of her blond hair coiled around carved wooden combs, and a painted gold eye glittered from the dark skin of her forehead.

"I've heard nothing new about Irsea's death since we last spoke," Yara said quietly.

Atreau nodded.

Months ago the elderly Haldiim holy woman had been found murdered near the Royal Physic Garden—six deep knife wounds punched through her frail back and a scrap of violet cloth clenched in her fist. The brutality of the crime outraged even the Cadeleonian populace of the city. In the Haldiim District, several prominent mothers had packed up their businesses and departed for Anacleto, while others offered large rewards for the identity of the Bahiim's killer. Informants whispered that Captain Yago or one of his underlings had committed the murder at the royal bishop's behest, and Atreau paid attention. Proof could have toppled Captain Yago and weakened the royal bishop's standing considerably. Several times Atreau came frustratingly close to securing evidence. But in the end the scrap of violet cloth was destroyed and none of the few witnesses possessed courage enough to testify.

When, a few weeks later, a Cadeleonian priest was decapitated at the south gate public sympathy swung back toward the church. The Haldiim holy woman's murder was quickly attributed to long-gone foreign sailors. The rewards were forgotten. Now only crows watched over the beautiful wisteria trees of the sacred grove and Haldiim citizens continued to slowly, steadily flee the city.

Despite that, Atreau had been impressed by how much information Yara had managed to discover through her Haldiim connections and how eager she'd been to see justice done. She struck him as just the sort of person he needed now.

"I was hoping you might do me a different little favor," Atreau said. "I'd be happy to pay a few coins for the trouble, of course."

"How many coins for how much trouble?" Yara cocked her head and smiled as if she wasn't certain whether to take him seriously or not.

"Not so much of either, I hope," Atreau replied. He pulled as embarrassed of an expression as he could manage. "You see, I was tasked with looking after a young fellow by the name of Narsi Lif-Tahm; it's his first day in the capital. But I've rather lost track of him. I was hoping that you might look out for him. He's all on his own and I noticed a number of Captain Yago's men in the Theater District, so I'm—"

"He's Haldiim, new to the city and alone?" Yara's expression lost all trace of humor.

"Half Haldiim. Very tall, with dark curly hair, and just arrived from Anacleto. As I understand it, he's got no family or friends here." Atreau suspected that Narsi wouldn't have been pleased to be portrayed as a hapless orphan. But he also knew the description would rouse sisterly concern in Yara. Her youngest brother had just been married off and sent away to a strange family in Anacleto.

"He's dressed in a physician's gray coat and he'll be carrying a medical satchel. He's nicely built . . ." Atreau almost mentioned the charming quality of his conversation and his remarkable capacity to hold his nerve but caught himself. Not only were those useless attributes for recognizing in a stranger in a city crowd, but throw in a reference to his sleek build and winning smile and Atreau would end up sounding half besotted. "What will stand out about him the most is his height. I'd say he's a good three fingers taller than I am."

Yara raised her brows and nodded, then asked, "Once I find him where should I take him?"

Atreau considered his own rooms at the Fat Goose but then thought better of it. There was a good chance that Yago would search there.

"If you would, simply keep an eye on him to ensure he doesn't fall afoul of any of our local roughs or Yago's men. You know how naïve southerners can be, and our Theater District can prove overwhelming, but tonight especially . . ."

"This would be quite a first night." Yara nodded at the men dressed as bulls. Behind them, a stagehand helped a young girl into a deerskin costume pincushioned with arrows. "I'll look for him and have the others do the same," Yara decided.

Atreau reached for his coin purse but Yara shook her head.

"Keep your pennies. Any Haldiim should do this much for another."

Atreau felt certain that most Haldiim, just like most Cadeleonians, wouldn't go out of their way to spend a festival night watching over a complete stranger. Yara had no idea of how remarkable she was, but it didn't serve Atreau to inform her.

"You have my thanks," he said.

Then he spied the three men who'd followed him from the Green Door. They prowled in behind a troop of drummers and several masked acrobats. All three stared at Atreau like hounds sighting a hare. A jolt of fear coursed through Atreau. If he ran they'd follow. Atreau pulled in a slow, deep breath and pushed back his old terror of being hunted through the halls of his own home. He'd been a boy then. Now he was a grown man and he had the wit to recognize that he could turn the situation to his advantage. If these men had to pursue him, then he could lead them where he liked, so long as he didn't allow them to catch him.

The panicked tempo of Atreau's heartbeat slowed to comfortable anticipation. He, not his pursuers, would master the situation.

So, Atreau took his leave of the gilded Candioro Theater. It seemed the simplest means of drawing Yago's three spies away before Procopio or some hungry understudy could be tempted to exchange one of Jacinto's unconcerned revelations—perhaps even Hylanya's whereabouts—for a small fortune.

He ranged across the south side of the city, making inquiries that he didn't care to keep from Yago or the royal bishop. He focused his attention on Captain Ciceron's possible enemies.

The man's distraught mistress wasn't accepting callers. However her freckled young maid assured him that neither of the pretty mistress's previous lovers could have murdered the captain. They'd both been elderly gentlemen who'd passed away before Ciceron began his visits.

"He always brought us lovely sweets," the maid commented as Atreau turned to take his leave. "I'll miss him."

"As will many," Atreau replied.

Down in the alleyways of the knife market, two light-fingered fences who often worked as his informants grinned at his questions. The brother and sister were both in their thirties, but lifelong poverty had stunted their proportions so that at a glance they looked like wizened children. One and then the other apprised him of the fact that a captain from the royal guard had already come down looking for the assassins and so had one of Yago's underlings.

"Of course they come around kicking over cook pots and threatening to haul half the row in for cutting the king's coins," the brother muttered. His scrawny sister scratched her arm and nodded.

"They didn't get anything," she said. "Nobody knows who it was. None of us would have done Ciceron over. He came from down here."

"Understood the value of accepting a bribe and keeping the peace," her brother added.

Atreau nodded. Glancing back over his shoulder, he noted that Yago's three men were pretending to shop through the stolen, banned and counterfeit bits of treasure mixed throughout stalls of scavenged trash. One of them purchased a battered rabbit mask.

Atreau set off at a quick pace, making them hustle behind him as he continued his inquiries.

He wasn't pleased with this latest news. If Yago sent men to investigate, that strongly indicated that he hadn't been behind Ciceron's murder. Atreau discovered the same news from Sabella's uncle when he visited the stained dueling circles of the Red Stallion sword house. There Yago's man had made the mistake of attempting to rough information out of a younger duelist. The youth's instructor and blademates had bloodied Yago's man and sent him running, with most of his right ear gone.

Atreau sighed. Simply giving Fedeles Yago's name would've made his life easier, but it wouldn't have changed the fact that some unknown group of assassins appeared to be loose in the city. He remembered

Hylanya's comment about enthralled assassins in the streets. How many were there and who controlled them? He wished Hylanya could have been a little more forthcoming. But there hadn't been much time and he'd had other matters to arrange with her.

He frowned and then glanced into a small windowpane to catch the blurred reflections of Yago's men. They looked bored.

Atreau dashed across the busy street, dodging between two donkey carts. He flashed an apologetic smile to a goose girl and took care not to startle her flock of rotund birds as he bound up onto the boards of the muddy walk. Shouts sounded from the road behind him as he darted into the shadows of an old stone staircase. The steps led to a raised walkway, but up in the open he knew his progress would be too easy to follow. Instead he stepped back into the small crowd gathered around a puppeteer.

He gazed up at the walkway, searching for one of Hylanya's feline familiars. But it was too early in the day. The *Red Witch* wouldn't have sailed yet. Until it did, Hylanya wouldn't send any messages.

He glanced back to the road. A moment later the honks and hisses of furious geese alerted him to the exact location of the three guardsmen whom Captain Yago had charged to follow him. He observed them closely, noting how long it took them to calm down and search the street for where he stood. They were clearly well prepared to chase a fleeing man down but not used to appraising their surroundings closely or calmly.

They were the kind of men whom Elezar would've taunted into overreaching in a duel.

Atreau smiled.

An hour later, he led them back into the heart of the Theater District. First night bell sounded from distant chapel towers. It had grown late enough that he needed to keep an eye out for any one of Hylanya's slinking little familiars.

As he progressed he found the streets filled both with brightly dressed entertainers and crowds of people hoping to witness Jacinto's parade. He heard folks in taverns toasting Jacinto nearly as often as his father, Prince Sevanyo. Vendors of sweet and savory delights set up impromptu food stands on corners. Enterprising seamstresses hawked flags made from pretty scraps of silk, while mask makers flogged their wares as memorabilia of Sevanyo's forthcoming coronation.

In the crush, Atreau had to slow his pace and backtrack twice after losing his three would-be pursuers. He was tempted to abandon them to their own devices, but then he spied Narsi's towering figure in the crowd.

The young man appeared to have just purchased a broad-brimmed hat and looked very pleased as he stroked the chin of a little alley cat.

Atreau indulged in a brief fantasy of strolling alongside the physician, commenting on the sights and noise of their surroundings. Then his gaze lit upon Narsi's medical satchel. A small surge of alarm quickened Atreau's heartbeat. He'd entrusted the stone of passage to Narsi's care to keep it secret—from his own companions as well as his enemies. The last thing he could afford to do now was alert Yago's men to his interest in Narsi—much less risk them discovering the stone of passage hidden amidst the collection of strange-scented powders and potions in the physician's satchel.

Atreau turned and, after ensuring that Yago's men still trailed him, sauntered down Oven Avenue, where the yellow brick walls of bakeries gleamed like gold in the late-afternoon sun. He bought three frogbuns from his favorite baker and ate them, feeling oddly satisfied by the fact that she took the time to chide him for abandoning the Labaran braids that he'd worn as a youth. Her own gray hair fell down past her waist in two neat plaits. His mother had worn her hair in much the same fashion, even on her deathbed.

At last, as the afternoon shadows lengthened and cool breezes began to whip up off the river, Atreau spotted one of Hylanya's familiars watching him from a raised walkway. The grizzled old cat yawned and stretched in a pool of dimming sunlight.

Atreau glanced back at the three men who'd trailed him so long and far.

"If we keep company much longer, gentlemen, gossips will mistake your presence for faithfulness and your pursuit for passion," Atreau called back to them. It was childish, he knew, but the shock in their expressions was rewarding after an entire day of bearing with them plodding after him.

Then he plunged into a crowd of costumed dancers and excited onlookers. He raced around a street corner and then dropped back into the shadowed alcove of a narrow doorway. He stood still and watched as Yago's men swore and shoved their way through the people thronging the streets. In a moment all three of them pelted past him and continued charging up the street. After a few moments Atreau lost sight of them in the crowd.

He backtracked to the raised walkway. At the top he found Hylanya's familiar. It turned three times in the little circle that assured him that the *Red Witch* had sailed. He scratched the old cat's cheek and took consolation in the fact that Hylanya, unlike another witch Atreau had met, didn't keep rats as familiars.

Then from the height of the walkway he thought he again spied Narsi. Yago's three men trailed him now as he strolled into the surrounding crowd of masked strangers and twilight shadows.

 **CHAPTER FIFTEEN**

Narsi spent the afternoon securing supplies and indulging himself. He explored the vast grounds of the Royal's Physic Garden, taking in the scents of sweet and pungent botanicals heightened to dizzying effect by the lingering traces of nightleaf. Several pale, officious conservators eyed him with suspicion at first, but their attitudes toward him warmed fantastically when Narsi mentioned taking kaweh with Prince Jacinto Sagrada and then produced one of the prince's favor coins.

Their assistance verged upon exuberant after they learned that Narsi's purchases would need to be delivered to the Duke of Rauma's residence. He didn't mistake the curators' obsequiousness for genuine warmth, but at least he managed to introduce himself to a few of the other physicians. Soon he found himself engaged in pleasant conversation and received two open invitations to dine with them.

He allowed a weathered, elderly gardener to convince him to buy three gold-pin-striped Labaran rosebushes, as he found the perfume of them intoxicating. Though one of the bushes punished his familiarity with a scratch across the back of his right hand. The old gardener commiserated, displaying the multitude of scratches covering his own hands and saying, "The flowers are so sweet and pretty, but their thorns make sure we don't take them for granted."

"I shall have to remember that," Narsi replied.

He left the garden in good spirits and to his delight he recognized the distinct scent of frying adhil bread drifting on the air. The fragrance led him to a section of the city where solstice lamps stood in most of the windows and many of the signs hanging over shops bore flowing Haldiim script as well as blocky Cadeleonian letters. Teahouses, printshops and bakeries, offering fragrant adhil bread as well as traditional Cadeleonian loaves, crowded the street. Clusters of dark-complexioned and fair-haired Haldiim women and men hurried between the buildings, engaged in their own conversations. A remarkable feeling of relief washed through Narsi. Until just this moment he hadn't recognized how tense he'd grown after even a day of being surrounded by only Cadeleonians. He didn't fit in perfectly among these people either, but just looking around him at so many people who resembled his mother and aunt, he grew more relaxed.

When he caught sight of a star-shaped pharmacy sign swinging over the door of a business, he was delighted. He'd not known that the Kir-Naham family operated a pharmacy here in Cieloalta. As he entered the cool, pungent interior of the pharmacy, he drew the curious gazes of the two women working behind the shop's heavy marble counter—but neither of them seemed unfriendly. The older woman looked about sixty and struck Narsi as the owner. She wore her white hair up in the crown of braids that was common among elder mothers of Haldiim communities. Both her long yellow vest and red trousers bore such detailed, fine embroidery as to resemble precious works of art. The younger woman resembled her closely, except that her jaw seemed a little more square and her eyes looked almost brown in color. Her clothes were cut from the same shade of golden silk, but only her sash sported rich embroidery. Her curly blond hair hung loose except for a silver comb.

"Welcome, young physician. I'm Mother Arezoo Kir-Naham. This is my niece, Esfir," the elder woman called, then she dispatched the younger woman to assist him.

Narsi provided his own name as well as his mother's. Mother Kir-Naham smiled, though Narsi wasn't sure if it was in response to his family name or his proper and immediate response. Male physicians weren't common in Haldiim communities and they nearly always came from or wed into the households of pharmacists, so perhaps she simply assumed he shared a background with her and her niece.

After turning Narsi's medicine list over to her aunt, Esfir offered him drops of fortune oil, which he accepted and rubbed into his hands. That welcoming perfume of camphor and cinnamon rose up as he worked the soothing oil into the dry skin of his knuckles. When the young woman brought him a small clay cup of tea, Narsi felt absurdly touched.

Then Esfir smiled at him and he was suddenly struck by how much her expression and round face reminded him of Querra's. He almost asked if they were related but then caught himself.

"Five minutes wait, child," Mother Kir-Naham told him as she studied his order.

"Thank you," Narsi called.

Mother Kir-Naham nodded and returned to carefully grinding down a bundle of dried herbs. The sharp smell of coinflower filled Narsi with a feeling of nostalgia. All the pharmacies in Anacleto had smelled just like this one.

He drew in a deep breath and closed his eyes. For just a few moments he felt as he had the first time his mother had brought him into a Haldiim pharmacy. The cedar shelves brimmed with ceramic jars and ornately carved boxes, all filled with mysteries of salvations and poisons.

Only now Narsi knew the names and uses for the herbs, potions and powders. He'd traded that initial thrilling sense of perilous mystery for an understanding of just how much and how little power he and all these medicines possessed. He opened his eyes, this time taking in just how different this pharmacy was from the one he'd frequented in Anacleto. He noted the names of concoctions that he didn't recognize and took a little time with Esfir to learn what he could.

He considered asking her if she had any idea how a medicine—like nightleaf—could affect something like a magically induced sleep. Then he realized how very much he would have to reveal just to offer the question in hypothetical terms. He shook his head and returned his attention to Esfir's fascinating lecture on the newest cloud-dust creams. Maybe later he could discuss the subject with Lord Vediya.

All too soon his orders had been prepared. Mother Kir-Naham pushed his refilled jars and tins to him.

"Coinflower that grows here is stronger than the southern plants, so use about a third less than you normally would," Mother Kir-Naham told him.

Narsi thanked her and paid.

As he left, Esfir called out to him, "Don't hesitate to come back anytime, Narsi. We'll be happy to answer any questions you might have."

"Thank you. I'm certain that I'll return very soon."

He ended up lingering in the tiny Haldiim section of town far longer than necessary and bought a case of new macroscoping lenses as well as a pill press that embossed the Cadeleonian script of his last initials into the medications he prescribed.

He'd always wanted one.

He took a lunch of adhil bread, lamb and lemonherbs. Then, attempting to find the sacred grove of wisteria trees that Lord Vediya had mentioned, he wandered the streets and soon found himself back in the Theater District. In a shop not too far from the Green Door, he discovered a black leather mask that reminded him of the cat that shared his rooms. He bought it as well as one of the simple wide-brimmed hats that he'd noted many men wearing.

The sun sank toward the horizon and the sky filled with messenger doves winging back to their evening roosts. Narsi strolled toward the Fat Goose. Though now he found the going quite slow. People of obviously different classes and vocations crowded the walkways. Here and there orange sellers hawked their goods. But most voices rose and fell in a stream of excited conversation. Speculation abounded about the procession that Prince Jacinto had arranged. People gawked up and down the empty road. Then a hush seemed to spread over the gathering.

Along with everyone else, Narsi quieted and listened as music filled the air. He wound his way between the clusters of people until he found a break, and he peered down the length of the dusty roadway. Groups of masked musicians and vividly costumed dancers paraded down the stairs of a theater. Steadily more and more came, filling the width of the roadway. Then they began marching up the street. Cheers rose through the surrounding crowd, but not even the roar of so many jubilant voices could overwhelm the swelling music.

Twenty flushed Cadeleonian youths hammered at the drums hanging from the bright blue baldrics slung across their chests. Haldiim pipers—both men and women—all decked out in royal blue marched behind them. On their heels came a group of ten sturdy Cadeleonian men carrying a platform festooned with bright yellow paper flowers. A little girl stood atop it, wearing a horned deer mask and a hide dress. She danced with a happy abandon that undermined the gruesome display of arrows jutting out from the chest and back of her costume.

Narsi guessed that the Cadeleonians surrounding him probably recognized the pierced deer as Summer Doe, the fawn goddess upon whom the heroes of the Great Hunt had feasted. But he and likely every other Haldiim knew her as Yah-muur, the goddess who tricked the hunters into firing all of their arrows into her immortal body and then led them on a fourteen-day chase while the great herds she protected fled to safety.

Father Timoteo had actually loved the Haldiim version of this story when he'd heard it, but Narsi didn't think too many devout Cadeleonians would have responded with the same delight.

"She who is ever reborn," Narsi murmured softly. Then he wondered what Lord Vediya would have thought of the story.

More masked men and women danced past him, shaking bells and pounding hand drums. Another platform followed, this one featuring two plump little boys who couldn't seem to suppress their laughter despite the fact that they were obviously meant to represent gold-dusted twin saints. A crowd of youths costumed as white stallions surrounded them. A giant of a man garbed as an ebony black bull followed. After him came dozens of masked women, all twirling so the delicate layers of their yellow skirts swirled wide like the petals of blooming roses.

Through the procession, Narsi glimpsed a man across the street. For an instant he thought it might be Lord Vediya, but then Narsi realized the figure was too slim, his face thinner and less lined than Lord

Vediya's. Though a woman very like Inissa leaned in toward him and the two kissed. Narsi looked away. It was hardly becoming to gawk at lovers on the street.

He wondered if Lord Vediya might be somewhere in the crowd or watching from one of the raised walkways. Considering the hour, he might have already returned to the duke's residence.

Though recollecting Lord Vediya's earlier words, he suddenly wondered if it was possible that the man had already set out to discover the identity of Captain Ciceron's assassins. Narsi scowled at the thought of Lord Vediya undertaking such a task alone as the surrounding shadows stretched into the darkness of night. Despite Lord Vediya's clever ruses this afternoon, Narsi couldn't imagine the man stalking the city streets in search of murderers like some avenging ruffian.

Wasn't it more likely that he'd retired to the privacy of his room in the Fat Goose to enjoy the pretty Suelita's company?

The idea pained Narsi a little and then made him feel annoyed at himself for harboring childishly romantic longings. He wasn't a boy anymore, and there were better ways to entertain himself than mooning over Lord Vediya.

All around him people among the crowd of onlookers adjusted their masks and then stepped out into the road, joining the dancers to become part of the procession. Narsi watched as a group of Haldiim men, clothed in little more than bright cloaks of pheasant feathers and loose scarlet breeches, bounded past. Among other Haldiim he might even find a fellow to share a bit of companionship, if only for this evening. He drew down his cat mask and fell in step.

Soon enough the procession reached the frothy, nautically themed tower of the Shell Fountain. It stood in the center of a large open square where the light of the sinking sun and the fiery cast of the torches turned the gurgling water red as rust. As Narsi caught sight of it, a cheer went up from the actors and actresses surrounding him. A complete stranger wearing a rabbit mask clapped him on the back. Narsi glanced back at the man, trying to see if he might be Lord Vediya or someone else from the Green Door. But then the crowd around Narsi surged and he was carried in a different direction from the masked man. Two Haldiim youths next to him pointed and cheered. Narsi realized what had drawn their attention.

Large wine barrels ringed the fountain like a wooden fortress. Several brawny Cadeleonian men dressed in the royal colors stood around the barrels, filling up and distributing clay cups of brandywine. Anyone who approached them and called out praise for *King* Sevanyo received a serving. Toasts were soon being shouted and cheered by the growing throng.

"Our Lord keep King Sevanyo!" seemed to be the preferred call of Cadeleonians, while Haldiim like himself hooted and added, "Long live King Sevanyo!" All of them were rewarded with more brandywine, which seemed to grow better-tasting with each refill.

A little back from the barrels, dozens of musicians gathered atop the stacked platforms that had made up the procession. Already couples in bright costumes and leather masks danced and whirled around the fountain. A sea of more sedately dressed people encircled them, drinking and clapping their hands with the music.

Narsi joined the large crowd watching the couples romping near the musicians. He pushed his mask up from his face and sipped his third brandywine. It tasted surprisingly strong and sharp. As the sun sank into darkness, more torches lit up from the edges of the square. The dancers took on a fantastic beauty. Shadows disguised the seams and laces of their costumes, making the square seem to truly be filled with mythic creatures and Old Gods.

After finishing his wine, Narsi felt warm and relaxed enough to consider approaching a stranger and requesting a dance. To Narsi's delight a strikingly beautiful Haldiim woman, dressed in a cascading cloak of peacock feathers, approached him before he said a word.

"We haven't been introduced before this, have we?" the woman's Haldiim words lilted and rolled with melodic inflections that struck Narsi as perfect for the stage. "I feel certain I'd remember meeting anyone as tall as you."

"No, I've just moved to the capital from Anacleto," Narsi admitted. In proper Haldiim fashion, he provided her with his mother's lineage and his name.

"Yara Nur-Aud." She brought one hand up in a sign of welcome.

Even in Anacleto, Narsi had heard stories about the dramatic Nur-Aud family; their audacity on and off the stage was said to have inspired scandalous affairs as well as political outrage.

Yara shifted and the torchlight fell across her cloak and thick curls of her hair as if gilding her. Narsi marveled at how perfectly she could find her lighting even off the stage. He struggled for something clever to say but found himself dumbstruck.

"How interesting that you've just come from Anacleto," Yara went on. "My mother is in the midst of searching for property there. The way things are with the royal bishop, it seemed wise to consider relocating to the south. If you don't mind me asking, what's brought you north? Joining your wife's family, perhaps?" Yara trailed off as she frowned down at the ring on his finger.

She seemed to then realize that it was a physician's signet that he wore and not a promise ring gifted to him by a spouse.

"I'm unwed," Narsi clarified.

"Oh." Yara raised her brows. "And your mother lives where? Anacleto?" Her firm tone reminded him of his aunt when he'd traipsed into her paper shop looking dusty and hungry.

"She passed away a year ago," Narsi replied. He wished immediately that he'd lied, because now he felt certain that he sounded like some sad orphaned child to Yara, instead of striking her as an accomplished traveler and charming conversationalist. "I've come north to accept a post as a physician in a noble household. The Duke of Rauma . . ." From Yara's expression he realized that the duke's hatred of physicians was very common knowledge. He added quickly, "Though it's the duke's priest who's employing me directly . . ."

Yara's concern bloomed to something very near horror at the mention of a priest. Again Narsi realized he'd erred in his attempt to subtly brag about his post in the Duke of Rauma's household and ended up making himself sound like an abandoned orphan who'd fallen into the clutches of a priest—and was now doomed to conversion.

"I'd love to dance, if you'd care to join me," Narsi said quickly before he lost all confidence in himself. To his relief, Yara smiled.

"It would be my pleasure." She took his hand. Her skin felt warm and a little rough. "You're familiar with Cadeleonian pairs dancing?"

"Passingly so." In fact he knew the Cadeleonian steps just as well as he did the gestures and turns of Haldiim circle dances, but he didn't want to sound like a braggard. Particularly not when the wine and uneven flagstones might very well make a fool of him. However, his assurance returned to him as he and Yara spun and reeled around the fountain.

Afterward Yara teased him for playing the part of a naïve lad when he was clearly a strapping charmer. Then she introduced him to a multitude of other Haldiim men and women. Narsi danced with many of them and shared drinks with even more. One earnest young man leaned a little against Narsi as they spoke. The heat of his fingers brushed Narsi's thigh and for a few moments Narsi struggled to follow the chatter flowing around the circle of Haldiim actors and actresses.

Then he focused his attention; the serious-looking older man had wondered if they wouldn't need to begin digging out "the roots" again. Narsi didn't understand the reference but also didn't feel comfortable enough to admit his ignorance. Fortunately, Yara swooped in with more clay cups of wine and an explanation.

It turned out that during the purge of Haldiim from the north, many of those trapped in the capital had dug tunnels, first as places for Bahiim to hide, then as a means of escape. To this day dozens of aged tunnels still wound beneath the city streets, though few had been maintained over the last hundred years. They'd largely been left to the interests of smugglers and rats.

"'Roots' referred to the underworlds of sacred trees, of course, but it was also a play on the Cadeleonian word 'routes.'" Yara inclined her head toward the pretty young man beside Narsi. "That way even when they were barred from speaking Haldiim, our ancestors could discuss escape plans as if they were talking about planting carrots right in front of the guardsmen keeping them captive."

Narsi found the thought ingenious but also chilling. So many people, like himself and those standing near him, all terrified to speak even a word of their native tongue. All trapped within the walls of this city, awaiting their executions.

The other Haldiim looked somber—particularly compared with the rowdy, cheering Cadeleonians all around them. Even Yara seemed suddenly uneasy as she stood in the shadows and frowned down at the clay cup in her hands. Then the young man beside Narsi straightened and lifted his cup.

"Once Sevanyo is king, he'll put the royal bishop in his place." He drained the last of his wine. "Why are we standing around like forlorn lambs? We should be celebrating!"

That roused spirits and several couples rushed to join the next dance, while Yara and two other actresses joked about the horrific wreck of a production they had been cast in. They delivered lines in quavering voices and Narsi laughed at their performances.

"I know a place where you could rest," the young man whispered to Narsi. "It's not too far from here."

Narsi gazed down at his light eyes and delicate features. He'd probably make a very obliging partner, certainly pleasant for one night's company. But he spoke with so much sincerity and hopefulness that it made Narsi uneasy. He deserved someone who wouldn't be thinking of another man while holding him.

Narsi turned the young man back over to the care of his friends and then found himself a carefree Cadeleonian seamstress to accompany him for the next dance. To his surprise a number of Cadeleonian women queued up to dance with him after that. Several flirted playfully and one jolly older lady asked him for a second reel around the square. Narsi obliged her happily, since she was quite fast and fun to dance with.

Belatedly he realized that with such poor light and so many people in costumes he didn't stand out as anything but rather tall and a perhaps little bulky with his medical satchel slung across his back.

When Yara came to wish him good night, Narsi thanked her sincerely for her company and introducing him to her friends.

"We have to look after each other. If you find yourself in a tight spot with the priest or the duke, you can always come find me at the Candi-oro Theater." Yara offered him a slightly inebriated smile. She began to turn but then stopped. "Is there anything that you need before we head home?"

Narsi shook his head, then realized that he did have a question; the delay made him wonder if he wasn't still a little drunk himself. "Do you know where I can find the sacred grove? I'd love to see the wisteria trees."

"Take the crooked lane past the fountain there. It's not far at all . . ." She yawned and then added, "Irsea, the Bahiim who tended the trees, died, so you won't wake anyone if you go visit in the moonlight."

Narsi wished Yara and her friends a good night. As they departed, Narsi noted that he was one of the only Haldiim who remained in the square. The tone of the music had changed as well, turning slow and sultry. Cadeleonian couples swayed close and embraced. A few men surreptitiously handed coins over to their dance partners before creeping beyond the torchlight to gasp and groan in alleyways.

The jolly woman who'd danced with Narsi for two very fast reels sat down on an empty brandywine barrel to pull her shoes off and fan her blistered foot.

Reflexively, Narsi swung his medical case down from his shoulder and opened it up to offer her a balm. As he glanced down into the satchel a jolt of surprise went through him and, had he been sober, he guessed he might have dropped the satchel. As it was, he stared into the leather depths, slowly processing the unexpected glow that Lady Hylanya's necklace gave off. Narsi snapped the satchel closed.

The jolly Cadeleonian woman didn't appear to notice at all. She called to a broad-shouldered man with a thick beard. A moment later they were both laughing as he hefted her onto his back, promising to spare her blistered feet the walk back to their home.

Narsi watched them go and wondered if he shouldn't try to find his way back to the Fat Goose and his horse. The music quieted briefly. Narsi noticed a figure moving through the weaving couples with a purposeful stride. Then he heard the distinct tread of boots ringing out behind him. He glanced over his shoulder but couldn't make out more than a group of large silhouettes. A flicker of torchlight illuminated a flash of violet cloth hidden beneath a black cloak. Instantly, Narsi remembered the men of the royal bishop's guard.

Had a group trailed him this entire time?

Yesterday he would have dismissed his alarm as too much imagination and brandywine. But after witnessing Captain Yago paying off two informants—and recalling Lord Vediya's caution—he knew he shouldn't ignore his fear. He needed to put as much distance between these men and himself as he could—particularly since he was carrying a necklace that not only belonged to Lady Hylanya but also glowed with illicit spells.

Moving as casually as he could, Narsi walked closer to the swirling rings of dancers. He felt certain that another figure followed after him. The man wearing the rabbit mask. Which meant both the lanes leading back to the stables at the Fat Goose were likely unsafe for him. Narsi's heart began to hammer in his chest.

Where could he go? How could he elude Captain Yago and his men?

Narsi danced between several couples, his growing fear lending him an unexpected speed. As he wove through deep shadows and whirling dancers, he noticed the mouth of the narrow lane that Yara had pointed out. The sacred grove.

Narsi took several casual steps away from the dancers and then darted from the flickering light of the torches. He hurried up the lane, wishing he could run but too uncertain of his footing to chance it. The cobbles felt decidedly uneven beneath his shoes. He passed what looked like shop fronts, all of them closed—though up on the second floors of a few buildings he noted faint candlelight burning. Here and there he noticed pale blossoms cascading down from flower boxes, and as he distanced himself from the music, he picked out the sounds of bats flitting through the dark sky. His own footsteps rang out against the cobblestones.

He couldn't be certain, but he thought he heard the tread of boots behind him.

The lane curved suddenly and as Narsi turned he caught sight of a dark rise looming up to his right. Moonlight shone down over a huge grassy hill and lit the magnificent sprawl of giant wisteria branches and flowers. Narsi raced up the hill, feeling absurdly reassured by the way the soft earth and grass muted his steps. The perfume of the trees washed over him as he took the rise and ducked beneath the streamers of cascading blossoms. He leaned back against the huge, gnarled trunk of the nearest tree and watched the road below.

He hoped that his figure would melt into the shadows of the twist-ed, bowed branches and the rough trunk. He silently repeated a Bahiim prayer twice to himself.

He waited. The street below the hill remained quiet and empty. Narsi began to feel foolish.

Then a dark figure turned the corner. A second followed and stepped briefly through a shaft of moonlight. This time Narsi saw the violet lining the man's cloak clearly.

"You're sure it was him?" Captain Yago spoke quietly, but Narsi still recognized his voice. "And he came this way?"

Narsi's heart began to pound in his chest. He hadn't just imagined it. The royal bishop's men truly were in pursuit of him. Did they know that he possessed Lady Hylanya's necklace? Or were they simply following him because he seemed like an easy target to vent their frustrations against? Neither thought offered any consolation.

"It looked like Atreau," the other man answered, but he didn't sound certain. "It's hard to say with so many of them wearing masks and cos-tumes."

Narsi wondered if some snitch had mistaken him for Lord Vediya? That seemed like quite a stretch. Neither he nor Lord Vediya had lost a limb and they were both clean-shaven men, but beyond that there was little physical resemblance between them.

"I . . . He might have turned down a different lane," the informant admitted and Captain Yago swore. Though Narsi thought that the man sounded almost as tired as angry.

"Maybe if we searched ahead up to Ochora Street—" the informant began, but Captain Yago turned away.

"You've wasted enough of my time tonight," Captain Yago ground out.

"What about the silver you promised—"

"Don't push your luck! As it stands, you're lucky I haven't paid you with a steel blade in your back." Captain Yago disappeared around the corner. The narrow-faced informant scowled, then followed Captain Yago.

Narsi leaned against the tree, feeling relieved for the shelter. He wondered if his prayers hadn't been heard—though just to be safe, he crept farther into sacred grove. The towering wisteria trees formed a cir-cle, and overhead, Narsi could see the moon.

He sank down to the ground beside one of the thick tree roots.

When he set his medical satchel down, a faint golden glow seemed to seep from it. All at once small gold letters lit up across an exposed section of the wisteria's gnarled root. Narsi stared at the faint, flickering letters and then quickly looked back behind him to make certain no one stood on the street below. Not only did the street remain empty, but he realized that the glow of the letters didn't reach far, and they dimmed after first igniting. Now they smoldered dull red, like dying embers.

Protection, Strength, Wisdom, Courage.

Narsi stared at the Haldiim words until they faded back to darkness. He remembered the night that the sacred grove in Anacleto had lit up like a forest of lightning and filled the night sky with golden blessings. But that had been in Anacleto, behind the thick walls that protected the Haldiim District; here in the open air of the capital Narsi felt nearly as frightened as he did awed. If some Cadeleonian passerby noticed the lights amidst the trees, Narsi felt certain it wouldn't go well for him.

And yet he couldn't keep himself from lifting up his satchel and setting it down a few inches farther away. Again gold symbols lit up along the roots, but this time they also flickered to life from between tufts of wild grass and weeds. Narsi glanced back over his shoulder, then cautiously opened his satchel. The dull green of Lady Hylanya's pendant shone like an emerald and the very tip of the stone gleamed bright white. The gold sparks on the ground leapt up like fireflies taking flight and circled around the open mouth of the satchel and hovered around Narsi's face. He heard a woman's melodic voice whispering in Haldiim through the branches of the trees.

"Have you come at last to rouse Wadi Tel and raise Meztli's shields again?"

"Uh . . . I—no?" Narsi barely managed to get any words out at all.

The grove stood silent and the golden blessings all around Narsi seemed to dim.

"You've not been sent to defend this place?"

"Defend? No. I'm just . . . resting here. Are you Irsea . . ." Narsi trailed off as he recalled Yara telling him that the Bahiim who had tended the sacred grove had died. Narsi peered around but couldn't make out who addressed him.

The shining gold blessings floating all around him seemed to cast deep shadows across the grassy ground. One of the shadows shuddered, almost like a living thing. Then it opened its yellow eyes and Narsi realized that he was being scrutinized by a large black crow only a yard from him.

Another shadow flapped its wings and two more shifted their sleek heads to peer at Narsi. There had to be twenty or thirty of the glossy black birds all gathered around him.

Bahiim kept crows as familiars and as vessels for their wandering souls; he'd been told that countless times, but somehow realizing that a human spirit studied him from the birds' bodies felt startling. After everything else he'd seen today, this shouldn't have so unnerved him. Yet his hands shook as he gripped his medical satchel.

He stared at the crows, trying to will them to either become completely solid or to recede back into flat shadows. But as the letters hovering over Narsi's hands flickered, the crows appeared to rise and collapse, like tricks of the light.

A warm breeze moved over Narsi. It whispered in his ear.

"You are no witch, though you carry one of their stones of passage. You are no Bahiim, though you bear our blessings. No priest, though you wear the emblem of their orders. Who are you, child?"

"I—I'm Narsi, son of Wadi Lif-Tahm. I'm a physician, and this necklace—" Narsi recalled what the voice had called Hylanya's necklace. "The stone of passage isn't mine. I'm just holding it for someone else." Narsi whispered the words, feeling both foolish and frightened at once.

"Ah, you are a courier. But you are too late to shelter here, child. My flesh lies in the ground beneath you. My spirit abides in my crows. We are besieged by enemy spells. All around us traps wait to take any Bahiim who comes to protect this grove."

Narsi's entire body tensed at the idea of a body lying beneath him. Was it rude to sit on the dead, even after their spirits had left behind their remains? The ghost didn't seem angry. She sounded resigned as she went on whispering in Narsi's ear.

"I am sorry, Narsi Lif-Tahm, there is little shelter I can offer you. What strength I still possess I must conserve for the battle to come."

"What battle?" Narsi asked.

"An old battle—a great battle begun in ages long past, but one that never truly ended. It can no longer be forestalled. The kings grow weak and their guardians no longer remember their calling. Songbirds tear apart the wards and the shroud will spread over us once more. This time it must be fought to the bitter end. It cannot be forestalled any longer.

"Oh, but child, this is no place for one such as you. Run from this place. Return to your mother and shelter beneath the oaks that blessed you."

My mother is dead, Narsi thought. Despite his fear, he resented being told to run away and hide like he was a hapless child. For all the strangeness of the situation, it actually reminded Narsi of his aunt, fretting over him with the best of intentions but also the unspoken assumption that he was utterly hopeless and helpless.

"Travel warily, child, for the night is full of spies."

The wind suddenly stilled. The shining letters darkened and fell across Narsi's hands like ash falling from a fire. He jolted at the contact but felt no pain, just a lingering warmth. A moment later his eyes adjusted to the darkness of the night. He glanced up at the moon, then gazed around him. No sign of the crows remained, but across the small glade, near one of the tree trunks, a man's silhouette rose up. Then it came striding toward him. Narsi rose to his feet.

How much had he seen? Anything was likely too much, Narsi realized, and he turned to make a fast retreat.

"You know I've been looking for you for hours now," the man said, and Narsi stopped.

"Lord Vediya?" Narsi turned to peer into the gloom. Yes, that was Lord Vediya's form. A distinct loose quality played through his steps. Even moving quickly, he conveyed an air of indolence.

"I wish you'd call me Atreau." He stepped into the clearing and moonlight lit his lined face. He glanced around the circle of towering wisteria and his expression struck Narsi as genuinely troubled. "I thought I saw a light flickering up here."

"You did," Narsi whispered. "The sacred trees reacted to the Lady Hylanya's necklace. And I think the Bahiim who guards—or guarded— the grove spoke to me from her grave."

"I do want to know about this, but not now and not here." Lord Vediya turned his attention to the street below them. "Who knows who else the lights might have attracted. We'd best move."

Lord Vediya turned back the way he'd come up the hill and Narsi walked alongside him. Together they descended to a narrow alley and then followed several flights of worn stone stairs up onto a walkway that spanned a dark rippling stream. Moonlight shimmered across the water's surface and lit the bare rocky banks.

Once they descended from the walkway they hastened along another series of alleys and raised walkways until Narsi caught sight of the large painted sign cut in the shape of a rotund goose. Just across the road stood the Green Door. Steam filled the windows and it looked as busy at this late hour as it had been in the morning. The scent of kaweh and wine drifted on the night breezes.

"You know, I had been counting on finding you here." Lord Vediya didn't make for the stable, as Narsi expected, but instead led him to the sturdy front door of the inn.

"Why?" Narsi replied. "We never agreed that I should come here."

"But I showed you where it was," Lord Vediya responded.

"You pointed out the Candioro Theater as well."

"So I did, but I didn't think that you'd be inclined to wander that far, much less join a public parade and then caper into the sacred grove."

"Why shouldn't I?" Narsi tried to sound reasonable but couldn't keep from adding, "You hardly seemed concerned about where I went when Prince Jacinto sent me away."

Lord Vediya paused and turned back to Narsi.

"It serves me not to show too much concern in front of men like Procopio. But that doesn't mean—" Lord Vediya broke off. He cast a searching look back to the dark street behind them.

Narsi glanced back as well. He noticed two men lingering on the stoop of a theater entry and a dog padding around a corner, but otherwise the lane appeared largely deserted—though very distantly, Narsi could still hear the strains of music rising from the Shell Fountain. And then it seemed to him that one of the shadows lying across a staircase very slightly resembled a crouching man wearing a rabbit mask.

Lord Vediya said nothing and didn't move.

After a few minutes the masked man rose and set off running after a shadowy figure farther down the street. Lord Vediya relaxed and continued walking and talking as if the interruption never occurred.

"I had assumed," Lord Vediya said quietly, "that you weren't so audacious a young fellow that you'd roam a city brimming with thieves, cutthroats and royal bishop's guardsmen while loaded down with gold and a stone of passage."

"You are *mop* my mother." Narsi repeated the words Lord Vediya had muttered to him while feigning drunkenness. Lord Vediya laughed.

"That I'm mop," he replied, and then he pushed the door of the Fat Goose open. Firelight and raucous voices poured from the crowded inn. Lord Vediya walked in and Narsi followed him, though not without drawing a few stares from several of the men seated at the bar. One heavyset, red-faced fellow glowered at Narsi with the unfocused gaze of a drunk making his last attempt at any coherent thought. He attempted to stand, but Narsi eluded him by simply taking several steps farther into the inn. The drunkard plopped back into his seat, his head lolling forward as if he'd just dozed off.

The slim man behind the bar watched him with an assessing expression. Narsi thought that he might have been the same fellow he had seen kiss Inissa. Then Narsi remembered that Lord Vediya had pointed the man out to him this morning. The handsome owner of the inn heralded from the Salt Islands and went by the name Spider.

"Yago was looking for you," Spider called.

Alarm shot through Narsi. Lord Vediya, however, didn't seem particularly concerned.

"I can't possibly have ensnared his affections so quickly, could I?" Lord Vediya asked, and he struck a coy pose.

The man behind the bar laughed, as did both women serving drinks to the patrons crowded around the gaming tables. Several men glanced up and snorted at Lord Vediya's posture.

"I let him have a peek through your pretty room upstairs and I think he must have seen all those love letters that pile up for you there." Spider grinned and then added dramatically, "he went away in tears."

"The poor man. No wonder he can't find Lady Hylanya. He only has eyes for me."

That inspired roars of laughter from all around the room. Then a hunched, white-haired old man called for new wagers on how much longer it would be before Captain Yago captured his quarry.

"You mean the lady or Atreau's heart?" demanded the taller of the serving women. She looked near forty but in very good health. Her shoulders seemed remarkably muscular to Narsi's eye. The men next to her chuckled, but the white-haired old man seemed to ponder the question seriously.

"Doesn't matter which," a short serving girl who looked to be in her teens called from near the hearth. "He ain't ever catching neither of them. I'll place a copper crown on that."

"All right then," the old man proclaimed. "It's two wagers that I'll put down in the book . . . though the odds on the second requires a number too long to write out. Still I'm taking all bets now." He sat back down and, to Narsi's surprise, a good number of men roused themselves from the bar to place their wagers.

Spider offered Lord Vediya a friendly nod before returning to his wine casks and beer barrels. The rest of the populace appeared far too focused on the cards and dice at their tables to spare either Lord Vediya or Narsi any further attention. As they passed between the crowded tables, Narsi heard a few men gossiping about the changes they expected when Prince Sevanyo took the throne, but most conversed about horses, the weather and popular operas.

Following Lord Vediya, Narsi climbed up a rickety winding staircase to a dim upper floor. Lord Vediya opened a door on the right without even needing a key. Narsi couldn't make out much of the space except that it appeared to be a chaos of weird shadows. As soon as Lord Vediya lit a small lamp, Narsi realized why the place had looked so odd. The velvet-upholstered chairs had been thrown onto their sides, and a dainty writing table lay completely overturned with its ink bottle leaking a dark pool and papers scattered all around. The mattresses had been pulled off the bed frame and heaps of straw stuffing spilled out from huge gashes. Captain Yago had certainly done more than merely have a peek at the place. Even the curtains seemed to be in tatters.

To Narsi's surprise, Lord Vediya laughed at the wreck.

Then he pinched out the lamplight, turned around and sauntered down the hall. He stopped about five yards farther and leaned against the hallway wall. For a moment Narsi wondered if he'd lost his strength or been somehow overcome. But then a large expanse of the wall paneling slid aside. Narsi followed him into the secret passage with a feeling of delighted wonder. This was exactly like something from one of his books. Just before the panel fell closed behind them, Lord Vediya reached back and placed his hand in Narsi's.

"Stay close, the footing's tricky in the dark," he said.

The panel snapped shut and gloom swallowed them. Narsi curled his fingers around Lord Vediya's hand and walked cautiously forward. After only a few steps he noted very faint seams of starlight seeping in through cracks in the wall ahead of them.

"There's a release hidden here." Lord Vediya reached out to the wall and Narsi traced his hand down to a notch in the rough wood of the wall.

"Slide it down," Lord Vediya instructed.

It took a hard push, but a solid click reverberated through Narsi's fingers and all at once a small circle of the wall in front of him slid upward. Beyond it lay another chasm of complete darkness, though Narsi could smell the faint scents of domesticity: woodsmoke, lamp oil and a hint of rose oil. Lord Vediya crouched down and then crawled through the opening. A moment later a lamp flared on the other side of the thick wall.

Narsi clambered after Lord Vediya, though his greater height and broader shoulders made it a very tight fit. He felt like a snake wriggling into a tiny mouse burrow. But then he pulled himself free and scraped out onto a hard wood floor. Lord Vediya dropped down beside him while Narsi sat up.

"The pull to close the door is here." Lord Vediya reached out and caught a yellow tassel hanging from a window sash. He pulled the tassel down with both hands and the heavy wood panel slowly descended to reveal a section of a painting depicting wild horses on a rocky cliff in a thunderstorm. The small section snapped back into place behind the large decorative frame, leaving only the presence of great strokes of lightning illuminating an unbowed herd of roan horses.

Narsi straightened and peered out the window, amazed to realize that he now stood in the building behind the Fat Goose. How the second floors of the two buildings adjoined was almost impossible to discern.

No wonder Lord Vediya had been so amused by Captain Yago's intrusion into the room in the Fat Goose. It was obviously a decoy. Before today the thought of maintaining a decoy room might have struck Narsi as almost laughably paranoid. But he was quickly coming to realize that Lord Vediya's real life was much more dangerous than that of the mere sensualist adventurer he'd made himself out to be in his books.

"Probably best to pull the curtains," Lord Vediya commented. Narsi drew them shut quickly. Lord Vediya set his oil lamp on a battered-looking bed table. Then he turned and dropped into one of the wood chairs near the stained writing desk. Just beyond that stood a dresser and bed. Both looked humble for belongings of a nobleman, though taking in the rest of the room, they weren't much out of place. Paint stains spattered the old rug lying near the small fireplace and the green basin on the wash table in no way matched with the orange pitcher beside it.

"We can speak freely here. Have a seat." Lord Vediya indicated the larger upholstered chair near the fireplace. Two patches covered the seat cushion and the back seemed a little threadbare, but Narsi found it quite comfortable.

"I take it the lady made it safely to her ship?" Narsi asked quietly.

Lord Vediya nodded. "Now we must simply pray that she and her brother will accept Prince Sevanyo's apologies for his brother's behavior."

"Do you think they will?" Narsi asked. The Bahiim ghost's words still seemed to flutter through the back of his mind. A battle to come . . . "They wouldn't fight a war over this incident, would they?"

Lord Vediya shrugged and then said, "It's hard to know what any common Cadeleonians would fight a war over, much less what Labaran witches like Hylanya and Skellan might feel is necessary." He stared down at his hands and then glanced to Narsi's medical satchel. "You still have the stone of passage?"

"Yes. But what is it exactly?" Narsi asked.

"It's a secret. One you should do your best to simply forget you ever saw." Meeting Narsi's curious gaze, Lord Vediya added, "It's a spell that provides safe passage as well as illuminating a path to whomever made it. In this case it's passage to Count Radulf's court."

"For further negotiations?" Narsi asked.

"Perhaps." Lord Vediya shrugged again. "If we can't outmaneuver the royal bishop, then Radulf County may be the only safe haven left. Considering the political environment just now, it's best if we keep the stone's existence between the two of us. It can't be traced back to the duke, you understand."

"Of course," Narsi replied automatically.

Lord Vediya looked tired, his expression uncharacteristically grim.

"Tell me about the lights in the sacred grove." Lord Vediya spoke in a soft tone, but Narsi didn't miss the fact that he hadn't bothered to disguise the order with niceties or flirtation. Had it been almost any other man, Narsi might have pointed out that he wasn't in the man's employment and expected a bit more curtesy in his conversations.

But there was a kind of exceptional candor in Lord Vediya's directness that Narsi suspected was rare. He'd only observed Lord Vediya to speak so frankly to Inissa, and then it had been in a lowered voice. But even if this wasn't a special glimpse of the real man beneath all his flattery and banter, Narsi still owed Lord Vediya a great debt. Even if Lord Vediya didn't remember Narsi's promise to repay him, Narsi intended to keep his word.

"When I took the necklace into the sacred grove, I heard a voice—I think it belonged to the spirit of the Bahiim who last cared for the grove. She asked if I'd come to wake Wadi Tel and raise Meztli's shields again. I'm not sure if she meant the Meztli who was mentioned in the Cadeleonian holy books or not." Narsi struggled to recollect the actual passages that mentioned Meztli, but it had been years since he'd last paged through a Cadeleonian holy book. "I have no idea where Wadi Tel is. But Tel in Haldiim is a hill or rise, and Wadi is a very archaic word for a guardian. I only know the word because it's my mother's name, but no one uses the term in common speech anymore."

"So she thought you'd come to do something with an obscure religious figure's shield possibly on some archaic Guardian Hill?"

Narsi nodded.

Lord Vediya stared at the fire with a distant expression. "This Wadi Tel could be Crown Hill. The Savior's forces rallied there against the demon lords. I don't know what the place was called during the Battle of the Shard of Heaven, but it was renamed Crown Hill after our first king was anointed there ten days later." Lord Vediya fell silent, then looked to Narsi. "Go on with your story."

"Well, I told her I wasn't who she was expecting. And then she told me that I should run back home because a battle is coming." All the strangeness of the day seemed unreal now as he put it into mundane words. A dead woman prophesizing war from the body of thirty crows seemed like it merited its own dialect, at least.

"A forthcoming battle." Lord Vediya's frown deepened. "I don't suppose she offered a date or mentioned who exactly would be fighting in this battle?"

"Not as such, no." Narsi tried to remember the exact words spoken to him. "Some kind of unfinished battle from a long time ago. And she said something about kings being weak and guardians forgetting their duties. Does any of that help?"

"It's something," Lord Vediya replied. "Hylanya mentioned the kings weakening as well . . . Though a Bahiim making the same comment worries me." Lord Vediya looked to Narsi. "As I understand it, they anchor curses and spells across entire groves or even whole forests."

"That's right. Trees represent the connection between the living world around us and the realms hidden from us—the underworld realms where their roots grow. But there aren't any Bahiim kings. Weak or otherwise."

"We've had plenty of Cadeleonian kings. The current one is certainly weak, but I don't think that's who she meant. As for an ancient unfinished battle . . ." Lord Vediya sighed but didn't say anything more.

"Lady Hylanya didn't indicate anything else?" Narsi asked.

Realization flashed across Lord Vediya's face for just an instant, but then he scowled.

"She was interested in the Shard of Heaven in the beginning. Perhaps those are the weak kings . . ."

"The Hallowed Kings?" Narsi asked. "You mean they're real?" The words were out before he considered them.

Fortunately, Lord Vediya merely laughed at his near-heresy.

"I can't vouch for their existence myself, but considering Hylanya's interest, I'd guess that the Hallowed Kings are more than myths or symbols. The fact that they might be weakening is troubling."

"Because they're supposed to be the guardians of the Cadeleonian nation? Or are you thinking of something more specific?" Narsi thought back on what he remembered about the Hallowed Kings and the Shard of Heaven. The creation of both had been the price of vanquishing ancient demon lords. Only one of those demon lords had woken in Labara just six years ago. "There couldn't be another . . ." Narsi trailed off as he met Lord Vediya's gaze.

His tanned face looked ashen and the pupils of his eyes flared to black pits of stark fear. Unlike Narsi, he'd witnessed a demon lord break free of the stone that had bound its body. He'd been there when towers collapsed and a city burned.

"No. That can't have been it." Lord Vediya shifted his gaze to the fire. "Hylanya and Skellan may be committed to freeing trolls, giant wyrm and Old Gods, but they wouldn't release another demon lord."

The majority of Narsi's ideas about Count Radulf had come from Lord Vediya's book. He remembered thinking that the count had sounded uncultured but also strangely egalitarian for a ruler. Though what stood out to him most had been the descriptions of the man striding across exposed city walls in all weather, clothed in little more than a red fur cloak for the sake of protecting his people.

"From what I remember of your book," Narsi commented, "the Labaran demon lord hadn't been defeated in the same manner as all the others—"

"That's right." Lord Vediya smiled. "God's tits, how could I forget? Yes, Javier said as much. He had been trapped, but all the others had been killed or driven back to their own realms."

"So, that can't be the ancient battle that the Bahiim referred to."

"No, indeed not." Lord Vediya's relief seemed to melt through the muscles of his body. He leaned back and stretched in his seat. His eyes drooped and a moment later he only half stifled a yawn.

Narsi wondered how long it had been since he'd slept.

"An unfinished war . . . it begs the question of when a war truly does end, doesn't it? How many battles, lost generations past, are raging even now in the hearts of people defeated or wronged." Lord Vediya closed his eyes.

Narsi contemplated his question but also wondered if he shouldn't just let the man relax. He was nearly exhausted himself. The heat of the fire seemed to wrap around him like a blanket.

"*Your nation calling, Your kingdom falling, Oh, come, young brash and brave, Run with me to an early grave . . .*" Lord Vediya hummed under his breath. The light melody seemed at odds with the grim lyrics.

"Is that from an opera?" Narsi asked.

"Maybe someday. Just now it's something I'm working out."

"The tune is nice." Narsi let his eyelids sink closed as he slumped back into his seat. Beside him Lord Vediya continued humming the low melody, almost as if he was singing a lullaby. Narsi's thoughts seemed to melt away into half-dreamed memories of Mother Kir-Naham's pharmacy and pots of Labaran roses.

He felt Lord Vediya's warm hand rest on his knee.

"The bed is better for sleeping in than that chair, I promise you."

"I couldn't take your bed," Narsi protested, and he let his eyes fall closed again.

Lord Vediya laughed.

"Lord, no. I'm not so gallant as to make that sacrifice. But I can certainly share it with you."

That brought Narsi's eyes open quickly enough. Lord Vediya already stood, with his back turned. He strode to the simple bed, sat on the edge and quickly stripped off his riding boots, shirt and breeches. His motions were neither graceful nor seductive, and yet somehow Narsi found himself fascinated. Here was the infamous libertine pulling off his undergarments with tired disinterest. He yawned and scratched his chest, utterly bereft of all polish and performance.

In this moment, more than any other, he reminded Narsi of the young man he'd been when they'd first met, more than a decade before: unstudied and sincere, with all his pretenses still years before him. He glanced back and only belatedly seemed to realize that Narsi studied him.

"Have I disappointed?" Lord Vediya asked.

As much as Narsi wished to arouse Lord Vediya's desire, he appreciated that a different, perhaps greater intimacy belied this moment—perhaps this entire day. While any number of people might inspire lust, it struck Narsi that very few merited Lord Vediya's trust. Narsi truly wished to number among those few. More than that, he owed it to Lord Vediya to rise above his own desire and prove himself a man worthy of relying upon.

"Not at all." Narsi rose and his legs felt leaden as he trudged to the bed and dropped down on the mattress opposite Lord Vediya.

In all honestly, Narsi doubted that he could've performed all that magnificently tonight even if Lord Vediya had propositioned him. Clumsy fumbling and thrusts of earnest exhaustion weren't experiences he most wished to share with any lover, but particularly not Lord Vediya.

Narsi stripped. Any burden to make a show of exposing his naked body had been allayed by Lord Vediya's own artless disrobing. Narsi felt strangely relieved. If only here and now, he wasn't required to impress anyone or be on guard against any betrayal of his genuine character.

Lord Vediya drew back the blankets and slid under them. A moment later Narsi joined him. He did his best not to take up more than his share of the bed, but he wasn't a small man and the bed itself wasn't particularly spacious. Lord Vediya's leg and buttocks bumped up against Narsi's thigh. His skin felt warm. The bedding smelled faintly of rose cologne. Lord Vediya snuffed out the bedside lamp, then settled back down, with his back pressed against Narsi's chest and his hair spilling across Narsi's shoulder.

"So is this an average day for you?" Narsi asked at last.

"Lying naked next to a handsome man I've just met?" Lord Vediya asked. "Not as much as you might expect."

Narsi laughed.

"No. All this intrigue, magic, ghosts and secret passages. Somehow I'd thought you spent more time penning strange and thrilling stories and less of it living them."

"Had I been blessed with a more fertile imagination, I probably would. But alas, for the sake of my art I must burden myself with an adventurous life."

"You say it so cleverly that I feel I should pretend to believe you," Narsi replied. "But none of what I've witnessed today could possibly be written about."

"Which is why I am forced to sell anonymous erotic tales to a local pearl-drop publisher," Lord Vediya muttered. "Not that I've had the time to even whack off one of those recently."

"You really published anonymously? I thought I had read everything you've written." Narsi couldn't keep the disappointment from his voice.

"Oh, trust me, they weren't masterpieces of forbidden beauty, not by any stretch of the imagination. Trash, actually." Lord Vediya sounded genuinely dispirited. "We needed money to buy into this place and the Fat Goose. The property belonged to a relative of one of my old classmates, so he brokered us quite a bargain. Still, it came dear."

"Morisio Cavada, you mean?" Narsi asked. He recalled that Morisio had come from a prosperous family of scholars and merchants before he'd joined the crew of the *Red Witch*. He even recollected a mention of the young man's uncle owning several taverns in the capital.

"God's tits." Lord Vediya gave a tired laugh. "You truly have read every page of my memoirs, haven't you?"

"More than once."

"You're just extraordinary . . . ," Lord Vediya murmured.

Narsi couldn't think of a response to that. Lord Vediya sighed and shifted his back against Narsi's hips. The sensation of supple bare skin against his naked body nearly undid all of his previous resolve. Then Narsi felt the tension of consciousness drop from Lord Vediya's muscles. His breathing slowed and settled into a decidedly unarousing snore.

   CHAPTER
SIXTEEN

Atreau floated at the edge of a dream, feeling safe and warm, but uncertain of where he now wandered. He could hear birds singing. Sunshine filtered through the leaves of an almond tree and the scents of a physic garden in full bloom drifted over him. Yellow coinflower blossoms peered out between the blue branches of succulent halda plants. The faint perfume of camphor and sweet cinnamon made him think that he must have traveled to Anacleto.

The idea filled him with relief.

He was no longer in Cieloalta—no longer responsible for the lives of Fedeles's agents and enemies. Nor had he betrayed his friends and family, fleeing to Labara while Cadeleon burned.

Somehow, all that was over and done. His life could be his own.

A man leaned against his back in easy familiarity. Atreau luxuriated in the sensation of naked skin grazing his own. He longed to run his hands over the other man's body but stilled with uncertainty. He tried to remember who it was that stood behind him. Atreau turned to glimpse his companion's face but the sun at his back shone too bright and he flinched away.

"Who are you?" Atreau whispered.

"Don't you remember?" the man asked.

Atreau tried to look at him again, but the sun had intensified to a blinding heat.

Now Atreau could smell smoke. Fear rose like bile in his gut. He remembered flames gushing up thatch roofs and bell towers collapsing. The garden was burning. Birdsong turned to screams. Willow leaves seared away. The man at his back cried out as the fire rolled over him. Atreau threw his hands over his clenched eyes, desperate to block out the ferocious light. But it seared through the flesh and bone of his arms.

He bolted upright, coming awake to find himself on a sagging mattress in a dark room. A long, lean body lay pressed against him. His companion breathed easily and released a contented sigh from the depth of sleep. Atreau squinted, picking out the lines and shadows of his face. The master physician, he belatedly remembered, Narsi.

God's teeth, he looked young in this faint light.

Then the burst of white light flared from beneath the crack in the door, followed by the sound of a pebble striking the wood. The light dimmed just a little.

Atreau glowered at the door. What would they do if he just refused to answer one day? What if he packed his bags and boarded a ship for Yuan, leaving all of this behind? What would it matter? But of course he knew—he'd been there when ancient spells shattered and the city of Milmuraille crumbled and burned. He'd treated the injured and carried the bodies of the dead to mass graves.

Atreau scrubbed his palms against his face. He'd gone too far to back out now.

Another pebble smacked against the bedroom door. Then a third and a fourth.

"Just one night," he muttered to himself. "Can't I sleep all the way through just one damn night?"

Atreau snatched his trousers from his discarded clothes and pulled them on. Had it been any other rap at his door he would have taken up his sword belt and weapons as well. But there was no point. He strode across the room and didn't bother to peer through the tiny spy hole. He knew exactly what he would see in the barren hallway.

Atreau stepped out and closed the door behind him as quietly as he could. The less he had to explain—or lie about—to the fetching and far too curious Narsi, the better they'd get along.

A dry, stale scent hung in the air, and where a bare white wall should have stood directly across from the bedroom door there now appeared to be a large, seeping black stain. The odor of mushrooms and loam wafted from the darkness. Then a pale rock came hurling out. Atreau managed to catch it before it smacked against his door.

"I'm coming," Atreau muttered. He stepped neared to the dark stain. The edges rippled and pulsed like something living—some shuddering, hungry maw wheezing a decayed dry breath over his face. His entire body tensed as he tried to stride into the darkness. An intense dread rooted him in place.

He knew that Javier couldn't step foot in Cieloalta without countless spells surging to life and setting off alarms all across the city. That would bring Yago's men directly down on him here and provide evidence that the royal bishop would use to accuse Atreau—and likely Spider as well—of heresy.

There was no option but for him to take that single step forward. Still he remained where he was, with his heart pounding like a drum and sick dread turning his muscles to lead.

Another pebble flew out, this one clipping his chest.

"God's tits! I'm coming!" Atreau charged in, his vexation offering him enough motive to overcome his instinctive horror.

In a single step he passed through the wall and into the darkness. Then he stood there, on the Old Road, as Javier and his fellow Bahiim called it. The Sorrowlands, as he and Elezar knew it. By any name it was a realm of darkness, where luminous blue mists slowly rose into the likenesses of the dead. They called in whispers and moans, pleading for help, for comfort, for a final goodbye. Already Atreau could hear the voices.

He glanced around him for Javier but saw nothing through the dark.

Then a haze of pale blue mist swirled into a familiar form. Atreau recognized his mother, though her dark hair hung over most of her wan face. In her gaunt arms she cradled the wide-eyed corpse of his stillborn daughter.

Atreau stared, feeling their presences as much as seeing them. They were both so weak, both starved for warmth and love.

"She can't sleep." His mother's pale lips trembled over the words. "Why won't you hold her? Don't you hear her crying?"

A gasping thin wail slowly rose. Atreau lifted his hands to cover his ears, but it made no difference. The broken sobs weren't real. Neither was the vision of his daughter and mother.

Atreau knew that the longer he concentrated upon them the stronger their presences would grow. Still he had to stop himself from stepping nearer. He raised his hands, almost offering to take the child from his mother as she struggled to rock the sobbing infant in her arms.

Then he caught himself and turned his back. He focused on the darkness in front of him, refusing to acknowledge the fading voices behind him. For an instant nothing but darkness surrounded him. Then a faint glow swirled up. Atreau's gut tightened. He prayed he would see Javier standing in a pool of white light.

Instead, Miro Reollos floated a few feet from him, as he always did. Beautiful, despite the blood pouring from between his full lips. He accused Atreau of nothing, but simply pulled open the folds of his robe, exposing his gaping wounds.

"I never meant for you to be hurt—" Atreau cut himself off.

This wasn't Miro. This vision just one of the countless devils that inhabited this hellish place, and fed by luring the living into their hidden jaws.

"Atreau, please," Miro's voice whispered. "Hold me one last time. I'm so alone here . . . how you left me . . . bleeding . . . dying alone. Please—"

A wave of radiant white light seared through the wispy blue image of Miro. The surrounding darkness seemed to writhe back from the growing sphere of light, exposing a featureless expanse of flat gray ground and bleak gray sky. Javier strode out from the center of the blazing white light. Despite how long his black hair had grown over the past thirteen years and the strangeness of the Bahiim robes he wore, he still looked like the undaunted nineteen-year-old youth whom Atreau had schooled with so long ago. He surveyed his surroundings with the assurance of a boy who'd ruled over a vast dukedom at seventeen and commanded the fires of the White Hell before he was twenty.

"Sorry about letting them creep up on you like that." Javier rolled two white stones between the fingers of his left hand and held a piece of blank paper in his right. "I went to fetch a few more pebbles."

"Not satisfied with beaning me in the chest just the once?" Atreau snapped. His heart was still hammering with fear and anger. Even knowing Miro's image was only an illusion, he'd still felt overwhelmed with guilt. It had been nearly six years, but this place made the horror fresh as it had been that night.

Javier shrugged and tucked the paper away into his cloak. "All the Labaran witches assure me that stones fall where they are fated to come down. So I couldn't possibly take credit. Or have I completely misunderstood Labaran fortune-telling?"

"If you mean casting a vei, then yes, you're going about it all wrong," Atreau replied. His mother had believed in veis and often insisted that destiny wasn't a preordained fate but a destination reached through a lifetime of the paths taken and choices made.

Here in the Shadowlands, Atreau could almost hear her whispering to him. *You forge your own vei, my darling. Be true to yourself and your destiny will be of your own making.*

She'd died brokenhearted and abandoned in a convent infirmary. Atreau didn't want to believe that she'd played any part in her own downfall. At the same time he knew that her decision to trust his father, despite countless betrayals, had been her undoing. More than that, her death had left Atreau and his siblings bereft of their one protector. After that, there had been few choices for any of them to build their destinies upon.

Javier drew near enough that Atreau briefly glimpsed the white bones shining through his pale skin. His dark eyes looked black as the hollows of a skull. Then his expression turned playful and he threw his arms around Atreau and pulled him into a firm embrace.

"It's so good to see you, Atreau."

Returning Javier's hug, Atreau felt his earlier resentment dissipate. Javier's lean body felt cold in his arms, and not for the first time Atreau wondered what it cost Javier to lay claim over the paths of the dead. Atreau reminded himself that he wasn't the only one who'd suffered loss or made sacrifices. Javier had been stripped of his noble title, his family and his home.

Javier released him just enough to gaze into his face. The affection in his expression seemed to wipe away the deathly quality of Javier's countenance. "Has it been bad in the capital? You look tired."

"The last two weeks were taxing. We lost Ciceron last night. Beheaded—"

"And Fedeles?" Javier tensed as if he meant to tear out from the sanctuary of the Sorrowlands and race to his cousin's side.

"He's sad but perfectly safe." Atreau gripped his arm. "I'm looking into Ciceron's murder. The man wasn't without his own enemies, so his death might not have anything to do with Fedeles or noble politics."

"You really believe that?" Javier asked.

"No. I'm almost certain that the assassins are connected to some conspiracy of the royal bishop's, but I've been wrong before."

"Not often," Javier replied. "You were right about Yago murdering Irsea, the Bahiim who guarded the Circle of Wisteria."

"But I couldn't prove it," Atreau replied; then he recalled everything Narsi had told him of his encounter in the sacred grove. "And speaking of Irsea, it seems that her spirit is still present in some form."

Atreau quickly related Narsi's adventure. He supposed it was telling that Javier appeared far more surprised by the description of the towering Haldiim physician than he did by the idea of a quavering Bahiim ghost warning him to flee before the capital was consumed by an ancient war. It further confirmed Atreau's fear that another demon lord lurked beneath the Shard of Heaven.

"So Hylanya has recovered?" Javier asked.

"Thanks to Master Narsi, yes," Atreau replied. "She and Kili sailed on the *Red Witch* this evening. They should be back in Milmuraille in a week's time."

"That's a relief at least." Javier's shoulders sagged slightly as tension seemed to drain from him. "I was afraid that we'd have to carry her across the Old Road. This realm is a nightmare for perfectly healthy men and women, but for someone on the edge of death . . ."

Atreau nodded. Earlier, they'd discussed the possibility, but only as a very last resort. Witches reviled the Sorrowlands—even Skellan refused to set foot on the path of the dead and had been carried by Elezar the one time he'd entered the desolate place. More worryingly, Javier hadn't been certain that he could keep Hylanya's spirit from abandoning her body to escape the Sorrowlands.

"And of course the place certainly isn't fit for entertaining nobility," Javier added with a grin. "I can't seem to ever burn enough incense to get the smell out."

Atreau laughed, but his amusement didn't last. Narsi's troubling conversation kept turning through his thoughts.

"Do you know what Irsea meant?" Atreau asked. "This unfinished battle?"

"I have a suspicion, but I can't be certain," Javier admitted. "Even if I tried to ask her I wouldn't receive an answer, much less a warm welcome."

"No?" Atreau asked. "Because you're Cadeleonian?"

"I'm hardly the first Cadeleonian who's converted. The problem is my master, Alizadeh. He's brilliant but not . . . roundly beloved among his fellow Bahiim. Particularly not among the elder practitioners here in Cadeleon. As his student, I'm unwelcome in certain sacred circles. In the capital my presence wouldn't be tolerated."

"But she was talking about a war. How can some dispute among Bahiim possibly be more important than averting that?"

"Obviously, I don't believe that it is." Javier frowned. "But the fact is that you and I are meeting here on the Old Road because there is an entire web of Bahiim wards that were raised against my master and his followers. Dead or alive, Irsea views my presence in the city as an immense trespass. I'm no better than the royal bishop as far as she's concerned. Possibly worse."

Atreau sighed. Why did it always have to be this way? People with so much in common hanging onto grudges when they would all be best served to make peace.

Even as the exasperated thought occurred to him, he recognized his own hypocrisy. How many times had Fedeles nagged him about putting his mistrust of Oasia behind him? But the fact that she'd tried to have him murdered wasn't something Atreau could easily forgive.

Then he suddenly wondered, what caused so many Bahiim to view Javier's master, Alizadeh, in the same way?

"Does Irsea have reason to suspect your master of bad intentions?" Atreau studied Javier's young face. Something like embarrassment flitted over his countenance.

"Ages ago, perhaps, but not now . . ." Javier paused as if weighing his next words carefully. "Long ago he belonged to a group of sorcerers called Waarihivu. They battled demon lords for dominion over a multitude of realms."

"And?" Atreau prompted.

"In a *few* cases they destroyed those realms rather than lose them to demons. But Alizadeh converted to the Bahiim faith ages ago, and since then he's kept true to the faith and—"

"Wait. Destroyed realms? You mean he wiped out whole kingdoms?" Atreau's nightmare fluttered through his memory. Buildings collapsing all across Milmuraille as flames consumed every living thing. There were old tales of kingdoms lost to floods and earthquakes as well.

"I mean entire worlds," Javier said at last. "They wiped out whole worlds. But only as a last resort."

Atreau stared at him, trying to come to grips with the idea that somewhere entire other worlds existed and that some had already been destroyed.

"It was a different time," Javier stated quickly. "And as I said, Alizadeh has since sworn himself to the Bahiim duty of protecting this realm and its sacred roots. He's no longer a threat, but some Bahiim still don't trust him."

Atreau nodded. It would seem that the Bahiim did indeed have good reason to view Javier's master with suspicion.

"So, Irsea is more likely to tell Narsi all her secrets than you or your master?" Atreau asked.

"Clearly. Though the fact that she responded to him so quickly makes me think that she's growing desperate. Her soul must be under immense strain, and it sounds like she has no hope of a living Bahiim reaching her to take guardianship of the sacred grove."

"Yes. She said there were traps set to capture any Bahiim who entered the city," Atreau agreed, though he wasn't certain of what stood to be lost if the sacred grove went without a guardian. When he asked, Javier looked grim.

"It's not by chance that the Circle of Wisteria and Crown Hill are aligned with the Shard of Heaven." As Javier spoke he rolled the stones between his hands. Tiny white sparks flickered over them. "From what I've read in the Radulf library and from what Alizadeh has said, it seems that the sacred grove and Crown Hill might serve as shields for the Hallowed Kings—"

"But the kings are Cadeleonian, not Bahiim or Labaran," Atreau objected.

"The kings who are currently interred at the Shard of Heaven are Cadeleonian, but that couldn't have always been the case," Javier replied. "The Cadeleonian church hadn't even been established when the Battle of the Shard of Heaven was fought. It was only after the battle that the first Cadeleonian cult sprang up to worship the Savior. But it was the combined power of Bahiim, witches, sorcerers and a multitude of mystics that actually defeated the demon lords and created the Shard of Heaven."

For an instant Atreau simply stared at Javier, feeling that he must have misunderstood his friend.

"I do not recall Father Habalan teaching us any of that," Atreau remarked at last.

"He wouldn't have, even if he'd known. And I promise you there are entire worlds of wisdom that Father Habalan is ignorant of." Javier flashed a boyishly gleeful grin. When they'd schooled together, Javier had always taken great pleasure in digging through ancient diaries and moldering records to find little-known facts that embarrassed teachers and contradicted sermons.

"So the Shard of Heaven would originally have been crafted by witches or Salt Island mystics or Bahiim?" Atreau asked. He could count on Javier and his master for information concerning Bahiim spells. Hylanya's many familiars might prove useful, if it came to matters of Labaran witchcraft. And he supposed he might be able to pry something out of Spider if it came to Salt Island mysticism. That was better than nothing.

"Likely a combination of all of them and more. The spells that encompass the Shard of Heaven are like a tapestry woven from thousands of different threads. And Crown Hill is much the same, though it has been neglected for far too long. I'm not certain of how many of the wards there are still intact. Did you know that in days long past it was known by another name—"

"Wadi Tel." Atreau remembered the name from his discussion with Narsi. "The guardian hill."

"Exactly." Javier grinned at him with delight. "The guardian hill that overlooks both the Shard of Heaven and the sacred grove. It's a place where power flows through the stones like water rushing through a stream. That's why the Savior's forces amassed there."

"Is that also why you've had Fedeles riding out there for the last few months?" Atreau asked.

"Yes." Javier nodded, though his smile faded. "Has it been hard on him?"

"Now that he has a wife he doesn't often turn to me with his private troubles, but I can see that he's grown more anxious of late." Atreau paused out of habit. But if anyone was safe to confide in about Fedeles and matters of magic, it was Javier. "His shadow disturbs him, and he's not alone in that. There are times when I swear that the thing is going to get up and walk off on its own. Only last night it killed two men."

"What?" Javier's horrified expression made Atreau suddenly aware of how accustomed he'd grown to the deaths all around him.

"They were assassins," Atreau added quickly. "Hylanya will tell you that the capital is full of them now. These two meant to murder Prince Sevanyo. Only Fedeles stood near enough to stop them. Fortunately the night was dark enough that no one could be certain of what they saw. No one dared accuse Fedeles of practicing witchcraft. But it was bloody—

both bodies slit open in an instant. Fedeles was shaking for nearly an hour afterward."

"But he didn't harm anyone else?" Javier asked.

"No. His attack was so precise that I would have said that Fedeles had perfect control of his shadow," Atreau admitted. "Except he looked so stricken. The entire time we walked together afterward he kept moving so that his shadow wouldn't touch me."

Fedeles's anxiety had in fact made Atreau more nervous than witnessing the two assassins being dispatched.

"No matter what it might look like, Fedeles's shadow isn't something separate from him." Javier shook his head. "It's the form that his power—his spirit—was channeled into, but it's not a curse, not anymore."

"Yes, Hylanya said much the same thing when she first came to the capital," Atreau remembered. "She called his shadow an astounding black witchflame. Said he had a soul like a thunderhead roiling with lightning."

"She's not wrong. There's power in him that many would envy. Though I know Fedeles wishes it was otherwise," Javier said. "If he could have his way, he'd be as ordinary as possible and spend all his time in the company of horses."

"And the occasional well-built man," Atreau added.

Javier cast him such a look of disbelief that Atreau laughed.

"What do you think he and Captain Ciceron were doing together? Holding hands and talking about ponies?"

"No, of course not . . ." Javier's pale face colored with embarrassment. "It's just difficult to think of Fedeles that way. To me, he's still a shy little brother."

Fedeles hadn't been anything close to *little* for nearly a decade. He stood as tall as Javier, with far broader shoulders. As for shy? Could a young man who laughed, wept and argued so openly ever have been shy? Atreau didn't think so, but he saw no point in arguing with Javier.

"The thing is that we can't allow Crown Hill or the Circle of Wisteria to fall into the wrong hands. Not when the Hallowed Kings are fading and so many wards around the Shard of Heaven have failed," Javier said a moment later. "If I could do this alone, I wouldn't embroil any of you in it, but I can't . . ."

Atreau considered him. Javier had always kept his own council and maintained an air of mystery, even back when he'd not had all that much more than any of them to hide. It would be like him to underestimate how much his friends could stand to know or endure. He'd always tried to shield them from both the truth and its consequences.

But none of them were boys anymore.

"We'll do what needs to be done. But it would help to know exactly what we're up against. If the wards fail and we can't keep control over the sacred grove and Crown Hill, will another demon lord break free? Is that what the Shard of Heaven and the Hallowed Kings keep locked away?" Atreau felt certain he already knew the answer.

Javier scowled, but then, to Atreau's surprise, he shook his head. His expression, however, struck Atreau as far more troubled than certain.

"Are you sure?" Atreau asked.

"Alizadeh says it's not possible for another to have survived. And I believe him—"

"But you just said that the Bahiim here in the capital haven't shared anything they know with him. So if a demon lord survived here, then he might not know of it."

"True. He and I could both be completely mistaken." Javier turned his gaze toward the dead gray horizon. Atreau thought he saw faint blue plumes of mist swirling in the distance. "But before I met Alizadeh, I stood on the Shard of Heaven along with Sevanyo and Fedeles. I don't suppose you've ever been?"

"I took Hylanya around it on the river, but I've never been inside the chapel."

"It's a powerful place. I can still remember the feel that emanated up from below my feet. It was nothing like the sanctum where Zi'sai lay trapped." Javier clenched his hand around the stones he held, and again white sparks fluttered over his fingers. "The Shard of Heaven felt like nothing I had ever encountered before. Not until that night in Milmuraille . . ."

Javier's gaze narrowed but remained focused far away. Atreau wondered if he wasn't gazing upon some nightmare of his own in those luminous blue mists.

"How does it feel, then?" Atreau prompted when Javier didn't go on.

"Numb and dry, like breathing in ash. Like losing all hope . . ." Javier's expression remained distant for a moment longer. Then he glanced to Atreau. "It was nothing like Zi'sai's thick coils of purple fire."

Atreau considered that.

"I don't suppose I'm making much sense to you," Javier commented.

"You are, actually," Atreau replied. "When I was taking notes for my book, I spoke a fair while with Skellan. He constantly described different sources of magic and spells in terms of colors and sensations. Even smells and flavors. I remember he said that your magic felt bright and cold as sunlit ice. Your spells are blazing white and leave behind a smell like snow lichen."

"Lichen?" Javier frowned and then, to Atreau's amusement, he sniffed his right hand. "Could be worse, I suppose . . ."

"Could be hot eel shit," Atreau replied, recalling Skellan's description of a particularly aromatic curse. "So, if the thing lurking down in the Shard of Heaven didn't feel like a demon lord to you, then what did it feel like?"

Atreau recognized the knowing look on Javier's face.

"Refusing to tell me just leaves it to my imagination to make up the worst of possibilities, you realize," Atreau said.

"Yes, I know. I'm not reluctant because I mistrust you . . ."

"And yet you still hesitate."

"All of this is based on a mere boyhood recollection. It may be entirely wrong." Javier sighed. "So, I don't wish my theory to pass as a fact. Particularly not if you uncover anything that indicates that I'm wrong—"

"I promise to doubt your perfection," Atreau replied. "Now please enlighten me."

"When Alizadeh belonged to the Waarihivu, he possessed a spell called the Black Fire. It was—is—a spell created to wipe entire worlds from existence."

"And?" Atreau could feel the blood draining from his face.

"The night Skellan destroyed Zi'sai, it was the smallest shard of Black Fire that he turned against the demon lord." Javier rolled the stones between his hands. "How well do you remember what happened?"

"I've been hard-pressed to forget a single moment of it." Atreau frowned, recalling what he'd witnessed that night, amid the fires and crumbling buildings. Skellan had stood atop a tower and lifted his hands toward the huge serpent that arched over him, shining like a sun. Flames poured from the monstrous demon lord's gaping mouth, but they guttered before Skellan's outstretched hands, and then Zi'sai himself washed away into the darkness of the night sky like smoke dissipating in the wind. Skellan toppled after that and Atreau didn't see him again until much later.

But he remembered people all across the city remarking that nothing had remained of the demon lord. Not flesh or bones, not even ash. Only the ruin he'd made of the city and people's lives persisted as testament to his existence. It was as if he'd been unmade.

"That was the magic your master practiced?" Atreau asked.

"Magic he has forsworn." Javier stated it firmly, as if he expected Atreau to offer some argument. Atreau wondered how often he had to defend his master to other Bahiim.

"Just making certain of the facts," Atreau assured him.

"Yes. Sorry." Javier sighed. "Yes, it was Waarihivu sorcery, and the one other place I can recall experiencing a magic that felt similar was in the chapel on the Shard of Heaven."

Atreau stared into the dark as dozens of luminous blue mists seemed to coalesce and then dissipate. Human figures stretched and twisted up from the blackness. Atreau shifted his attention back to Javier before he could recognize the agonized faces.

"If it is the Black Fire, and the wards fail, what do we do to stop it?" Atreau asked. "Could your master destroy it? Or even Skellan?"

"I don't know if any of us could stop it. At least not before it destroyed half our world. Alizadeh is searching for answers. The few surviving Waarihivu dispersed with their secrets long ago, but some traces of their spells may linger in places like this." Javier gestured to the murky darkness behind him. "Hylanya will likely have a great deal to share with us when she arrives. But nothing is certain at this point, except that Crown Hill and the Circle of Wisteria played key roles in keeping Cadeleon safe for hundreds of years."

"In other words," Atreau said, "the dead Bahiim is desperate for good reason, and if someone doesn't take over the Circle of Wisteria soon then we're all fucked?"

"You always did have such a way with words," Javier replied. Then he drew the paper he'd held earlier from his cloak. To Atreau it appeared blank. But seeing the way Javier studied it, he had no doubt that troubling correspondence lay across its surface.

"For Fedeles?" Atreau asked.

"I'm asking so much of him . . . ," Javier murmured. Then he looked up from the page. "This is for him." He held the paper out and Atreau took it. It felt like a sheet of frost against his palm.

"Is there anything I should tell him?" Atreau asked.

"Tell him that I miss him and that all of us in the north are safe and well," Javier replied. "But don't share my theories with him—particularly not about the Black Fire."

"Why not?"

"Because he's already afraid of how much power he wields and what harm he could do. If he knew that so many lives were in his hands, I don't know that he could stand the burden," Javier said quietly. Then he added, "And I could be wrong, after all."

He wanted to be wrong, Atreau realized. For all their sakes, he was hoping to be wrong. The thought made Atreau all the more certain that he wasn't.

Atreau nodded and folded the paper away.

"This is for you to keep other spells at bay." Javier lifted the two white stones to Atreau's bare chest and they melted against his skin, leaving him shivering and the hair on his arms standing on end.

Then without warning, Javier grasped him in a crushingly tight hug, as if this was a last goodbye, forever. His frigid body chilled Atreau and a sense of hopelessness seemed to seep into his heart. Javier knew more than he'd said—and had reason to fear that this might be their final exchange.

"What is it that—"Atreau began to ask.

Javier shook his head, then placed his hand against Atreau's chest and gently pushed him back a step.

And in an instant Atreau was standing alone in a dim hallway. His lungs ached and his mouth tasted like it was full of dust. His muscles shuddered to shake free of the icy chill that had permeated him. Belatedly he realized how unusually light the hall appeared.

He turned to see Narsi peering out from the bedroom door, holding his small oil lamp. His curly hair stood in disarray. An inviting warmth seemed to radiate from the bare skin of his chest.

"I thought I heard a knock." Narsi glanced down the hall.

"So you did, but I'm afraid my caller has already come and gone."

"Was that . . . ," Narsi began, but then he appeared to change his mind. "You look half frozen, are you all right?"

Atreau opened his mouth to assure him that he was fine. This once the words didn't come. Narsi set the lamp aside and stepped nearer to him. The gentle concern in his expression was no doubt a reflection of his training as a physician; he probably possessed a very charming bedside manner. But just now Atreau didn't care if Narsi's compassion merely reflected his professional skill. He needed something—anything—to purge the cold futility that gripped him.

"Indulge me, will you?" Atreau asked.

"Of course, what can I—" Narsi went quiet as Atreau leaned into him, wrapping his arms around the warm skin of his bare back.

To Atreau's immense relief, Narsi remained quiet and returned his embrace, with a welcoming affability. He gently rubbed the chill from Atreau's skin, his long fingers tracing over Atreau's shoulders and back. Where Javier's grip had filled him with despair, Narsi's touch sent thrills of heat coursing along the small of his back and down his thighs. Atreau leaned into Narsi's naked body and felt Narsi's breath catch with excitement. Atreau's pulse quickened as longing throbbed through his loins.

He'd nearly forgotten what it felt like to hold someone without weighing the strategic value of their desire. Narsi asked nothing of him and offered nothing but shared company. His caresses were affectionate and honest.

Atreau basked in the possibilities before the two of them. The bed stood only a few feet away. Couldn't they both do with a little respite from a world of growing trouble? What harm could come of filling a few hours of this desolate night with companionable pleasure?

Then the ghostly, bleeding image of Miro filled Atreau's mind. Sincerity, pleasure and affection carried their own dangers, he knew that—and shouldn't have let himself forget for even a moment. He released Narsi at once and quickly walked past him back into the bedroom.

He was aware of Narsi's perplexed expression, but he didn't look back to him. It would be better for them both if the young physician took Atreau's abrupt withdrawal as a personal rejection. Atreau went to his washbasin and splashed tepid water in his face. As he toweled dry, he caught Narsi's gaze again. He appeared surprisingly serene, as if he'd expected to be released. Atreau couldn't decide if he was relieved or vexed that the intimacy of their embrace hadn't moved Narsi enough for him to feel irritated by its brusque ending.

Atreau pulled on his shirt and then caught up his sword belt.

"Do you truly mean to leave? In the middle of the night?" Narsi sounded almost amused. Then he offered Atreau an oddly gentle smile. "You don't have to flee. I swear that I can restrain myself even if we return to sharing a bed. Or I could take the flo—"

"I'm afraid that your wiles are not what compel me to dash away," Atreau said quickly before the lie could sound in his voice. With an effort he managed to meet Narsi's gaze. "My visitor brought news, which requires me to return to the duke's residence."

"Will anyone there even be awake at this hour?" Narsi appeared rightly skeptical.

"If you want to stay and sleep, you can." Atreau pulled on his boots. "Just lock the doors behind you when you leave in the morning. And try not to let anyone see you exit this particular building."

"I appreciate the offer, my lord, but I rather think you overestimate the allure of your aged and empty bed. And I'm already awake, I might as well ride along with you," Narsi replied. Then he swept up his own clothes.

In a matter of minutes the two of them left the building and found their horses in Spider's stables. The mounts were far less genial about being roused than Narsi had been, but soon enough they were out on the streets.

Even in the dark they rode roundabout to the Gado Bridge. Atreau watched for the flutter of violet silk or the silhouette of any masked figure following their progress. They encountered neither. On the resplendent avenues of the north side, they passed numerous mansions where perfumed lamps lit golden interiors and shadowy figures. Atreau thought he recognized a few of the figures. His eldest brother, Lliro, laughed from up on a minister's balcony.

Then the glossy black gates of Fedeles's home came into sight. Atreau slowed his horse and drew nearer to Narsi.

"If we undertake further excursions," Atreau said quietly, "we should agree now that if we're separated as we were today then we'll meet up either in the Fat Goose or my more private rooms."

"I will look forward to it," Narsi replied with a rather dashing smile.

The guards at the gates provided them with a lamp to light their way and the two of them continued on together. Narsi yawned. Atreau resisted the need to do the same and then failed. Narsi laughed and, for no reason he could name beyond sleep-deprived delirium, Atreau, too, suddenly found their exchange amusing.

They walked side by side from the stables to the walled garden that opened to Narsi's rooms. Atreau wondered if Narsi would invite him in, and if not, how best to request the stone of passage from his medical satchel.

Then, just ahead, a long shadow bounded from the path and up into the dark branches of a tree. The figure moved with such speed and so silently that Atreau thought it a figment of his exhausted imagination, until a moment later when he saw the body sprawled across the flagstones.

All at once he was wide awake.

"Assassin!" Atreau shouted. "Assassin on the grounds!"

As Atreau raised the alarm, Narsi raced ahead and knelt beside the supine man. With a flick of his belt knife he opened the man's shirt, revealing a deep puncture wound, still wet with hot, dark blood.

Lamps in the windows of the mansion and distant outbuildings lit up. Dozens of voices rose in a cacophony of groggy confusion and alarm. Dogs barked, geese honked and someone back near the ovens seemed to think something had caught fire. Master Narsi gave no sign of noticing any of it as he leaned in over the fallen man's chest, attempting to stanch the flood of scarlet blood.

The cloying iron odor of the open wound washed over Atreau and he knew that Narsi wasn't likely to succeed. No minor injury filled the air so distinctly; that was the pungent stench of a mortal wound, gushing up life's blood. Atreau remembered the smell hanging over the red muck of battlefields. And washing across polished floorboards of his rented room. As long as he lived he didn't think he'd ever forget that scent.

"Murder!" Atreau bellowed.

He heard guards racing toward them across the pebble path. When they arrived, Master Narsi would still be here to tell them what had happened, Atreau decided. But he was wasting time waiting for them—standing here filling his lungs with the stink of death.

He dashed across the pebble path after the shadowy figure fleeing through the trees. Delicate branches laden with dewy flowers slapped at his face. His lamp swung in his hand, throwing out flashes of brilliant illumination all around. Tree trunks flared into view. A rabbit bolted. Atreau thought he glimpsed a man's figure just ahead of him—very broad shoulders filled out a dark cloak. But an instant later the lamp revealed only the crooked branches of an apple tree. The assassin seemed to melt away in the darkness.

When Atreau burst from the cover of trunks and limbs, he found the open grounds ahead of him standing empty and calm in the moonlight. Had the bastard crossed the grounds in seconds? No, not even a mounted rider could have managed that. So either the assassin had veered off to the duchess's wing of the mansion—where a small army of guards roamed the halls—or he'd doubled back. That would put Master Narsi and his patient in the murderer's path, Atreau realized.

Could this damned day get any more tiring?

He spun around and charged back the way he'd come. His heart hammered in his chest as much from fear as exertion. If this was one of the assassins who'd murdered Ciceron, then Atreau would be in for a hell of a fight. He gripped the hilt of his sword as he bounded out from the trees.

But all he found was Master Narsi still kneeling beside a dying man. An odd mix of both disappointment and relief washed over Atreau as he realized that the assassin had eluded him. He shook his head at his own foolish impulse to give chase. *I'm acting like a fisherman who thinks he can land a whale.* He glanced again to Master Narsi, and it occurred to him that the flattering quality of the young man's company might have swayed him to emulate the heroic men whose feats filled his books. It took him aback to realize how fond he'd already grown of the other fellow.

Atreau frowned.

The young master physician seemed oddly still. Was it possible that he'd never seen a murdered man before? Was there something unspeakably disturbing that Atreau couldn't make out through the gloom? Ciceron had been decapitated, he remembered.

"Master Narsi?" Atreau started forward.

"Stay back!" Narsi called out. "There's muerate poison in his wound and I think the assassin dropped a vial of the stuff. There's a pool of it here and shards of broken glass."

Atreau stopped immediately. Lady Hylanya's recovery aside, muerate was not a poison to trifle with. It had been known to kill people who simply handled the stuff with their bare hands.

"He's not breathing. I can't feel his pulse either." Master Narsi paused as he leaned over the man's chest. "The wound in his chest is small, but quite deep and very precise. I believe his heart is bisected. I can't . . . I can't do anything for him."

"What about you?" Atreau lifted the lamp higher and carefully walked nearer. As the lamplight fell across the prone man's body and glassy-eyed stare, it became obvious that there was no hope for the guard. Still Master Narsi pressed his hands over the wound in the man's chest out of some reflex. His expression was drawn, but not wild with terror. At least not yet.

As Atreau moved the lamp lower he noted, with growing horror, that the muerate poison was already blackening and inflaming the physician's hands. His fingers looked painfully swollen and blisters bubbled up across the backs of his hands.

"I've definitely gotten a dose through my skin, but it's the cut on my right hand that's the real problem," Master Narsi said in the slow, careful manner of a man intent upon maintaining a calm air. "I'm . . . I'm experiencing some difficulty moving. I may not remain conscious much longer. It . . . it's important that I not be declared dead too quickly. I'm guessing—hoping—that I haven't absorbed a fatal dose. I'm relatively large and in good health, so there's a strong chance that I'll regain consciousness within . . . two days. My hands and this man's body need to be rinsed with bonechalk water before anyone handles . . ."

Narsi's eyes rolled and he swayed, but then he took in a sharp breath and locked his gaze on to Atreau.

"Make sure you and anyone else who comes near wears oiled gloves . . . watch for the glass shards . . . and, Atreau, don't forget your . . . stone of . . ."

He sat back, then collapsed onto his side.

An instant later two parties of household guards rushed up. Atreau could hardly tear his gaze from Narsi's still figure to look at any of them. He'd just met the young man; and he'd truly enjoyed his company. It seemed horrific that he would die now.

"What's happened?" One of the guards asked, while the other just stared at the bodies lying on either side of Atreau.

"An assassin has entered the duke's house. We interrupted him only moments ago, but he already killed one man."

Atreau couldn't allow himself to think about Master Narsi. He forced his attention to the guards, scanning all of them quickly for any sign that one of their number had been in a scuffle before this. No, it didn't appear that the assassin hid among them. Atreau ordered the majority of the guards to begin searching the grounds for the assassin immediately. He sent the remaining two to fetch Fedeles.

"And send someone to me with oiled gloves!" Atreau shouted.

A better man than himself would have crouched down beside Master Narsi and felt along his throat for a pulse. *Most likely that better man would also get himself poisoned for his efforts.* Even with that thought, Atreau stepped closer and held out the lantern. Master Narsi's chest rose slightly and then fell. He still drew breath. But for how much longer? While the muerate remained on his hands he would be taking in more poison.

Master Narsi had mentioned chalk water, hadn't he?

Atreau noticed the physician's satchel laying near his right foot. He snatched it up and rifled through the contents—Hylanya's necklace and the collection of gold coins were useless to him right now. Just as he found a jar of powdered bonechalk a large group of maids arrived— several wearing only their nightshirts. Atreau gripped the bottle of bonechalk and snapped the medical satchel shut.

Querra, the woman in charge of the kitchen gardens, and a group of strapping groundsmen charged up and nearly trampled the maids surrounding Atreau.

"Don't touch either of them. They've been poisoned with muerate," Atreau warned them all.

"That's Dommian," Querra commented as she took in the dead guard's face. Atreau vaguely recalled hearing the man's name previously, but he couldn't recollect where exactly.

"Oh no! Not young Master Narsi as well!" The expression of sorrow in Querra's face made Atreau think that he wasn't the only one who'd taken an immediate liking to Master Narsi. "Oh, but the boy only just arrived."

"He's not dead," Atreau assured her. She dropped down beside Master Narsi's head and whispered something in Haldiim.

"Where are the guards?" a ruddy gardener asked. His gaze darted across the swaying shadows cast by the surrounding trees. Many of the maids appeared anxious as well.

"They're already hunting for the assassin." Atreau returned his attention to Querra and Master Narsi. "We need water to wash away the poison . . . and oiled gloves."

Querra nodded and dispatched several groundsmen. Two maids raced away with them to wake the rest of the household and further the search for the assassin.

Querra shoved her tangled silver hair back from her face. "Lift the lantern a bit higher and to the right, will you, Atreau?"

Given something to do, Atreau obeyed immediately.

"He—Master Narsi—said that he and the guard should both be washed with bonechalk water." Atreau held out the medical jar.

"Well, young Master Narsi certainly kept his wits about him, didn't he?" Querra nodded and took the jar. Despite her easy words, her expression turned mournful as she glanced to Narsi's hands. The swollen flesh looked almost charred and blood seeped up from the pores of his skin. Atreau had seen far worse injuries, but still he felt horrified. A physician's hands were his tools. He shifted his gaze to Master Narsi's face. How tranquil and calm he looked.

"A shrewd fellow wouldn't have endangered himself for the sake of a mere guard, but that shows you the quality of the man. Father Timoteo is right about him." Querra spoke softly, then she craned her head back to call to the remaining maids. "We'll need to make the master physician's room ready for him. And we'll need waxed cloth to carry Dommian's body away from here."

Atreau heard her and noted the maids rushing away, but his attention remained on Master Narsi's slowly rising and falling chest. His own breathing felt tight, as if the guilt gripping him was an ever-tightening band of iron. If he hadn't drawn Narsi into his plans then the young physician would never have been in this place at this hour. If he'd not brought Narsi . . .

Then no one would have woken Hylanya and Yago would have seized her. Inissa and Atreau would both have been jailed and Cadeleon would be at war with Labara in less than a week.

Even filled with regret, Atreau knew he'd made the correct decision in choosing Narsi—even if this was the cost. He had sacrificed other agents to achieve far less; he despised himself for that, but it was true.

Narsi had accomplished so much in just one day that Atreau had felt a flutter of brash confidence and optimism return to him for the first time in years. For a few hours it had seemed almost as if he'd returned to that long-ago boyhood when he'd believed that he and his friends could overthrow the cruelty and corruption of the entire world.

Now he might lose Master Narsi when they were just beginning . . .

The groundsmen returned with troughs of water and Atreau focused himself on the need to treat Narsi's hands. Querra took a pair of oiled gloves for herself and handed another pair to Atreau.

"Strip him while I mix the water," Querra said, and Atreau set to work at once. Fortunately a lifetime of undressing both drunks and injured men granted him an expertise in doing away with clothing in seconds. He didn't think that Narsi had contacted the muerate anywhere but his hands. But he wouldn't chance being wrong. And to Atreau's eye he possessed a handsome enough figure that the guards, maids and groundsman who glimpsed it should count themselves lucky.

Years earlier Atreau imagined he would've indulged in a lingering perusal of the physician's sleek muscles and comely endowment. But now his heart hammered with fear for the man's life as he almost frantically searched every inch of Narsi's body for a trace of burning black muerate poison. For just an instant he thought a droplet of poison had eaten through Narsi's thin trousers to his thigh, but relief swept through him as he realized that he held his lamp up over a small bluish birthmark. Vaguely, he recalled glimpsing it earlier in the evening.

"The poison's only on his hands," Atreau pronounced.

Querra measured out the bonechalk, poured some into one wooden trough, and then dashed a second dose into the other. A cloudy blue froth bubbled up as she stirred the water with her arms. Atreau claimed the first trough, plunging Narsi's arms into the cold water. Narsi's head fell back against Atreau's shoulder and Atreau felt the rise and fall of his slow breathing against his chest.

As he moved Narsi's arms through the water, involuntary shudders of pain shook through Narsi's hands. For an instant his eyes opened, and he attempted to jerk free of Atreau's grip. Atreau held him in the water. A moment later he slumped back against Atreau. Blood and black fluid foamed up to the surface of the trough. Atreau pushed it away from Narsi's exposed arms with his gloved hands.

Two groundsmen followed Querra's directions and dumped the second trough of treated water over the dead guard's bloody, blackened chest. Querra moved to Master Narsi's side and joined Atreau, skimming the bloody foam off the water, causing a young gardener to yelp and jump back.

"The muerate is dissipated. This stuff's no worse for you than frog-spawn," Querra snapped. "We need to clear it away so we can see our master physician's hands." She took up the lamp Atreau had set aside and peered into the water. Atreau noted that several of the gardeners and maids looked too.

In the yellow glow of the surrounding lamps the water took on a green tinge. Beneath that Master Narsi's hands appeared swollen stiff and almost blue. Jet-black muerate stains discolored his nails and stretched up his fingers in long, inflamed streaks.

"No new blisters. That's good. The poison's not spreading." Querra sighed and then offered Atreau a brief smile. "We got to him in time, I think."

"Thank you for your help," Atreau murmured.

"If he lives it will be your doing much more than mine," Querra responded. "Though we won't know for days yet—"

The rest of her words were cut short by a wail of horror.

Atreau and Querra both turned to see the gaunt figure of Holy Father Timoteo looming from the darkness, his white hair looking wild. His eyes were wide and horrified. Brother Berto and a flock of prepubescent acolytes trailed him. One of the acolytes wore his black robe inside out; another had donned only long underpants. Brother Berto was dressed in his nightshirt and stocking feet.

"Narsi?" Timoteo stared at the master physician's slumped form. "Oh Lord, no! Narsi!" He raced ahead with alarming speed. Querra scrambled aside as Timoteo crashed down to his knees. He reached out and pulled Narsi's wet body from Atreau's arms. Narsi's head flopped limply against the Holy Father as he cradled Narsi to his chest.

"Oh Narsi, my child! Oh, God in Heaven! Narsi, speak to me!" Timoteo's voice shook and tears gleamed in his dark eyes. When Narsi gave no response, Timoteo bowed his head to Narsi's hair and wept.

Querra attempted to assure the Holy Father that Narsi might still recover, but he hardly seemed to hear her. Atreau straightened to his feet, unable to bear the sight of such obvious grief.

Timoteo's open display disturbed him, rousing shame and guilt, as well as a strange sort of envy.

Even if they hadn't resembled each other so strongly, this display made it abundantly clear to Atreau that Narsi was Timoteo's child, and dearly beloved. Certainly more cherished than Atreau had ever been. Atreau's own father had never shed a tear on any of his children's accounts. Nor could Atreau claim that he heaped his only surviving offspring with any affection. At least he knew that both Fedeles and Oasia adored the boy. The best Atreau could do for him was to keep away lest anyone note a passing physical resemblance.

Atreau edged back from where the Holy Father knelt weeping and rocking his son in his arms. His boot knocked into Narsi's medical satchel and he picked it up.

"What on earth have you done to Narsi?" Brother Berto stormed up to Atreau. The young acolytes followed behind like goslings trailing a squawking mother goose.

"Atreau saved his life, most likely," Querra stated. "But you'll have to offer him your heartfelt thanks later, Brother Berto. Right now we need to carry the master physician to his rooms and get him covered up before he catches a chill."

Berto looked between Atreau and Querra in confusion for just a moment, but then his attention narrowed in upon Father Timoteo. He went to the older man, urging him to let the groundsmen take Narsi's body to his rooms. Timoteo hardly seemed to hear him at first, but at last he wiped the tears from his face and looked around himself as if the rest of them had just materialized from the shadows.

And thinking of shadows, Atreau glanced over his shoulder. What was taking Fedeles so long to get here? Just as he wondered as much, he noticed the flickering lamplights and the silhouettes of a large party hurrying from the main house. He peered into the crowd of armed guards, handmaids and half-dressed ladies-in-waiting and recognized several of the women, Delfia Plunado among them. However, he couldn't locate Fedeles anywhere in the crowd. Instead it was the duchess, the loathed Oasia, who met his gaze as the group drew near.

She glanced over the guard's corpse as impassively as if he were a heap of fallen leaves. However a sliver of a crease lined her brow when she noted two brawny gardeners lifting Master Narsi from Father Timoteo's arms.

"What has happened here? Is the physician dead?" Oasia inquired. She stared a little past Atreau, as if she could not quite bring herself to look on him.

"No. At least not yet," Atreau replied. "Where is Fedeles?"

Oasia's dark eyes narrowed.

"Lord Quemanor," she stated in plain rebuke, "has finally fallen asleep after I made a draught for him. He's already endured too much strain this day and I will not have him distressed any further."

"I think that an assassin roaming the grounds of his house merits disturbing him," Atreau retorted. Even as he spoke he recognized that Fedeles wouldn't be in any condition to receive Javier's missive. Still, he wasn't about to allow Oasia to overrule him on the matter of a murder in Fedeles's house. "The mansion must be searched and each room—"

"My wing of the mansion is perfectly safe. We've just come from there and everyone is just where they should be—including the duke. I've dispatched the guards to search farther out across the grounds."

Atreau opened his mouth to argue the foolishness of assuming that anywhere in the mansion was safe before every room was searched, but then stopped himself. Oasia and he often clashed, and not just because their very public antipathy made Sparanzo's true paternity seem unthinkable. Genuine injury fueled their animosity. Atreau recognized that he had sparked the conflict. Six years ago, he'd instigated a playful affair with her first husband—the fair but far-too-serious Miro Reollos. In response Oasia had drugged and seduced Atreau, and that in turn had led Miro to attack him in a jealous rage. Some days Atreau almost wished that he'd not been the one to survive that fight. In the end Miro had died, leaving Oasia a very wealthy widow.

Of course, Fedeles readily offered up excuses for Oasia's actions, but none of them could undo Miro's death—or lessen Atreau's guilt. He couldn't forgive Oasia any more than he could forgive himself.

They were both monsters.

Even so, he knew that the petty pleasure of contradicting him wouldn't be enough to inspire Oasia to risk her son's safety. She wouldn't have sent guards away unless she knew absolutely that her wing of the mansion was perfectly safe.

But how could she be so certain? Unless . . .

Atreau considered how completely composed she not only sounded but appeared. The maids and groundsmen surrounding them looked unkempt and hastily dressed—their hair a mess, buttons misaligned and their expressions both confused and frightened. Atreau's own sleeves dripped with water and cold sweat now clung to his skin.

Oasia's resplendent clothes betrayed no signs of frantic assembly. The snowy white sleeves laced to her bodice peeked out perfectly from the stylish slashes that decorated the green silk of her gown. Her braids and curls nestled neatly among gold and emerald combs. Only a single glossy curl hung loose.

Nor had she betrayed any alarm when she'd seen the dead guard. In fact it was only Master Narsi's fallen form that seemed to have given her the slightest pause. Atreau frowned at her with a growing certainty that she'd expected to learn of the guard's death. What he didn't know was whether she simply had an informant who'd made her aware of someone else's plot—and she'd done nothing to stop it—or had she arranged the assassination herself? She certainly didn't fear the assassin, so quite possibly she sheltered and employed the man.

That begged the question of what threat the guard Dommian might have posed to her. Atreau wished to God that he wasn't so tired or that he could remember where he recalled the guard's name from. Had it been Spider who'd mentioned the man? He thought it might have been, but exhaustion dulled his recollection of the exact conversation. He would need to leaf through the decorative ciphers that littered his diary.

Though not tonight. His curiosity, the secret missive from Javier and the stone of passage would all have to wait until tomorrow. He hefted Master Narsi's medical satchel over his shoulder.

"It is a pity about the master physician," Oasia murmured to Delfia. "Though I suppose this is the sort of thing that befalls people who aren't scrupulous about the company they keep."

Mistress Delfia's mournful expression made Atreau think that she didn't find Narsi's demise amusing. The rest of Oasia's retinue weren't nearly so solemn. Several ladies-in-waiting laughed at Oasia's remark and more than one guard chuckled.

Outrage flushed through Atreau.

"At least he doesn't serves a mistress so callous as to besmirch his good name after he's risked his life to save another member of her household," Atreau snapped. "Can you imagine what a monstrous injustice that would be?"

Atreau didn't remain to see what if any reaction his words provoked. Instead he turned on his heel and marched after the train of acolytes hurrying to join Father Timoteo in Master Narsi's rooms. He knew that he didn't fit in among the kind and pious folk who seemed drawn to the young physician, but just now he preferred them to the company of these beautiful, heartless nobles.

CHAPTER
SEVENTEEN

Early-morning sun lit the dust motes and slivers of straw that drifted across the stable grounds, making the air seem alive with glinting forms. Ariz imagined that hidden amidst the dirt and hay, tiny spells darted like flies waging their secret wars over the destinies of the men and women who walked through them unaware. Ariz watched a little whirl of dust dance and then die at his feet.

A pair of young grooms strode past. Ariz listened intently to their conversation while maintaining the pretense of nodding off next to his horse. The grooms, like the rest of Lord Quemanor's house staff, had been shaken by the previous night's murder. One of the grooms wondered if the physician who'd discovered the body could actually have been the culprit.

"He's a half-breed Haldiim and dark as the duke's charger. I seen him."

To his credit, the second groom regarded his companion with a skeptical expression.

"By that reasoning, the duke's horse is as likely to have done the deed, ain't he? Master Narsi didn't even know the man. And Querra says that he poisoned himself trying to save the fellow. Got muerate on his bare hands and all. That's courage, that is . . ."

The groom's voices distorted and faded as they continued along their way to the indoor arena. Ariz didn't strain to hear their further speculation about how the retainer got himself murdered. It had been common knowledge that the man had accrued a variety of gambling debts even in the short time he'd been a member of Lord Quemanor's household. Likely he owed even more all across the city. The experienced gamblers among Lord Quemanor's staff all whispered about the Salt Island Spider, who ran a travelers' inn where dangerous men gathered, brawled and gambled away fortunes. A fellow who held out on the Spider wasn't likely to live a long life.

While it reassured Ariz that most people wanted to place the blame far from the members of Lord Quemanor's household, it vexed him that the murder had come to light at all. If only Atreau and Master Narsi had tarried even a few moments longer. Then Ariz and Delfia would've had the body out of sight. By this hour, the corpse should have been drifting out to sea on the same tide that carried so many merchant ships from the river to open water. Days, perhaps even weeks, would have passed before anyone in the Fueres household learned of the man's absence. But as matters now stood, if Hierro didn't already know that he'd lost an assassin, the news would filter to him by the day's end.

Ariz doubted that Hierro would blame some Salt Island moneylender. The Spider was famous for employing poison, but not muerate, whereas Delfia had learned to distill and handle muerate on the Fueres estate. Ariz had no way of knowing if or when Hierro might connect that fact to the death of his man, but he feared it could occur all too soon.

Pondering how Hierro might respond filled Ariz with an anxiety that had kept him from sleep most of the night and lent a nervous quality to his normal stillness.

His dappled stallion snorted at him, as if catching a little of his uneasiness. Then Ariz noticed the glossy mare prancing in the nearest paddock and realized that he'd mistaken the cause of Moteado's flared nostrils and tense posture.

Ariz squinted at the chestnut mare as she flicked her tail and then pranced back toward another paddock where one of Lord Quemanor's young stallions stood.

"She's just teasing you, old man." Ariz stroked the stallion's jaw and let the horse steal a sweet yellow bird-apple from his hand. He provided a second after Moteado attempted to lip his way into the pocket of Ariz's hazel-brown coat. The stallion was growing bored with waiting.

As the sun climbed a little higher, Ariz wondered why he'd bothered to come here. Lord Quemanor's offer to ride with him out to Crown Hill had probably been long forgotten in the wake of not one but two murders. Likely Lord Quemanor would not ride at all today but instead busy himself having the death in his household investigated. The chance that he even recollected his offhanded offer struck Ariz as slight. Certainly not something he'd put money on.

He should've just slept in.

But since he was already up and had put Moteado through the annoyance of bit, bridle and girth, he supposed he ought to take himself and his horse out to ride. If he truly wished, he could find his way to the ruins on Crown Hill alone. Though that would put him temptingly near count Zacarrio Odalis's property. His brand smoldered to life as the thought crossed Ariz's mind.

Would a third death, one removed from any relation to Lord Quemanor, move suspicion from the household? Or would it simply inspire a panic? Ariz supposed that would depend upon how natural the count's demise could be arranged to appear. The burning sensation fluttered across his chest, but it had not been long enough for it to grow too agonizing for Ariz to resist. Count Odalis could keep his life this morning. Ariz would ride the grounds of Lord Quemanor's property simply for the pleasure of it.

He swung into his saddle.

"Master Ariz!"

Lord Quemanor's voice stilled him before he could rein Moteado ahead. Ariz turned his stallion back to the stables to see Lord Quemanor dressed in riding clothes and leading a tall black warhorse out into the morning light.

"My lord." Ariz bowed over the low pommel of his saddle. "I had not thought that you would ride today."

"I need to get out." Lord Quemanor sprang easily into his saddle despite his mount's height. "And I've been looking forward to showing you the Crown Hill ruins. So few people indulge me in journeying out to the old wreck."

"Then it would be my pleasure." Ariz glanced past Lord Quemanor and frowned when he caught sight of no retainers or courtiers. "But certainly after . . . you aren't going to ride unescorted?"

"Of course not." Lord Quemanor offered him a trusting smile. "I have you with me, Master Ariz."

The idea of time alone with Fedeles Quemanor filled Ariz with pleasure, but Lord Quemanor's habit of riding alone or with only a single companion at his side was dangerous. Ariz feared that very soon it might prove the death of him.

"It would be wiser—"

"Come now, Master Ariz." Lord Quemanor nudged his mount into a canter and called back to Ariz. "If you can catch me before the red gates, then I will turn back and accept any escort of your choosing. If not, we will ride on unaccompanied."

At once Ariz lit after him. They tore across the carefully maintained lawns and through a bed of moss roses. Ariz closed the gap between them. Lord Quemanor glanced back at him, looking flushed as the wind tossed his dark hair about his face. He grinned at Ariz and then in an instant Lord Quemanor's mount bounded ahead, taking the ground with magnificent strides. The warhorse carried Lord Quemanor over a low yew hedge that Ariz had to circle around.

By the time the ivy-entwined arch of the red gate loomed ahead of them, Lord Quemanor rode a good furlong ahead of Ariz. He halted just outside the enamel red gate and then turned back to beam at Ariz with a smile so self-satisfied and boyish that it made Ariz think of Sparanzo. Ariz didn't bother to tax Moteado in pursuit of a lost race. He allowed the stallion to set his own pace, though pride kept the horse from slowing to an amble. Instead he cantered through the gate and turned once just to display himself.

Outside the gate the grounds grew wilder. Grass and wildflowers cascaded down the rolling hills to edge the worn dirt path. Moteado stole a few mouthfuls of bright yellow broom blossoms from a rangy shrub.

"What is he called?" Lord Quemanor favored Ariz's stallion with an affectionate gaze, then nudged his own mount forward.

"Moteado." Ariz rode alongside Lord Quemanor, studying the ground ahead of them.

The dirt path led them beneath fluttering shadows cast by a stand of large old willow trees. Out of habit Ariz searched the branches for the figure of some spy or assassin. Finding no one, he allowed himself to relax slightly.

"He looks very at ease with you," Lord Quemanor commented.

"He's been mine since he was two." Ariz allowed himself a little pride in remembering that he'd picked Moteado from a half-wild herd brought to the fair by Irabiim traders. At the time not even Ariz's uncle had thought that the shy horse would make much of a mount. But Moteado had carried Ariz through tournaments and hunts alike. Though recently he'd only carried Ariz quietly and discreetly to knife shops, fighting halls and dark alleys. "He's nineteen this year."

"It's good to ride with an old friend," Lord Quemanor said. He patted his own mount with an amused expression. "Believe it or not, Firaj here is in his thirties."

Ariz had heard rumors about Lord Quemanor's unnaturally long-lived warhorse, but he'd not put too much merit in them. People liked to gossip and details often became exaggerated in the retelling of a story. He'd assumed that the glossy horse's age had been doubled a few times for dramatic affect.

But to hear directly from Lord Quemanor that Firaj was over thirty astounded Ariz. Firaj ran and leapt like he was hardly eight years old. His eyes seemed bright and clear, his entire body toned. Now Ariz wondered if the warhorse hadn't benefited immensely from near constant contact with Lord Quemanor's powerful shadow.

"He's a beautiful creature," Ariz commented, then, noting Lord Quemanor's frown, asked, "You think not?"

"He's such a dashing scoundrel that he's charmed half my grooms into sneaking him extra apples." Lord Quemanor's expression turned a rueful. "I was thinking of something else for a moment. I hadn't realized it showed plainly on my face."

Ariz made no comment; he certainly wasn't going to admit to watching Lord Quemanor so closely that he recognized even the slightest change of expression. Though in truth Lord Quemanor rarely seemed to mask his feelings. He was a refreshingly sincere man.

"I was thinking of Atreau." Lord Quemanor's gaze followed the sway of wind-tossed willow branches, then he looked to Ariz. "You don't keep company with any of his circle, do you?"

If ever there was an unlikely association, that was one. Atreau cultivated exceptional company: a scandalous prince, a cursed duke, lauded playwrights, stunning courtesans and infamous duelists. Whereas Ariz maintained as dull and unremarkable of a presence as he could, going so far as to stain his auburn hair with walnut dye. Though Ariz supposed that an acquaintanceship might not have seemed so very implausible had his family not been stripped of their nobility. The fourth son of a baron wasn't so different from the second son of a count's cousin. Both of them minor aristocrats, circling the perimeter of the brilliantly wealthy and powerful like moths courting candle flames.

But where Atreau had charmed himself—and by extension his dissolute father and ambitious brothers—into the company of the crown, Ariz had fallen from noble dignity to the rank of a mere servant. Not even Atreau would have bothered to recall his acquaintance, had they ever had any.

"No, my lord," Ariz replied. "I've had the pleasure of hearing Lord Vediya sing on the occasion of your last birthday, but beyond our allegiances to yourself, I do not think he and I have much in common."

"Not particularly interested in literature?" Lord Quemanor asked.

Ariz responded with a shrug.

He wasn't inclined to feel too fascinated by the kind of aggrandizement that so many famous Cadeleonian tomes indulged in. So many authors wrote far too flippantly of violent death and the ruin of families and nations.

"You've not read *any* of Atreau's books?" Lord Quemanor inquired.

"A few pages of his earliest memoir," Ariz admitted. In truth he'd read certain passages of that book so many times that his fingers had smeared and dulled the printer's ink. His awareness of masculine beauty and his recollections of lying alone in the night filled with anxious longing had seemed to Ariz to speak to a temperament like his own—if only for a few paragraphs. Ariz didn't delude himself that he and Atreau Vediya shared any deep similarity of character. Atreau seemed to admire beauty in any form and eroticized everything from comely widows to heavily hung fruit trees. Still, those few sentences were precious to Ariz.

Though he expected that for Lord Quemanor, the memoir represented something else entirely. Between lush and lurid descriptions of orgies and reckless camaraderie, Atreau merely hinted at Genimo Plunado's betrayal of his friends as well as the horrific effects of Lord Quemanor's descent into madness and possession. He'd written it all beautifully, but it had still made Ariz sick to think of. Countless tragedies had arisen during the days that Atreau recounted as largely sensual and carefree.

"And?" Lord Quemanor held his gaze.

Ariz didn't wish to bring back bad memories for Lord Quemanor, or indeed for himself.

"I think that you boys at the Sagrada Academy ate much better than we did at Yillar. There were hardly any mentions of cabbage stews."

Lord Quemanor laughed.

"We downed plenty of the wretched stuff, but I suspect Atreau hates to recount it since it always made him fart like a pig."

Ariz felt the corners of his mouth tug up slightly at the thought of the famously seductive libertine blasting out volleys of gas in some lovely's bedroom. A dry rasp of a laugh escaped his throat.

Then, he noted Lord Quemanor studying him with that expression of bright-eyed curiosity. For a foolish and vain moment Ariz wished that he'd dressed himself in a more flattering doublet than this brown, padded sack that he habitually wore. He looked quickly away from Lord Quemanor to take in the clearing ahead of them. The dirt path seemed to end there amid sprays of yarrow, wild oat and mounds of flowering sage. A hawk took flight from the wooded hill beyond the meadow and Ariz noticed a wild hare bound suddenly for the cover of the willow trees.

"I called on Father Timoteo in the new physician's rooms earlier this morning and came upon him discussing Atreau with Brother Berto. It seems the holy brother much prefers your company."

"Brother Berto's preference probably stems more from his affection for my sister than time spent in my company," Ariz replied. He'd heard the holy brother refer to him, rightly, as *dull as dirt*. "And I think he feels a little jealous of Lord Vediya's ability to engage Delfia in lively conversation."

"Likely you are correct." Lord Quemanor shook his head in a rueful manner. "A surprising number of men seem to regard Atreau as their romantic rival, even when he's done little more than exchange a few words or won a laugh from a woman."

"So charming a man as Lord Vediya makes most of us far too aware of our deficiencies."

"Certainly not you, Master Ariz." Lord Quemanor glanced at him and his expression was flatteringly warm. Though Ariz found the idea of himself as a challenger to Atreau's charisma almost hilarious. If he could have burst into laughter he would have. Lord Quemanor might as well have suggested that a sack of laundry could challenge Atreau's handsome form and delightful conversation.

"I have it on good authority that I am a rather dull fellow. Not much different in bearing than a sack of potatoes." Ariz took no offense at such comments; after all, he cultivated his lackluster air.

But to his surprise Lord Quemanor's cheeks colored with offense. "If you believe such a thing, Master Ariz, then you have deeply undervalued the pleasure of your company. You possess immense grace and rare composure. Though I think perhaps you are burdened by too much humility."

Ariz felt as though his entire body ignited with the flush those appreciative words inspired, but he accepted the response with a shrug. To argue would have only seemed an awkward attempt to fish for further compliments.

They rode side by side into the clearing and Lord Quemanor lifted his head into the sun to watch the hawk circling high above them. Ariz studied the ground for signs of a trail. Lord Quemanor rode this way only yesterday and his tracks remained scattered between the wildflowers.

To the east he noted the wooden fencing that enclosed the pasture where many of Lord Quemanor's mares and foals grazed alongside aged geldings. Most of the animals had been purchased from dissatisfied owners or even snatched up in front of slaughterhouse doors. Few, if any of them, would ever carry a rider. Still, Lord Quemanor was said to have spent a fortune on the shelter that protected this herd of scarred, overworked horses.

Lord Quemanor smiled at several of the animals as they grazed.

A few yards away a low stone wall marked the boundary of Count Odalis's land. A smoldering burn crawled through Ariz's chest. He was so very close.

Ariz reined Moteado into the long shadow cast by Lord Quemanor and his mount. He felt a cool relief fall over him. Ariz lifted his gaze from Lord Quemanor's shadow and a golden afterimage shone briefly before his eyes. He turned his attention to the man himself. This close and in bright sun he noticed that Lord Quemanor hadn't shaved quite as meticulously as he normally would have, and a cast of blue weariness hung beneath his eyes. Likely he'd not slept since the alarm had been raised last night.

"How is your arm?" Lord Quemanor asked.

"It's much better." Ariz held up his hand, as if it proved that he'd recovered completely. "Master Narsi certainly knows his business."

"Hmm." Lord Quemanor's expression clouded. "You've heard he was poisoned during last night's murder?"

"The grooms gossiped of little else." Ariz knew he couldn't deny knowledge, though he'd rather not have discussed the subject. Dommian's death had been swift and had freed him from Hierro's cruelty, but Ariz hated the thought that the young physician's compassion now left him to die slowly.

"My wife tells me that Dommian, the slain guard, had only recently arrived as a gift from her brother, Hierro. You served in Hierro's household yourself for some time, didn't you?"

"Yes, young Lord Fueres was my upperclassman at the Yillar Academy, but after . . ." Ariz decided not to mention the loss of his rank and simply went on. "He employed me briefly as a fencing partner. I joined your wife's household soon after that—to be nearer my sister. I don't think that I met the dead man while I served in Lord Fueres's household. I'm not certain that any of us here knew him very well."

"There's speculation that he crossed one moneylender too many," Lord Quemanor said.

"The Salt Island Spider is what I've heard," Ariz agreed.

Lord Quemanor did not look particularly convinced.

"You think otherwise?" Ariz asked.

"I do." Lord Quemanor shifted in his saddle and Ariz felt his gaze moving over him like a breeze. It wasn't a searing spell that Hierro might have hurled against him, but there was definitely more power in Lord Quemanor's study of him than the mere effect of dark eyes and arched brows. Untrained, and likely unaware of his actions, he pulled at Ariz's thoughts as he searched his face.

Ariz flexed his right hand and sharp pangs sang out as his raw flesh pulled at his stitches. It seemed the smallest discomfort to Ariz, but Lord Quemanor's brow knit with concern and his attention dropped to Ariz's arm.

"Are you certain that it doesn't hurt you too badly?"

"The arm?" Ariz shrugged, wishing he could flash a confident grin. "Not at all. A twinge once or twice, but certainly nothing so great that I would miss my chance to ride with you."

Lord Quemanor's expression brightened. Ariz had to look away from him to keep his happiness at seeing Lord Quemanor's smile from showing in his hapless stare. Fedeles was a well-made man, though he was not as handsome or polished as Hierro. But there was something about his smile that lent him an overwhelming radiance. Ariz didn't know if the transformation was only in his perception or if the stunning effect of Lord Quemanor's happiness was another unconscious work of magic. But even the horses seemed to move at livelier gaits, and above them the hawk soared and dived as if delighted in play.

"Let us tarry no longer, Crown Hill awaits," Lord Quemanor decided. At once his warhorse charged ahead. Ariz followed as Lord Quemanor led him up through stands of gnarled oaks and ancient-looking yews, and then across a weather-worn stone bridge and into a narrow ravine that the trees had previously hidden from view. Sunlight filtered through the branches overhead and rivulets of water trickled down the rocky walls that rose on either side of them.

Though Ariz knew they hadn't left Lord Quemanor's estate, much less Cieloalta, he felt transported to an older wilderness, where the holy church had not yet stamped out all the strange creatures of the mythic ages. The air smelled rich and the stream twisting its way through the ravine seemed to murmur and echo with soft voices.

Frogs, perhaps, Ariz told himself. Or maybe birds.

Then Lord Quemanor slowed and pointed to two stones jutting up from the rocky walls. Generations of moss and lichen coated their blue-gray surfaces, but Ariz could still make out the forms of two immense torsos, as well as the outstretched fragments of raised arms. The giant horned head of one of the statues lay a few feet away, half sunken into the earth and mulch. Shards of the other littered the ground.

The sight reminded Ariz of the interior of the Shard of Heaven and a shudder wriggled down his spine.

"They're supposed to have been the giants who guarded the way up the hill," Lord Quemanor commented. "The Savior was said to have placed them here as guards. They've remained even after the first royal bishops raised a chapel on the ruins of the heathen temple standing there."

"What a strange world it must have been then." Ariz tried to imagine these hulking giants walking through the forest, dwarfing the trees.

"It is strange still in some places."

"You mean Count Radulf's lands?" Ariz recalled that Lord Quemanor had sailed there five years ago. He'd been one of the first Cadeleonian noblemen to recognize the count's claim to his lands and title despite his heathen ways and savage upbringing.

"You wouldn't likely believe me, if I even attempted to tell you all that I saw there." Lord Quemanor shook his head. "Trolls as big as these stone fellows wander the woodlands, and nearly every soul practices some kind of witchcraft. It's like walking into a storybook."

"One where the houses are made of butter and candy, or the sort where one wrong step off the righteous path lands you in a monster's larder?" Ariz asked.

"A little of both," Lord Quemanor replied. "It was interesting to visit Radulf County—particularly in the safety of the count's company. The air, earth and water seemed alive and endlessly whispering. It was beautiful and vibrant, but after a time the ceaseless strangeness of the Radulf lands made returning home feel like a relief."

"Was the count himself as . . . odd as folk say?"

"Skellan? He's not a wild animal, as the royal bishop would have you believe. Nor is he a scheming, wicked witch." Lord Quemanor paused. "But his character is quite foreign to a Cadeleonian temperament. He's neither mannerly nor subtle. Almost insultingly direct upon occasion. But that also makes him refreshingly frank, and I found his sense of humor and friendliness quite charming. Politically, he can seem naïve, even hapless. But then you witness him call flames from cobblestones or crush a cannonball with a motion of his hand. And you realize that he can be easygoing and indulgent because he commands the power of an Old God. Perhaps he is actually one of them reborn into human flesh."

"He sounds dangerous."

"He could be. There's no question of that, but he could also be the best of allies; that depends upon how we treat him and his subjects,"

Lord Quemanor admitted. "The mythic creatures of Radulf County are not monstrosities. They're living beings. They have their places in the world just like any creature. Some of them are even charming."

"Really?"

Lord Quemanor nodded.

"Once when we were out riding we encountered a weathra-steed. It shone like a star and looked incredibly fierce, but it allowed me to stroke its flank and feed it an apple before it bounded back up into the clouds. It was beautiful." Lord Quemanor smiled, but then the happiness seemed to fade from his expression. "No creatures like them survive here. Not anymore. All the people of Cadeleon are much safer because of that. I'm glad for it. But . . ."

"My lord?" Ariz asked when Lord Quemanor went quiet.

"Forgive me." Lord Quemanor pulled a quick, self-conscious smile. "I was merely pondering the wonders we traded for our security, when the Savior expelled magic from our lands."

Ariz nodded. He'd heard no end of fantastic stories concerning Count Radulf and his wild lands. But unlike many Cadeleonians, Ariz harbored no illusions that the Savior had purged their nation of all forms of magic. Ancient spells—like the brand that Ariz bore—lay hidden all around them just waiting for men like Hierro to exploit. He would have thought, though, that Lord Quemanor had personal reasons to dislike Count Radulf.

"Did it pain you to see . . ." Ariz almost stopped himself from asking the rest of the question. But there was a part of him that needed to know Lord Quemanor's answer. " . . . your friend Lord Grunito bewitched by the count?"

Everyone knew about it. How the once brave son of Cadeleon had been enthralled by sorcery and become a traitor to his homeland. Count Radulf turned Elezar Grunito into his consort. Countless broadsheets scattered across the city regularly parodied the couple. Elezar Grunito's abdication of his noble title had been conclusive proof of his utter enslavement to Count Radulf.

To Ariz's surprise, Lord Quemanor gave a snort of laughter.

"You shouldn't believe everything you read. Elezar is his own man. More so now than he ever was when he had to live under Cadeleonian holy law. He loves the count with his whole being and Skellan dotes upon him. Theirs is a love match, as shocking or unthinkable as that might seem to some."

"I didn't . . ." Ariz could hardly admit that his shock at the idea of such a pairing wasn't revulsion, but relief. "I only asked because I felt certain that you wouldn't have accepted a friend remaining enthralled by sorcery."

"Given that it happened to me?" Lord Quemanor finished. His expression softened and again Ariz felt that searching gaze upon him. "If that had been the case, then I would have done everything in my power to free Elezar. No one should ever live under a thrall—on that point I agree absolutely with Father Timoteo . . . and Skellan as well. But Elezar needs no rescuing. He's happy. Life as a Labaran warlord suits him far better than a comfortable courtly appointment ever could."

Ariz only remembered Elezar Grunito from school tournaments, but even as a youth he'd been a towering giant, possessed with terrifying strength. Imagining him as a full-grown, battle-hardened warlord was frightening. Particularly since Ariz knew how many assassins Oasia had once dispatched to kill him and Atreau Vediya. None had returned to claim their rewards.

"He would make a deadly foe." Ariz pondered how he would have killed the man, had Hierro compelled him to. Then he felt disgusted with himself. Elezar Grunito had been one of schoolmates who risked their lives to free Lord Quemanor from the thrall placed upon him.

"Certainly." Lord Quemanor inclined his head but didn't appear at all disturbed by the thought. "If he chose to lead Skellan's armies against Cadeleon, I have no doubt that we would see our cities in flames. But despite how much he's been ridiculed by our countrymen, Elezar is likely our nation's greatest ally. His presence shields Cadeleon greatly from Skellan's most dangerous idealism. He's a dear friend."

"That's fortunate," Ariz managed. The conversation was a mire, but Lord Quemanor's earlier statements rang through him. *No one should ever live under a thrall . . . I would have done everything in my power to free Elezar.*

If only Ariz could find some way to communicate his own enslavement to Lord Quemanor . . . A shock of pain withered the thought before it could even begin. The brand would kill him before he could ever get the words out.

"You know"—Lord Quemanor's voice dropped to a whisper—"there are even some men who consider Elezar's story quite romantic. Atreau told me there's a dueling house here in the capital where Elezar is held up as almost a patron saint. Perhaps you've heard of it?"

Ariz knew exactly the place. He practiced there regularly and was known as 'Corpse.' Under normal circumstances he would never have admitted any awareness of the sword house, but Lord Quemanor's curiosity and blatant hope made Ariz want to please him.

"I've heard of it," Ariz admitted.

Lord Quemanor studied him intently and Ariz found himself unable to look away.

"I have the strangest feeling, Master Ariz, that there's something you want to tell me." Lord Quemanor's expression softened further, and as he leaned forward, Ariz felt the comforting pull of Lord Quemanor's unconscious magic. "Whatever it is, you can confide in me."

Ariz parted his dry lips. A paroxysm of crushing agony hammered through his chest. He struggled to pull in breath.

"The Red Stallion," Ariz gasped.

Lord Quemanor drew back in confusion. "What?"

"The name of the dueling house, it's the Red Stallion." The pain eased and Ariz managed a deeper breath. "You'll have to improve your footwork if you want to spar there."

"I didn't mean . . ." Lord Quemanor blushed, seemingly at a loss. Then he pointed to a slab of white stone jutting from a spray of wildflowers "Look! We've arrived."

"So we have."

"That's the only remaining step from the original temple path. The rest were dug out and carried up to make the chapel." Lord Quemanor returned to playing the part of his guide. He pointed out a few other features as he led his stallion up a nearly invisible track in the east wall of the ravine and Ariz followed. In a matter of minutes they reached the summit.

Great blocks of white marble and fallen columns lay scattered across wildly overgrown flower beds and herb gardens. Crooked flagstones wound in broken trails, winding through the fallen walls that had once supported a Cadeleonian chapel. Ariz recognized the stone steps of a pulpit, and a few weathered stone pews still stood.

Oddly, the remains of the older, heathen temple appeared in far better condition—perhaps because the larger chapel had sheltered them from the brunt of winter winds. An archway and a small circular chamber from the temple appeared in near perfect condition, though the timber doors and roof that had once enclosed it were long gone.

They hitched their horses in the shade of a few saplings and left them to graze on the summer grass.

As they wandered the grounds Ariz spied numerous intricate carvings covering the temple structures as well as the flagstones that lay scattered beneath weeds and wildflowers. He recognized a number of them, from the books that Hierro had kept in their shared room at the Yillar Academy. These were incantations and spells, Ariz felt certain. It frightened him to look at any one of them too long.

But Lord Quemanor seemed drawn to them. He reached out and traced their shapes as he strolled the ruins. He walked a full circle and twice paused to replace an upended piece of stonework. Then he paused only a foot from Ariz and ran his fingers along a string of symbols that curled between the weathered reliefs of two winged mares.

"Do you think these were their names?" Lord Quemanor asked.

"Blessings granted in their names, I believe," Ariz replied.

Lord Quemanor looked to him with a questioning expression.

"Those two symbols"—Ariz pointed but took care not to touch the carved stone—"I believe they're the archaic forms of blessings. Bishop Seferino wrote about them. He thought that the symbols came down to us from the days when the Old Gods were dying and our Holy Cadeleonian Church was just arising. So you see them in both heathen ruins and very old chapels."

"Really?" Lord Quemanor gazed at the carved script and Ariz wondered if it didn't speak to him in some deeper way. Did his heartbeat quicken in the proximity of so many dormant spells? Did the magic flowing in his blood respond in some way to all this potential for it to take form?

Ariz dropped his gaze briefly to Lord Quemanor's shadow, noting how it curled into the recesses of the carvings. It seemed darker and stronger here, so that Ariz could almost feel the solidity of where it brushed over his ankle.

"You are a student of languages as well as a sword master?" Though Lord Quemanor's expression remained friendly, a tension played through his voice. Genimo had studied languages; he'd been fluent in the ancient tongue in which these spells were written. Ariz had no wish to be equated with his cousin.

"I'm afraid that trivia is the full extent of my knowledge," Ariz replied quickly. "I just happened upon it back in school when I was sifting through old classics looking for anything new to say about Bishop Seferino."

"Ah. And what did you end up writing, do you recall?" Lord Quemanor appeared to relax a little.

"Sadly, what I told you was nearly the full extent of my paper," Ariz admitted. "I think I tried to pad it out by throwing in a few instances of 'by the will of Our Holy Savior' and 'Lord bless us,' but even so I don't think I ever managed to turn out an essay longer than a single sheet of paper."

Lord Quemanor laughed but then seemed to think he shouldn't have, because he cast Ariz an apologetic look.

"I could hardly put my own name down to paper, so I don't know what I think I'm laughing at, forgive me."

"No need," Ariz replied. "I've no illusions as to my scholarly prowess. Honestly, I'd be happier riding, or dancing or fencing, than receiving any number of accolades for puttering about in a musty library."

"There's the truth," Lord Quemanor agreed, but his gaze lingered on Ariz's face. "You don't smile readily, do you, Master Ariz?"

Ariz shrugged, but out of reflex he bowed his head, hiding his dead, plain face.

"It isn't that I'm unhappy, my lord. It's just that my feelings don't easily show."

"I envy you. Mine betray me all too readily," Lord Quemanor admitted. "Any passing stranger can know exactly what I'm thinking. Even Sparanzo can see through my bluffs when we play cards."

"Well, he is a particularly canny boy." Ariz hoped that his affection conveyed through his tone if not in his expression.

"Indeed he is." Lord Quemanor's fingers absently played over the carved blessings. "He's utterly smitten with you, did you know?"

"He seems to enjoy his classes," Ariz replied.

"He does nothing but talk about you for most of his dinner. Did I know that Master Ariz can walk on his hands? Did I know that Master Ariz can juggle five knives at once and never drop a single one? Was I aware that Master Ariz can run up a wall and flip over to land back on his feet?" Lord Quemanor gave Ariz a slight smile. "He has suggested—in all seriousness—that I purchase a carnival tent where he can sell tickets and you can amaze onlookers and the two of you will make me a fortune."

Ariz snorted at the thought of making a living, much less a fortune, in such a manner.

For some reason Lord Quemanor looked incredibly pleased with himself. He turned away but then beckoned Ariz to follow him to one of the pews. Lord Quemanor sat and Ariz joined him, though he didn't dare sit as near as he would have liked.

"Here is the view that I promised you," Lord Quemanor said.

Ariz took in the rolling hills below them, where horses ran free. They made a lovely sight. But looking farther, Ariz realized that he could see all the way across the expanses of noble households to pick out the gold spire of the ancient chapel perched atop the Shard of Heaven.

"If you look far out across the river"—Lord Quemanor pointed to a distant green circle in the midst of all the cluttered yellow and blue architecture in the southwestern Theater District of the city—"that is a Haldiim sacred grove called the Circle of Wisteria. I think sometimes that it's a mirror to the green circle of this place. Though I suppose when they were both founded ages ago, nearly all the land was open, wild and green."

Ariz nodded. Three points of power so perfectly aligned wasn't likely an accident, but what ancient purpose it might have served he couldn't have said. Though he remembered how vexed Hierro had been by the thought of Lord Quemanor controlling this old ruin.

"I'm glad that a few wild places have survived," Lord Quemanor said. "It's pretty up here. And blessedly quiet."

When Ariz looked he realized that Lord Quemanor gazed up at the blue sky and billowing white clouds.

"What do you see?" Lord Quemanor asked.

Ariz peered intently into the sky, trying to pick out the flash of a dove's wing or the shreds of a torn banner. But all he could make out were the masses of clouds.

"I see a ship." Lord Quemanor raised his hand and traced the curve of a cloud. "There's the bow and the mast. The sails are getting tattered as the wind takes them."

Ariz peered at the clouds, then suddenly he saw the large ship. A simple but delightful wonder lit him and he studied the clouds overhead anew. He remembered that very long ago, when he'd still been a child, his uncle had sat with him after sword practice and pointed out pictures in the clouds overhead. It had been decades since Ariz had allowed his concentration to wander up into the sky.

The wind pulled and tugged the masses of clouds into new forms.

"There's a wolf's head." Ariz pointed. "It's howling."

"Ah, yes, I see it," Lord Quemanor said, then he pointed to a string of small round clouds in the west. "It must be why those rabbits are leaping off into the horizon."

"Likely you are right, my lord."

"Call me Fedeles, will you? It's only the two of us, and this morning I don't feel much like anyone's lord or master."

Ariz considered Lord Quemanor. He looked tired but also languid, leaning back against the pew, his face lifted into the morning sun. How tempting it was to reach out and brush that stray lock of black hair back from his brow. But indulging such thoughts would lead him to ruin.

"You may not feel like it at this moment, but you are my lord," Ariz said.

He didn't want to argue, but he was also extremely wary of overstepping his place. Directly after Ariz had been stripped of his nobility, Hierro had taken a particular pleasure in punishing him for behaving in a manner that was suddenly inappropriately informal. And though he didn't believe that Fedeles Quemanor was the kind of man to encourage familiarity only to punish him for it—there were many other nobles among

Lord Quemanor's entourage who would not hesitate to beat a servant for assuming he had the right to address his better as an equal.

Lord Quemanor scowled up at the blue sky, then turned his gaze to Ariz.

"If I weren't, would you call me Fedeles?"

"What do mean? How could you not—"

"I mean if our circumstances had been different." Lord Quemanor returned his attention to the air overhead. "If, for example. you had attended Sagrada and Genimo had been sent to Yillar. Do you think we might have been friends?"

There was a fantasy so near everything Ariz longed for—and so impossible that it struck him like a blade driving fast and deep to the very core of his body. For just a moment Ariz couldn't even speak.

"I . . . Yes. I would have been the best friend to you that I could have been—" Ariz cut himself off before he said anything even more foolish. He glowered down at his ugly boots, feeling like an idiot.

This, he rebuked himself, was the problem with indulging his desire to be near Lord Quemanor. Thanks to the letters exchanged between Hierro and Genimo, Ariz had been aware of Fedeles Quemanor since the very beginning of his school days. Lord Quemanor had been the one other soul whom he knew bore as great a burden as himself, and he'd felt a bond with him that had only grown since entering the man's service. He'd thought so much about Lord Quemanor that now his every little word or motion carried too much importance for Ariz. Particularly when he was already so tired and dispirited.

"I'd like to imagine that we would have been friends as well." Lord Quemanor sounded wistful but also distant—as if he were again speaking of illusions passing over wind-tossed clouds. "I didn't really live those years with the others, you know. I've read a little about them in Atreau's memoirs, but . . . I never had the opportunity to grow close to my peers. By the time the curse was broken I'd become a duke and the friends who'd saved me were gone—exiled."

"I'm sorry, truly—"

"No, please. I don't want an apology or sympathy. I'm not telling you this to make you feel bad for me, but because . . ." He trailed off with an exasperated shake of his head.

Ariz said nothing, but simply sat beside him, giving him time to think and speak if he felt like it.

"I'm not good with words," Lord Quemanor said at last.

"That we have in common," Ariz replied and Lord Quemanor laughed.

"God knows how we're going to muddle through a conversation, eh?" Lord Quemanor offered Ariz a wry smile. "If only we could, I don't know, dance a conversation."

Ariz imagined the two of them performing wild, rhythmic panto-mimes back and forth, and again that ugly rasp of a laugh escaped him.

"Sir, you know I am an excellent dancer." A grin undermined Lord Quemanor's indignant tone. "If anyone could strut and pirouette a dis-course, it is I."

"Of that I have no doubt," Ariz replied. "Any failure to understand would be all on my part."

"No, I've seen you dance when you were instructing Sparanzo. You're a sight to behold."

Ariz felt his face heat.

Lord Quemanor cocked his head to the side. "Speaking of instruc-tion . . . do you think you might be able to take me through the steps of a quaressa?"

"The ballroom dance?" Ariz asked, though he knew the dance full well. It was a standard of Cadeleonian courtship, and most young men learned the steps in school, if not even before then. A slight flush colored Lord Quemanor's face.

"Yes, you see, the way I was at the academy, I never learned."

Ariz felt immediate sympathy. How unmanning must it have been to have to admit ignorance of something most boys mastered before they reached sixteen years of age? Doubtless, many other gaps existed in Lord Quemanor's education and experiences. But this one Ariz could easily remedy for him. He rose to his feet.

"I'd be happy to teach you. We could do it right now, if you'd like."

Lord Quemanor's face lit with a truly stunning smile. Then he leapt up.

"I entrust my education to you, Master Ariz."

For just a moment Ariz hesitated to remove his coat, but they were alone and likely to hear anyone approaching. Without the coat Lord Quemanor could much more easily see the exact motions on his arms. Ariz stripped it off and lay it across the pew, taking care not to let its weight show. Then he strode out to a flat expanse of stonework that had likely once been a chapel floor. Lord Quemanor followed him.

First Ariz took him through the steps, keeping time by clapping his hands. Then he demonstrated the simpler changes of holds that accom-panied the two turns that made up the full circle of a quaressa. Lord Quemanor picked up the entire thing with remarkable ease.

"You're a quick study," Ariz commented, and again Lord Quemanor colored just a little.

"Perhaps. But isn't the real test dancing with a partner?" Lord Quemanor asked.

Ariz's heartbeat quickened at the prospect of holding Lord Quemanor in his arms. His throat felt too tight to get a word out, so he simply nodded and then held out his hands.

Lord Quemanor stepped up next to him and took Ariz's left hand in his right. His skin felt warm and fine against the hard calluses of Ariz's fingers. His grip was surprisingly gentle. Then Lord Quemanor drew Ariz against his chest with a hand curled around his waist. Pressed so close, Ariz felt the heat of Lord Quemanor's body and caught the faint mingled scents of sweat and soap. He bowed his head toward Ariz just slightly. Ariz lifted his gaze to meet Lord Quemanor's scrutiny. His eyes were like polished onyx beneath the shadows of his lowered lashes; his full lips curved ever so slightly in a smile. He seemed both inscrutable and inviting at once. Ariz felt his face again heating with a flush, his blood raced through his veins, turning his entire body rigid and hot.

They stood holding one another, staring into each other's faces. The foolish desire to shift his hands from the careful pose of a dancer and truly embrace Fedeles Quemanor rushed over Ariz, and for just an instant he thought he sensed a similar longing in the tension of Lord Quemanor's graceful body.

But the danger of even entertaining such a thought, much less acting upon it, quickly brought Ariz back. As Duke of Rauma, and the favorite of Sevanyo, Lord Quemanor could discreetly do as he pleased with whomever he chose. If called out, he might pay a fine that he could easily afford and go on as he always had done. But common men like himself faced long prison sentences of hard labor for indulging in such vices—they rarely survived the ire of their fellow Cadeleonians, even if the brutality of their prison terms didn't kill them.

"You lead, my lord," Ariz prompted.

Lord Quemanor immediately lifted his head, his expression tensing, and then he swept Ariz into the rhythm of a quaressa. No one would have believed that Fedeles Quemanor only learned the steps minutes ago. In fact, Ariz began to doubt it himself.

Lord Quemanor led him in the double circle with graceful, quick steps. After three turns around the stones, Ariz couldn't resist testing Lord Quemanor's skill by doubling their pace, and to his delight Fedeles Quemanor matched him perfectly. When Ariz threw in a few showy spins, Lord Quemanor laughed but still managed to keep up. Then Lord Quemanor improvised several elegant kicks, which Ariz took up as well.

Their shadows skipped and whirled at their feet as they steadily transformed the staid, simple quaressa into a singular dance of their own. More than once they knocked knees or nearly tripped as they shifted the direction of their promenade and traded the lead in the dance back and forth. And yet neither of them stopped; neither of them released the other. Lord Quemanor's wide smile looked radiant and his low, rich laughed seemed to rumble through Ariz's body as if it were his own joy.

Caught up in the moment, Ariz forgot his shame at the raw ugliness of his own laughter and the slow, stunted quality of his smiles. He felt so free and happy that for a time he forgot even the brand, burning against his flesh.

"I knew you would be a delight to dance with, Master Ariz," Lord Quemanor told him.

"Did you?" They spun together far faster than would normally be proper.

"I should confess to spying on a number of the lessons you gave Sparanzo." Lord Quemanor offered him an expression of mock repentance. "It looked so graceful and such fun that I must admit to feeling a little envious."

"Really?" Ariz almost missed a step at the thought of Fedeles Quemanor wanting to dance with him. Perhaps even arranging this entire thing to dance with him. Ariz couldn't credit it. Still he found himself asking, "You didn't claim not to know the steps just to . . ."

"I might have exaggerated my ignorance," Lord Quemanor replied. He looked like he might have said more, but from below a strident voice called Lord Quemanor's name, breaking the morning quiet like the shriek of a jay.

Both of them stilled. Their hands remained linked, their bodies too close. Ariz was aware of Lord Quemanor listening—just as intently as himself—to locate the direction of the call. And now the sound of approaching horses rose to them. At least three riders, Ariz realized, ascending the hill from the west side.

"Fedeles!" This time Ariz recognized the voice as belonging to Prince Jacinto Sagrada.

Lord Quemanor said nothing. His hand tensed just slightly against Ariz's hip.

"Fedeles! Damn it, where are you?"

With a sigh Lord Quemanor released Ariz and strode to the edge of the hill. Ariz studied the ground around him, assessing how much of their dance remained visible. A few trampled wildflowers and scuffed clumps of moss were all that attested to their passage over the weathered stones. No one was likely to suspect anything of that. Still, Ariz caught his coat from the stone pew and pulled it back on. Then he withdrew to stand near the horses, as if their needs explained his presence in Lord Quemanor's company.

"Come around to the east face," Lord Quemanor shouted down the hill. "The footing will be easier for your mounts."

In a matter of minutes Prince Jacinto Sagrada spurred his white stallion over the hill. Behind him came his two constant companions, the mismatched Helios twins, Cocuyo and Enevir. All three looked dressed for court in fine silk breeches, snow-white shirts and brocade doublets, but wore strained expressions. Their mounts were dull with sweat and breathed heavily from the exertion of racing up the steep hillside.

Prince Jacinto swung down from his horse and tossed the reins in Ariz's direction. Ariz stepped forward to catch them and then led the prince's stallion to the shade of the nearby saplings.

"You must come at once!" Jacinto proclaimed.

Lord Quemanor silently arched a dark brow in response.

"I'm not joking this time," Jacinto continued. "Uncle is holding audience with father and demanding that he denounce, excommunicate and arrest the Grunitos of Anacleto. All of them. Every single one."

"Even the ladies," Enevir added from his place atop his horse.

Ariz wondered if the royal bishop's action against the Grunitos was related to Hierro's plot or if this was some madness the royal bishop had concocted on his own. The last time a Cadeleonian king and his royal bishop had attempted to wrest control of Anacleto from the Grunitos, both the crown and church had soon found themselves outmaneuvered and bankrupt. The Grunitos and Anacleto had never been brought to heel.

But the powerful Dukes of Rauma and Gavado had both taken advantage of the situation by extending the royal bishop and the king large loans at exorbitant interest. The four decades of civil war that had followed soon after had only served to strengthen the dukes.

Hierro had loved to read over histories of that bloody age. No doubt he would welcome something very like it again.

"Excommunicate?" Lord Quemanor's expression turned furious. "On what grounds?"

"He only has gossip. But he knows that father needs him in order to ascend to the throne and that you aren't expected to attend court until tomorrow." Jacinto shook his head and went on in a grim tone. "Father is so tired of fighting. And after losing Gael . . . he doesn't have it in him to resist Uncle like he used to. He may well give in if you aren't there to bring the might of Rauma down against Uncle."

"The Grunitos are as loyal to the king as the sun is bright," Lord Quemanor stated, though Ariz found it telling that he didn't make any such comparison of their obedience and faith in the royal bishop.

"It's all the rumors about Cadeleonians in Anacleto converting to the Haldiim religion—it's called Bahiim, the faith . . . at least, I believe it is." Jacinto frowned as if surprised by his own uncertainty. "Or perhaps that's just what they call their holy men and women—"

"Jacinto, what does the royal bishop actually accuse the Grunitos of doing?" Lord Quemanor snapped and the prince tensed as if coming to attention before a war master.

"It seems he ordered his clergymen in Anacleto to confront Nestor Grunito about having converted. Apparently Nestor has not denied the accusations, though he's been given numerous opportunities. Even Father's spies tell the same story, and Uncle knows as much. Now it seems that he's deadly serious about having the entire Grunito family arrested."

Both the prince and Lord Quemanor's expressions turned bleak and a quiet filled the air.

Jacinto went on. "The earl and Lady Grunito refuse to disavow him or to turn him over for trial and excommunication. So, of course, Uncle wants a royal decree against them all—"

"No. Not so long as I live." Lord Quemanor strode toward his stallion, his expression a mask of furious determination and his shadow bristling beneath his feet. Ariz noted the way it traced certain inscribed stones as it stalked at Lord Quemanor's heels. Without any doubt, that shadow reflected and responded to Lord Quemanor, not as a spell cast over him but as an extension of his being.

Prince Jacinto followed Lord Quemanor, looking relieved, even a little pleased. Almost immediately the prince returned to his habit of maintaining a stream of chatter. Ariz sometimes wondered if the man could keep quiet for an hour or if the strain of it would kill him.

"Maybe it if was that ruffian Elezar, but dear young Nestor—can you imagine? The man and his wife are an absolute joy! Who cares if they sneak off into the woods and dance naked around a couple trees from time to time? I certainly don't. But Uncle, you know how the old bastard is."

Lord Quemanor mounted his stallion while the prince took his reins from Ariz.

Briefly, Lord Quemanor glanced to Ariz. He looked apologetic but said nothing. His shadow fell across Ariz like the caress of a cool breeze. Then Lord Quemanor turned his mount down the hill. The prince and his attendants followed after, leaving Ariz alone amidst the ruins.

Chapter Eighteen

Fedeles strode past the royal guards lounging on either side of the ornate doors of the throne room. A youthful attendant in royal blue pelted ahead of him, attempting to clear a path through the crush of courtiers, priests and servants who filled the palace like clouds obscuring the summer sky.

Gold and sapphire light streamed through the panes of stained glass windows and reflected across the polished shields adorning the far wall. Below them, gilded statues struck graceful poses with raised swords and glinting spears, while overhead, frescoes depicted heroes of Cadeleonian lore atop their resplendent mounts and doing battle. Throughout the throne room savage wars were transformed into sweeping, elegant art, where even the dead lay in lovely poses.

Ahead of Fedeles a sea of silk, velvet and jewels seemed to flow from the foot of the twelve large marble steps leading up to the gold throne. At the very height, King Juleo sat, stiff and glassy-eyed as a corpse. A circle of white-robed attendant priests knelt at his feet, whispering the binding prayers that trapped his fluttering, pale soul in the husk of his dying body. Fedeles couldn't remember a time when the king had been more than a gasping revenant. According to Prince Sevanyo, the old king had once been a vibrant, lively man. He'd been responsible for the mechanisms that proliferated throughout the palace gardens as well as the multitude of Haldiim scholars and foreign dignitaries who had brought so much knowledge and beauty to the capital. Now though, most of the old ruler's favorites lay in their graves and his surviving allies had long since shifted their attention and ambition to his two eldest sons.

Nobles and courtiers jostled around one another, edging as near as they dared to Prince Sevanyo and his brother, the royal bishop Nugalo, where they stood on the tenth step of the stairs.

"Fedeles, do slow down, will you?" Jacinto whispered. "I can hardly keep up with these damned spurs clattering at my heels."

Fedeles nodded but didn't slow. Too much time had already been wasted by the niceties of throwing on proper clothes and slipping past the hordes of priests that the royal bishop had scattered throughout the palace as simpering impediments to his passage. Thankfully Jacinto commanded a vast train of courtiers and retainers who now swarmed around him, jogging after Fedeles. They cloaked him and deflected priests intent upon waylaying him with their pretenses at prayers and philosophical questions.

The attendant glanced back as Fedeles closed in on him. The boy broke into a sprint. A moment later he skidded across the gleaming marble floor, coming to a halt just short of a woman dressed in yellow pin-striped silk. The attendant slammed the butt of his gold staff against the floor and a resounding clap echoed through the throne room.

"May it please Your Highnesses! Fedeles Quemanor, Duke of Rauma, has arrived!" The attendant bent briefly to catch his breath, then straightened and went on. "His Highness Prince Jacinto Sagrada, Their Lordships Cocuyo and Enevir Helio, His Lordship—"

"Fedeles!" Prince Sevanyo called over the attendant's ongoing introductions. Even from the stairs, Sevanyo's pleasure seemed obvious. Beside him, the royal bishop's handsome countenance turned sour.

Fedeles met the man's glower with his own disdain. It was strange that he could adore Sevanyo so deeply and at the same time feel a physical repulsion at the sight of the prince's brother. Outwardly the two resembled each other greatly—the royal bishop looking a little more crisp and youthful even in his sixties. But to Fedeles they were as opposed as paradise and the three hells.

As a youth of eighteen Fedeles had been brought before the royal bishop—his spirit trapped within his own body and screaming from years of torture. The royal bishop had gazed into him. He had seemed to see Fedeles's suffering, had even pulled his hands back from Fedeles's shoulders as if utterly repulsed by contact with the malevolent curse possessing him. His sickened expression had assured Fedeles that the royal bishop felt the murderous curse that held him captive. But it had not suited the royal bishop's ambition to free Fedeles or even acknowledge his suffering. Instead he'd feigned ignorance so that Fedeles could be used as a weapon against Prince Sevanyo's most ardent supporters.

So many lives had been destroyed by that decision.

As much as Fedeles despised the physician who'd possessed him and the classmate who'd betrayed him, he loathed the royal bishop even more. It would have cost Nugalo nothing to have intervened on Fedeles's behalf. With a gesture of his hand he could have ordered his hundred attendant priests to perform an exorcism. But the merciless old man had only smiled and abandoned Fedeles's soul to shriek in a cage of fire and madness.

Once Fedeles had been freed, the royal bishop had seen to it that Fedeles's only true family—Javier Tornesal—was sentenced to exile for his part in Fedeles's salvation. Nugalo had then condemned Hylanya, and likely he'd paid the assassins who took Captain Ciceron's life. And now he pointlessly turned his ire on the Grunito family despite the fact that it could ruin the nation.

The outrage of it all felt too much to tolerate. Fedeles longed to wrap his hands around the old man's neck and strangle the life from him.

Fedeles felt his shadow bristle with rage. To his shock he realized that the time in the ruins had roused it too much already. Now it slithered ahead of him, making for the stairs. With a jolt of horror Fedeles fought to call the shadow back. Murdering the royal bishop with magic wouldn't just cost Fedeles his life; it would also condemn his entire household. His wife and son would burn alongside him.

He wouldn't be able to protect Sevanyo, Nestor, Atreau or anyone else, much less ever meet again with Master Ariz.

Fedeles averted his gaze from the royal bishop and groped for something calming and comforting to think on. He focused on the sensation of Master Ariz's callused hand in his own and the joyous revelry of dancing with the man. For a few minutes he'd been taken out of himself completely. He'd not thought of his obligations or the murder in his own household. He'd simply danced, as warm breezes rolled over him and the pleasure of holding another man's body in his arms filled him.

He had held such hope for today. He felt certain that the sword master returned some of his attraction. If only they'd had a little more time. Perhaps he might have won a kiss from the solemn Master Ariz. Perhaps more.

Fedeles felt his shadow retreating and coiling back beneath him, as if it too longed to bask in the warmth of that memory. He lifted his gaze to Prince Sevanyo and then the royal bishop. This time his composure held.

"Dear cousin, come to me, will you? I would hear your opinion on a matter that is much upon my brother's mind recently." Sevanyo extended a hand.

"It would be my honor," Fedeles replied.

Fedeles strode through the crowd of nobles. It took some effort not to stare at his brother-in-law, Hierro Fueres, as he passed him. A wan light illuminated Hierro's eyes and something flickered between his ringed fingers. A spell? Or just a trick of reflected sun dancing through the throne room?

Fedeles hoped the latter but feared the former. Though making such an accusation would only serve to warn the Fueres family and the royal bishop that Fedeles could perceive their manipulations. Better to wait for the letters to be translated and produce evidence of their treachery—their involvement in the very witchcraft they decried and condemned—in a form that any man could see.

Fedeles mounted the stairs to Sevanyo quickly. As a duke and a blood relation of the royal Sagradas, he could have claimed the tenth step and stood shoulder to shoulder with both Sevanyo and the royal bishop. The eleventh would have required Prince Sevanyo's explicit invitation, and the twelfth step could only be taken by the king or at his command.

Out of reverence to Sevanyo he stopped on the ninth step and bowed to the prince.

"How timely you are!" Sevanyo raised his voice just a little. "My dear brother and I were just discussing your neighbors, the Grunitos of Anacleto."

"Were you indeed?" Fedeles asked, though he doubted anyone having witnessed him storming into the throne room would have imagined he hadn't known as much and come to defend his allies. This conversation had become a piece of theater, and he understood his part in it.

"It seems that my brother has heard no end of rumors of the family participating in wild orgies of Haldiim heresy and swearing their loyalty to the Bahiim priestesses, as well as Count Radulf in far-off Labara." Prince Sevanyo raised his voice to carry over the multitude of attendant nobility surrounding them. At the same time Fedeles searched for a response. Then he remembered a story Atreau had penned.

"Rumors? What are rumors but lies, too salacious to resist retelling?" Fedeles quoted, and a little of his tension eased. He'd feared that physical proof of Nestor's conversion had surfaced. He forced a hard smile at the royal bishop. "Were every rumor a truth then the royal bishop would have fathered bastards into every noble house and I would number among his many sons."

Suppressed laughter sounded from the nobles gathered below, particularly those surrounding Jacinto. The royal bishop scowled, but didn't allow himself to be drawn out by Fedeles's deliberate provocation.

Prince Sevanyo lifted a silken kerchief to his mouth and feigned a cough to hide his amusement. He would not publicly disdain his brother—not when his own coronation hinged upon the royal bishop's decision to release the king from his mortal body and shepherd his soul into the company of the Hallowed Kings.

"It is not a matter of gossip alone." The royal bishop glowered at Fedeles. "Six years have passed since Elezar Grunito allowed himself to become enthralled by the heathen Count Radulf, and still the Grunito family has not denounced him. Now the heir to the earldom, Nestor, is said to practice Bahiim rites. And again the Grunito family refuses to submit him to our holy judgment or to repudiate him."

"As would anyone. Your charge against Nestor is without proof. You can only claim anonymous hearsay such as 'it is said.'" Fedeles felt such anger that he nearly took the next step to loom over the royal bishop. But physically intimidating an old man wouldn't win him the support of the gathered nobles. Not the way mocking him would.

"*It is said*," Fedeles went on with a forced smile, "that your queen mother refused to suckle you at her breast lest your foul mouth poison her. *It is said* that Nestor Grunito is secretly a Bahiim. *It is said* that Hierro Fueres is a witch and that all Labaran girls are enchanted cats. Any amount of slander can be aired by anonymous nobodies who *say* so much without proving a word."

Sounds of amusement and approval rose from the gathered crowd. Sevanyo beamed and the royal bishop continued to glower at Fedeles.

"There is no smoke without a fire—" the royal bishop began.

"Has Cadeleonian justice now been reduced to aphorisms, your holiness?" Fedeles demanded. "If so, then isn't the kettle as black as the pot it accuses?"

Again a hushed laughter answered Fedeles. The royal bishop's face flushed with anger. He parted his lips as if to restate the case against Nestor, but Fedeles went on—though now in a more respectful tone, if only for the sake of appearances. "We are men of law and reason. Both require proof to convict any citizen of this nation of any wrongdoing. If we accept anything less as grounds for prosecution, then we betray the very tenets of law that uphold our rights to rule over this nation."

"Indeed," Prince Sevanyo agreed.

"You cannot simply dismiss this matter," the royal bishop snapped, and for an instant Fedeles thought he saw a faint light flicker over the old man's thin lips. A spell again? Fedeles glanced down to see Hierro Fueres studying him with an amused expression. Why would Hierro choose to cast an enchantment against his own ally, the royal bishop? From his elevated position Fedeles noted Remes, just behind Hierro, looking equally pleased—as if he'd somehow hoped for this outcome.

Fedeles felt suddenly very uneasy. He'd thought before that this entire interaction had seemed like a performance. Now he wondered if Hierro and Remes had engineered it. If so, what were they intent upon showing the gathered audience?

The royal bishop straightened and turned to look directly at Sevanyo.

"I demand that Nestor Grunito be summoned to testify under holy oath before the Hallowed Kings."

Fedeles only half heard the royal bishop's demand. His attention remained on Hierro. It almost looked as if Hierro murmured the words an instant before the royal bishop proclaimed them. Fedeles looked to Sevanyo, but he gave no indication that he'd noticed any of Hierro's flickering spells.

"He must give an account of himself and his family!" the royal bishop demanded.

Fedeles lifted his head to argue, but Sevanyo answered before he could say anything.

"Fine," Prince Sevanyo agreed. He looked tired of all this already. "But it will be my royal guards who summon him and escort him, not men sworn to the church. The last time your men-at-arms attempted to take the Grunito home, far too much blood was spilled. He will be summoned as my guest and be treated with the utmost respect."

The royal bishop appeared vexed by the imposition, but down in the crowd of nobles and courtiers, Hierro Fueres smiled like a cardsharp holding a winning hand. With a feeling of dread, Fedeles realized that he'd miscalculated and played into Hierro's plan.

He opened his mouth to argue that no military escort would be required to summon Nestor; simply extending him royal invitation to attend the king's court would ensure he came to the capital.

But Prince Sevanyo caught his eye and silenced him with a small shake of his head. Fedeles relented, though he did not like it. The royal bishop had only grudgingly blessed Sevanyo's ascendance to the throne; he could still change his mind. Now was not the time to refuse the royal bishop's demands, but rather to reassure him of his importance and influence. Recognizing that, Fedeles accepted that it was vital for Prince Sevanyo to make at least one public show of siding with the royal bishop over one of his own supporters. He didn't enjoy being the supporter whom Sevanyo chose, but that was largely his own fault for storming into the throne room and demonstrating such open disdain for Royal Bishop Nugalo.

He recalled Timoteo's fear that Sevanyo couldn't be relied upon to take a strong stand against the royal bishop, but he resisted thinking on it now. Fedeles bowed his head and kept his mouth shut. At his feet his shadow rippled like dark troubled water.

"Thank you so much for speaking your mind, dear cousin," Sevanyo told him. "No matter how strongly we might agree or disagree, I always know that my brother and I can be assured that you will offer your honest thoughts and opinions. These days, truth is a precious gift."

"It is an honor to serve my prince, in any way I can," Fedeles replied. He couldn't bring himself to look at the royal bishop.

"Please don't let me take up any more of your time now, dear cousin." Prince Sevanyo dismissed him easily. "But we will have to speak again soon. I must know what you plan to wear for this year's masquerade. The theme of the Great Hunt offers so many splendid opportunities."

"I will look forward to it." Fedeles bowed low and then withdrew.

As he descended to the fifth step, he noted a figure dressed in gold and green silk striding through the vast crowd. He lifted his hand in return to his wife's silent greeting. Even surrounded by so many beautiful courtesans and expertly coifed ladies, Oasia stood out from them with her dignified poise. She could have dressed in filthy rags; her proud bearing and direct gaze would still have marked her as the eldest child of a royal princess and a ruthless duke.

Very purposefully, she and her entourage cut through the courtiers who gathered around her brother, Hierro. From the way one insolent young man jumped back, Fedeles felt certain that Oasia and her ladies freely wielded their dagger-sharp, emerald-studded hairpins to ensure that the crowd opened before them, allowing them passage into the fold of Jacinto's large retinue. A moment later Fedeles reached the floor and took his place at his wife's side in the tight press of bodies.

Oasia held out her hand and Fedeles bowed and kissed her fingers. As always, that won him a soft laugh. It amused her to no end that he still publicly treated her as he had when they first began courting. She continued to hold his hand after he straightened.

"God's teeth, how can you two still be so enamored with one another?" Jacinto shook his head. "It makes a man wonder if sharing a marriage bed might not be so bad a thing after all . . . so long as he was lucky enough to share it with the two of you, I mean."

Several of the young noblemen who ran with Jacinto roared with laughter, while Oasia's ladies-in waiting made small scandalized noises and glowered at the amused men surrounding them. It wasn't the sort of comment that would do any of them honor if it carried to Hierro's followers.

Oasia didn't dignify Jacinto's words with any reaction at all. She simply gazed coolly past Jacinto—as if he were a pane of glass. Jacinto's grin faded at once. Fedeles didn't know why, but where reprimands or outcries of affront only served to inspire worse behavior in Jacinto, Oasia's indifference never failed to bring him to heel. Perhaps it was simply her resemblance to his long-dead mother.

"Forgive me, I mean no offense, m'lady," Jacinto said quickly.

Oasia only blinked at him and then leaned into Fedeles. He placed his arm over her slim shoulder, playing the part of the protective husband sheltering his delicate wife.

"The kingdom has fallen upon hard times indeed if a royal prince must hire himself out as a bed warmer just to find a place to sleep," Fedeles commented.

"Don't be like that, Fedeles." Jacinto pulled a pained face. "You know I'm only joking."

"I suppose I do know that," Fedeles relented with a smile. He didn't have it in him to take umbrage with Jacinto. He was a man of good intentions, and though he despised the formality and propriety of the king's court, he'd taken it upon himself to wade into this sea of disapproving nobles for Fedeles's and Nestor's sakes.

He'd not changed much since they'd all schooled together in the Sagrada Academy. Then he'd been Atreau's upperclassmen and something of an inspiration to all the wild reckless youths who, after his graduation, would call themselves Hellions. In the years since then, Javier had gone into exile, while war and a Labaran witch had lured Elezar from their fold, Morisio had fled their enemies to live at the mercy of foreign seas, and even Atreau no longer possessed the lusty carelessness that had once so marked his character. Only Jacinto, the eldest of them, remained ever the ebullient, brash boy.

"It's all just so dreary here in grandfather's palace. I can't help myself." Jacinto scowled down at his leather boots and then tapped his heels, making his golden spurs ring like bells. "And you were the one who brought up my dear, departed granny's tits, after all."

"I'm not sure those were my exact words, but I take your point." Fedeles noted Jacinto's sly smile. No doubt Jacinto had been thrilled to have the story of his grandmother's refusal to nurse the royal bishop aired so publicly.

"All for a good cause, though." Cocuyo Helio had clearly missed Jacinto's amused expression. Beside him, his slender brother nodded.

"Who knows what might have happened if you hadn't argued against the royal bishop," Enevir added. "He did seem intent upon arresting the Grunito family without any proof of his charges whatsoever."

"I thought as much myself," Lady Elenna Ortez commented from amidst Oasia's pretty, dark-haired ladies-in-waiting. "Thanks to God that Lord Quemanor arrived when he did."

Fedeles scowled. He couldn't shake the feeling that, if anything, his presence had played exactly into Hierro Fueres's designs. Could it have always been Hierro's intention to manipulate Sevanyo into sending away a large number of his royal guard? Surely not even he imagined that he could get away with directly assaulting Sevanyo?

As if sharing his thought, Oasia shook her head. Then she lifted her face slightly to meet his gaze.

"Won't you escort me around the heavenly fountains, dear hus-band?" Oasia asked. "I would love to see the devotional statues and all the blooming flowers. But I fear my womanly eyes would not discern their holy symbolism without you to guide me."

"What greater purpose can I serve than to gratify your every wish, my dearest mistress?" Fedeles bowed deeply before her, which won him another one of her rare soft laughs. In truth she knew far more than him about holy texts and sacred symbolism, but the fountains' cascades produced more than enough noise to ensure that the words whispered between them would not be easily overheard—not even by Oasia's six ladies-in-waiting.

Fortunately Prince Sevanyo kept the gathered courtiers in atten-dance for only another quarter of an hour, while he announced that in honor of his father's final year as king, all the gardens of the royal palace would be opened for masquerade festivities; in previous years the drunk-en tramping of revelers' feet had been limited to the tough hedges and hardy lawns of the Royal Star Garden. The colognes to be worn for the fourteen days of festivities were limited to oakmoss, meadowsweet and rockrose, in observance of the theme of the Holy Savior's Great Hunt. Then the royal bishop spoke briefly of their Savior's great battles to bring wild, heathen creatures to heel and warned those gathered to guard themselves not only against the savage leanings of their own hearts but against genuine abominations awakening abroad and at home.

"As I recall, isn't that just the opposite of what it actually says in the holy texts?" Elenna Ortez whispered. Oasia nodded and both of them glanced to Hierro with a look of suspicion.

While the royal bishop completed his odd, impromptu sermon, Fed-eles edged nearer the doors, leading Jacinto and Oasia, as well as their attendants. They escaped the throne room well ahead of the rest of the crowd and made their way to the rolling hills where long lines of bowed laburnum trees supported arches of wisteria. The gold and violet-blue flowers of both hung from the branches spreading over crushed-shell paths. Every few hundred yards the paths opened to expose huge foun-tains filled with gilded figures, cascades of fresh water and sprays of huge blue and gold irises.

"Oh look, there's a dragonfly sleeping on the nose of the Savior's charger," one of the ladies pointed out. Fedeles smiled at the sight of the brilliant insect's repose amid a scene of charging cavalry and naked swords. Several frogs appeared to have taken up residence as well. Ene-vir Helio shifted his weight from his cane and rested on the edge of the fountain.

"It is all rather pretty, I suppose," Jacinto commented, but he didn't appear particularly impressed with the sights he'd known since his early childhood. Cocuyo quoted some popular poem, which no doubt Atreau would have recognized but Fedeles found too much like every other poem comparing a desirable young woman to dewy blossoms, or perhaps it was to limpid pools—something wet, in any case. Fedeles never possessed much of an appreciation for poetry, but he did admire the powerful masses of the towering statues.

One gracefully balanced figure, half hidden behind a frothing cascade, reminded him of Master Ariz. The muscular statue appeared to be bursting with intensity even while standing perfectly silent and motionless.

"The guard who was killed last night," Oasia whispered. "Hierro intended him to murder Sparanzo. I only discovered as much late yesterday, but I acted at once."

Fedeles stifled a shock of horror at the thought of an assassin stalking Sparanzo. His shadow bristled at his feet. He took a deep breath. There was nothing he could do with his fear. The threat to his son had already been destroyed before he'd even known of it.

"I suppose it was only a matter of time before Hierro stooped so low." Fedeles wondered what it said about the age that they lived in that the information didn't surprise him. Fedeles couldn't quite hide the tension in his voice, but none of the people surrounding them seemed to pay any mind to him and Oasia. "You must not accept any more *gifts* from your brother."

"Many have proven useful to us," Oasia replied. She gazed down at a cluster of blue irises. "And others have proven an ideal means to disseminate misinformation."

Though Fedeles knew Oasia loved Sparanzo, he also understood her to be far less sentimental and much more ruthless than himself. Even in private she treated the boy with formality that Fedeles had never achieved since the day Sparanzo was born. On one occasion Atreau had suggested that Oasia would sacrifice Sparanzo—along with the rest of the household—to save herself from falling under Hierro's dominion again. He could almost hear Atreau now saying, *She can always have another child, after all.*

"No person, however useful, is worth risking Sparanzo's life to acquire," Fedeles whispered.

Oasia's head came up and she held his gaze.

"This entire kingdom will crumble into the sea before I allow *any* harm to befall our son. He is safe." Her expression softened and she smiled. "The threat was dealt with quickly enough, all thanks to previous gifts that my brother sent. Hierro's cruelty makes those who have served him willing to betray him and happy to see him fail."

"Do I owe my gratitude to Mistress Delfia or her quiet brother or both?" Fedeles asked.

Five years of observing the siblings had shown Fedeles how innately they acted in tandem. They reminded him of a team of horses trained to pull a carriage, so practiced at moving in unison that they did it even when unaware. It had been a miracle that he'd managed to lure Master Ariz out alone this morning without Delfia finding an excuse to follow them.

"You should allow me to think that I have my secrets," Oasia said.

Fedeles laughed. No doubt his wife kept much hidden from him. They shared a mutual priority in their son and a mutual enemy in Hierro Fueres, but Fedeles didn't flatter himself to believe that Oasia limited her ambitions to the quiet realm of his sedate aspirations. Though for just a moment he wondered if he couldn't ask her to reveal more of Master Ariz's history in the Fueres household. Had he truly been nothing but a classmate to Hierro?

What had it done to him to be stripped of his nobility?

But he didn't know that he wanted those answers—particularly not from a source other than Master Ariz himself.

"I had planned on informing you of all of this first thing in the morning, but Elenna summoned me here with important news . . ." Oasia quieted as Jacinto wandered nearer them. "Shall we see the next fountain?"

They all strolled on through another tunnel of bowed branches and flower streamers. Butterflies flitted through the air and at some distance Fedeles heard the clear peal of Hierro Fueres's laughter.

Jacinto and his friends plucked blossoms from the bowers and tossed them at one another. Fedeles caught a fistful of wisteria before they could strike Oasia's cheek.

"My apologies!" Cocuyo colored like a beet as he realized how far the afternoon breeze had blown his throw off its target. Jacinto crowed with laughter. Oasia plucked the violet flowers from Fedeles's hand and hurled them into Jacinto's dark hair. Elenna and Enevir laughed.

Then they reached another immense fountain. This one erupted with contorted waves of tangled, naked bodies all falling back before the resplendent armored figure of the Savior and his chosen few companions. The damned cascaded down along with tiers of flowing water and spilled out into a pool of lily pads.

"Do you think that ancient devils actually went to battle buck naked?" Jacinto sauntered around the fountain. "Or do you think it's an artistic convention that allows us to ogle all this bare flesh while still feeling devout?"

Fedeles didn't catch Cocuyo's response, as Oasia leaned into him.

"From what Elenna has reported to me, I believe that the royal bishop is after much more than just destroying Nestor or his nearest relations," Oasia whispered.

"Yes?" Fedeles bowed his head down next to hers.

"He's after the Grunito earldom—their very right to rule Anacleto. He seems intent on rooting out some secret that they've buried out on the Salt Islands. Something to do with the inheritance of the title. I suspect that he believes that it could give him more legitimate grounds to seize the whole of Anacleto in the name of the church."

Alarm shot through Fedeles like icy chill. If the royal bishop claimed Anacleto, then the Haldiim population as well as any Cadeleonians who had converted to their faith would be doomed.

"How did Elenna come by all this?" Fedeles asked. It seemed both too much information and also far too great of a threat for him to have heard nothing about it previously. Certainly Nestor or Elezar would have hinted at something if there was a family secret that required protecting.

"One of the bishop's dove keepers alerted us. The young man is completely smitten with Elenna," Oasia whispered. "He copies messages he's been entrusted with and passes them on to us."

"How much does he ask of Elenna in return?" Fedeles wasn't so naïve as to expect that he could protect his family or secure Sevanyo's rule without stooping to deceit, manipulation, theft or outright assassination. But those were not ideal means to accomplish any end. And he would rather not add pimping out a young girl to the ignoble list.

"Not more than she is happy to provide," Oasia responded. "He was already half in love with her at first sight and he's a kind man. Elenna endured far more odious lovers when she was still under my father's control, I promise you that."

Across from them Jacinto invited Oasia's ladies to brave the spray of water to see the details of the fountain where the artists had hidden obscenely endowed little devils. Elenna smiled and appeared as happy as any of them. Laughter filled the air as Jacinto dropped into a splayed squat and pointed out his own resemblance to one creature on the base of the fountain.

Fedeles returned his attention to Oasia.

"But what is it exactly that the royal bishop thinks he'll find on the Salt Islands?" Fedeles asked.

"We don't know yet. This only began yesterday at dawn," Oasia replied. "A young priest demanded admittance into the royal bishop's chambers and spoke with him for more than an hour in secret. Afterward the old man apparently went wild, sending message after message to his agents on the Salt Islands. He seems to be searching for a particular person who served the Grunito family some twenty or thirty years ago. A physician, I think."

Fedeles frowned. Twenty years ago Nestor would have still been a child and even Elezar only a boy of ten. So what secrets other than Nestor's conversion did the Grunito family hide? Without knowing what it might be, Fedeles couldn't discern how damaging the information might be or how best to keep it from the royal bishop.

"I don't have a reliable agent on the Salt Islands," Oasia said; then she sighed, as if speaking further was some kind of burden to her. "I understand that Atreau may have contacts there, so I'm passing along copies of the messages for you to give to him."

She drew the bundle of thin notes from a fold in her dress and handed it to Fedeles. He slipped the notes away into his coat.

"Thank you," Fedeles said. He suspected that it pained her to have to rely on Atreau for information; she made little secret of her doubts about Atreau's ability to remain loyal to any one master.

"Just be certain that he shares everything he discovers," Oasia said.

Fedeles nodded.

When they reached the fifth fountain, Fedeles stilled beside the towering statue of a deer standing defiantly despite the dozens of arrows that pierced her body.

"I understand that there are other letters that have fallen into your hands. Concerning Royal Bishop Nugalo's search for certain relics?" Oasia asked.

"Yes. They're locked in my library, if you want to look them over. From what I've read, it would seem that the old man is seeking out relics that are oddly out of character for a royal bishop." Fedeles frowned. After witnessing Hierro manipulate Nugalo, he had to wonder how many of the royal bishop's actions were actually Hierro's.

"All her life Clara has collected strange relics," Oasia murmured. "Even as a little girl she would obsess about ancient ruby shields and some Old God's horns—"

"The horns of Summer Doe?" Fedeles raised his brows.

"Yes." Oasia nodded. "The Summer Doe. One of the four great champions who accompanied the Savior in the Battle of Heaven's Shard. She died but was born again, wasn't she?" Oasia gazed at the stone deer before them. "She was mentioned again in holy writings. The reindeer that sustained the heroes of the Great Hunt by allowing them to kill her and devour her flesh again and again?"

Fedeles nodded. "The Bahiim version of that story is quite different. She's said to have lured the hunters away from their intended prey and tricked them by taking a new body each time she was slain. They ate her flesh, but her radiant soul forever eluded them." Fedeles paused a moment, wondering what, if anything, these ancient stories truly told them. "She's still worshiped by a few Irabiim tribes but has passed into myths for most Bahiim. All that I could find out about her horns is that she was supposed to shed them when she passed on into a new life. They sounded rather more metaphorical than real."

"Clara believed that they were real enough, I remember that." Oasia rarely displayed her sorrow, but as she spoke her younger sister's name, Fedeles thought he glimpsed a little of her grief. "She would go on and on about how we would be free once she found the horns . . ." Oasia shook her head and looked away as she quickly wiped her hand across her eyes.

"I'm sorry," Fedeles whispered. He'd never had the opportunity to know his own little sister, but it had still hurt him when he'd received news of her death in childbirth. He couldn't imagine how much greater a loss Oasia felt, being so estranged from the sister she'd known and loved in childhood.

Fedeles extended his hand and Oasia grasped it. She drew in a slow breath and squared her shoulders.

"You've nothing to be sorry for, my darling." Oasia turned her attention back to the statue before them with a supremely composed expression. "So the royal bishop's choice of the Great Hunt for the masquerade may well carry some greater importance."

"No doubt it does," Fedeles agreed. "But I don't know what that might be."

"It doesn't make sense," Oasia murmured. "Why would a zealot like the royal bishop want a symbol of pagan witchcraft? An Old God, at that?"

"Perhaps to destroy them?"

"That's a great deal of trouble to go to, since the relics are apparently long lost and largely forgotten," Oasia replied.

"Atreau thought that Lady Radulf might have been looking for the horns as well," Fedeles confided. "And he felt certain that her search had something to do with the blessings that enshrine the Shard of Heaven."

What they knew—and the majority of Cadeleonians did not, thanks to Atreau's second memoir being burned—was that all of the demon lords had not been destroyed in the ancient battles recounted in holy books. At least one had survived, sleeping for centuries beneath the city of Milmuraille. Hardly six years ago, Labaran conspirators in Radulf County had woken the towering, fiery serpent with the intention of unleashing it upon the Cadeleonian royal court. The demon lord, however, had not proven so easily controlled and the current Count Radulf had nearly died destroying it.

"You don't think that there could be another demon sleeping beneath Cieloalta . . ." Oasia quieted, as if she feared to even voice the thought aloud.

Fedeles understood her anxiety. She had to have seen the roiling golden spells that churned within the Shard of Heaven—just as he had. Something magical and immense writhed beneath the blue spells that the souls of the Hallowed Kings maintained.

Hylanya had warned them that the Hallowed Kings were growing weak, and both Javier and Alizadeh feared the unknown force that would escape if the kings' spells faltered.

"Perhaps. Alizadeh said that if the Hallowed Kings fail it could mean the destruction of all of Cadeleon," Fedeles whispered. "But by what, he could not say."

"No . . . not so long as you and I draw breath," Oasia whispered. Fedeles could see the fear in her eyes. But then she lifted her chin in defiance. "We will find the means to rebuild the wards. If it means seizing these shields and horns, then that's what we will do. Enevir has connections with several Irabiim caravans, he might be able to find out more for us—" Oasia cut herself off as loud shout boomed across the grounds.

Through the splash of water and chatter of his companions, Fedeles recognized Atreau's voice. Both he and Oasia stilled, listening.

"How now, Hierro. What a bright little knife! I daresay my own preference is for penetration of a much more metaphoric nature." Atreau's words rang with a theatric amusement and carried clearly past the cover of flowering greenery. "We truly shouldn't meet like this in broad daylight. The royal bishop might grow suspicious of us shaking the hedges with so much passion."

Hierro's response didn't carry clearly, but tones of enraged obscenities penetrated the hedges. Fedeles thought he heard the ring of clashing blades.

Oasia went rigid, faint blue flames lighting up between her fingers. Her ladies hurried to her. Elenna snapped open a silver-ribbed fan like she was drawing a dagger from its sheath, while two handmaids slid long steely combs from their hair. Jacinto and the Helio brothers followed them.

"Was that Atreau I just heard?" Jacinto gripped his sword hilt.

"He may have displeased my brother, I fear." Oasia cupped her hands together and the pale light intensified to a blaze. Fedeles felt his shadow surge forward and had to restrain it from reaching out in Atreau's direction. None of them could afford to act rashly in broad daylight—not in the royal court.

The bushes rustled. Branches cracked. Then boot heels hammered across cobbled stones and spurs chimed like frantic bells. Atreau pelted through the archway of a rose bower with a grimace of a smile plastered across his face. His hair looked wild with rose petals and leaves tangled through his locks. His doublet and shirt front hung open. Atreau gave a crow of delight as he caught sight of Fedeles and his company. He charged to the fountain.

Hierro and three of his noble companions pelted through the arch with knives drawn and murderous expressions. Hierro stopped just past the rose bower. His gaze went to Fedeles and he smirked. His two friends stilled as well, though they appeared more concerned by Jacinto's presence. Both sheathed their knives and the older of the two muttered an apology for approaching the prince with a weapon drawn. Hierro made no such concession to Jacinto's rank.

Atreau jogged around the fountain once as if taking a victory lap. Then he made a show of kissing the hands of each of Oasia's ladies. As always he kept his distance from Oasia herself.

Oasia crushed the flames between her hands and relaxed next to Fedeles.

"I fear that Lord Fueres does not appreciate my sense of humor." Atreau slouched against the wall of the nearest fountain. Prince Jacinto beamed at him.

"Perhaps you tease him on too tender a point?" Jacinto commented.

"Your Highness may well be correct. But he must know that his overture is far too public not to inspire gossip and even incite jealousy. After all, I already have Captain Yago's ardent desires to consider."

Jacinto and his companions laughed.

"You are filth," Hierro growled at Atreau.

"Filth indeed, sir. But we all know that blossoms thrive best with their roots buried deep in dirt and shit." Atreau's reply inspired several giggles from Oasia's ladies and Jacinto's loud guffaw. The Helio brothers and Hierro's two companions seemed to consider each other with an uneasy civility. Feigning amusement while their hearts still pounded in readiness for a fight obviously did not come easily to any of them. But they all knew that a brawl on the palace grounds would only result in the whole lot of them spending a night in the king's dungeon—or worse were anyone of them killed.

Already the commotion drew several other parties of noble onlookers. Fedeles recognized Atreau's eldest brother—Lliro—standing in one group alongside the minister of the navies. A cluster of eight royal guards marched in their direction as well.

Only an idiot would attempt to fight now. Hierro was many things, but Fedeles did not take him for a fool.

In fact, Hierro's pursuit of Atreau struck Fedeles as out of character. Dispatching an assassin in the dark of night seemed more in his nature—certainly he wasn't normally prone to making a public display of his murderous impulses. That would have destroyed the image of scrupulous refinement that he so carefully maintained at court.

A faint half-formed spell appeared to be fading from where it had been hastily traced between the torn remnants of Atreau's shirt. It was a strange shape, eight shivering points flickering within the confine of a sphere, and yet something about it reminded Fedeles of the spells that had once been used against him. Had Hierro attempted to enthrall Atreau?

Had he succeeded, it would have meant ruin for a multitude of Fedeles's agents. But the likelihood that Hierro would have prevailed where so many lovestruck Labaran witches had failed was slim. And to attempt such a thing while the royal bishop and a multitude of priests were in attendance at court was reckless.

So Hierro had grown either too desperate or too assured to fear royal condemnation.

Neither thought pleased Fedeles.

Then he noticed the faintest glints of white light flickering from a scrap of torn paper gripped in Atreau's fist. Even crumpled, it still radiated the silver white script that was so unique to Javier. Another secret missive. Or the torn remains of one.

Quite possibly this was the very thing that had inspired Hierro's attack and now seemed to make him loathe to sheath his dagger.

In fact, Hierro already gripped a shred of the paper. The shining blue flames that glinted on his fingers like sapphire rings nearly hid the white script. Noting Fedeles's gaze, he made a show of slipping the paper into his coat pocket.

Then as the royal guards approached, Hierro turned his knife in his hand to cut a large red rose blossom from the bower beside him.

"I'm afraid that I have other business to attend to just now. But we will finish this another time. Soon." He tossed the rose in Oasia's direction, but

Fedeles slapped it aside. Thorns grazed the back of his hand and the flower fell onto the pebbled path. Tiny blue curses wriggled from between the petals like hungry tapeworms.

Hierro turned and strode away; his two companions offered quick bows to Jacinto and then hurried after him.

"He's grown too confident," Oasia murmured.

Fedeles scowled at the rose at his feet, then allowed his shadow to roll over it, crushing out the blue flames and shredding the fragile red petals to a pulp.

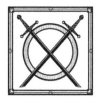 CHAPTER
NINETEEN

After returning from Crown Hill, Ariz attended his duties schooling Sparanzo in both dance and swordplay. Done with the lessons, he decided to look in on the physician, Narsi. The young man had treated Ariz with a gentleness that he rarely encountered. If there was something he could do to ease the physician's suffering, then he would do so. If Master Narsi was recovering, then it would do Ariz good to see as much for himself and to be able to reassure Delfia, as well.

Though he'd not considered how many other well-wishers might be visiting the master physician. Father Timoteo, Brother Berto and Atreau Vediya all stood in the hallway just outside the master physician's open door. Two maids' voices rose from the chamber.

Ariz immediately thought better of his concerned impulse. He didn't trust the holy men or feel comfortable under Atreau's scrutiny. He certainly didn't want any of them connecting him to Master Narsi's poisoning. Unfortunately, Atreau spotted him.

"Master Ariz! Don't slink away like a wet cat. I promise you we are not such grim company that you need to dread passing us in the hall."

Ariz turned and offered Atreau and the holy men his most bland stare. He let his arms hang slack as he joined the others outside the physician's door. As he came closer he noted the maids were nearly finished cleaning the examination room. They sprinkled blessed flowers and salt over the windowsills.

Brother Berto watched the women with a dissatisfied expression. Ariz had noticed him angling the same concerned gaze at Delfia now and again. He didn't know if he should interpret Brother Berto's expression as worried for his sister or as consternation directed at her. That uncertainty made him wary of the man's motivations, though Delfia found him good company and a pleasant dance partner.

Holy Father Timoteo steepled his fingers as if preparing to pray—or perhaps the gesture was habitual for the priest. Always gaunt and hollow-eyed, this afternoon the Holy Father struck Ariz as an embodiment of Death Walking among the Living, except that Ariz couldn't imagine the skeletal specter ever wearing so sorrowful of an expression as the one the Holy Father now turned on the master physician's bedroom door. Beyond the door, Ariz could just make out the foot of a bed and the shape of motionless legs hidden beneath a blanket.

Like the Holy Father, Atreau appeared unusually sober and pallid. He hunched against the door jamb with his arms crossed and angry tension in his expression. He'd clearly slept as little as Ariz but likely wasn't as accustomed to the deprivation. His shirtfront looked rumpled and torn, as if he'd just wrenched himself from a tussle. He didn't even cast a lewd glance after the young maids now departing the examination room. Only when one of the women lingered beside him did he rouse himself to flash a flirtatious grin.

"Thank you for airing the rooms out for him," Atreau said. "I'm sure Master Narsi will appreciate the improvements once he wakes."

"It was no trouble at all, Atreau," the maid replied. Ariz sensed that she took a certain pleasure in addressing Atreau so directly and informally—as if she was his peer. From her companion's scandalized expression he wondered if she hadn't done it on some sort of a dare.

"You are kind to indulge the rest of us in the illusion that your service is of little importance." Atreau smiled at both the maids and offered them a rather elegant bow. "But having attempted to keep my own rooms in any semblance of cleanliness, I'm certain that we would all be lost in filth and soot without such care as you provide."

The maids laughed, but both of them seemed to stand a little taller and hold their heads higher when they took their leave.

Ariz had to admit that Atreau's appeal went beyond possessing a handsome visage and glib tongue. He appeared genuine in his warm demeanor and ability to perceive beauty in nearly everyone he encountered. That capacity lent his dissolute temperament and undisciplined character a certain charm. No doubt he appealed to the sorts of people who yearned to domesticate lanky alley cats.

Ariz found him pleasant enough to look at but didn't like how curious he could turn or how observant he was, even when staggering drunk.

Sober, he might well prove dangerous.

"I thought you'd gone away to amuse yourself at court," Brother Berto commented to Atreau.

"Sadly the company there proved less diverting than watching you dig through Master Narsi's belongings while he slept," Atreau drawled.

"I was looking for medicines!" Brother Berto pinned Atreau with an expression of outrage, and then he caught himself as his gaze fell on Ariz. He forced a smile. "It's good to see you as well, Master Ariz. Does your sister plan on joining you?"

Ariz shook his head and Berto hung onto his smile though his disappointment was obvious. Since he'd developed a fondness for Delfia, Brother Berto had made a point of paying Ariz more attention than he normally would have—which was to say, any at all. Ariz returned Brother Berto's smile with a blank stare before dropping his gaze to the floor.

They all fell silent for a moment.

Atreau yawned, then he called to the Holy Father, "Tim, is there anything I can do for you or Master Narsi?"

Father Timoteo offered him a wan smile, demurred any niceties and thanked Atreau for his offer; then he added, "I know he's not expected to wake . . . soon. But I thought it might help him to hear our voices. I'm going to read to him from a few of his mother's letters. But as I recall he admired your writing greatly. Perhaps later you would read something of your own to him?"

"Of course," Atreau replied.

The Holy Father nodded and then stepped into the master physician's exam room. Brother Berto started after his master but then glanced to Atreau.

"He loved your description of Lord Grunito's wedding and how you all escaped the royal bishop's guards that afternoon," Berto said. "He was there, you know. We both were, actually."

"Really?" Atreau studied Berto as if trying to recall him from some distant memory.

"We were just servant boys," Berto said quickly. "I doubt you'd recall us. But Narsi was very impressed when you and all the Sagrada Hellions stayed at the house."

"Well, I would be happy to read that selection from my first memoir to him," Atreau replied. "Just tell me when Tim needs a break."

Brother Berto nodded and then hurried after the Holy Father. In the following quiet Ariz clearly heard Brother Berto chiding the Holy Father for standing when he should take a chair. A few moments later Father Timoteo's low voice rumbled as he read from some quiet, meditative letter.

"So, you've come to visit Master Narsi as well?" Atreau favored Ariz with his handsome interest. But there was something cold about his appraisal, almost as if he suspected Ariz of having harmed the young physician in the first place.

Ariz shrugged.

"Between Mistress Querra and half the chapel looking after him, I'm beginning to think that our Master Narsi makes the most enchanting of first impressions." Atreau indicated for Ariz to enter the exam room with a motion of his hand.

"I . . ." Ariz shook his head. "Just came to find out when I could cut out my stitches. I thought he might be awake by now."

"No. According to the man himself, he won't likely wake until tomorrow," Atreau remarked.

"He knew how long he'd be ill?" Ariz didn't want to betray interest but he couldn't help himself. Master Narsi must have had some experience with muerate to be so clear-headed—or perhaps he'd just made the pronouncement in a state of shock.

"I could hardly believe it myself." Atreau favored the examination room with a crooked smile. "He warned me to stay back because there was muerate poison on the body and then told me that he was going to lose consciousness but ought to regain his senses within two days' time. And not to allow anyone to pronounce him dead unless he'd been unresponsive for at least that long."

"How . . . level-headed." Ariz wondered if he could have remained so collected himself. Master Narsi might be a good man to keep in mind when Hierro's orders came and it became vital to treat the many people who would suffer. "He seems suited to his calling."

Atreau nodded and then glanced again into the exam room. Ariz thought that his attention rested on the examination table. Then he saw the black cat curled up there and watching the two of them over its tail. For a moment they both simply stood there, Atreau lingering for no reason that Ariz could discern and Ariz remaining because exhaustion made it easy to simply stand with a blank expression and think of nothing much. Then it occurred to him that if Atreau had any concern for the physician he might be in a position to squelch bigoted rumors before they could drive Master Narsi away.

"Gossips are torn between blaming the murder on the Salt Island Spider and Master Narsi himself, it would seem," Ariz informed him. "One of the younger grooms and a group of women who tend Lord Quemanor's goats seem too ready to blame Master Narsi."

Atreau's brows rose.

"But you know better, Master Ariz?"

Was there an accusation hidden in that question? Ariz knew better than to respond as if there had been.

"Dommian was deeply in debt, but Master Narsi hadn't been with us long enough to number among those he owed money to. I'm inclined to think it was the work of the Spider."

Atreau gave a shake of his head and Ariz wondered if it wasn't true that Atreau kept very close company with the moneylender. The man seemed to enjoy the society of every other sort of reprobate, so why not an infamous bar owner and loan shark?

"Oh, I nearly forgot." Atreau reached into the pocket of his coat and drew out a stiff white kerchief that looked largely soaked with dried blood. Even so Ariz noted the pattern of white swans that decorated the costly square of silk. "I think this might be yours."

Again Ariz suppressed the urge to deny any knowledge of the kerchief. They both knew that it had been the one he'd clutched to his bloody arm two days ago. Lying about it would only make the Fueres heraldry seem all the more damning. Ariz reached out and took it from Atreau. He pretended to study it.

"I think it must be one of my sister's," Ariz said. "I don't know if you can see the swans for all the bloodstains, but I recognize them. I think the duchess gifted this to her. She's going to be vexed that I bled all over it." He tucked the kerchief into his pocket. He'd burn the thing later.

"Perhaps it could be dyed to hide the stains." The subtle tension in Atreau's expression seemed to fade. "A clever mistress of mine swears by madder dyes for such things."

"Thank you. I'll be sure to tell Delfia as much." Ariz couldn't think of anything else to add. For his part Atreau seemed lost in contemplation of the exam room.

"Well, I should be on my way," Ariz said after several moments passed in silence. "I'll come back later to ask about the stitches."

Atreau nodded. Ariz left him standing at the threshold of the doorway, looking in as if some troubling mystery awaited him within. He didn't know Atreau well, but it struck him as strange that the man should concern himself with a physician he'd only just met. Perhaps Master Narsi's arrival at Lord Quemanor's house didn't mark their first meeting. The young physician was obviously related to the Grunito family, and Atreau was famous for his friendship with the infamous duelist Elezar Grunito. There was a chance that Master Narsi and Atreau would have met previously in the Grunito household. They could well know each other better than either let on.

But why bother to hide that? Unless it was to protect Master Narsi's reputation, though if that was the case, Atreau was hardly doing the young man any favors by spending days and nights with him.

Ariz felt too tired to think much on the idea, so he allowed it to simply float in the back of his mind. Later it might prove important. For now he just wanted to go to his room and steal a few minutes of rest.

He'd only reached his own door when Delfia found him and handed him a note that a beggar child had been paid to carry to Lord Quemanor's household and see handed over to Ariz.

"I gave him a cake and lifted it off him," Delfia said. "When he thought he'd lost it he fled."

Ariz noted the cracked wax seal with great relief. He trusted Delfia to read messages sent to him and shield him from laying eyes on any command from Hierro that would endanger her or the children. This missive came from Hierro's sister Clara. Ariz knew her handwriting. Without mentioning any specific name she informed him of her husband's evening schedule.

The last lines read: *After that matter is settled, I should like a word with you. It would be to your advantage not to keep me waiting another day.*

"You'll do it tonight, then?" Delfia asked him.

Ariz nodded. A third death in as many days would hardly set anyone at ease though. The count's passing would have to look natural.

Delfia took the note to the fireplace and fed it into the embers smoldering there. She used a poker to ensure that no trace of the fine linen paper remained. Then she turned her attention back to Ariz.

"Be careful of her, little brother. She's as ambitious as Hierro and more of a zealot than the royal bishop."

Again Ariz nodded. He knew this had to be done, but part of him wished that he'd just stayed up on the ruin watching clouds roll overhead.

"Have you slept at all?" Delfia asked him.

"An hour or two."

"Sleep now," she told him. "I'll see to Sparanzo's extra dance lesson."

"Won't the duchess have need of you?" Ariz didn't admit aloud that the possibility of Lord Quemanor seeking him out made him hesitant to accept her offer. Silently Ariz chided his own wishful turn of mind. Fedeles Quemanor would likely be at court the entire day. And even if he weren't, he would no doubt have better things to do than call upon him.

"No, she's gone to the king's court to meet with her agents there," Delfia replied. "She received another missive from Elenna Ortez. This one seemed urgent."

"What's the matter, do you know?" Ariz asked. He prayed that another threat to his nieces or Sparanzo hadn't been discovered. Not that he wouldn't deal with it.

"Something on some distant island. It's nothing to do with you or me. So get some rest, while you can."

Ariz sat down on his bed and pulled off his boots. Noticing his sister lingering, he asked, "Is there something else?"

"Shall I pack you an elixir for tonight's errand?" Delfia whispered.

"That would help. But not muerate. There's been too much of that already."

"Duera then." Delfia said. "Enough to quiet him so that you can make it seem . . . natural."

Ariz nodded. His eyelids drooped. He already knew how he would end count Zacarrio Odalis's life. While the countess entertained her friends in the late afternoon, the count would retire for his habitual nap in his library. A dose of duera and the firm application of a pillow over the old man's face would leave an unmarked corpse and the general impression of a man who died quietly of a failed heart. He would be the fifth soul Ariz had smothered to death, two of Hierro's young stepmothers numbering among them. Ariz's stomach rolled with revulsion at the memories. The murder wouldn't be difficult. Ariz supposed that was a large part of what made it feel all the more terrible to him. He didn't want to be such a monster that he could take a life as easily as packing a trunk.

Delfia took his hand in hers and squeezed his fingers.

"I know . . ." She didn't say any more, but the concern in her expression reminded him of his reason for doing all of this, instead of slitting his own throat. Delfia had already endured too much at Hierro's hands. Ariz had to do all he could to shield her and her children from Hierro's anger and avarice. So long as he made himself available, Hierro wouldn't bother to employ spells to make Delfia or her children into his agents. The longer he could endure, the more time he bought for Delfia to secure an escape for herself and the girls.

"It will be fine." Ariz returned her grip. "I'm just tired."

"You should sleep then." Delfia released his hand and withdrew to his door. "I'll lock the door behind me."

Ariz nodded and lay back, still dressed but too exhausted to care. He closed his eyes and slept, his dreams filled with twisted white clouds churning through blood-red skies.

He awakened to hear the chapel bells ringing out midday. He rose, dressed and then set out to smother an old man to death.

∾∾∾

The perfume of melting beeswax hung through the warm drawing room but didn't quite cover the sharp scent of the birch oil burning in the table lamps. The light haloed Clara Odalis and made each of the demure combs holding her black hair glint like a knife's edge. The shadows of her two ladies-in-waiting and the four men amusing them at a card table bounced and sprang across the silk screen that separated the countess from her guests. She'd withdrawn, claiming a terrible backache, when she'd spied Ariz awaiting her in a corner. As the others laughed and teased each other, the countess commented to them occasionally from her velvet divan.

With a gesture of her pale hand she indicated for Ariz to approach her. He edged around the lamplight, watching where his own shadow fell and keeping it hidden within dark masses of the surrounding busts and decorative columns. Several cages of exotic birds blocked his path, but Ariz ducked around them and the birds continued sleeping, with their golden-plumed heads tucked beneath their emerald wings.

"Procopio, I am depending upon you to win a hand of hearts for me," Clara called sweetly. "I shall be devastated if you give up the game before you've won at least one."

"I will endeavor to do so for your sake, my lady." The nobleman's enunciation sounded amused but also eroded by alcohol. "But I should warn you that your companions are the most outrageous cheats."

The ladies-in-waiting giggled in response and the gray translucent shadows of full glasses were raised and drained, before another hand of cards. One of the men picked up a lute and plucked after some melody that Ariz felt had truly eluded him. The man's mediocre singing made Ariz suddenly appreciate Atreau Vediya's immense musicality. It elevated the whole standard of entertainment at Lord Quemanor's estate.

Ariz knelt at the head of the divan. Clara's dry perfume of iris root and calendula flowers drifted over him.

"Is it done?" she whispered.

Ariz nodded. Clara's large dark eyes moved over him quickly, likely searching for a gory weapon or bloodstains. Ariz held up his spotless hands and leaned forward to whisper in her ear.

"He's in his chair in the library. There is no sign of violence to be discovered."

Clara stared into his eyes and for a moment—if even that—he thought that he might have frightened her, for her pupils had gone so wide and her breath had seemed to catch. But then he recognized the flush spreading across her face. She leaned closer so that the tender skin of her cheek brushed his jaw.

"Did you see his soul rise from his body?" Her breath fluttered across Ariz's ear.

Ariz shook his head, though he'd not expected such a question at all. Clara sighed regretfully.

"I wish I could have witnessed it to be sure where his spirit went. Zacarrio was cruel, but so are many men whom our holy books name as saints. Perhaps paradise had a use for him. I wonder, will there be a place for you, Master Ariz . . . ?"

Ariz said nothing. He didn't move even to blink. He'd learned long ago not to arouse the interest of any member of the Fueres family. He crouched still as stone, staring ahead at the shadows wavering across the silk screen. One of the ladies-in-waiting stole a card while the other distracted the men at the table by exclaiming over a button that had burst open on her bodice.

"Tell me that you made Dommian's death quick at least, won't you?" Clara whispered.

Ariz hadn't expected Clara to know the guard's name, much less concern herself with his fate.

"It was fast. He didn't fight," Ariz said after a moment.

"No, he wouldn't have." Clara glanced to the shrouded silhouettes of her birdcages. "If he could have had his own way, he would have led the simple life of a history scholar. But this world is unfair to those of us without power. Dommian hated what Hierro made him into; likely you did him a kindness."

Ariz found it strange to take any comfort in Clara's words, but he did.If someday, some other swordsman took his life, he would feel only relief at the prospect.

"Hierro will be furious when he discovers that you killed Dommian. He's not to be trifled with." Clara drew back just slightly from him and crossed her legs beneath the folds of her silken dress; even so Ariz noted the black bruises that mottled her slender calf. "I'm sure that we both have the scars to prove as much, don't we, Master Ariz?"

Ariz nodded and Clara seemed to relax again. She leaned into him once more.

"I can claim that I ordered the killing," Clara said. "I can protect you and your sister."

The offer took Ariz off guard as no threat or revelation of horror might have. He met Clara's gaze. She smiled, but there was something dull and dead about her eyes. Extending protection to him and Delfia brought her no pleasure.

"He'll be furious," Ariz said.

"He can't afford to murder me yet, not with Prince Remes paying me court. I can manage him. But . . ."

"You need something in return," Ariz said.

"Yes." Her eyes flicked to the shadows cast across the silk screen, then returned to Ariz. "I need you to ensure that Sparanzo Quemanor is protected."

Clara reached out and picked up a silken coin purse from the desktop. She handed it to Ariz. Inside Ariz found a gold locket on a gold chain strung with stones the color of rubies but oddly shaped and cracked. The locket too appeared battered and scratched, but even so Ariz was able to pick out the weathered symbol incised across its face. A null symbol.

"These shards contain ancient blessings, and the locket is said to be one of the last crafted by Bhadia before the Battle of Heaven's Shard."

Ariz recalled Clara mentioning Bhadia's locket the evening he'd delivered Ciceron's head. She'd implied that the royal bishop might be searching for it but also that it was long lost.

"It is so precious to me, you cannot know. But I must not deprive Sparanzo of its protection." Clara reached out to briefly touch several of the ruby stones. She drew her hands back with an expression of regret. "All I need from you is to ensure that he wears it from this day on—"

"I'm not his dresser—"

"Give it to Oasia, then." Clara scowled at Ariz, but her annoyance seemed to melt at once into soft-eyed melancholy. "She may have abandoned me to Hierro's mercies, but surely she wouldn't do the same to Sparanzo. Tell her that I am offering her son the protection I so desperately sought when we were children. The least she can do is ensure he survives when judgment comes."

"When will that be, my lady?" Ariz asked.

"How can it matter for you, Ariz? Your life isn't your own, and Hierro will never free you. Your demise might as well have come decades ago." Clara held Ariz's gaze, and this time her expression did seem to turn a little kinder. "But you aren't asking for your own sake, are you?"

Ariz said nothing but Clara must have perceived something through the mask of his blank face. Her composed expression wavered and for an instant her eyes looked a little too bright. She turned her face to the screen.

"Does your sister know how fortunate she is to have such a brother?" Clara whispered. "How I envy her."

Ariz didn't doubt that. Neither Oasia nor Clara had known the sort of affection and adoration that both he and Delfia had grown up with.

"If you could ferry her and her children from Cadeleon, perhaps you could buy them a little time. But I don't believe they'd elude Hierro for long. It might be a greater kindness to let them live out what remains in the relative shelter of Oasia's household. Better that than their last days being spent in Hierro's grasp, don't you think?" Clara attempted a smile, but it came out as a pained grimace. "If it's any consolation, know that Hierro will get what he deserves. Not before the corrupt Sagrada bloodline is washed away, but his time will come."

After the end of the *entire* Sagrada bloodline? Ariz wondered if that was part of Hierro's plan or a separate goal of Clara's own devising. But he knew better than to comment. Already her expression had closed to him. Ariz took the coin purse.

"Why Sparanzo?" he asked.

"He is innocent and the one child whom I have the capacity to protect. If I could I would save every innocent child, but my power is limited and my position is precarious." Clara didn't meet his gaze this time. "Even monsters like you and I have our little conceits of morality, Master Ariz. Mine is to save the boy. And I do not think that his survival is contrary to your own wishes, is it?"

Of course he wanted to protect Sparanzo. Though not Sparanzo alone.

"I would see him saved, yes."

"Then do this thing for me and let us both be the instruments of some shred of redemption for ourselves." Clara drew back from him and then rose and approached the silken screen. She raised her voice to a sweet, bright tone as she called, "I'm feeling so much better. But I'm missing my darling Zacarrio. Let us go and rouse him for a game!" She drew back the screen and the late-afternoon light flooded the alcove.

Ariz fled into the shadows.

CHAPTER
TWENTY

Narsi lay at the edge of wakefulness, hearing a low, warm voice speaking familiar words. Lord Vediya was reciting one of his old adventures. He wasn't as Narsi had imagined he would be, and now a strange new sense of secrecy and cunning pervaded the story that Narsi had thought he knew so well.

Dappled lamplight fluttered over Narsi's eyelids. He thought he was about to wake. Then his bed rocked and he realized he was afloat on a swelling sea. The sliver of a moon shone overhead and thin, luminous clouds drifted across the dark sky.

The black cat that shared his room leaned over him; its yellow eyes seemed huge and its paws blazed with heat as they pressed into his chest.

"I repay your kindness, Master Narsi. Not only will you live, but your hands will heal," the cat said. Narsi wasn't surprised that the creature spoke; this was a dream, after all. Though he'd not expected its voice to be that of a woman, or its words to sound so distinctly Labaran. "Now let us curl up and sleep. We both have long undertakings ahead of us before the sun rises."

The bed heaved with the rolling ocean and Narsi slipped away into a deep unconsciousness.

When he next woke it was with only a vague awareness of an ache in his right hand. Again he heard the low tones of men whispering somewhere near him. But the cadence of their words no longer sounded in the artful tempo of prose. Brother Berto and Father Timoteo, Narsi realized. They were in his examination room and discussing Haldiim funeral rites. A comfortable lethargy washed the significance of the conversation far from his grasp. His eyes remained closed. The effort of lifting his heavy lids seemed a monumental task and unlikely to result in any reward better than the soft warmth that presently cocooned him.

Something had happened to him, he vaguely recalled. Someone had been poisoned and there'd been something important about the corpse. But now Narsi couldn't remember, and the harder he tried, the more the memory seemed to dissolve away into the confusing images from half-forgotten dreams. He probably wasn't ready to be awake yet.

He relaxed to drift back to sleep.

If only it weren't for that hard, hot little weight compressing his chest. What was it? Now that he focused on the sensation it seemed all the more strange. Had someone placed a bed warmer on his chest? Was it ever so slightly vibrating against him?

He drew in a deep breath and felt the prick of tiny claws against the bare skin of his shoulder. At once his eyes opened to meet the yellow gaze of a black cat. The thin creature lay curled on Narsi's chest, watching him over its tail. Then it closed its eyes and Narsi felt its body relax against him.

"And he rises from the darkness like a new moon."

Narsi rolled his head to the right and caught sight of Lord Vediya reclining in a wooden chair near his bedside. The morning light filtering in from the window lent a particularly golden tone to the man's skin and turned the gray streaks in his dark hair bronze. He struck Narsi as looking better rested than he'd been the last few times they'd met. The realization made Narsi feel suddenly self-conscious of his disarrayed hair and sweat-soaked body. He hoped that he hadn't been snoring and farting all the time he'd been unconscious.

The fragrance of Lord Vediya's rose and musk cologne mixed with the lingering scent of an astringent wash.

"How long have you been here?" Narsi made an attempt to pull his nightshirt straight, but his right hand felt almost like a stranger's, groping numb and clumsily at the thin white cloth. The cat shot him a disapproving glare and then slunk down to the foot of the bed.

"Dearest fellow, I've never left your side," Lord Vediya replied. "I've waited like a champion kneeling in vigil, praying for your recovery." For the briefest instant his sincere tone and concerned expression touched Narsi—but then Narsi caught himself, recognizing the utter implausibility of the words.

"Wept yourself dry as dust, as well? Careful, my lord, lest a sudden breeze blow your sad body away like ash," Narsi responded.

"No fooling you, is there?" Lord Vediya grinned at him with a truly delighted expression. "I took advantage of the comforts of your exam room the last two nights but heartlessly abandoned you to Tim's care on numerous occasions. He's all but held vigil over you this entire time."

Narsi looked to the closed door, his groggy mind slowly rousing to the idea of a larger world beyond this room. Lord Vediya eyed the door as well, but his expression appeared much more furtive than Narsi would have expected. Lord Vediya leaned closer to the bedside.

"I don't know how close you are with Berto—or Tim, for that matter—but they seemed a bit too at ease with your things, so I've stowed your medical satchel in my private rooms." He stole another glance to the door, then returned his attention to Narsi. "Also, this might be none of my business, but your friend Berto found a letter addressed to Father Tim and opened it. I caught him at it and he handed it over to the Holy Father. Maybe it's nothing, but I wanted you to know."

"Thank you." Narsi's thoughts rolled sluggishly over the idea of a letter, and then all at once he remembered the missive. He'd fretted over it so much, it surprised him to have forgotten its existence even briefly. The idea of someone, even a friend, opening the letter that he'd been so careful of didn't sit well with Narsi. And yet he supposed that Berto regularly opened and read Father Timoteo's correspondences. Likely he'd simply acted out of habit. Still, Narsi would have liked the chance to hand it over himself.

Perhaps he might have even summoned the courage to ask Father Timoteo if the contents revealed the identity of his father.

Or maybe—considering how doggedly his own mother and Timoteo kept the information from him—this was a favor to them all. Narsi sighed. Was it better to always live with this uncertainty or to discover some terrible heritage? His gaze fell on the cat at the foot of the bed. He likely hadn't known his father and didn't seem to care a jot.

"But it would do your feline pride some damage to find out he was a dog, wouldn't it?" Narsi murmured. In response the cat scratched its ear.

"Pardon?" Lord Vediya asked.

"I'm just having a joke with the cat," Narsi replied. He wondered if he ought to go ahead and give the creature a name. Perhaps Tariq, which meant "whisper" in Haldiim.

"You're an odd one, Master Narsi." Lord Vediya's amused expression made Narsi think this might not be a bad thing. "We really ought to discuss a few things. There's a proposition that I'd—"

The handle of the door turned and Lord Vediya went silent and slouched back in the chair. Father Timoteo leaned in.

"Narsi!" Father Timoteo's mournful expression lifted as he met Narsi's gaze. He hurried into the room and very gently settled on the edge of the bed. "How are you, dear child?"

"Good," Narsi replied.

"Your hand?" Father Timoteo asked.

Belatedly Narsi again remembered the poisoning and the strange ache in his right hand. He lifted his hands from beneath the blankets. Father Timoteo gave a soft gasp of horror. From that reaction Narsi guessed that Father Timoteo hadn't been the one who'd rinsed Narsi's hand and removed his ring after he'd collapsed. Both his hands would have looked far worse earlier, with blood seeping from his pores and his fingernails cracking and blackening as if burned. In fact, he felt both relieved and surprised to see that he'd not lost his right hand completely.

His left hand sported fading bruises and still felt slightly stiff, but otherwise it appeared normal. But his right hand looked like it belonged to a bare-knuckles boxer who'd gone a round against the interior of a chimney. The joints of his fingers and wrist were too inflamed to bend easily and the mass of bruises discoloring his palm and the back of his hand lent his skin sickly purple and yellow tones. The faint line where a rose thorn had scratched him now stood out as a jet-black streak of scar tissue running from his first knuckle down to his wrist. Happily he'd only lost one fingernail—the smallest—though the others each bore several tiny blackened pockmarks.

He closed his eyes and carefully pinched each of his fingertips. A wave of relief washed through him as the fingers of his right hand registered the sensations. He'd not lost the use of his hand.

"Ugly," Narsi said. "But nothing lasting. The swelling will go down in a day or so and the bruises should fade in a matter of weeks."

"It looks . . ." Father Timoteo trailed off with a pained expression.

"Hard to imagine you having much joy waxing your pole with that sad flipper," Lord Vediya commented.

Father Timoteo shook his head at Lord Vediya but Narsi laughed.

"Some might say that this is just the reason we are gifted with two hands," Narsi replied.

"The good Lord's wisdom knows no bounds. Though a good friend might—" Lord Vediya began, but his words were cut short when Brother Berto shouldered the door open and came in carrying a tray laden with dishes.

"Is our lad up at last?" Berto asked, though his broad smile faltered as he caught sight of Narsi's right hand. "Lord . . . your hand looks like you've just pulled it out of the Black Hell, Narsi. Does it hurt very badly?" Berto stepped past Father Timoteo and rested the tray on Narsi's bedside table.

"It's a little stiff but not too bad, considering." Narsi lowered his hands back into the folds of his blankets. "Am I being presumptuous in assuming that tray is for me?"

"It is. And this time it was sent with the duke's compliments." Berto regained his pleased expression. "Your errand of mercy to the captain's widow must've won him over to your side."

Narsi struggled to recall what Berto referred to. A widow? He couldn't remember visiting any widow recently. Then the jumble of events that had led up to his poisoning seeped back to him and he recollected that the excuse for his flight from the duke's house had been to succor a widow. In truth he'd done nothing of the sort.

Uneasy of speaking too much while his memory still felt so unreliable, Narsi turned his attention to the tray. A leg of roast goose and a great heap of mashed carrot and turnip filled a plate. Beside that stood a server brimming with gravy and several smaller dishes heaped with nuts and freshly cut herbs. A cup of some fragrant warm tisane steamed beside a tiny silver pitcher of cream.

"Well, this all smells lovely," Narsi commented, then he added to Berto, "Thank you."

Berto offered him a reassuring nod with such a concerned expression that Narsi suddenly wondered just how ill he'd appeared.

Using his left hand, Narsi took up the silverware provided and managed to scoop out an inelegant mound of mash and deliver it to his mouth. Having three other men and one cat watch made him feel particularly awkward. However the rich flavors of carrot and butter that filled his mouth along with hints of warm spice made it all seem worth the self-consciousness.

"You three should talk among yourselves," Narsi said. "This deserving meal may require all my attention." Narsi focused on serving himself a portion of gravy and then poorly carving away a hunk of the goose leg.

"Good weather we're having," Father Timoteo said into the quiet of the room. When that inspired no response he added, "I hope it will hold through the masquerades."

The other two men nodded. At the foot of the bed the cat stretched and then bounded down to the floor and sauntered out the door.

"Should I put the creature out of doors?" Berto inquired.

Narsi almost laughed at how obviously Berto struggled not to show his repulsion for the small beast. Clearly offering to touch it was a sacrifice he only considered out of friendship.

"No need. It seems to have found its own way of coming and going," Narsi replied, then he returned to the surprisingly difficult matter of feeding himself with his left hand. Had he been alone he would have snatched the goose leg up with his bare hand and simply gnawed on the thing instead pushing it around his plate with clumsy manipulations of his silverware. But Cadeleonians tended to judge others by their table manners and often held Haldiim and foreigners to an even more demanding standard than they met themselves.

"You need some kindhearted soul to cut that damn thing up for you," Lord Vediya commented, though he made no move to leave his seat. Instead he propped his feet up on the edge of Narsi's bed as if it were a footrest. Berto shot Lord Vediya a look of disgust.

Father Timoteo moved to Narsi's side.

"Would it help you, child? Or are you hoping to improve the dexterity of your left hand?"

"I suppose I ought to use this occasion to do just that," Narsi replied. "Though I fear I might starve before I see much improvement at this rate."

"Well, then please allow me." Father Timoteo took the cutlery from Narsi and quickly stripped the meat from the bone. He returned the silverware to Narsi and then returned to the stool near the bedroom window.

Narsi ate with much greater ease, though it still made for slow going. After he'd finished off the meat and mash, he managed to clasp the cup with both hands and enjoy a few gulps of the tisane.

He didn't find it odd that Father Timoteo remained quiet and appeared lost in thought as he regarded the garden view outside Narsi's window. He was a man of contemplation and prone to long periods of quiet between his orations. But the silence between Berto and Lord Vediya was hardly an easy one. Berto glowered like a suspicious guard dog, while Lord Vediya slouched in his chair like a youth bent upon provoking a schoolmaster.

As the silence stretched on Narsi began to wonder why the two of them seemed so intent upon remaining here. Their worry for his welfare made for a flattering motivation. But Narsi doubted it, since neither Lord Vediya nor Berto had insisted upon remaining by his side all the time he'd been unconscious and in the most danger of succumbing to the poison.

Bells sounded from the chapel across the grounds. Lord Vediya scowled and cast Narsi an oddly exasperated glance. Then he swung his long legs down from Narsi's bed and stood.

"I can see that you aren't likely to be up to treating my little concern anytime soon, Master Narsi." Lord Vediya shot Berto a lewd smile as he tapped his fingers over the silver buckle of his low-slung sword belt. "But when you're back on your feet, do remember to call upon me. Preferably privately. I wouldn't want to shock the children." Again he turned his gaze to Berto, who glared back but said nothing. For his part Narsi wondered how Lord Vediya managed to woo so many lovers when he so blithely and constantly implied himself to be riddled with merrypox. He really didn't seem to give a damn about his reputation or society's respect.

"I'll see to the treatments as soon as I can, Lord Vediya," Narsi replied.

Lord Vediya nodded and then sauntered from the room. A moment later the click of the hallway door sounded and Berto made an obscene gesture at the door.

"Berto!" Father Timoteo shook his head. "Atreau only acts so brashly because he knows that it provokes you. He's always been a bit of an attention seeker, you know. But there's never been any real malice behind his incitements, I don't think. He's much more of a sensitive soul than he lets on. Wouldn't you agree, Narsi?"

"Me?" Narsi felt oddly alarmed and guilty being asked his opinion of Lord Vediya's heart. Perhaps because he knew more than he should have and had come by the knowledge in a manner that would embarrass both himself and Lord Vediya, though for very different reasons. "I've really only spent a day with him, but he does seem . . ." Far more politically involved and personally complex than I ever suspected, Narsi thought. Aloud he said, "... sensitive, just as you say. Yes."

"He rubs me the wrong way. He always has." Berto scowled at the door, but then some movement outside the window drew his attention and his expression brightened. Narsi looked to see several workmen hauling wheelbarrows brimming with botanicals in heavy pots past the weedy beds of the medicinal garden. Tanned-faced youths sprinted past them with hoes and shovels, while a plump gray-haired woman directed them. Narsi squinted through the warp of the glass panes and decided that the woman had to be Querra. If he listened he could just hear her chiding a young man to be very careful with the dogseye plants.

"Have my botanicals arrived already?" Excitement rose in Narsi's chest.

"They've been showing up all through the day," Father Timoteo told him. "Mistress Querra has directed the gardeners in uncrating them and preparing the beds, but she didn't want to presume so much as to take charge of the actual plantings."

"That's so good of her." Narsi took another slug from his cup and set the tray and his cup aside as quickly as he could manage. Then he pushed back his blankets and swung his legs off the edge of the bed. "I should go and thank her. And see that the plants are laid in as soon as possible."

He managed to stand and even take several steps before the room seemed to tilt under him. All at once his footing failed him and he lurched. Alarm lit Father Timoteo's expression and Berto bounded to Narsi's side to support him.

"I'm not sure you should be up yet," Berto said.

"I suspect it will do me good to move around and work through what lingering numbness remains." Narsi carefully stretched each of his limbs in turn, testing their stability.

"Or Querra could easily come here to you and give your orders to the gardeners," Berto suggested.

Narsi shook his head and was pleased to note that it didn't induce another wave of vertigo. Berto looked to Father Timoteo and, a little to his own annoyance, Narsi found that he did as well—as if they were both still boys, expecting the Holy Father to know what was best in all things.

"Would you advise a patient of yours to leave his bed and go about under the same circumstances?" Father Timoteo asked Narsi.

"If he were young and healthy, yes . . . ," Narsi replied, but, meeting the Holy Father's gaze, he faltered. "Though I'd caution him not to go alone and to rest often the first few days. But a walk out to the physic garden is hardly a great distance, and there's a small stone bench near the fountain where I can sit and oversee the plantings."

"That sounds reasonable. Let us all three get a little sun and fresh air then." Father Timoteo nodded and rose to his feet. "I dare say Mistress Querra will be amused by our company just so long as we don't get underfoot."

Querra did take their attendance well, though Narsi suspected that was due to her possessing an indulgent and patient nature. She even managed to maintain her pleasant expression in the face of Father Timoteo inquiring after the name and special properties of every single plant specimen, whether it was going into the garden beds or being weeded out. To Narsi's pleasure Querra informed him of the seasonal shifts of the angle of the sun and how they differed from those in Anacleto. Together they decided which of the raised beds would best suit each of the botanical specimens. Steadily the air filled with the scents of rich soil and bruised mint leaves.

More than once Narsi slipped into speaking his native Haldiim with Querra. They were both more familiar with the Haldiim terms for various plants. As he and Querra discussed which herbs to harvest for the household and which to trade with Mother Kir-Naham, it began to feel almost as if he'd never left Anacleto. It seemed natural to chat about Summer solstice. Narsi was delighted when Querra insisted that he should join her in celebrating with Esfir and Mother Kir-Naham.

Though the curious glances of the surrounding workmen brought him back to his true situation. And then Cadeleonian conversation reasserted itself. Several of the workmen worried over the condition of Narsi's fountain. Father Timoteo pointed out the little clusters of songbirds that all the digging had attracted. He identified several more from their calls.

Berto remained at Narsi's side for a time, but then he caught sight of an auburn-haired woman—Mistress Delfia, Narsi realized—escorting two dark-haired children past the garden and excused himself. Narsi felt heartened to see the excitement with which Mistress Delfia greeted his friend.

Narsi leaned back into the cool shadow of the fountain, listening to the conversation a little absently as he admired the display of lustrous leaves, flower buds and young vines. Mere days ago he couldn't have hoped to afford even half the bounty that spread before him. Now if all went well, in a year's time he'd be able to distill, harvest and process nearly any medicine he could wish for. All of this was his, now.

Querra waved over two burly gardeners, who joined the three already shoveling bone and blood meal into the dark soil of the only remaining empty plant bed. She paused a moment, frowning, as a gardener wheeled in the three Labaran rose specimens Narsi had paid so much for. She cast a questioning look at Narsi and he averted his gaze, feeling unreasonably guilty. How likely was it that anyone would assume that affection for Lord Vediya had inspired the purchase?

He gazed at the black cat lounging in branches of the overhanging willow while Querra stood over the roses, contemplating the little yellow striped flowers.

Labaran roses didn't possess the enormous blossoms of the hundred-petal varieties that adorned so many of the duke's arbors and pots. But even at a distance their perfume filled the air.

"Those are Labaran roses, you realize," Querra commented.

"Yes, a groundsman at the Royal's Physic Garden assured me that they are very winter hardy and produce the finest of distillates."

"That is all true." Querra tucked a lock of graying hair that had come loose from her matron's braids back behind her ear. "But Labara is not so popular a place just now."

"The flowers are hardly to blame," Narsi responded. It surprised him to see Father Timoteo too contemplated the fragrant small blossoms with a troubled expression.

"Nor is the color red," Querra replied quietly. "But there are still more than a few idiots going around the city hurling shit and calling folk traitors for wearing Count Radulf's color."

Narsi almost argued, but then he remembered that the only Cadeleonian whom he could recall wearing red had been Inissa—but even that had been a ploy. Were all citizens of the capital really that opposed to Count Radulf, or was it simply easier for most of them to give up wearing red and avoid the wrath of a few outspoken bullies?

"I'm not going to kill my roses for fear of some shortsighted bigots," Narsi replied.

"And rightly so," Querra responded. "They're wonderful flowers. But maybe we should plant them nearer your window and farther from the wall where all and sundry passing by will see them."

Narsi considered the proposition, feeling annoyed and uneasy with the thought of having to take some imagined idiots' hateful reactions into consideration. But he was already an outsider to most of the surrounding Cadeleonians. It would be foolish for him to flaunt a Labaran affiliation when he'd been warned against it, and—the memory came back to him again—he'd actually assisted Lady Hylanya to evade the royal bishop's men. It wasn't as if he didn't have anything to hide, he realized.

And he liked the idea of being able to smell the roses from his bedroom window.

"All right, let's plant them back away from the wall," Narsi agreed. Querra nodded and then offered Narsi a sympathetic smile. He suddenly realized that she, too, had to weigh the risks she took by simply speaking Haldiim to him.

"Who would have imagined that foreign politics would dictate my garden layout?" Narsi commented.

"Count Radulf's actions have had a greater effect than even he can likely imagine." Father Timoteo's gaze drifted up to the bright blue sky overhead. "Between the count freeing so many banished monsters in the northlands and the Bahiim waking Anacleto's White Tree in the south, many Cadeleonians have come to see themselves as surrounded by growing threats of heathenism and witchcraft. Monsters and demons at our gates."

Narsi found the idea of the holy White Tree being demonic or threatening to anyone absurd. It was a source of blessings and offered protection and respite. Though recalling how eerie he'd found the Circle of Wisteria, he had to acknowledge that not every aspect of Bahiim mysticism was innocuous and nurturing. The Bahiim had once been a warrior sect who battled demons and Old Gods. Even so, Bahiim beliefs represented no threat to Cadeleonian lives.

As for Count Radulf, Narsi knew little of the man personally, but Lord Vediya's book had not depicted the trolls, frogwives and weathra-steads he liberated as monsters, but as creatures kept too long in bondage. Obviously Lord Vediya's memoir being banned and burned deprived all but a small population of Haldiim readers in Anacleto of that knowledge.

Narsi wondered if that might have been the very reason that the royal bishop had condemned the book.

"Fear can make some people violent and cruel." Father Timoteo sighed. "It blinds them to beauty and allows them to see new things as threatening."

"But not all people," Narsi said.

"No, not all, but men like you and women like Mistress Querra are more rare than I think either of you imagine." Timoteo offered them both a slight smile before returning to his contemplation of the heavens. "If I'm honest, I must confess that uncertainty frightens me as well, some days. But I've seen where giving in to imagined threats can lead. No, as a man of faith, I must believe that these new happenings are part of our Lord's plan. It may take time, but we will find the divine within the strange. We will be all the stronger for accepting both the wonder of the White Tree in Anacleto and the awakened ancients of the northlands. We will learn from them, and they from us."

Timoteo seemed unaware that his words had caught the attention not just of Querra and Narsi but also of the surrounding workmen and gardeners.

"But they're heathens, father," a young gardener with a sunburned nose and shaggy brown hair objected. Other men stilled in their work, clearly waiting for Father Timoteo's response.

"Yes, they are." Timoteo smiled in that indulgent way that Narsi remembered so well from his boyhood. "But then again, aren't we heathens from their perspective?"

Not unsurprisingly, the young man and most of the other workers looked confused. Querra sighed and Narsi suspected that she'd already heard Timoteo's thoughts on the subject. Narsi made himself comfortable. Once Father Timoteo got going, these discussions could range on for a long while.

"No church, religion or holy book is without error," Father Timoteo said. "Not even our own. Why, only a few years ago the most blessed royal bishop failed to notice that Fedeles Quemanor had been possessed, despite Fedeles standing before him. It required the intervention of a heathen Bahiim to see the truth. Such failings are not rare, though men in power often try to hide them. Throughout our history ordinances have been withdrawn and holy texts altered to remove false predictions and outright mistakes. But if we consider that these writings are supposed to originate directly from our all-knowing, all-seeing divine Lord, then that presents a problem."

Timoteo paused, but no one spoke in the quiet. Narsi had no doubt that the Holy Father held the rapt attention of the devout workmen surrounding him.

"Either we must accept that our Holy Lord has made numerous errors and does not even know the true size of the very ocean he created, or we must recognize that *our* understanding of our Lord is imperfect. Now, I don't see the wonders of the world around us as the creations of an inept deity, do you?"

Narsi briefly entertained the thought of a religious order that did worship a bungling, clumsy god. He smiled and cracked his eye open briefly to see all of the groundsmen shake their heads. Several of them sat on the stonework of the raised beds with their tools in their hands, while a few others leaned on their shovels as if they were staffs.

Narsi closed his eyes again, and the sunlight shining through the willow branches played across his eyelids. The warmth felt good on his skin. The fountain at his back murmured soothingly, like a slow-flowing brook.

"It's not hard to accept that we—not our Lord—are the source of errors and misunderstandings in our holy texts and teachings," Father Timoteo went on in that low, assured tone of his. "It only follows that being flawed, mortal creatures, we cannot perfectly comprehend the divine. We understand a little of his instruction; we see glimpses of him in the world around us and in each other. But we cannot grasp the whole and so we have only fragments of truth. But then what do we make of other religions and peoples?

"We know that when our Lord created us all, he imparted instructions to us. If we recognize that we misunderstood some of those instructions, then no doubt so have other peoples—likely that is why we have many different beliefs across the world instead of only one. At the same time, we ought to recognize that as we have grasped some divine truths despite the confusion, then other people must have as well."

Narsi didn't bolt upright, but only because he was still recovering from poisoning. He met Querra's wide-eyed stare with his own. Clearly this was not an opinion either of them had heard Father Timoteo voice aloud before. Seated beside Narsi, Father Timoteo appeared so serene that it seemed almost impossible to believe how near heresy his words brought him. And the Holy Father just kept talking.

"If that is the case, then every religion and every people possesses some aspect of true holiness. It would be up to us not to reject heathens but to look into their ways for those jewels of our Lord's whole wisdom that we have lost."

"Like fitting together pieces of a broken crock from shards scattered all across a floor? Is that how you mean?" a leathery, middle-aged gardener asked.

"Yes. Exactly," Father Timoteo replied. "I think that all the peoples of all nations are in possession of parts of a whole, and if we wish to know and serve our Lord, we must seek those pieces out by exchanging ideas and teachings."

To Narsi's surprise, the men gathered around Father Timoteo didn't outrightly reject his suggestion. Some appeared skeptical, but most wore almost dazed expressions, as if the Holy Father had performed some magic trick that they still struggled to comprehend. The young sunburned man appeared troubled. At last he spoke in a nervous whisper.

"But, Father, them Salt Islanders turn men into women and such things. That ain't in no way natural or godly."

Father Timoteo gave a soft laugh and indulged the young man with an affectionate smile. "Have you visited the Salt Islands, Usto?"

"No, sir. But I heard stories . . ."

"Yes, I know what you mean. I was very nervous the first time I visited the islands myself, for much the same reason. I would make a rather homely nun, wouldn't I?"

That won Father Timoteo a loud laugh from all the workmen. Even Querra snorted.

"But then I went to their Butterfly Temple and saw the truth for myself." The admiration in Father Timoteo's expression seemed to wipe away the heavy shadows of his face and reveal his youth. "The priestesses there only transform people who have come to them because they have been trapped in the wrong bodies in the first place. I met several young people undertaking the transformations and I saw with my own eyes how joyous they were when they were given their true forms. It was the exact opposite of what I'd feared. Not boys and girls being disfigured but being freed to grow up as they were meant to. It was truly moving."

"You've been there and seen it?" The sunburned gardener, Usto, gaped at Father Timoteo. The Holy Father simply nodded and then returned his gaze to the sky, his expression still filled with happiness.

"Visiting the temple made me all the more awed by the Lord's kindness in gifting the priestesses with the power to help those who came to them."

For a few moments the rest of them in the garden, Narsi and Querra included, remained silent, considering Father Timoteo. Narsi had never been all that inclined to deep religious thought. As a boy he'd seen the holy texts as something to memorize alongside the Haldiim histories his mother taught him in the evenings. Even so, he wondered at the possibility of all religions arising from a single source. He frowned down at his own bruised hands.

How could the god who instructed Cadeleonians to punish men for their own sexual inclinations be the same as the radiant nameless first Bahiim who blessed all unions? Could cats and mice alike have been born—one to hunt and one to die—from the desire of a single god? If so, was that deity one deserving of worship?

His mother had always maintained that Cadeleonian priests and the Bahiim mystics drew their powers from different sources and served different causes. She moved between them as her needs dictated: Cadeleonian chapel to ease her grief, the White Tree of the Bahiim to bless her child.

But it seemed to him that at least half the groundsmen were taken with Father Timoteo's idea. Usto appeared stunned. Querra nodded to herself once, then she straightened and clapped her hands, drawing everyone but Father Timoteo's attention.

"Best get those roses in the dirt," she directed.

At once the groundsmen sprang to action. Narsi managed to stand and join them. He observed as they transplanted the three rosebushes into the dark soil. The perfume of the blossoms rolled over him as he contemplated companion plants for the roses. Fleabane to keep insects at bay, but perhaps some thyme and lavender as well. The work hardly took a quarter of an hour to complete, but by the time Querra and the gardeners departed—with Narsi's thanks—Narsi felt exhausted.

Once again he settled back down on the bench beside Father Timoteo and closed his eyes. The fountain continued its soothing murmur. He could feel his muscles relaxing in the warm sun. His thoughts wandered between careless whimsies as he drifted on the edge of sleep. He wondered where Lord Vediya roamed now. Had he ventured back across the bridge into the Theater District, or could he be up in his rooms, only yards away from Narsi even now? What proposition had he been about to offer Narsi, before Father Timoteo had come upon them?

"Did your mother show you any of what she wrote to me?" Father Timoteo's voice drifted over. Narsi cracked his eyes open just a little. Father Timoteo didn't look at him but leaned forward on the bench to pet the black cat at his feet.

"No, she didn't," Narsi admitted. "I thought that perhaps it was to do with my father . . ."

Father Timoteo nodded but still didn't look at Narsi. He scratched the cat's chin.

"Are you going to tell me?" Narsi asked.

Father Timoteo turned to face him at last, his expression so troubled that it sent a thrill of alarm through Narsi.

"Is it truly so bad?" Narsi asked. "Was he so horrible that you can't even say his name?"

"No! He wasn't. Your mother must have told you. He was a very good young man." Father Timoteo's gaze moved over Narsi's face intently. Narsi felt certain that Father Timoteo sought aspects of that dead young man in Narsi's flesh. "He was the best of us."

"Then why keep his identity from me?" Narsi asked.

"Because matters are rarely simple. Good men can leave their sons terrible legacies."

A terrible legacy? How was that supposed to serve as any kind of answer? That only added another layer of mystery for Narsi to speculate upon for hours on end. Narsi felt the familiar surge of frustrated anger, but today he didn't have the strength to maintain it. He simply shook his head and studied the branches of the willow tree as they spun in the light breeze.

"You don't think that by this point you'd just do me the kindness and offer me some random name to call father," Narsi commented. "I always thought I looked like I could pass for Miralindo's son."

"Miralindo?" Father Timoteo sounded almost offended, though as far as Narsi knew the man was a distant cousin of Lord Grunito's—an illegitimate and something of a rascal but generally harmless and good humored. "Lord, no! Your good mother would never have . . . never."

Narsi shrugged and dropped back against the bench. The black cat wound around his feet, then settled a little distance away in a pool of sunlight on the fountain's edge.

"And in any case, Miralindo's still alive," Father Timoteo went on. "If he were your father, don't you think the Grunito family would have made him pay for your schooling and care?"

"This does nothing to ease my curiosity, you realize," Narsi replied.

"I know." Father Timoteo scowled. "It's not my intention to toy with you. I just don't want to lie to you—"

"But you don't want to tell me the truth either," Narsi commented.

"I . . . No. I don't," Father Timoteo admitted. "Truth isn't always a kindness, and sometimes it only opens the way for greater harm."

"Well, then you might consider lying." Narsi offered the Holy Father a halfhearted smile.

"I've never lied to you, Narsi. Not once."

Narsi believed him, and he supposed that he ought to have felt reassured to know that the Holy Father had never misled him. If he'd been even two years younger, he would have been delighted. But since he'd been practicing medicine he'd come to realize that there were times when a lie was a kindness. Certainly no grieving widower needed to learn that his beloved newborn was likely another man's child. No one benefited from having all hope stripped from them after a diagnosis. Sometimes the only good a physician could offer was to allow a place for people to believe in rare possibilities and miracles.

Revealing the absolute truth in such cases only served the physician's vanity and often came at the cost of breaking a patient's spirit. Perhaps it seemed different from a priest's perspective.

"Miralindo likely has a few other children, I can't see the harm in adding myself to their number," Narsi murmured. "He might even be pleased if I began sending him solstice gifts. He might teach me a few card tricks—"

"Oh, Narsi." Father Timoteo shook his head. "You must not allow such a story to start up. It would sully your mother's name and open the way for folk to deem you illegitimate."

Narsi suspected that his mother had been well past caring about her reputation among Cadeleonians even before she died. And as for his own reputation, who didn't think him the illegitimate offspring of some member of the Grunito family?

He almost said as much, but Father Timoteo reached out and gripped his knee with a gentle squeeze. He leaned in toward Narsi and whispered. "When the time comes—when it's safe for you—I will do all I can to deliver your rightful inheritance to you. That was what your mother's letter asked of me."

"My inheritance?" Narsi's thoughts had been so far from such matters that he couldn't quite understand what Father Timoteo could possibly be referring to.

"She sent me the certificates and proofs of her marriage and your birth," Father Timoteo went on, though his expression grew grim, as if just thinking on the matter exhausted him. "It will not be easily achieved nor without cost, but you are your father's rightful heir."

Was this the terrible legacy? Narsi wondered. He patted Father Timoteo's cold, bony hand.

"I have a source of income of my own now. I don't think that I need to demand any inheritance—certainly not one that comes at a cost to other people. I think that I'd be happy just to know my father's name."

Father Timoteo's expression wavered.

"I'd like to be able to name him in my nightly prayers," Narsi said, despite the fact that he'd not recited evening prayers since he'd turned ten. Father Timoteo's amused expression and dry laugh assured Narsi that he knew as much.

"Isandro," Father Timoteo whispered. "That was his name. But for your own safety you must not tell anyone. Certainly not now, with the royal bishop already so opposed to the growing Haldiim influence in Anacleto."

Isandro. Narsi hardly heard the rest of Father Timoteo's words. The name seemed to echo through his mind. *Isandro* . . . There had been a fruit seller who'd gone by that name—a tall, very tanned Cadeleonian who'd seemed to travel in a mist of lemon oil. But he'd been only a few years older than Narsi. He recollected a wiry, half-Mirogoth rat catcher who might have been called Isandro . . . But no, it had been the name of the man's snarling little rat hound . . .

Isandro . . .

And then Narsi remembered. In the Grunito family chapel, a large window of brilliantly stained glass memorialized Lady and Lord Grunito's firstborn son, Isandro Grunito. Before he'd been murdered by highwaymen, *that* Isandro had been heir to the earldom of Anacleto. Afterward, the title had been refused by Timoteo—who as a second son was already consecrated to the church—then the title was again abdicated by the infamous swordsman Elezar and at last settled upon the charming fourth son, Nestor.

Narsi stared at Father Timoteo. For one of the few times in his life he couldn't think of anything to say. The shining figure from the stained glass window blazed up in his mind, looking so handsome and heroic, but nothing like the vague few memories he possessed of being held and rocked against a warm body. Dark hair and dark eyes defined a pale face, but nothing else came to him. He felt certain he would have remembered, even at the age of three, if his father had worn the blazing armor and shining helmet of the figure in the window.

"Isandro Grunito?" Narsi asked, and he half expected Father Timoteo to laugh and inform him of his mother's marriage to some tinkerer or troubadour who'd shared the glorious Isandro Grunito's given name. Instead, Father Timoteo nodded.

"My older brother, yes. You are my nephew."

"But if I'm Isandro Grunito's . . ." Narsi suddenly recalled Father Timoteo's comment about the importance of his legitimacy, and then the full implication of that sank in. He was the firstborn son of a firstborn son. According to Cadeleonian law, that made him the heir to the earldom of Anacleto. "Who else knows?"

"The priest who performed your parents' wedding passed away before your father did, and the physician who attended your birth moved to the Salt Islands fifteen years ago," Father Timoteo replied.

"That's rather convenient," Narsi commented as a joke, but Father Timoteo cast him a guilty glance.

"Mistress Kir-Khu was always fascinated by the medical innovations of the Salt Island temples; I merely provided her with the funds to move there and study," Father Timoteo replied. "Father Posco was simply very old."

Narsi nearly asked why Father Timoteo would bother to send the physician away, but then it occurred to him that there was far more at stake than just his ability to give a name to the few vague memories he possessed of his father.

Lady Grunito had often regarded Narsi with the suspicious expression of an eagle finding a skunk nesting with her eaglets. But how furious would she be to discover that a gangly half-Haldiim servant boy was her grandson? Even if she accepted that, she certainly wouldn't delight in the possibility of him displacing her son Nestor.

Nestor and his wife, Riossa, had been unfailingly kind to him and had gone out of their ways to present gifts to both him and his mother even after he'd left the Grunito household. The last thing he wanted was to take Nestor's title from him.

And yet that seemed to have been his mother's dying wish.

The enormity of it all left Narsi feeling at a complete loss. He looked to Father Timoteo—his uncle. He'd always adored Father Timoteo as if he were his family, but now, discovering that they were blood relatives, the idea felt strange and somehow unnatural.

"I don't know what I should do about this," Narsi admitted.

"I don't either." Father Timoteo offered him a brief smile. "I agree with your mother that is it without question wrong to deny you your rightful heritage and to keep you from claiming the resources of your family—"

"But I don't want to take Lord Nestor's title."

"You could abdicate in Nestor's favor as Elezar did. Though I would insist that you retain at least the barony of Navine for the security of income," Father Timoteo responded, but his expression didn't become any less troubled. "Though even that might not be enough to protect you from the royal bishop and his followers."

"Because I'm Haldiim."

"Yes and no. The trouble is that you aren't Haldiim enough to exclude you from the nobility on grounds of heathenism." Father Timoteo quieted a moment as someone passed outside the garden wall. He went on in a hushed tone. "You're legitimate and have been blessed into the Holy Cadeleonian Church. Legally, you are as much a nobleman as the Duke of Rauma or the king himself. You have every right to associate with your peers and even take a Cadeleonian noblewoman for your wife."

"I'm not about to do any such thing."

"Whether you would or not doesn't matter. It's the fact that you could—that you are within your rights to stand among the lords of this land. Your intentions will have little bearing on the royal bishop's outrage." Father Timoteo sighed heavily. "Even if you were to take holy vows and live as a celibate, I fear that the royal bishop would still view you as a threat to the purity of the Cadeleonian aristocracy. Your legitimacy sets a precedent. And that opens a door for other Haldiim—and any number of foreigners—to enter the nobility and bring with them values from outside the narrow confines of holy law. As nobility you— or others like you—could alter laws and even withhold funds from the clergy. From the royal bishop's point of view you would be the first crack that could bring down the great wall of his church."

Narsi stared at the dancing shadow of the willow branches. This all seemed more than he could absorb. He was no one—a common physician of no significance—how could his mere existence somehow threaten so formidable a man as the royal bishop? Powerful witches like Count Radulf and his sister were the sorts of important people who inspired such animosity.

"And moreover, now is the worst possible time for our family to reveal your exact relationship to Isandro," Father Timoteo said.

"Why is that?" Narsi didn't miss Father Timoteo's wording. *Our family.* Except Narsi had never been considered a member before this. He wasn't sure he wished to be included now.

"Yesterday the royal bishop demanded, on pain of excommunication, that Nestor come to the capital and swear before the king that he has not converted to the Haldiim faith."

"Should that be a problem?"

Father Timoteo leaned close. "Yes. Because my brother is stubborn, naïve and unrealistic and I fear he will not recant—not even to save our mother and all the rest of the family from excommunication and war. If at the same time it's revealed that you are the family heir, then that would put you at the very center of the conflict that Nestor has stirred up. You see why I hesitated in telling you?" Father Timoteo asked. "It's too much of a burden for you. Especially now."

"I . . . It's a great deal to take in," Narsi admitted. Only moments ago he'd felt so wise and worldly about rightfully withholding and dispensing the truth. Now he struggled to think of a way out from under all this knowledge. He wondered what Lord Vediya would have done under these circumstances. He probably wouldn't have troubled himself over predicaments that were mere potentialities when he had actual difficulties to face.

"Well, if it comes to the worst, I suppose we can all sail north to join Elezar for a family reunion in Labara," Narsi decided. "Throw a few stone chisels into my medical satchel and I'll be all set to begin doctoring to a growing population of troll patients."

Father Timoteo made a noise that was halfway between a laugh and a sob.

"Your voice is so like his. So optimistic." Father Timoteo gave Narsi's knee another gentle squeeze. "I've done all I could to keep this a secret, to protect you, but the capital is full of spies and informants. You must be very careful. Try to take greater care in the future, even when you are treating a dying man. You can't know if he's been placed before you as a trap—"

"I doubt that I was the intended victim of that guard's murder," Narsi replied, but even as he spoke he remembered the shadowy figure lurking on the path directly ahead of him. What if the body had been placed in Narsi's path not by chance but design? Narsi shook his head. Wouldn't it have been a thousand times simpler to attack Narsi directly? Certainly an assassin skilled enough to silently murder an armed guardsman could have killed Narsi even more easily.

"No, but that doesn't mean that feigning an injury wouldn't be a ruse to lure you to an isolated spot." Father Timoteo kept his voice low. "Mere highwaymen didn't murder your father. He died at the hands of his peers. Six friends who discovered his marriage to your mother. I don't know if they acted on a bishop's orders or of their own volition, but if I hadn't hidden you and your mother . . . What they did to him, Narsi—" Father Timoteo's deep voice quavered and he didn't seem able to go on speaking.

"I'll be careful," Narsi said. He didn't want to see Timoteo brought to tears on his account. "And I have no intention of pursuing the matter of an inheritance at this point. So all should be well. As far as anyone here knows, I'm just a Haldiim physician in your service and I'm more than happy to keep it that way."

Even as he spoke Narsi wasn't certain of his words. The idea of having any heritage to claim from his father felt too new, too strange, for him to really grasp just yet. But at the same time was he wasn't sure he wanted to abandon it completely and forever.

"The Lord will protect and guide us." Father Timoteo wiped his eyes and then patted Narsi's knee again.

Slumped on the edge of the fountain, the black cat cast Narsi a skeptical glance. Then it bounded away through his newly planted garden. Narsi studied the grounds, taking comfort in the future harvests all the greenery promised. This was his real life, here and now, not some worrying political game of inheritances and assassinations. He wondered if his father would have been proud of him for that or disappointed.

"What was he like?" Narsi asked after a few moments. "Isandro?"

"He was . . . joyous." Father Timoteo smiled slowly as he gazed into the distance. "He was the laughter of the Grunito household, full of jests and quips and pranks. Whenever our father was taken with fits or our mother seemed at the very limit of her endurance, he cheered them. I don't know that there was anyone he feared offending. He'd often turn his wit against his own peers, and even his elders if they belittled servants or beggars. But he did it with such good humor that people rarely took any offense.

"Of course, I was the snotty, jumped-up exception. I couldn't see the affection in his teasing, nor did I appreciate his wisdom when he'd warn me against cultivating a morose outlook upon life. I was so young then and convinced that everything sober was profound while happiness resulted from shallow thoughts and simple minds. If only I had known then how wrong I was . . . how precious he was . . ." Father Timoteo's voice gave out and the glassy shine of unshed tears filled his eyes.

Alarm rushed through Narsi. He'd not intended to distress Father Timoteo with his question.

"I didn't mean to bring back bad memories—" Narsi began.

"No, you haven't, my dear boy. They are good recollections, all my memories of Isandro are full of his charm and laughter," Father Timoteo replied. "It's only thinking of the time after he was . . . gone. When the entire Grunito household stood desolate and no one—not even a scullery girl—could manage to smile. When Isandro was in the ground and Elezar lay at the edge of death . . . it was only then that I realized how worthless all my dour sermons truly were and how miraculous had been Isandro's gift of joy. I felt so useless. So guilty."

Father Timoteo wiped away the tears that trickled down his cheeks and closed his eyes. Then he drew a deep breath and went on. "You were sometimes my only respite in those days. I can't tell you how greatly it buoyed me just to see you playing and hear your laughter."

Father Timoteo gazed intently into Narsi's face, and for the first time in his life Narsi realized that the Holy Father's expression of open affection wasn't just for him but for Isandro too. He supposed that explained those odd instants when Father Timoteo's kind expression wavered and turned almost regretful.

"You are so very like him. It nearly breaks my heart with happiness just to know you are in this world."

Narsi placed his left hand over Father Timoteo's. His thin fingers felt cold and dry as kindling, but slowly they seemed to warm against Narsi's hand. For several minutes they remained there, sitting side by side, hands clasped in quiet affection.

Would they have cared so much for each other if Isandro hadn't died? Would they have lived completely different lives—been strangers to each other? Would Father Timoteo have been so supportive if he hadn't been mourning Isandro when he first met Narsi and his mother? Or had he already known of them?

He must have, because how else would he have rescued them or even known they were endangered by Isandro's assassins?

Perhaps Father Timoteo had witnessed Isandro's marriage or even Narsi's first blessing in a chapel. The thought of that comforted Narsi. Maybe Father Timoteo's signature appeared on one or more of the papers that his mother had entrusted to Narsi to deliver to the Holy Father.

Then a troubling thought roused in Narsi's mind. How *had* Father Timoteo known the intentions of the men who'd murdered his brother? Why would they have confided in him, unless—

No. Narsi stopped the direction of his wandering thoughts immediately.

Some questions weren't worth the price of their answers. He didn't have it in him to disturb the love he shared with his uncle for the sake of solving some long-past mystery—not just for the sake of a father he hardly remembered. The past tragedy had already taken too much from both Narsi and Father Timoteo. Narsi wouldn't sacrifice their present happiness to it as well.

The past gapes like an open grave
from whence regret's ghosts arise.
Howling, hungry, the dead cry and crave
to feast upon our present lives.

Wasn't that what Lord Vediya had written?

Narsi closed his eyes and basked in the sensation of the sun's warmth on his skin. A breeze rustled through the willow branches overhead. The faint perfume of roses filled the air and then was gone.

Chapter
Twenty-One

The setting sun smoldered between the blue shadows of the city's skyline and lit the yellow roofs like a wildfire. At the south gate, guards rang the first bell of night, declaring the city closed off until daybreak. Atreau studied the evening populace as he strode past a noisy alehouse. A few merchants peopled the walkways and several cart drivers urged their animals ahead through the gloom. But none of them struck Atreau as useful to his purposes.

Four houses farther, two women, wearing their hair loose and cascading over their bare shoulders, lounged in a doorway. A pimp's small, black tattoo stood out on the pale skin of each of their necks like a brand. At least they seemed happy in each other's company.

Atreau tipped his hat as he approached, which won him an amused smile from the younger woman. He paused briefly and made inquiries. The older woman recognized his name and offered her own hilarious version of one of his better-known poems. They laughed together and after a little more conversation the two women shared what they knew with him. Atreau played at the ardent fascination that these lively women deserved. It seemed almost a shame that after so many years of calculated seductions, he felt little more than tired at the prospect of bedding either of them. Very likely they felt much the same about him.

He thanked both of them and paid them more than he probably should have.

But he enjoyed being magnanimous when he could afford it. The black eye the younger women had tried to hide beneath face powder made him feel that generosity had been in short supply for these gracious women. Of course, a block later, a scrawny youth who was likely as sharp-eyed as he was light-fingered flitted to Atreau's side. On a different evening Atreau might have indulged in the dance of keeping his coat pocket half a step ahead of the young man's hand, but tonight he didn't have time to waste. Nor was he willing to risk the youth somehow managing to finger the stone of passage hidden in his cheat's pocket.

The youth reached. Atreau caught his fingers and held them just hard enough and long enough to assure the pickpocket that he wouldn't tolerate a second attempt. The young man dropped back to trail a merchant sporting a velvet coat.

Atreau turned down a narrow lane and mounted the worn stone steps leading up to a raised walkway. Night-blooming jasmine cascaded down the walkway walls and the perfume of the white blossoms turned the smell of the street sweet.

Captain Batteo Ciceron's home stood three streets away, and the second-story landing offered Atreau a view of the alley where he'd been killed. A thin woman with long, unbound brown hair paced slowly between the arches of the raised walkways below. She looked a little past thirty and didn't appear too drunk just yet.

Atreau descended the stairs.

"Esevia?" he asked. The two women who labored for the same pimp had apprised him of her name as well as her fondness for very sweet wines and the fact that she regularly worked the lane where Captain Ciceron's decapitated body had been found.

"Yes?" Esevia smiled, but wariness lingered in her gaze. Atreau understood that expression innately. Any man who approached her held the potential of income but also the threat of a violent assault. Atreau remained at arm's length from her, offering her space to feel safe.

"Your friends Nanya and Chella told me I ought to speak with you. I'm called Atreau."

"You're welcome to talk all you like, but my time isn't free." Esevia crossed her thin arms over her chest like a shopkeeper shuttering a window against thieving passersby. No doubt many men wasted her time ogling and making lurid innuendos without concerning themselves with the fact that it was necessity—not desire—that forced her to endure their company.

Atreau offered her a half bow and added, "Naturally, I'll pay you for your time."

"Fair enough." She shrugged but didn't lower her arms. The pose made her look cold, and just a little like his mother, as he'd last seen her shivering in the Sorrowlands. Atreau resisted the urge to offer her his coat. He really couldn't spare it.

"What do you want to talk about?" Esevia's tight expression told him that she expected him to attempt to shock or titillate her. As a boy he'd endured that same experience in the company of truly depraved older men. It pained him a little to think that he inspired the same dread he'd once felt.

"I was wondering if you were in this area the night Captain Batteo Ciceron was murdered?" Atreau asked. "If you were, I was hoping you could tell me if you saw or heard anything?"

Esevia's hard expression turned briefly surprised, then she shook her head.

"No. My daughter fell sick that evening. I stayed with her." Esevia shrugged again but seemed to relax a little. "Sorry."

"No reason for you to be sorry," Atreau assured her. "I hope your child is feeling better."

"She is, thank you." Esevia cocked her head and gave Atreau a more appraising look. "You aren't a city guard or one of the royal bishop's men. Why are you inquiring about Captain Ciceron?"

"He was a friend of a friend," Atreau replied. "And I was asked if I could find anything out."

"He was hardly a saint, you know," Esevia commented.

"Not many of us are." Atreau would have been among the last men to argue Captain Ciceron's virtuous merits. He'd been a brutal man and an unrepentant murderer. But he'd also numbered among Fedeles's most loyal supporters and had doted on his daughters. "His wife and children miss him, in any case."

"True enough, I suppose." Esevia scratched absently at her bony shoulder. "Still, I wasn't here, so there isn't much I can help you with."

"Well, I appreciate you taking the time to talk to me." Atreau reached for his purse.

"Although . . ." Esevia's expression turned thoughtful. "It might be nothing, but there was something, not that night. Earlier . . ."

"Yes?" Atreau stilled, almost afraid that a sudden motion might break her concentration and scatter the memory Esevia seemed to be slowly luring back to life.

"There was a man here the night before the captain was cut down." Esevia scratched her shoulder again. "Yes . . . and now that I consider it . . . I think the same man was here a few evenings before that, as well."

"Just one man?" Atreau asked.

"Yes, a shadowy fellow all on his own. He wasn't really much of anyone." Esevia looked uneasy as she recollected. "I don't rightly recall anything about his face, and usually I can remember a face. But him, he looked like . . . nobody. I looked at him and he looked at me, then he vanished like a shadow. A few moments later the captain came past."

Not exactly the skulking team of assassins that were suspected of the captain's murder. But Atreau was inclined to trust the intuition of women like Esevia who worked alone through the night. The vulnerability of their lives often honed their instincts for recognizing danger in an instant.

"Can you describe him at all?" Atreau asked.

"Not really. I think he might have been about your height, but not a flashy fellow, and there wasn't much light." Esevia squinted into the distance but then shook her head. "I can't think of anything that stood out about him, except he was so fast and so quiet. He didn't seem natural. A shadow cut out of the night."

The simile didn't make sense, but Atreau grasped her meaning.

He paid Esevia and gently demurred to join her for a drink in the nearby tavern, less for her sake than his own. He'd grown wary of his own penchant to waste days and nights drinking. He made poor and impulsive decisions when drunk and he was no longer so young that he could expect to be forgiven his foolishness on account of inexperience.

So, he bid Esevia a good night, and then he made his way back toward the Theater District. Despite the growing darkness, his work wasn't done. He still needed to secure an agent to investigate the royal bishop's interests on the Salt Islands. Atreau had already arranged an interview at the Green Door with a brawny sailor named Xavan. The man had proved himself dependable in the past, and his ship would be setting sail for the islands tomorrow.

If that went well, it might leave him a little time to consider how best to handle the sacred grove. From everything Javier had said, he'd realized that they needed more information from the Circle of Wisteria. Yara was well-positioned, but Atreau was certain that she'd be refuse to turn informant if she felt she might be betraying her Haldiim community. Narsi, on the other hand, seemed to understand that something even larger was at stake. Also he appeared to enjoy making and sharing discoveries. If only he could be positioned in the right company, he might prove exceptionally valuable.

A cold breeze whipped through the narrow alley and sent a shiver down Atreau's spine.

Six years ago, when the witch queens had marched to war, unseasonably chill winds had risen from the far north too. But he didn't think that this could be Count Radulf's doing, not yet at least. Once Hylanya reached her brother, it might be a different matter. But this evening the wind seemed to herald only another passing summer storm.

His rooms would be cold when he returned to them tonight. Then he wondered if Narsi was keeping warm and frowned at the speed with which his mind turned to the young physician.

As Atreau walked on, sedate streets fell away behind him and the air filled with the noise of playhouses, gambling dens and opera halls. Stanzas of music and the scent of spilled wine floated around him. Atreau noted masked figures loitering in the mouth of an alley. His thoughts returned to Ciceron's shadowy assassin. He compared the man's description to what he remembered of the swift, dark figure that had disappeared in an instant, leaving a dead man at Master Narsi's feet. That fellow had reminded Atreau of the fleet whisper of a man who'd attempted to stop Hylanya Radulf's poisoning. But could they all have been the same man?

He strongly suspected that Oasia controlled the man who had murdered the guard, Dommian. Why? He still didn't know. Nor could he see Oasia's stake in Hylanya's welfare. Oasia and the young woman were hardly acquainted. Ciceron, on the other hand, Oasia had not even pretended to like—Atreau himself had felt hard-pressed to tolerate the man some days. There was no doubt that Oasia had been relieved to learn of his murder. But had she ordered it?

Could all these murders have been committed by the same man? Atreau scowled at the thought, but then, the other possibility wasn't a better one to ponder. Was the capital now breeding nests of silent, swift assassins from every shadow?

Atreau's preoccupation dissipated as a shriek split the air, carrying over the noise of the surrounding opera houses and theaters. Then a very familiar voice roared out a string of obscenities in both Cadeleonian and Labaran.

Spider.

Atreau's pulse leapt and he raced to the open street. There, through the twilight gloom, he spied the figures of two armed men wearing the royal bishop's star on their helmets and dragging a woman between them. Past them, another of the royal bishop's guardsmen grappled with Spider. Then Atreau realized that the woman slumped between the men was Inissa.

Had the royal bishop's men returned to have their revenge for being made fools of, or had they come hoping to scare information up in Jacinto's absence?

For just an instant Atreau's hand went to his sword hilt as he weighed his chance of overpowering the soldiers. He could have taken one from behind easily enough but wasn't confident about three. Nor did he imagine that demanding the men explain themselves would accomplish anything. The want of a lawful writ would hardly stop the royal bishop's men from attacking a barkeep or abducting a courtesan in the dark of night.

No, the best hope for saving Spider and Inissa would be to expose their attackers to immediate, mass scrutiny. Call the sort of attention to the royal bishop's guardsmen that a mere street brawl never garnered in this part of the city.

"Free wine!" Atreau bellowed. "Free wine for the first folk on the street with me!"

The royal bishop's men turned and the one fighting Spider lost his grip. Spider leapt back from him and staggered to the support of a nearby building. Atreau prayed that his brother hadn't been badly injured. Another of the royal bishop's men dropped his hold on Inissa's arm and launched himself at Atreau. His fist loomed into Atreau's sight and Atreau ducked to the left, shouting, "Who'll have a drink on me?"

The bishop's man lunged for him again and this time landed a hard blow against Atreau's side. Sharp pain cracked across his ribs, but didn't stop Atreau from slamming his knee into the other man's gut. The royal bishop's man gasped and collapsed to his knees.

"Free wine!" Atreau bellowed, though now his ribs ached as he drew in a deep breath. He felt the wet heat of blood seeping down his left side.

The door of the Fat Goose swung open, as did several other taverns. Streams of golden lamplight poured across the dark street, lighting the six of them on the street as if they were a tableau on a stage. People spilled out from the Green Door and immediately shouted for others to join them. Crowds hurried out from all around. Most appeared more curious than enticed, but all of them drew others behind them. In a moment the empty street filled with light and witnesses.

The man still holding Inissa's arm released her as if he'd suddenly realized he gripped a burning poker. Inissa immediately bounded to her feet and raced to the crowd gathered outside the Green Door. Pepylla embraced her and then they both disappeared inside.

"It seems the lady would rather not keep your company, but I daresay her friends here wouldn't mind having a word with the three of you." Atreau grinned at the nearest of the royal bishop's guardsmen as he struggled back up to his feet. The man who'd grappled with Spider started toward Atreau, his hand on the hilt of his sword. Atreau didn't back away from him, but edged nearer the left side of the street, where he could just make out Spider, swaying on his feet.

Someone in the crowd pelted the soldier with an apple core. A stone followed that, just missing Atreau. Then a brick and more stones sailed through the air. They battered the guards' armored chests and backs like hammers striking anvils. The royal bishop's men glowered at the crowd, but as rocks and hunks of horse droppings pelted their faces and helmets, they seemed to quickly surmise that they weren't in a defensible position. All at once the three of them fled down the street toward the river. The crowd gathered outside the taverns hooted and jeered as they passed.

Atreau hurried to Spider. In the dark, the blood spilled across his face looked black as tar. Spider stepped toward Atreau, but then his knees started to buckle. Atreau caught his brother in his arms and, despite Spider's protests and the ache of his own ribs, didn't let him go. Instead he helped Spider walk back into the Fat Goose. A small crowd of regulars from the Fat Goose trailed them inside, congratulating one another on so easily defeating the royal bishop's men.

"The first round of drinks is on my tab!" Atreau called to the two women behind the bar.

"Have I extended you that much credit?" Spider murmured, but he didn't object.

Atreau hauled his brother up the stairs to Spider's office and lowered him down into a battered oak chair. Spider slumped back and Atreau felt a jolt of fear, unable to see the extent of his brother's injuries in the dark room. He dug his tinderbox from his coat pocket and lit the fat little lamp squatting on Spider's side table. In the flickering yellow light Spider looked even smaller and paler than usual. His delicate nose appeared scraped but not broken, and a little blood trickled from his nostrils. He'd obviously taken a few hard blows, but aside from a bloody graze in his scalp, he appeared to have fought fast and smart. Armed with his belt knife, he'd kept himself clear of knife edges and sword blades.

"Will you stop gawking at me like a worried mother hen," Spider muttered. "I'm fine. Or I will be after a drink."

Atreau glanced around the room for a bottle of Spider's favorite ruin, a harsh Salt Island liquor that smelled like liniment and tasted like spite.

Thick ledgers covered much of Spider's desktop, while bundled stacks of papers filled his bookshelf. Several small, new paintings decorated the walls and Atreau recognized Inissa's hand in the detailed wings of moths and butterflies. He spotted the distinct blue bottle on a shelf and brought it to Spider, who pulled the cork and gulped down a swig. Then he set the bottle aside and wiped at a trickle of blood dribbling down the side of his face.

Atreau drew a kerchief from his coat and wiped the blood from the side of Spider's nose and the side of his face. He half expected Spider to shove him away, but this once he allowed Atreau to tend to him.

"I didn't think they'd come after you," Atreau said. He'd not gone to pains to hide the fact that they were brothers, but as far as anyone knew Spider numbered among dozens of bastards sired by Atreau's father and held no particular importance to the family.

"They didn't," Spider replied. "I was stretching my legs when I saw them grab Inissa."

Atreau scowled. What had Inissa been thinking going out alone at such a late hour? Jacinto's favor could only protect her so much. Then another thought occurred to him.

"Tell me she wasn't meeting you," Atreau said.

Spider didn't answer, but his angry expression might as well have been an admission.

"Idiot!" Atreau snapped. "You do realize that Inissa is completely dependent upon Jacinto's money to keep her out of debtors' prison, don't you? And it's only been his protection that has prevented the royal bishop's men from attacking her before this. Likely it was fear of his reprisal that sent them running tonight. What do you imagine would become of Inissa and you if Jacinto turned against you?"

"She wants to be with me," Spider snapped back.

"She has no idea what she really wants! One moment it's all true love and undying faith, the next it's gold coins—"

"You don't know!"

"I do and better than you—" Atreau began, but Spider cut him off again.

"She chose me, not you!" Spider shouted. "And that's what you're angry about. Just admit it! You can't stand that I'm the better man!"

"For fuck's sake! This isn't about me or you." Atreau had to resist the urge to grab his brother and shake him hard. "Inissa is Jacinto's woman! She likes to pretend that she's not, that she could leave him anytime, but she's as much his as his foreskin—"

Spider struck Atreau hard across the jaw and sent him stumbling back several steps. Pain ground through Atreau's battered ribs. For a furious moment Atreau grappled with the urge to slam Spider's head down into the hard wood of his desktop and punch a dagger into his chest. He was the stronger of the two of them, and while Spider had scrapped in street brawls, Atreau had trained in dueling rings to kill his opponents. His fingers already curled around the hilt of his belt knife.

But the last thing he wanted was to harm Spider, ever.

Atreau released his knife and stepped back from his brother. Spider glowered at him, his face flushed and his breath coming fast and angry. Blood dribbled from his gashed scalp and formed a scarlet track down the side of his face. He looked half mad and half beaten, a man stripped of civility and dignity by passion. Atreau had seen that expression before and nearly died for inspiring such fury.

"Don't you dare . . ." Spider's voice trailed off. Perhaps even he didn't know what he would do or say. Atreau tossed his kerchief to Spider.

"I imagine you can manage for yourself then." Atreau turned and started out of the room.

As he reached the door, a sense of utter futility filled him. He wanted to protect his older brother, to help him as he never could have when they'd been young and their father's abuse had driven Spider out of their home. But the fact was that they'd not been close then and after twenty years apart they hardly knew each other now. The regret and tenderness Atreau felt was for a fantasy of the family that he and Spider should have been to each other. Their brotherhood existed more as a hope than any reality. And yet he treasured that hope.

"Wait, Atreau," Spider called.

Atreau turned back. The rage in Spider's expression seemed more like anguish now. He gripped Atreau's discarded kerchief but didn't bother to use it to stanch the slow trickle of blood dribbling down from his scalp.

"You don't understand her," Spider said. "Not like I do."

"No, I don't suppose I do," Atreau admitted. His relationship with Inissa hadn't been built on the kind of long conversations and trust that seemed to underpin her romance with Spider.

Atreau and she had shared a bed and a child and had briefly considered marriage, but they had never done so amiably. They'd been too alike in their inconstant hearts—too alike in their need for powerful and indulgent protectors and in their insecurities as well. They'd neither of them remained faithful to the other and, when they'd attempted to temper their infidelities by sharing their bed with a patron, they'd ended up hissing and snapping at each other like alley cats fighting over the remains of a rat.

When their tiny daughter had arrived into the world stillborn, the heartbreak hadn't brought them closer. It had only made them both feel shamefully relieved to escape each other's dreary company.

"She's done what she must to survive," Spider said. "But deep down, she is strong and caring and loyal. She's a good woman."

"I know," Atreau agreed. Despite their failed romance, he still counted Inissa among his dearest of friends. Now as all his anger drained away he was left with only his fear for the lives of two people whom he dearly loved. "She deserves to be happy. You both do."

"If you truly believe that, then why are you so set on keeping us apart?" Spider demanded. "Why won't you help us?"

"I'm hardly in any better position to defy Jacinto than either of you are." Atreau shook his head. "This entire degenerate little district of the city only thrives because it amuses Jacinto to shelter us. You know that."

Spider took another gulp from his bottle.

"We could sail back to the Salt Islands. There we could live free from the grasp of this corrupt, bigoted Cadeleonian court." Spider didn't meet Atreau's gaze as he spoke, but instead he continued to fix his stare on the bottle.

"Really?" Atreau didn't laugh, but it wasn't easy to suppress his sour amusement. "Has Inissa told you that she'd be willing to give up everything she has here, abandon her friends and patrons to settle down with you in a shack and gut fish for a living?"

Spider glowered, but his silence assured Atreau that he'd gotten it right. The simple ways and grinding labor that made up much of life on the Salt Islands couldn't hold much allure to so cosmopolitan a woman as Inissa. Atreau hadn't lasted a month there, himself. And Inissa was an artist who yearned to have her paintings displayed in great halls and palaces. How would she attain that recognition when she was hidden off on some smoldering island?

He pinned Spider with a hard, assessing gaze.

"For that matter, what in the three hells would you do back on the Salt Islands? You returned to Cadeleon for a reason, didn't you?"

"Well, I didn't come here just to make sure you were still alive." Spider stated it almost as if he expected Atreau to accuse him of such a thing. "I came for money. But I'd rather be poor with Inissa at my side than possess a room full of gold."

How easy it was to say such a thing when a room overflowing with gold wasn't on offer, Atreau thought. Though studying Spider's expression, Atreau suddenly feared that his brother might just be willing to sacrifice all he had for Inissa's sake.

"I'm not sure you have the option of either," Atreau replied.

"I have connections on the Salt Islands. The temple looks after its own." Spider dabbed at the side of his face and belatedly pressed Atreau's kerchief to the gash in his scalp. "If you truly wanted to, I know you could help us."

This time Spider raised his glare to Atreau's face.

"Again I ask, what do *I* possess that could possibly benefit either of you?" Atreau asked.

"You could purchase my share of the Fat Goose." Spider said it so quickly that Atreau had no doubt he'd been mulling over the idea for a long while. "You would own this place and provide Inissa and me with enough money for us to start fresh on the Salt Islands. I have friends in the temple who are looking for someone to take over their hostel. With their blessing, I could own the only hostel on the entire Flower Road. I just need enough gold to buy it."

Atreau laughed. Not at Spider's business plan, but at the idea of the wretched parcel of land his paltry finances would procure. One of those Salt Island fumaroles that was forever belching out black, rancid gas? Or perhaps a little pool of boiling yellow mud and biting flies.

"Are they selling the place for ten pennies?" Atreau asked.

Spider glowered at him.

"You have money, I know it! I've seen you handing fat purses of coins over to everyone but me!"

No doubt he had noticed Atreau doling out the payments Fedeles provided, but not a single coin of that had belonged to Atreau.

"You've seen me paying off interest on my considerable debts, I'm sure," Atreau replied. "But have you once noticed a single soul paying me?"

Spider opened his mouth but then caught himself. Atreau could almost see him trying to recall a single occasion when Atreau had received so much as a copper coin from any of his acquaintances.

"I've not," Spider admitted rather begrudgingly.

"I haven't either, brother of mine. I'm skint!" Atreau pulled the small purse from his coat pocket and tossed it to Spider's side table. The four copper coins inside made a pathetic clink as they struck the wood. "There. You and your lady love may enjoy the spoils of my fortune with my full blessing!"

Spider scowled at the limp purse.

"You run with dukes and princes, how on earth can you still be so poor?"

"You could ask the same of Inissa, couldn't you?" Atreau went on before Spider could summon an outraged response. "It costs to keep up appearances in noble company, and the rewards aren't always monetary. These days, most of us ply our asses just to ensure protection from the royal bishop's men. It's only the Duke of Rauma's favor that kept me from burning along with my books last year. If I weren't under his protection you can bet I'd already be dead. Money is the last thing I could ask of him or Jacinto at this point."

Spider picked up the coin purse with a crestfallen expression. He sighed heavily, then he tossed it back to Atreau.

"I'm going to be the one to make a fortune for us all, I suppose." Spider managed a wan smile.

Atreau tucked the coin purse back into his coat pocket. He considered his brother through the flickering lamplight. Bloodied but still defiant, Spider seemed hardly changed from the delicate, beaten child he'd once been. He'd always been honest and courageous—willing to fight for what was just, even when he knew he'd be thrashed.

He deserved so much better from life and from Atreau.

Atreau considered the bundle of copied letters that Fedeles had turned over to him. Likely his sailor was already waiting in the Green Door, ready to take on the matter. But now Atreau pondered the reward Fedeles had offered. He didn't want to involve Spider in any of the wreck of his own life. He'd never wanted Spider to number among the anonymous multitude of agents whose entire lives were so often sacrificed for the sake of dukes and princes. At the same time, Spider needed money and Atreau needed someone with connections on the Salt Islands. All Fedeles asked for was information, not an agent.

"If told you that I know of a nobleman willing to pay a large sum to have a physician on the Salt Islands located, what would you say?" Atreau asked at last.

Spider cocked his head and regarded Atreau as if he'd thrown down a truly curious hand in a game of cards.

"What does he want the physician for?" Spider asked.

"He has no idea," Atreau replied. "He only knows that agents of the Cadeleonian church are hunting for a physician on the Salt Islands and that he needs to find her before they do."

Again Spider studied Atreau with that assessing gaze. A distant memory of meeting that same expression as Spider knelt beside him to wash the blood from his scraped knees wafted through Atreau's mind. They'd done their best to care for each other, but they'd both only been children.

"Please tell me that you're not working as a spy for Count Radulf," Spider said. "Because that's treason and you will get yourself hanged if anyone finds out."

"I'm not working for Count Radulf," Atreau replied and for a moment he believed it himself. Then he remembered his bargain with Hylanya. He wasn't *primarily* working for Count Radulf, he supposed. "I appreciate your concern."

"Of course I'm concerned. I have read your books, you know." Spider glanced to his bottle but didn't bother to drink from it. "Magnificent Elezar and radiant Javier dragging you across all three hells on their vainglorious escapades, then leaving you to bury the dead or ply your way across an ocean full of pirates. You're always falling for arrogant bastards and their appalling plans."

"I really don't think that was the conclusion of any of my memoirs," Atreau replied. "And it's certainly not my current situation."

"You might not think it is, but I'll bet one of your dear friends has you doing his dirty work, like always."

Atreau said nothing but Spider read him all too well.

"How you have the gall to chide me for being reckless, I've no idea. You're obviously up to your neck in someone else's troubles." Spider muttered the words under his breath as he dabbed a little blood from the side of his face. Then he narrowed his gaze. "You haven't allowed that handsome Haldiim fellow to embroil you in a plot to assassinate the royal bishop, have you?"

"What?" The suggestion was so far removed from any of Atreau's intrigues that he almost laughed. He couldn't imagine how it had occurred to Spider.

"There's no end to the rumors going around about Haldiim plots against the church." Spider shrugged. "More power to them, I say."

Atreau nodded. Spider loathed the Holy Cadeleonian Church, and with good reason.

"I'm not currently entangled in any assassination plots." Atreau hesitantly drew the bundle of letters from his coat pocket. "I'm doing just what I said. Trying to locate the physician mentioned in these missives before the church gets ahold of her. I have almost no information about her, except that she may have been employed by the Grunito family twenty-five years ago and she immigrated to the Salt Islands some fifteen years back."

Spider glanced down at the letters but didn't take them from Atreau.

"Your nobleman will pay well, you're sure of that?" Spider asked.

"If you can deliver the information he needs, then he'll pay you in gold. Enough that you won't need me to buy out the Goose."

Spider took the letters, untied the string holding them together, and then leafed through them.

"If she kept practicing medicine then she would've had to train at the temple. Though most folk who move to the Salt Islands go to make new lives, so . . . ," Spider said quietly. He turned back through the small pages two more times, then frowned and shook his head.

Atreau wasn't certain if he was relieved or disappointed that Spider refused the work. As much as he wanted to find this physician, he didn't want to embroil Spider in the battle between Prince Sevanyo and the royal bishop.

"That's all right," Atreau decided. "Honestly, I might be able to scrape up some money for you and Inissa. Not right away, but after the coronation. I might see an investment of mine come in then." Once Prince Sevanyo's reign was secured, Fedeles would likely receive so many royal favors that he'd not begrudge Atreau a generous loan—even if both of them knew Atreau could never repay it. "We'll talk about what it would cost me to buy the Fat Goose then, all right?"

Spider appeared almost startled, and then a rare smile brightened his angular face.

"Of course, we can talk about it, when the time comes. But for now I think I'll pen a few letters to my friends at the temple. It's not too hard to guess where your physician would likely have ended up, and her name sounds rather familiar to me."

"But I thought—"

"I was shaking my head at how ignorant this fellow writing the letters must be to think that Cadeleonian missionaries are going to find anything that the temple doesn't want found," Spider said.

"So you'll look into this, then?"

"I will," Spider agreed, and then he grinned. "By the way, you realize that you'll have to pay off your tab before I sell you the Goose, don't you?"

Atreau laughed, and it hurt his ribs but came as a relief.

He left the Fat Goose a few minutes later and crossed to the Green Door. He briefly searched through the parties filling the many tables for Sabella. It had occurred to him that a swordsman as skilled as the assassin who'd slain Captain Ciceron would need to train almost constantly and against the very best of opponents. The best place for that would be the Red Stallion. The sword house was a breeding ground for ruffians and assassins, hosting countless unsanctioned duels and regularly providing fat purses of prize money to the most ruthless sword masters.

Unfortunately, Sabella was nowhere to be seen tonight. Since she'd taken to sheltering Suelita, her sociability had shriveled to nothing. Especially in the evening. But he couldn't begrudge Sabella her recent excess of hours spent in bed. She'd been lonely for a long time, and there was no telling if or when Suelita would wake up and realize she'd left all hope of safety and leisure behind and return like a penitent to her family.

Though Suelita did seem more sincerely dedicated to avoiding both marriage and the convent than the last couple of women Sabella had become entangled with, so perhaps hope was in order? It wasn't for him to say . . .

Atreau turned his attention to locating Xavan; if Spider's friends at the temple couldn't find the physician, then Atreau would still have another agent to fall back on. But the sailor and his big beard was nowhere to be seen. Then one of the serving girls caught his eyes. She knew Xavan well and when she beckoned Atreau back toward the kitchen, he guessed that the man had left a message for him with her. Perhaps the street brawl with the royal bishop's guardsmen had put Xavan off.

Atreau made his way back to the steamy, fragrant kitchen. Before he could speak with the serving girl, Pepylla caught his elbow and pulled him aside. He didn't mind, since Pepylla only wished to reassure him that Inissa was a little muddied but otherwise perfectly fine.

"She just needs rest now . . . though what she was doing out on the street, alone at this hour, I have no idea." Pepylla shook her head.

Reading her expression, Atreau felt certain that she harbored a suspicion and it didn't please her. Pepylla liked Inissa, but she couldn't have cared less for Spider's welfare. Jacinto claimed her true loyalty and also ensured her livelihood. If she came to believe that Inissa or Spider had betrayed Jacinto, she wouldn't keep quiet about it.

"That was my fault," Atreau told her. "I wanted a word with her about certain things that might have been left in her room by another lady."

Pepylla raised a white brow but then nodded as she realized that Atreau referred to Lady Hylanya and why he would be evasive about it.

"I was late meeting her," Atreau went on. "I didn't think that anyone would—"

Pepylla hit him, her tough hand striking his jaw just where Spider had laid into him half an hour ago. Atreau swore at the pain but Pepylla paid him no attention.

"You idiot! She could have been killed, you realize that!"

Wasn't there an irony that he now stood here taking the very words he'd shouted at Spider? Atreau kept his mouth shut and glanced meaningfully to the two serving girls standing only a few feet away, gaping at them. Pepylla scowled at the servers. The balding cook lounging near the roaring fire began to whistle a loud, nervous tune.

Pepylla shook her head and then returned her attention to Atreau.

"I didn't hit you that hard." A slight motherly concern showed in her expression. Atreau could feel the side of his face throbbing and had no doubt that a noticeable red weal now stood out on his cheek.

"No. Not so hard as Inissa would have, I imagine," Atreau replied, and in truth his bruised face didn't hurt nearly as badly as his ribs. "Tell her I'm sorry to have left her waiting for me, will you?"

Pepylla nodded and an idea occurred to Atreau. He couldn't do much to aid Spider and Inissa monetarily, but he might keep Pepylla—and Jacinto by extension—from suspecting too much if they met again. He leaned closer to Pepylla and said softly, "I've made arrangements with Spider across the way at the Fat Goose, so that Inissa can leave anything of importance in my rooms there—during the day, of course. Will you pass that on to her as well?"

"Of course," Pepylla replied, then she added. "I suppose you could go up and tell her yourself."

That Atreau guessed was as close as he'd come to Pepylla offering an apology.

"I'd better not, just yet. My delicate features can only stand so much righteous outrage in one night."

Pepylla laughed and over her shoulder one of the serving girls cast Atreau a sympathetic smile.

"Well, take care of yourself tonight," Pepylla told him before she turned her attention to arranging the complex assortments of little dishes meant to accompany the steaming pots of kaweh. The cook's whistled tune quieted and the serving girls each snatched up the side dishes as they called out drink orders to the cook. Pepylla just waved her hand when Atreau bid her good night, but outside of the kitchen, the serving girl sidled up to him.

"Did Xavan leave a message for me?" Atreau asked.

"No. Haven't you heard?" The serving girl lowered her voice. "He and two other sailors were attacked and branded last night."

"Branded?" Atreau scowled at the thought. Hadn't Hylanya said something about assassins bearing sorcerous brands? Then he remembered Hierro grasping the front of his shirt and the burning sensation that had seared across his flesh. Thankfully, Javier's icy white blessings had won him a moment's reprieve to tear free.

"That's not the strange part," the serving girl whispered. "A few hours later all three of them abandoned their friends and went loping after some nobleman's carriage like dogs. No one's seen a hair of them since."

A deep dread fluttered through Atreau.

"I thought I should tell you. Better watch your back when you're out on the streets alone."

"You too," Atreau replied.

The girl offered him a very sweet smile and thanked him for his concern. Then she was called away to a table and Atreau departed.

He collected his horse from Spider's stable and rode back to Fedeles's mansion in a wary silence. The thought of what Xavan and his friends were now enduring was terrible, but so too was the thought of what they might be able to reveal to Hierro Fueres. Atreau avoided narrow, empty alleys and took pains not to show how badly his ribs hurt him. The cut in his side broke open and bled a little more, but not so much that it soaked through his coat.

He wondered if Narsi wouldn't have a poultice for him and then reminded himself that Narsi was hardly out of the sickbed himself.

At the mansion, the guards allowed him past with a mere nod. Atreau didn't particularly feel like making merry conversation with every soul he passed, nor was he certain that his bedraggled appearance would pass without remark if he walked through the well-lit corridors of the house. So he skirted the grounds, making his way to a section of wall at the back of the building where a hedge of yew obscured several feet of carefully carved stonework.

Atreau found his key and slipped it into a hardly visible niche. As the hidden door opened, the slim shadow of a black cat slunk from the hedge and circled Atreau's boots.

"Creeping back to the charming physician's bed, are you?" Atreau whispered to the creature. The cat kept its own council but it followed Atreau into the secret corridor. As he made his way through the narrow space and up the stairs toward his own chambers, he heard the cat pad away. For just a moment he considered following it and intruding upon Narsi.

I should make certain that he's not feeling ill again . . .

Even as the thought occurred to Atreau he recognized the self-deception in it. He knew perfectly well that Father Timoteo and Brother Berto would look after Narsi. He wasn't hoping to sit at Narsi's bedside and play nurse any more than he honestly expected Narsi to tend the gash in his side. No, he simply wanted the young man's pleasant company to lift his own flagging spirit. It had been a long time since anyone had intrigued Atreau or entertained him as much as Narsi did. The young physician possessed such a quick mind and the sort of laugh that seemed to warm an entire room. And the way he gazed at Atreau when he didn't think he was being observed was so very flattering.

But indulging the impulse to pursue Narsi's company would only feed a fledging affection that could do neither of them any good.

Atreau had already involved Narsi in one deadly enterprise. And Narsi had performed so capably that Atreau planned to use him again, particularly after witnessing how well he controlled his own terror in the face of muerate poisoning. He could prove to be a highly valuable asset for Fedeles, and Prince Sevanyo.

Growing too attached to him would be about as wise as befriending a mayfly. No one as upstanding and daring as Narsi lived long in the capital. Being Haldiim on top of that . . .

No, Narsi wouldn't likely last a year. Atreau knew that he would no doubt play a large part in the other man's demise. For the sake of their nation—perhaps their world, if Javier was to be believed—sacrifices had to be made.

Atreau leaned against the cold stone of the dark passage and drew in a deep breath of the stale air.

Will I even remember the names of all the lovely dead left behind me?

Atreau shook his head at his morose turn of thought. After all he'd seen in the Labaran War, how could he still fret over sacrificed agents and spies? He had no right. Not when he thought of how Elezar had led hundreds of his best men to their deaths for the sake of a nation that wasn't even his own. Compared to that, what burden did Atreau bear? A mere handful of promising lives lost to ensure that hundreds of thousands thrived in a better, more tolerant kingdom.

There's an irony in how many murders are required to maintain the illusion of a great and peaceable land. Or perhaps tragedy is a better word for it.

He climbed the steps and emerged in his cold rooms a moment later. The narrow chambers were familiar but never felt welcoming to him. When he had the time for it he did most of his writing in his comfortable, run-down room at the Fat Goose. Here, he existed solely as an instrument of Fedeles's needs and, by extension, Prince Sevanyo's ambitions.

He'd dressed the chambers like the set of a stage play; the desk displayed an assortment of inks and randomly penned pages, while the books filing the crowded shelves largely served as decoys, disguising the few hollowed volumes where messages from Elezar and Javier lay hidden. A mildly obscene tapestry, depicting pretty maidens frolicking in a dewy garden, hid the door to the passage he'd just exited and the four little bare-breasted figurines posing on his dressing table contained vials of deadly-potent duera—in case escape prove impossible.

Starlight glowed through the narrow gaps between the heavy drapes hanging over his two windows. A pitiful stash of coins weighted the decorative trim of the curtains—certainly not enough to purchase the Fat Goose, but sufficient to hire a boat to carry him and his horse out of the capital if the need for flight arose. The stone of passage offered him another route, but Atreau knew better than to ever depend upon a single ally for salvation.

The transaction still made him uneasy. It came very close to serving two masters. But Atreau reassured himself that he was not working against Fedeles. Hylanya had already placed spies all across the city without his aid. Now, at least, he held some sway over her familiars and spies. He could keep his own agents and hers from working at odds to each other. Already, one of Hylanya's familiars had ensured Narsi's full recovery.

And if everything went wrong, he still possessed a means of escape that Oasia couldn't undermine.

Through the gloom, the pale blankets of his empty bed struck Atreau as the only authentic testament to the life he led.

He gladly sat down on the bed and then lay back to stare up at his blank ceiling. He closed his eyes. A melody rose from the music room below. It should have been dance music, played to accompany Sparanzo as he practiced his steps for the coronation ball, but tonight it sounded strangely like a dirge.

 CHAPTER
TWENTY-TWO

As midnight approached, Atreau still lay staring at his ceiling, willing sleep to come to him. When a knock sounded at his door, he welcomed the distraction from insomnia. Probably Fedeles expecting him to have something worth reporting. He sighed and hauled himself up to his feet.

A sharp, resentful pain flared from his ribs as he strode across the room.

He opened the door with a carelessness that he knew should have concerned him. Only two days ago a guardsman had been murdered in the mansion; at the least he should have asked who called and peered through the tiny spy hole hidden in the door's decorative inlay. Instead he simply flipped the latch and swung the door wide.

Lamplight flooded in from the hall and lit Narsi in a golden halo. He certainly cut a striking figure; tall, dark and handsome enough to breathe a new life into the tired turn of phrase. The curly dark hair framing his face reminded Atreau of a whirling thundercloud, and two of the buttons fastening his simple white shirt remained undone. His gray physician's coat hung open. Between the warm light and Narsi's easy smile, Atreau almost overlooked how ashen Narsi's complexion still appeared. He rather casually tucked his injured right hand behind his left.

"I apologize for calling on you so late in the evening, but you'd mentioned a proposition that—" Narsi's pleasant expression became troubled as he leaned nearer. The clean, astringent scent of coinflowers drifted from him. "What happened to your face?"

Belatedly, Atreau recalled that his cheek had taken a few blows and likely now displayed the beginning of a bruise.

"The wages of my life of sin and delight," Atreau replied.

Narsi didn't look convinced but he didn't argue either. Instead he simply stepped into Atreau's room and then, lowering his voice, commented, "I came for my medical bag. You said that I should—"

"Yes, yes, I did. Come in. Have a seat." Atreau shoved the door closed behind Narsi and flipped the lock closed out of habit. For a moment they were both plunged into darkness. Atreau silently cursed himself for failing to light a fire when he'd first arrived in his rooms. Now he went quickly to his mantel and lit the two lamps there. The flames flared up in gold tongues and set shadows all across the room flickering and jumping.

"Is that blood on your tunic?" Narsi pointed to Atreau's chest. Atreau glanced down and realized that a dark splotch of dry blood stained the side of his shirt.

"Damn it. Blood never washes completely out from these snow-white fabrics." Atreau supposed the shirt could be dyed to hide the stain, but just now only the very whitest of shirts were deemed acceptable for the resplendent company of princes and dukes. "I just bought this damn thing."

"Should I even bother to ask what you've gotten up to since we last spoke?" Narsi inquired. "Or is it all a secret?"

"Less secret and more pointless as far as anything worth telling goes," Atreau admitted. "Let me fetch your bag."

He crouched down to his bedside and, reaching under, found the small trapdoor in the floor. As he slid aside a wooden panel he noticed Narsi pause next to one of the three chairs near the fireplace. He didn't sit but instead knelt beside the log rack and set to work kindling a fire from the ash-encased embers in Atreau's hearth.

Atreau fished Narsi's medical bag from a compartment hidden in the floor and then slid the trapdoor closed again. As he stood he felt the bite of his abused ribs. He drew next to the fire and sank into one of his chairs. He saw how carefully Narsi used his left hand to feed pieces of plum wood into the fire. The injured right he kept folded close to his chest.

Aren't we a pair . . .

Narsi glanced up at him and offered another of those easy, winning smiles, as if he was thinking the very same thing. Then he snatched up his medical bag and stood over Atreau.

"I think it will be simplest if you just take off your shirt and let me have a look at your chest."

"Hardly here a minute and already having your way with me, are you, Master Narsi?" Atreau dropped down into a chair.

"Yes, indeed. Resistance, at this point, would only inflame my medical longings further." Narsi set his medical bag on the nearby side table and then went to Atreau's washbasin. He rinsed his hands and then brought the pitcher and basin back to the side table. "If you aren't careful I might well rub a balm on your cheek and actually treat that case of merrypox you seem so attached to."

"Oh, you want me out of my trousers, as well?" Atreau offered his most salacious smile as he pulled off his shirt. Though he couldn't suppress a brief grimace when the movement stretched his left side and the fabric of the shirt came away with a crust of scab that had closed up his cuts.

Narsi just shook his head, as if he were humoring a doddering old man. His expression turned more sober when he knelt at Atreau's side and gently sponged away some of the fresh blood.

"Can you take a deep breath?" Narsi asked.

Atreau did so, though it hurt some to expand his chest.

"Is the pain acute?" Narsi asked.

"Not so sharp as when I cracked a rib back in school," Atreau replied. "Nothing broken, I don't think."

"That's good." As he spoke Narsi brought a tincture from his bag and applied several drops to Atreau's wound. The medicine stung briefly but then seemed to slow the flow of blood and relieve much of Atreau's discomfort. "These scrapes look like they're from the back of a steel gauntlet."

"Well spotted." Atreau doubted he would have been so precise in recognizing the scrapes, and he'd been cuffed in the same manner more than once.

Narsi nodded and then rose to his feet.

Craning his head back to meet Narsi's gaze, Atreau couldn't help but remember all those school days he'd spent gazing up at Elezar, admiring his powerful build and great height. But unlike Elezar, whose attention forever turned to their classmate, Javier, Narsi studied Atreau in return.

"I'd guess that the bruise on your jaw came from a very hard slap, or you were punched but the blow was more glancing." Narsi narrowed his attention upon the side of Atreau's face. "It's oddly shaped. You weren't hit twice by any chance, were you?"

"Slapped twice," Atreau admitted, but then he added, "by different people. I didn't just stand there and take it two times from the same hand."

"Good to know. Were they lining up to have a go at you?" Narsi dabbed a sweet-smelling salve over Atreau's sore jaw. His touch felt surprisingly light and warm. As he drew back, Atreau's skin tingled and then numbed slightly. Narsi hesitated beside the chair opposite Atreau's.

"No need to stand on ceremony with me, Master Physician. Sit your fine ass down and enjoy this lovely fire you've built." Atreau beckoned him down to the seat.

"If it isn't an imposition . . ."

"Not at all. I could do with some friendly company."

Narsi graced him with another of his flattering smiles. Atreau felt certain that, given a little practice and polish, Narsi's natural charm could be honed into quite the effective tool—though just now there was something disarming about how unstudied he seemed.

Narsi took the chair opposite, yawning and stretching as he did. His long legs brushed briefly against Atreau's calves, but then Narsi quickly retracted from the contact, offering Atreau a politely apologetic glance. There was no faulting the man's manners.

"So you've had an adventurous evening, I take it?" Narsi commented.

"Hardly. I simply made the mistake of annoying Pepylla after having already offered unwanted advice to my brother."

"I thought you weren't on speaking terms with your brothers," Narsi commented.

"Espirdro isn't like the rest of them," Atreau replied, but then he frowned at Narsi. He didn't recall having told him exactly how estranged he'd become from his father and brothers. Though it wasn't a secret, and people liked to gossip. Still, this wasn't the only oddly personal piece of information that Narsi seemed to possess concerning him.

Narsi returned Atreau's puzzled gaze.

"Do you mean Espirdra?" Narsi asked. "Your runaway sister?"

Now Atreau had to stop himself from gaping. No one remembered Espirdra anymore; their father had gone to immense lengths to erase all trace of her existence. Only Atreau and his father knew Espirdra had not been one of the hundreds of people who succumbed to bluefever. His three oldest brothers had been away at sea or school. Noble peers hardly noted her disappearance, since she'd not yet been presented to the royal court. In the years since, her name had been relentlessly expunged from any records and recollections.

Narsi didn't offer him a smug smile—as a blackmailer might—but seemed genuinely confused. Clearly someone, somehow, had let one of the Vediya family's deepest secrets slip out within earshot of Narsi. But who? And what other dangerous information might have spilled out beside the fact that Espirdra hadn't died?

"Who told you that?" Atreau asked.

Narsi raised his brows.

"You really don't remember?" Narsi asked; then, with a slightly chagrined expression, he added, "*You* told me."

"I did no such thing." Atreau could hardly credit that Narsi would expect him to believe such a claim. "Take it as a compliment, Master Physician, for I clearly recall the few conversations you and I have shared. Not once did I mention any such thing—"

"Not here, not now, but the first time we met. At the Grunito house, when you came for Lord Nestor's wedding . . ." Narsi cocked his head. "You really don't remember any of it at all?"

"Nestor's wedding was eleven years ago." He stared intently at Narsi and tried to drag up any recollection of the other man. The Grunitos had employed a large number of Haldiim servants, but Atreau doubted any of them could have been quite as striking as Narsi. Though he would have been younger—twelve or thirteen—but his hazel eyes would have been the same, and likely he would have stood half a head taller than most of the serving boys.

All he recollected of the day was a sickening patchwork of feeling deeply hungover and then clinging to his horse as he raced ahead of the royal bishop's men. They'd been intent upon killing Javier Tornesal, and for some idiotic reason Atreau had taken it into his head to impersonate his friend and draw the murderous soldiers away so that Elezar and Javier could escape. He'd very nearly died.

"I don't . . ." Atreau trailed off as a faint glimmer of recollection stirred. There was something almost familiar about the set of Narsi's mouth, the tempting fullness of his lips . . . All at once disjointed memories seemed to filter through his mind. The night before the wedding, during all the loud festivities and chaos of boisterous guests, when the wine had been flowing like scarlet streams, he'd trailed after a tall young man who'd wandered between shafts of moonlight beneath the apple trees. The figure had reminded him of Elezar when they'd first met. Yes. Now he remembered. The youth had greeted him with that same charming smile and curious expression.

Atreau had been so drunk that he could hardly recall any other details, but he now felt certain that more had passed between the two of them, and it worried him.

"Were you by the apple trees? And I . . . walked over to you?"

"Staggered, really." Narsi appeared amused. "Is that all you remember?"

"At the moment," Atreau admitted. "Why don't you tell me about it. Perhaps it will rouse my memory."

"If you don't recall"—Narsi shifted his troubled gaze to the fire—"I don't know that I should bring it up. It might not have been the finest moment for either of us."

Dread crept through Atreau. All his life he'd promised himself that no matter how low he sank, he'd never stoop to the drunken debauchery of the wealthy men whom his father had slyly admitted to his rooms when he'd been a youth. But now a wretched uncertainty seized him. Had he been so deep in his cups that he'd assaulted Narsi—or at least attempted it? Considering his state, he might well have failed on several counts.

"Did I . . ." Atreau couldn't even say the words, they sickened him so. "If I . . . harmed you, I know that I can't possibly apologize enough to make things right. But—"

"No! Nothing like that at all!" Narsi rose to his feet and laid his hand gently against Atreau's arm. He looked just a little self-conscious. "I mean, I did beg a kiss from you, but you only obliged me after a long laugh, and even then it was the most chaste kiss I've received outside of my mother pressing her lips to my brow."

Relief washed through Atreau. He released a breath that he hadn't realized he'd been holding. Narsi looked decidedly embarrassed, but now the entire thing struck Atreau as funny.

"So I staggered up and you asked me to kiss you?" Atreau wished that he could remember how that exchange had gone. "And then for some reason I told you all my family secrets?"

"Not all, I don't suppose," Narsi replied. "And it went the other way around. First you staggered over to me and sort of fell on the ground at my feet."

"After that dashing entrance I can see why you might beg a kiss of me." Atreau couldn't help but laugh. Narsi laughed as well, but he still seemed embarrassed.

"It was the first time you'd noticed me, but not the first time I'd noticed you. The scullery girls were forever pointing you out when you came to visit." Narsi shrugged. "That night you weren't at your best, I admit, but you were troubled by Elezar's talk of having to fight to the death to protect Javier—as though neither your life nor his own was as valuable as Javier's."

Atreau scowled at the idea that he'd so blithely announced all this to a random youth. He certainly hadn't been anything approaching a spymaster at nineteen.

"You told me that you didn't want to die, not even for Javier. I assured you that it wasn't fair of Elezar Grunito or anyone else to extract such an oath from you. Then I admitted my own guilt for not wanting to take vows, not even for Father Timoteo's sake. You assured me that if Timoteo deserved my affection, he'd respect my decision and do what was best for me. And then you explained how it had taken you losing Espirdra for you to realize that despite everything your father said, he didn't truly care about any of his children more than his own wealth and comfort. If he'd loved Espirdra, he would've helped *him* instead of driving him away and then declaring him dead."

"I managed to say all that when I could hardly walk?" Atreau asked. Despite the years that had obviously passed, he felt mortified at just how much he must have poured out to Narsi.

"Our conversation wandered, but it wasn't unpleasant," Narsi said. "We talked about all sorts of things, from our favorite dishes to our hopes for our futures. You already knew you'd be an author, but you feared that you would never possess enough wealth or social status to ensure you'd never have to curry favor from anyone."

Atreau nodded. His younger self had been justified in this concern.

"So it was and so, it seems, it ever shall be. But tell me, what did you desire for your future?" Atreau inquired. "An empire built upon importing exotic fruits? Or perhaps a career charming secrets from loose-lipped Cadeleonian nobles?"

Narsi laughed and shook his head. "I wanted to leave service in the Grunito chapel and study medicine in the Haldiim District. I'd passed their entry test, but I didn't have the money to pay the tuition." Narsi paused and glanced to Atreau with a particularly searching expression.

"And?" Atreau prompted, because a man didn't look like that if there wasn't more to be said.

"You really don't remember at all?" Narsi asked, but then he shook his head. "You told me to wait for you and you staggered off. I waited and began to think you'd forgotten about me when you reappeared and handed me a coin purse filled nearly to bursting with silver—"

"Are you serious?" All at once Atreau recalled the frantic hours, two days later, when he'd rummaged through his pack unable to find even a single coin of the little treasure he'd so carefully saved through all of his years at the Sagrada Academy. He'd been devastated and had miserably reconciled himself to the thought that he'd lost the purse when he'd fled from the royal bishop's men. How absurd to know now that his drunken youthful self had actually committed the theft and given everything to a boy he'd just met. A very handsome boy, no doubt, but still . . .

"That's where all my money went?" Atreau murmured.

"I swear. You handed it over to me and declared that if you could not be free to follow your own desires, then at the very least I should pursue mine."

"How very charming of me. I can see why you would feel the desire to give me a kiss." Atreau laughed. The color that rose across Narsi's cheeks was very appealing.

"You did make a rather indelible impression," Narsi admitted, though he sounded more nostalgic than infatuated. "I probably shouldn't have accepted the money, but at the time, I'd just been so stunned and happy. You changed everything for me in just a few minutes and you didn't ask anything in return."

"Lord, I sound like an idiot," Atreau muttered, but then he added, for Narsi's benefit, "I suppose I must console myself that at least I possessed the wit to invest my own foolishness in your wisdom, Master Narsi. I can only hope you won't charge me too much for today's treatments."

"I'll not charge you a thing. That was part of the promise that I made to you. The one I asked you to seal with a kiss." The fact that he'd made such a request, and what it implied that Atreau had granted it, seemed to hang in the air between them for a quiet moment. Then to Atreau's relief Narsi went on. "I vowed that when I completed my schooling I'd find you and come to help you as repayment for all you did for me that night. I know it must sound childish to hold to such an oath, but you really did save me and I truly do feel I owe you a great debt. That's why I came to Cieloalta. To keep my promise to you."

Atreau had no idea of how he ought to respond. He'd made and broken so many oaths that he'd long since stopped believing in the worth of his own word or anyone else's. Yet here Narsi stood holding himself to a decade-old promise that only he remembered; if that wasn't the test of an honorable man Atreau didn't know what was.

"I sound rather trite, don't I?" Narsi commented. "But there it is. If I seem to know too much about you, it's only what you told me yourself."

"And I told you about Espirdro?" Atreau could hardly credit it. He'd not confessed to anyone. And he'd certainly had plenty of drunken occasions to do so.

Narsi nodded. "So, I take it she—or he now—made the journey to the Salt Islands and that you two found each other again?"

"Yes, a few years back," Atreau admitted. "Despite how changed he was. I knew him at once. He's called Spider by most of the folk who know him—"

"Yes! The owner of the Fat Goose. I thought that the two of you resembled each other. He has a very handsome smile." Narsi frowned then. "But why did he slap you?"

"I presumed to offer him advice on matters of the heart and he didn't like what I had to say. To be fair, I didn't word things as nicely as I should have. He's quite protective of his lady love."

Narsi looked like he might ask more, but then he shrugged and leaned back in the chair. "Sometimes advice from the people closest to us is the hardest to hear."

Atreau acknowledged the fact with a nod. Though in this case it was likely far more complex.

"It's complicated by the fact that the lady in question is a courtesan and she and I have a past *association*. The romance between the two of us is over. I wouldn't have introduced them to each other if it hadn't been, but I think it still bothers Spider."

"It doesn't trouble you?" Narsi asked. He wore a thoughtful expression, which seemed to suit him and lent the flattering appearance of fascination to his curiosity.

"Not in the way you probably expect." Atreau found himself answering honestly, though really he had no reason, except that it had been so long since anyone had seemed to care about his private life; there was always so much more at stake for more important people. "She and I are long past entertaining romantic illusions of each other. We have been for years. We're too much alike, really. She can be quite clever, quite calculating—but no more than I've been. So when it comes to my brother—" Atreau wasn't certain of how to express the conflict he felt. His desire to protect Spider tangled up with his hope for Inissa's pampered future, and both seemed always at odds with his wish for happiness for them both.

"If she's truly like you and does love your brother, then I'd say he must be a very lucky man to have won her affection."

Atreau laughed and Master Narsi looked briefly affronted.

"Oh, don't look like that," Atreau said. "You can't honestly think anyone fortunate to be caught up with a scoundrel like me."

"Merely caught up—as you say. No. Though it could be an enjoyable enough way to pass a few hours," Narsi replied. "But to be loved, that would be a different thing altogether, I think."

"Altogether worse," Atreau couldn't keep from adding. "Unless that bout of poisoning somehow burned all memory of my reputation from your mind."

"I'm aware of your public reputation. However my personal knowledge of you differs from the stuff of hearsay and gossip. Considering how greatly I've profited from the briefest time in your company, you must admit that I have grounds for my belief."

"Between a chaste kiss and forking over a great purse of silver, yours is certainly not the average encounter. I'll give you that." Seeing Master Narsi's satisfied expression, Atreau felt a strong desire to fluster him. He stood and leaned close to Narsi. "Perhaps it's time I rectify your impression of me?"

To his surprise Narsi smiled playfully and stood as well, leaning forward, so that his face was nearly against Atreau's.

"Perhaps it is."

Earlier, he'd resisted the urge to spy on Narsi, not wanting to sink to the level of a perverted old voyeur or further stoke his own fascination with the young man. But occasions when he might safely admire another man—particularly one whom he found so pleasant—were rare and had grown dangerous since he'd left his school days behind.

So for just a moment Atreau indulged in a long, shameless study of Narsi's tall, lean body. What Narsi's modest clothes hid, Atreau could remember from that first time he'd visited Narsi's rooms and caught him naked: a broad chest, taut buttocks and such a splendidly heavy prick that it left Atreau's mouth dry. But since then he'd found himself as fascinated by the young man's intellect and resilience as his physical beauty. Atreau recollected the sensation of Narsi's hands on his bare skin. He'd been gentle but unquestionably assured.

He wondered how Narsi's full lips would feel on his flesh. How would he taste? A surprisingly powerful surge of arousal coursed through him. His heartbeat quickened in a mixture of excitement and alarm. It had been years since he'd experienced so strong of a stirring or allowed another man to distract him so completely. There was an undeniable thrill to feel desire and sense that it was returned.

Atreau reached out, drawing Narsi's body to his own. At the same moment Narsi embraced him in return. They kissed deeply, tasting and inviting each other with lips, teeth and tongues. Narsi tasted of smoky tea and felt blood-hot and breathtakingly assured. For all his youth he was no neophyte. His strong fingers traced the Atreau's spine, sliding down to the curve of his ass and guiding Atreau's groin to brush against his own. A ravenous desire surged through Atreau.

He pulled from Narsi, but only far enough to shove Narsi's shirt aside and grip the buckle of his belt. Narsi stroked his shoulders and smiled at him slyly.

"This morning, when you said you had a proposition for me, was this what you meant?" Narsi asked.

For a hazy aroused moment Atreau had no idea to what Narsi referred. He just wanted to get both their clothes off and feel the glorious heat of thrusting, naked flesh. He nearly agreed. But then Narsi's actual question registered and he remembered.

The proposition he'd intended had been to make an agent of Narsi—to use him as he'd planned to use Xavan and to endanger his life just as flagrantly. The thought of Narsi holding himself to an idealistic, youthful promise made it all the worse. All Atreau had truly done to earn Narsi's admiration was to drink himself sloppy and misplace his money.

If he took advantage of that, would he really be any better than his father? Here he was ready to slake his lust while knowing that he'd use and discard his lover like nothing more than a playing card. Atreau's arousal chilled as self-loathing flooded him. He drew back from the warmth of Narsi's arms.

"No. It wasn't anything like this." Atreau's own half-hard flesh repulsed him now. "Actually, I can't . . . this won't work between us. I'm sorry, but it can't . . ." Rarely did words fail Atreau, but just now, with his intellect and his heart at such odds, he struggled and stumbled. He found himself simply shaking his head.

"Can't it?" Narsi asked gently, as if coaxing a bashful virgin. "We're doing no one any harm."

"You certainly do no harm, Master Narsi," Atreau replied. "But I cause myself and others no end of suffering with my dalliances. Too often I allow things to go beyond reason, making romances out of what should have been no more than jokes—"

Seeing the hurt in Narsi's face Atreau found himself backtracking. "Not that you are a joke, far from it. But *I* am. Worse, actually, because at least a joke ends with laughter. Despite all the amusing bedroom scenes I've put to paper, the truth is that as a lover I'm selfish and cowardly and inconstant. My affairs end soon and badly. Violently . . ." Atreau swallowed hard against everything he left unsaid. Miro's bloody body, his daughter's grave, men and women whose names he hardly recalled but had still kissed and sent to die for the good of Cadeleon.

All trace of desire had drained from Narsi's face. Now, he studied Atreau with the coolness of a judge—or perhaps it was a physician's assessing gaze that he turned on Atreau. He said nothing, waiting as if he knew there was one more thing for Atreau to say. The inevitable cliché.

"If I could, I would rather be a friend to you," Atreau managed at last. He tensed, expecting anger and frustration, feeling that he deserved Narsi's ire. To his surprise Narsi merely sighed, then stepped back entirely out of Atreau's reach.

"I suppose," Narsi said, "it rather defeats the point to offer any argument when the issue is one of mutual enthusiasm."

Atreau shook his head, more at his own contradictory desires than in response to Narsi. It wasn't lack of enthusiasm that worried Atreau but far too much.

"Well . . . if that's how it is"—Narsi took a moment to straighten his shirtfront—"then it's for the best that you told me, before we progressed to any positions that would've made the conversation awkward and possibly unintelligible."

Atreau laughed as much from relief as the idea of hungrily sucking at a stiff cock while attempting to groan and mumble a claim of disinterest.

"You're taking this with remarkable grace," Atreau told him.

Narsi flashed a wry smile. "I suspect that my ability to feel too distraught by anything short of poisoning is at a low point just now." Narsi turned his gaze to the dancing flames of the fire. "It could be an aftereffect of the muerate."

Atreau doubted that. He'd not noticed Narsi to betray shock or alarm under most circumstances. Perhaps that reflected a physician's discipline in calmly dealing with gruesome wounds as well as doomed patients.

"Speaking of the poisoning," Narsi went on quickly, pushing them both away from the awkward brink of intimacy and rejection. "You didn't happen to get a chance to look at the dead guard's body after I lost consciousness, did you?"

"His body?" The change of subject caught Atreau off guard but was welcome. "I saw him briefly laid out in the churchyard, while the staff was debating what to do with his poisonous remains. Why do you ask?"

"Because I'm certain that I saw a symbol branded into his chest. The same one that Lady Hylanya drew for me when she was describing the enthralling spell she'd glimpsed on her would-be assassin. Do you remember?"

Atreau nodded, though he was thinking of Xavan and his fellows.

"But it wasn't her assassin who was branded," Atreau corrected, "it was the fleet, shadowy fellow who drew attention away from the assassin."

"Ah, yes. You're right." Narsi nodded. "But I think that we can assume that the assassin and the shadowy man are comrades. After all, he knew what the assassin was going to do, when and where. Also he endangered himself to protect her."

"It's not a faultless assumption, but I'll accept it for the time being," Atreau allowed.

"How kind of you." Narsi smiled. "But what I'm wondering is whether the murdered guard and the shadowy man who protected the assassin could have been the same person?"

"Maybe . . ." It didn't seem quite right to Atreau. Dommian's killer—not the stocky, dead guard himself—had seemed more like the fleet figure who'd eluded and outdistanced Hylanya's defenders. He fit the description of Captain Ciceron's assailant, as well. That brought Atreau back to considering Oasia's connection in all these assassinations. He scowled down at his empty hands. If he was going to accuse Oasia of any involvement in Ciceron's and Dommian's murder, he would need to be very sure, very careful and in possession of solid proof. Fedeles wouldn't be convinced by anything less. Years ago he might've simply trusted Atreau's intuition, but now Oasia held too powerful of a grip on him. Atreau felt certain that any error on his part would present Oasia with an opportunity to tear down the last bonds of Fedeles's friendship, upon which Atreau depended completely.

"You think I'm wrong. I can tell by your expression." Narsi appeared more amused than chagrined. Atreau had to admire how quickly Narsi shed any possible resentment and slipped into the role of conspirator. How refreshing it felt to be able to disagree without inciting anger. Narsi dropped back down into his seat by the fire. "Come along then, tell me why."

"Because I believe the man who murdered the guard might have murdered Captain Ciceron as well as being the fellow who protected Hylanya's assailant."

Narsi leaned back in his seat with a thoughtful expression.

"But we know both Dommian and the unknown man were under the control of the same thrall, which implies that they were agents of the same person. Why would one kill the other?" Narsi asked at last.

"I couldn't say," Atreau admitted. Though a suspicion gnawed at the back of his thoughts. Dommian had originally come from Hierro Fueres's household, and he wasn't the only member of Oasia's personal staff who'd previously served Hierro. Perhaps conflicts between brother and sister had followed Oasia into Fedeles's household. Atreau thought again of that blood-soaked kerchief he'd handed back to Master Ariz. Oasia eschewed all traces of her family's heraldry, and yet that square of cloth had clearly displayed the Fueres swan.

"Do you think we could somehow get into his room? Dommian's room, I mean," Narsi clarified before Atreau could ask. Narsi leaned in closer, and his eyes seemed to light up like the flames dancing in the hearth. "I happened to have discovered that he belonged to the duchess's personal guard, so he was housed in the main building not the barracks. With a private room, he might have felt secure enough to keep a journal or leave letters lying about. There might be something there to indicate either who his master was or why he was murdered."

It wasn't a bad idea, but Atreau wasn't keen to drag Narsi into the enterprise. Not when he knew so little of what they would be up against.

"How did you come by this knowledge?" Atreau inquired.

"It's customary for a physician to offer condolences after losing a patient. When I went to the barracks to do so, the men-at-arms told me."

"You are very clever, aren't you?"

Narsi's smile took on a rather smug curve in response to the compliment, but then his right hand bumped against the arm of the chair and he winced in obvious pain.

"Shouldn't you still be in your sickbed?" Atreau asked, and Narsi rewarded him with a sour expression.

"I'm sick of my sickbed," Narsi pronounced. "And if we tarry, someone else may well clear out the guard's room before we have any hope of discovering anything."

Atreau bridled at how quickly Narsi assumed he should be the one directing matters. At the same time, his assessment of the situation was correct and astute.

"I even know which room he was assigned to." Narsi made it sound like an enticement and Atreau laughed.

"Very well. Give me a moment to find a clean shirt. Then we'll see if we can't make something of a dead man's worldly goods."

ཀ ཀ ཀ

An uneasy air seemed to haunt the duchess's wing of the mansion— or perhaps it was merely a draft stoking Atreau's uneasiness at anything having to do with Oasia Quemanor. Only seven years ago she'd dispatched mercenaries to murder him and Elezar. And though Fedeles had since settled the matter, Atreau knew that the duchess would still like to see him dead.

To be fair, Atreau felt much the same about her.

So much beauty and poison, she makes oleander pale with envy and puts the bronze asp to shame.

"The inlay on these hallway walls is quite pretty." Narsi traced a finger along the polished wood panels as they walked. Then he added, much more quietly, "Do you think one of them might hide the entry to a secret passage?"

"More likely that would be nearer the duchess's suite, above us."

"Oh? What makes you think so?" Narsi asked.

"Because the mansion was rebuilt just after the Mirogoths had been driven back out of Cadeleon. At the time, all the noble families were at pains to have a means of secret escape in case the armies of witches and shape-changers invaded again."

"But is there just the one, or do you think there might be several?" Narsi asked.

"Who knows?"

"Well, I'm beginning to suspect that there's a passage or something like it that leads to my exam room. I don't know how else the cat is coming and going." Narsi quieted as two footmen came around the corner of the corridor. The youths bowed their heads and did their best to appear busy with their duties but Atreau didn't miss the set of dice one of them carried. He and Narsi passed them, and when they came to an intersecting passage, they turned down the darker corridor on the left.

Twenty feet along they stopped at an unassuming door on the right.

Atreau had brought his lock picks, but as he neared the door he noted a faint glow seeping from beneath it. He leaned close to the wooden panel and listened but heard nothing. Narsi cast him a questioning glance and Atreau silently pointed down at the seam of light shining from within. The light flickered as someone in the room passed near the door. Someone had already beaten them into the place. Atreau stepped back.

Probably best to slip away before anyone saw them here.

Narsi nodded. Then to Atreau's surprise, he stepped up and gave the door a jaunty rap. For several moments no response came and Narsi lifted his hand as if to knock again. The door suddenly swung open.

Mistress Delfia gazed at them from the other side. A kerchief covered most of her auburn hair and a dark apron shielded her simple dress. She'd rolled up her sleeves and obviously had been engaged in some heavy work.

"Master Narsi and Atreau." She greeted them almost as if announcing their presences, though Atreau saw no one with her in the cluttered room. "Whatever can I do for you?"

Atreau's mind raced for an excuse. He couldn't claim any relation to the dead guard. Though perhaps he could say the man owed him money from a wager.

"I'm afraid that I insisted that Lord Vediya bring me here." Narsi stepped past Mistress Delfia as if she'd invited him in. "I feel I owe it to the fellow to know something of him . . ." Narsi paused a moment, his expression turning genuinely sad. "There was so little I could do for him other than witness his demise. I didn't even learn his name."

"He was called Dommian." Mistress Delfia stepped aside as Atreau followed Narsi into the small room.

A single lamp on the small dressing table lit the space, though deep shadows still filled the corners and added to the feeling of abandonment and disarray. Stripped bedding lay strewn across the floor and the mattress flopped on the bed frame at a haphazard angle. The wardrobe doors hung open, displaying traveling clothes, a winter coat and leather armor. The guard's personal weapon rack bristled with spears, pikes and blades, more in keeping with the armory of a mercenary than a simple house guard. The collection of books piled on the man's dressing table bespoke more than a passing interest in Cadeleon's early history as well as the ancient holy scripts.

The place reeked of stale, alcoholic sweat—sweet, filthy and very familiar to Atreau in the worst of ways.

"Did you know him?" Narsi asked Mistress Delfia.

"Not well, no." Mistress Delfia's posture embodied feminine humility—head bowed, arms close to her sides—but also served to keep her expression shadowed and her strong hands hidden. She stepped after Narsi.

Before Mistress Delfia had brought her bloodied brother to Narsi's exam room, Atreau might not have noted just how silently the woman moved. But that evening Atreau had recognized in her a strength and self-possession that reminded him far too much of Sabella to be ignored. Now, he noted the toned quality of the woman's shoulders and forearms and he recognized that the flowery sheath of her belt knife disguised just how long of a blade she wore tucked into the folds of her dress.

Mistress Delfia's meekness struck him as an artifice equal to his own pretense at drunkenness.

"I'd hoped that someone in the household could tell me a little about him," Narsi said.

"He'd not served the duchess long," Mistress Delfia replied. "And as far as I can tell his only close companions were his dice. Not that they showed him much kindness."

Narsi frowned at Mistress Delfia's cool assessment of the guard—though Atreau felt that it was likely quite perceptive. No doubt there had been much more to the man; the quality of his weapons and quantity of books implied a measure of discipline and thoughtfulness. People were rarely so simple that a single sentence could sum them up.

"I'd hoped to find out if he had family that I might contact to offer my condolences." Narsi edged closer to the table. Atreau started to comment on the title of one of the larger volumes but then stopped himself when he realized that something on the dressing table clearly caught Narsi's attention.

"There is no family that I know of," Delfia stated. "Only outstanding debts. The duchess asked me to look through his room to see what, if anything, could be sold or passed along to settle his accounts."

"It would reflect poorly upon the Quemanors to have troops of money-lenders and gamblers gather at the gates waving bills, I imagine." Atreau offered the comment to draw Mistress Delfia's attention away from Narsi and whatever it was that he found so fascinating. "Or is our beloved duchess the superstitious type who worries that unsettled debts can draw a ghost back from his grave?"

"No, you had it right with your first guess. She doesn't want odious persons hanging about," Mistress Delfia answered him but then started to turn back toward Narsi.

"This halberd looks well enough made, don't you think?" Atreau added quickly. He stepped closer to the weapon rack and ran his hand over the polished wood of the shaft and Mistress Delfia's attention leapt to him.

Yes, she was a woman who knew better than to look away from a man with his hand on a weapon. She couldn't help herself but to watch him.

"Worth a few silver at the very least. I certainly wouldn't mind owning such a weapon." Atreau lifted the halberd as if to test its weight.

All at once a man's hand shot out and gripped the halberd's shaft, stopping Atreau. Master Ariz seemed to materialize from the shadows of the weapons rack. With horror Atreau realized he'd been standing there—deadly still and silent—the entire time. So close he could have slit Atreau's throat without fully extending his arm.

Across the room from them, Narsi gave a short gasp and then laughed nervously. "I didn't see you there at all, Master Ariz. You're quiet as a shadow."

Wasn't he just, Atreau thought.

"I didn't want to intrude upon your conversation." Master Ariz's words were courteous, but his expression struck Atreau as empty, almost slack—more the face of a fresh corpse than a man of living passions.

Atreau released the halberd and drew back, so as to place Mistress Delfia partly between himself and the line of the weapon's strike. Emotionless as he appeared, Master Ariz still didn't seem the type who'd risk cutting down his own sister to get at an opponent.

"Did Dommian owe money to you as well, Atreau?" he asked.

"No. Sadly, I haven't any grounds to claim his fine halberd or that lovely winter coat, hanging there behind you. Though I do think we two frequented some of the same gaming houses." Atreau resisted the urge to look to Narsi to see what he might be up to. Instead he did his best to keep the conversation flowing between the Plunado siblings and himself. "He may have owed quite a large sum to the proprietor of the Fat Goose."

"The Salt Island Spider, you mean?" Mistress Delfia said. "Yes, he gambled and lost at the Fat Goose every chance he got. From what I've heard those debts may well have cost him his life."

"You think?" Atreau pulled a slightly theatrical expression of horror. "If so, then I may not have long for this world myself. My losses at the card table there have been startling of late. All too soon you and your brother may be searching through my tatty rooms for anything worth throwing to my slavering debtors."

"I doubt it would come to that." Mistress Delfia offered Atreau just the hint of a smile. "Anyone so foolhardy as to attempt to do you harm would no doubt find himself attacked on all sides by armies of barmaids, actresses and goose girls. You should not fear."

"Indeed. Goose girls can be quite fierce," Atreau responded.

"Ferocious as their charges," Mistress Delfia agreed.

Out of the corner of his eye he noted Narsi turn casually from the table. Atreau wondered if he hadn't stolen something, for he looked just a little too studied in his innocent expression.

"Well, I suppose there's nothing more I will learn of Dommian here," Narsi said. "I'm sorry for the intrusion, Mistress Delfia, Master Ariz. We probably shouldn't keep you from your work any longer. Thank you so much for indulging me."

Mistress Delfia nodded politely, but she eyed Narsi with a certain suspicion as he worked his way through the chaotic room and back to the door. Atreau offered the woman a half bow and then hastened to follow Narsi out and away from Master Ariz. Neither of them said a word as they hurried down the hall. Just as they reached the turn in the corridor, Master Ariz's voice sounded far too near their backs.

"Master Narsi," he called.

Both of them turned back. Master Ariz stood hardly a yard from them, slack-faced and dull-looking as a potato sack. Had Atreau not seen the man's bare body previously, he never would have given him a second thought. But now the purposeful deceit of his appearance struck Atreau as particularly sinister. Not since he'd gazed up at Elezar had Atreau laid eyes on so magnificent a musculature or such brutal scars. Master Ariz's body belonged to a man of ceaseless action—a man hardened by violent combat—not a children's dance tutor.

It could have been a coincidence that Master Ariz had been injured the same night Captain Batteo Ciceron had been murdered. No doubt any number of people all across the city had suffered falls, cuts and bruises that night. But the white swans emblazoned upon the kerchief that Master Ariz had clutched to his bloody arm nagged at Atreau.

He couldn't help but wonder at the true natures of the Plunado siblings and whether they were part of Oasia's machinations or if their loyalties lay far beyond the Quemanor household altogether. Either way, they both held positions too near Fedeles for Atreau's liking.

"Yes, Master Ariz. Can I help you?" Narsi asked, and he managed to sound only a little nervous. He started toward Master Ariz and Atreau had to resist the urge to catch his hand and pull him back.

As it was, Narsi came alongside Master Ariz and they engaged in a very soft-spoken and brief conversation. Atreau overheard Sparanzo's name and the mention of an early-morning hour. Then Narsi nodded and Master Ariz turned and walked back to Dommian's room. Atreau watched him go.

He noted that Narsi too stood as if rooted in place, observing the man's retreat. Only after the door closed behind Master Ariz did Narsi turn to Atreau and rush back to his side. Neither of them said a word. They all but raced from the duchess's wing. More than once Atreau caught himself stealing glances back over his shoulder to ensure that Master Ariz was not creeping silently behind them like a murderous shadow.

They reached Narsi's rooms moments later. There, Narsi locked the door behind them and then released a heavy sigh, as if he'd been holding his breath the entire time.

"I half expected Master Ariz would demand that I give back the book I took." Narsi dropped down into one of the chairs beside his warm hearth. The black cat lying beside the fire stretched and sauntered to the chair so that Narsi could scratch its head.

"I thought he might well run you through and then do away with me as well," Atreau admitted.

"I don't think he's so bad as that. All he actually wanted was to ask me to visit the dueling rooms tomorrow morning to look at the duke's son. It seems his right leg bothers him."

"Yes. Sparanzo does his best to hide it, but he tends to limp when he's tired. It trips him up from time to time. Lliro, my oldest brother, had something much the same but outgrew the trouble by the time he was six. Now you'd never know he ever walked with a limp." Atreau took the seat across from Narsi and went on before Narsi could make too much of any connection between young Sparanzo and Atreau's family. "Now, what about this book that you've liberated?"

"Here it is." Narsi shook the cuff of his physician's coat and a leather-bound journal slid from his sleeve into the palm of his hand. Stained and battered, the thing reminded Atreau of the little charm-books that many lifelong gamblers kept to record their favored horses, lucky stars, bad omens and the names of marks who were still easy to cheat.

"It's too bad that the duchess was so conscientious or we might have had the room to ourselves and had a greater opportunity to search the place." Narsi turned the little book over and carefully untied the leather thong that held it closed.

"I doubt conscientiousness had anything to do with the Plunados being there," Atreau replied. "They were obviously tossing the room in search of something."

"You think so?" Narsi's expression brightened but then turned concerned. "Do you suspect they were involved in his murder?"

"I don't know." Atreau scowled at the small journal for lack of anything better to focus his uncertainty upon. They were definitely involved in something. "Oasia—the duchess—controls her own agents and has her own designs. From what Fedeles tells me, she and he are aligned in their ambitions and she keeps him abreast of all she knows . . ."

"But?" Narsi prompted.

There was so much—too much—that Atreau could have told him. But to give voice to any of it would have only revealed the part he'd played in the death of Oasia's previous husband. Seven years of sick, shameful guilt churned through him, but he'd had enough of mulling over that tonight.

"I don't trust her. That's all. I just don't trust her and I don't know why Fedeles does."

"She *is* his wife," Narsi suggested. "He likely knows a side of her that others don't."

"That or he's been beguiled by her." She'd managed to drug and nearly destroy Atreau, despite his considerable experience with lovely and clever women. God only knew how well she could manipulate a man as pure and sincere as Fedeles.

Thankfully Narsi didn't pursue the subject beyond a shrug. Instead he opened up the charm-book. Numerous pages had been torn out and other pieces of paper stuffed in between the pages. Odd symbols and tiny cramped notes darkened the pages to the point of near illegibility. On top of that, it appeared that most of the writing had been angrily blotted out.

"Do you think this is a kind of cypher?" Narsi asked. "Or was he just incredibly frustrated? He's nearly torn through the paper here where he scribbled these lines out."

Between the flickering light, the defaced pages and his own exhaustion, Atreau found the charm-book almost impossible to read. He leaned in closer, as did Narsi. Atreau felt his head just touch Narsi's, but neither of them drew away. Atreau squinted at the sepia ink. Narsi started to turn the page when a darker blotch in a corner caught Atreau's eye.

"Wait. There." Atreau lifted his finger but couldn't bring himself to touch the symbol that he discerned from beneath a frenzy of scratches.

Narsi studied the mess of ink and then his eyes widened. "It's the spell Lady Hylanya showed us—the symbol I saw branded into Dommian's chest."

"The thrall that made a slave of him," Atreau murmured.

Once he recognized the shape, Atreau found himself picking it out again and again, from beneath angry scrawls. No wonder Dommian obsessed upon it and at the same time tried to blot it out of existence.

"I'm not certain of what this will tell us, aside from the fact that Dommian was a deeply unhappy man," Atreau commented. "At least that's all I can discern between the poor light and my wearied faculties. It's been a long day, for us both, I think."

Narsi nodded, but his attention had once again returned to the charm-book. "I wonder . . . how do you think a person actually works magic? How can this symbol drawn here command no more power than any random scribble?" Narsi tapped the page in his hand. "But as a brand—or even traced out in the air by Lady Hylanya—it becomes alive and deadly?"

Atreau glanced to the black cat, but it appeared to have fallen asleep beside the fire.

"Obviously one is magical and the other isn't," Narsi went on. "But what is magic, really?"

"I'm hardly an expert," Atreau said "But as far as I've seen, it seems that magic is simply a natural force—like the wind or rain—something that flows and pools through the world. Most of us rarely sense it, much less manipulate it. Then there are a rare few people who appear born with the potential to control it."

"Like Hylanya Radulf and Javier Tornesal," Narsi commented and Atreau nodded.

"Yes, those are two who have certainly honed their potential, but I don't think everyone with potential goes on to become a mystic or witch. Some folks probably don't even know that they could."

"How do you mean?" Narsi closed the charm-book and turned his full attention to Atreau. Meeting his gaze, Atreau felt a little of his exhaustion slip away. He straightened in his chair.

"I suspect it's like being born with a gift for music or dance or art. There's potential, but whether it's developed depends on a person's character and surroundings." Atreau remembered what Javier had said about Fedeles. If the choice had been his, he never would have entered the realms of magic and political conspiracies. But seeing Narsi's intellectual excitement, Atreau let go of the forlorn pondering and continued. "Just like a painter working her oils, I think that every person who shapes the magic around us into spells adds individual qualities to those spells."

"Thus the colors, sounds and scents of spells that you wrote about in *Five Hundred Nights in the Court of the Scarlet Wolf*?"

Atreau nodded. Narsi leaned back in his chair and peered up at the shadows of firelight flickering across his ceiling. Atreau watched too, feeling the dance of light and shadows soothe him like the murmur of a brook.

"That still doesn't answer the question of how such people physically sense and interact with . . . for lack of a better term, let's call it free-floating magic," Narsi said.

Atreau almost laughed. Clearly, he and Narsi thought of entirely different things when they contemplated shadows and firelight.

"From autopsies on Bahiim," Narsi went on, "we know that they don't possess any new or unusual organs. They don't possess better hearing, taste, sight or sense of touch than other people either. So how do they interact with magic and create spells?"

Atreau grinned. Wasn't it just like a Haldiim physician to take on the mystic realms with reason, logic and fact.

"A thousand Labaran witches will tell you that they work magic through their witchflames," Atreau informed him. "Their souls."

"Yes, but we all have souls," Narsi replied. "If you believe certain Bahiim mystics, every living thing, no matter how small or nasty, has a soul. Plants. Flies."

"Well, perhaps we're all just a little bit magic but we don't know it," Atreau replied with a grin. "Maybe we live in a world built entirely from countless spells crafted by everything from mosquitoes and roses to Old Gods."

Narsi stared at him as if he wasn't certain whether the idea was idiotic or ingenious. Atreau laughed.

"Would you like to know one thing I've always found rather intriguing, but I've never written down?" Atreau said.

"Of course." The gleam of fascination that lit Narsi's eyes was surprisingly rewarding. Atreau found himself glad that he'd never shared this observation with anyone else.

"I've noticed that the ability to perceive and use magic also seems to create certain blind spots. A friend of mine once showed me a symbol—" Atreau snatched up a graphite stylus and pulled a scrap of thin paper from his pocket. He drew a simple circular symbol. "It's a null sign, very much like the Haldiim mathematical naught—but for many witches it can act like a spell that becomes almost invisible to them."

"Really?" Narsi appeared skeptical, as Atreau had been when he'd first encountered that fact. "Your friend wasn't having a joke?"

"I might have thought so," Atreau replied, "if Count Radulf hadn't used this very symbol to render himself invisible to the demon lord Zi'sai when they battled."

Narsi stared at the scrap of paper and the little graphite mark.

"So, I could walk around with that and render myself invisible to anyone magical?" Narsi still didn't sound completely convinced.

"This one, drawn on a flimsy bit of paper? Probably not," Atreau admitted. "But if it were cut into one of those ancient stones that magic pools into? Then perhaps it might render you invisible to witches, other magical folk, even common people . . ."

Atreau ran his finger over the null sign. "Though I have a theory that even this little sign that I've written is somehow difficult for such people to perceive. I know, it sounds daft, but the fact is that I've met a fair number of magical people from different places and with different understandings of magic and power. But the one thing I noticed is that they've all had trouble with mathematics. And it's almost always because they become confused by null signs or other symbols that represent nothing."

Narsi stared at him, then suddenly sat upright. "Do you think that it's possible that they might actually be making the symbols into spells just by reading them?"

"Yes, that is my theory." Atreau nodded. "The more they concentrate on the symbol, the more likely they are to infuse it with magic, and then the more invisible it becomes to them. Eventually if enough magic has been concentrated into the symbol, it may become a true spell . . . and possibly never be seen by anyone again."

Narsi laughed but then looked thoughtful. "All those Labaran spells set in stones and the Bahiim wards woven through the wood of sacred groves. It could be that they're in those places because that's where free magic flows. That's where it can be shaped into specific spells . . . like your naught sign."

Atreau nodded and stifled a yawn. He knew he should get up and return to his own rooms, but it felt so comfortable here with Narsi.

"I wonder if Dommian was trying to work some small magic of his own, crossing out the symbol that oppressed him over and over and over again," Narsi murmured. He gazed down at the charm-book. "Or was this little journal the only place he could express his pain? His only confidant?"

A confidant . . . What troubled man didn't long for someone to confide in?

The idea stirred a memory. It had been Spider who had mentioned the guard's name to him previously.

"And who knows what he might have been forced to do," Narsi murmured.

"Nothing good, I would imagine." Atreau's thoughts raced back to what Spider had told him several days ago—before Captain Ciceron's murder had absorbed so much of his time and attention. *He wears Duke Quemanor's colors. A guard, from the look of him and his blade . . . drank himself nearly legless last night and then . . . started to blubber about not wanting to kill the kiddies.*

"The kiddies . . . ," Atreau realized.

Narsi cast him a questioning look.

"Dommian did confide in someone—thought it seems he had to drink himself legless to do so. A few days ago he slurred something to Spider about not wishing to kill the kiddies."

"He was ordered to murder children?" Narsi's face lit with alarm.

"Yes, and I think that order was what got him killed." Atreau felt almost certain as he spoke aloud. "The children who Dommian had ready access to were Sparanzo Quemanor and his playmates, the Plunado twins. Master Ariz's student as well as his niece and nephew."

"Yes, I see what you mean." Narsi dropped his voice to a whisper. "A man who threatened those children wouldn't be long for this world, would he? So, you think Master Ariz somehow uncovered Dommian's intention and murdered him?"

Atreau nodded.

"But why not reveal the truth to the duke and duchess? Why murder Dommian in the dead of night?" Narsi's frown deepened. "And weren't you thinking that the person who killed Dommian was the same man who Lady Hylanya said was under a thrall?"

"Yes. I'm now convinced that man was Master Ariz," Atreau admitted. "He bears a burn scar."

"True, but the scar on Master Ariz's chest is too mangled to identify."

Narsi's attention shifted to the black cat, as the creature stretched and then padded to Narsi's side. Narsi scratched its head and stroked its back.

"Master Ariz *is* disturbingly quick and quiet." Narsi seemed to weigh the thought. "But if Master Ariz is the same man, then why would his master bother to involve Dommian? Master Ariz has even more direct contact with all three children. Why not employ him?"

"That I don't know," Atreau admitted. "Perhaps he resisted too much . . ."

"Or could Dommian and he have been enthralled by different masters?" Narsi suggested.

"Maybe." Atreau considered for only a moment. "But no. If I'm correct, then these brands can't be the work of different men. Not only do both Dommian and Master Ariz bear similar markings, but they were both enthralled by someone who clearly enjoys the fact that they know what he's doing to them. If nothing else, Dommian's charm-book shows us that Dommian understood what was being done to him and struggled against it. Hylanya described the other man struggling as well. No, I think both thralls are the work of a singularly sadistic individual."

Given that Hierro Fueres had tried to sear some kind of spell into his own chest, Atreau thought he knew which sadist they were dealing with, but why had Hierro ordered the execution of Ciceron? The more they discovered, the less sense it all made. And he still had no real proof.

"Aren't all thralls rather sadistic though?" Narsi asked.

"I'd say thralls could be described as controlling but not directly sadistic," Atreau replied. "This particular thrall is very unusual. According to all of the witches I've ever met, an ideal thrall is one that goes unnoticed. It steadily shifts the desires and motives of the person under its influence to align with those of the witch who cast it. A strong enough thrall can fill a person with such intense devotion that he will undertake mad, reckless actions and endure agony, but he'll do it all happily."

"A little like falling in love." Narsi sighed, then leaned from his chair to scratch the cat again.

"In the very worst way, but yes. Much the same."

When Narsi straightened the cat leapt up onto his lap, where it curled up and eyed Atreau over its folded paws.

"But we don't really know that Master Ariz is enthralled," Narsi commented. "He might just be strange."

"He's the man. I'd bet my balls on it."

"Both balls? You *are* confident. Perhaps I'll be able to sound him out a little more tomorrow."

Atreau scowled at the thought of Narsi placing himself in Master Ariz's grasp. He all too easily remembered the deep pang he'd felt when he'd seen Narsi collapse beside Dommian's body. He should still have been in his sickbed, regaining his strength. At the same time he knew that Sparanzo's guards as well as numerous courtiers would be in attendance.

"Be careful," Atreau said. "Whatever you do, don't allow him to lure you off alone."

"You think he's going to risk murdering me in broad daylight?" Narsi cocked his head and smiled as if he found Atreau's concern droll. "I'm not sure why he'd bother."

"He may have noticed that you took that charm-book from Dommian's room. If he suspects that something in it could expose him, he might take the chance," Atreau said.

"By that reasoning, isn't he much more likely to creep up into your rooms? You were my accomplice, so aren't you just as likely as me to have read its contents? And you're in a far better position to expose him than I am, since I'm not likely to know anything of enthralled assassins or spells. You, on the other hand, have literally written a book on those subjects."

Atreau hadn't even considered that and it irked him.

"I very much doubt that Master Ariz numbers among the privileged few who read my latest book before it was burned," Atreau replied. "Even if he somehow did, let me remind you that I've accumulated a lifetime of experience in eluding furious men intent upon ending my life, whereas you are a physician through and through. I'd bet my eye-teeth that you'd reflexively open your door to anyone claiming an injury, no matter the hour or what danger he posed to you."

Narsi frowned, but he didn't look frightened so much as vexed at finding himself unable to refute the point. In fact, he seemed altogether too amused for Atreau's liking.

"Just because the man looks like a slack-jawed clod doesn't mean he's not dangerous," Atreau said. "If I'm correct, he's murdered two men in as many days, and both of them were accomplished soldiers."

"Fear not, my lord, I have no intention of provoking Master Ariz's ire, whether he's the man you think he is or not." Narsi turned his attention to the sleek cat in his lap. He stroked its chin and it stretched across his long thighs.

"Good." Atreau leaned back in his chair, feeling just a little envious of the indulged cat.

"Still, if I can discover a little more about him"—Narsi glanced up, meeting Atreau's gaze—"that would be useful to you, wouldn't it?"

Not at the cost of your own life, Atreau thought, and yet when he answered it was only to say, "Yes."

 CHAPTER TWENTY-THREE

Deep in the still of the night, Fedeles walked alone to the top of Crown Hill.

He unfolded the worn paper and watched as white script blazed up from the surface. The glow of the letters intensified as he ran his fingers over them, rereading Javier's instructions. Even with a quarter of the page ripped away it was clear what his cousin desired of him.

The guardian of the sacred grove at the Circle of Wisteria is fading. The power of the circle must not fall into enemy hands. Cadeleonian churchmen must be prevented from defiling the grove at all cost.

The next section had been ripped away and only partial sentences remained.

. . . secure the circle until we can find a new guardian. The spells in the old temple on Crown Hill are partners . . .

. . . through them safeguard the grove.

The sign that Javier normally used as a signature was missing, but Fedeles hardly needed it to recognize his cousin's writing as well as his tendency to make huge requests in quick little sentences, as if all things were easily accomplished. Perhaps to Javier's mind they were. But Fedeles felt overwhelmed by dread.

Ancient spells glowed up through the wildflowers and tall grass. Most shone no more brightly than fireflies. Certainly none of them could rival the stars that spread over the hilltop, or even the silver crescent of the waning moon. They were as aged as the temple stones that held them. Fedeles felt sympathy for them—abandoned to stand guard here long ago. Their valiant defense of the surrounding lands and people was almost entirely forgotten. No one venerated or celebrated them any more than anyone recalled the names of the gallant chargers who had carried kings and heroes into battle. These spells, like countless warhorses, had been taken for granted and discarded once their service passed.

Despite that, they still lit with golden warmth at his approach, like faithful old hounds welcoming their master home.

Fedeles knelt and stroked the rough stones. When the blessings and wards reached up to him, he smiled at the soft warmth of their touch. He took his time, making much of each of them and lavishing them with his admiration. In response the spells seemed to brighten and grow more energetic. The shining gold forms reminded him of the playful sprites that had populated many of his grandmother's bedtime stories.

These were good spells born from good magic. Nothing like the savage, polluting monstrosity that lived within himself. These incantations deserved a better master than him. It should have been Javier who crouched here, or Alizadeh. But neither of them would have been safe entering Cieloalta, much less working magic within the city.

Not for the first time Fedeles indulged in the brief fantasy of asking Oasia to take up the task. She made a better guardian than he did, and he thought that she would have liked these eccentric spells. Even if their feral natures didn't appeal to her, their odd forms would have fascinated her. But she already carried the burden of protecting Sparanzo and the rest of their household. Her wards spread across most of the city, and unlike himself, she was not famous for cantering off to wild fields and hills alone. Such sojourns would only attract suspicion to her when she could least afford it.

He had no right to ask her to also shoulder the work that Javier requested of him. Not even if the undertaking terrified him.

He sank down to the support of a stone pew. The blessings that now knew him so well circled his feet, dancing in rings around him. Fedeles reached down and cupped the gleaming light between his hands. A curling symbol radiated against his palm—Fedeles didn't know its original meaning, but he liked to think of it as *Courage*. He felt more assured when he held it and it seemed to grow more brilliant as it danced in his hand. After a moment Fedeles set the blazing symbol back down among the other blessings.

He felt glad that he'd roused and befriended all these old, forgotten spells on Crown Hill. It had taken him some time to tame them from the fleeting, shy little sparks he'd first encountered. Now they knew him and he liked to think that they had grown to care for him just as he cared for them.

They'd been forged long ago, in an age before Cadeleon had existed as a kingdom, much less possessed a codified church. According to myths it had been a time when witches, Bahiim, visionaries and even Old Gods had formed desperate alliances to free their world from the dominion of demon lords. The eldest of the blessings here on Crown Hill hadn't belonged to any order or faith but had been made for all. A Bahiim like Alizadeh, or a witch like Hylanya Radulf, could've woken them just as readily as Fedeles had. But even so, Fedeles would never have claimed the brave little spells had they belonged to another faith.

The sacred grove of the Circle of Wisteria belonged to the Bahiim— without question. To reach out to it, even if only to safeguard the place, seemed wrong to Fedeles. And what did it even mean for a Cadeleonian to *secure* a holy place that belonged to the Haldiim people? Fedeles gazed out to the south, remembering the two times he'd glimpsed the small grassy hill and towering ring of trees up close. The gnarled wisteria had stood like a giant crown of thorns while flowers, leaves and spells glittered throughout like emeralds and amethyst. The grove was indescribably beautiful but also a place where a creature such as himself would be utterly malapropos. He did not belong there any more than a horse belonged in the sea. Even now, miles away, the thought of stepping foot in the sacred grove sent a shiver up his spine.

Blessings flared up around Fedeles's legs. *Courage* rose up like a golden flame reaching to the height of Fedeles's knee. Another spell— he called this one *Fearless*—climbed onto the top of his boot, bristling and throwing off sparks as if challenging an attacker. Fedeles reached down and caressed and soothed them both as he would have petted an excited pup or his young stallion, Soluz.

"It's all right. There's no enemy to take on. I'm only making myself uneasy. Fool that I am."

The spells remained bright but both shrank back down. After a little time they returned to skipping over the stones of the old temple as if playing a game.

Fedeles watched them frolic and tried to take reassurance in seeing that he'd not corrupted these blessings or any of the hundred others that flashed all across the stonework of the abandoned temple.

But he couldn't stifle his fear of what might happen if he followed Javier's directive and attempted to use Crown Hill to lay any sort of claim on the Circle of Wisteria.

Not only was he Cadeleonian but he carried within him the corrupted shadow of a Bahiim curse. What might happen when that shadow curse united again with the power that had created it? What would it do to the sacred grove to be held by a creature so filled with murderous rage? If the shadow curse arose in him with that power, he feared that it would take complete possession of him as it had when he'd been a student at the Sagrada Academy.

Fedeles felt his heart begin to pound in his chest. He didn't possess the strength to fight it again. Merely contemplating the possibility terrified him. He clenched his fists to stop the tremors shaking through his fingers. A tight ache flared across his forearms. Glancing down, he realized that the sensation coursed through the old scars that disfigured his wrists. It had taken him years to overcome the terror and despair of his youth. Vivid memories still haunted him, as if they too were spells, carved into his flesh and all too ready to awaken again.

Fedeles purposefully opened his hands, willing himself to release the grip of his past.

He wasn't a child anymore, he reminded himself, and the men who'd tortured him were dead. Fedeles had personally seen their corpses buried deep in the cold earth. Neither Genimo nor Donamillo could ever use him again. Their machines had been torn apart and then burned into formless wreckage.

"The past is long done with and I have left it far behind me," Fedeles whispered to himself. "I won't be a captive still."

He stood and strode to the center of the old temple. Spells all around him lit as he passed them. A few followed him, like little guards. *Courage* and *Fearless* marched on either side of his riding boots.

"We're going to try to contact some relatives of yours." Fedeles found talking to the spells soothing. Whether they understood him at all he didn't know, but more and more they always seemed to respond to his voice. "At least that's what Javier claims. Though I honestly don't think he's ever been to the sacred grove in the capital. He makes assumptions, you know. And it's a fact that his master, Alizadeh, hasn't been here since the city walls were built because there are wards raised throughout the city that bar him specifically. He practiced some very bad magic once upon a time. Apparently the Bahiim here still don't trust him enough to allow him near their sacred grove."

Courage gave a little flutter that to Fedeles's eye looked like a kind of nod.

"Though I do wonder if they wouldn't rather have him than me . . . ," Fedeles muttered.

He stepped through a stone archway and wards carved in the temple floor and walls unfurled like flowers blooming all across a field. They illuminated the crumbling vault of the temple's central chamber so brightly that Fedeles easily discerned a pair of barn swallows sleeping up in the remnants of the eaves.

At the heart of the temple four concentric rings of red spells flared up from the flagstones like bonfires—only their flames were made of countless symbols, tangled and intertwined like walls of ancient thorns. For an instant Fedeles imagined that he could hear them each whispering in foreign languages, but when he strained to pick out individual words they seemed to melt away into the night breeze. All that remained for him to hear then was the gurgle of a nearby stream and the far-off calls of foxes.

Both *Courage* and *Fearless* drew to a halt outside the rings of other spells.

Fedeles too paused. Dread, like a spreading chill, sank through his body. He drew in a deep, steadying breath. Once again his heart began to race. The longer he studied the walls of spells, the more furious they seemed to grow. He felt his confidence draining into a cold sweat.

"Now or never," he whispered to himself.

He bolted forward before his nerve could fail him. As he raced through each of the four blazing circles, light gushed over him and tendrils of spells wrapped around him, like strands of fiery cobweb. Spells gripped him and stung him, but he tore through them one after another. At last, gasping and drenched in sweat as if he'd clambered up a mountainside of thorns, he reached the simple carved circle at the center of the temple. Strands of faint light clung to him like spider silk and red welts marked his hands and burned across the bare skin of his face. Smoke drifted from a few scorched locks of his hair.

But the shadow curse had not awoken.

All at once the surrounding rings of spells stilled, the gaps in one ring aligning with spells in the next, so that they formed a single sphere around Fedeles. He could see only shadows of the temple. Overhead the sky looked unnaturally black. Fedeles tried not to think of what might happen if he couldn't leave this orb.

Again faint whispers brushed over him. But this time their tone was not warning so much as curious. He felt their question more than he heard it.

"I wish to see the sacred grove." Fedeles's mouth was so dry that his words came out in a low rasp. The filaments of spells that clung to his body from his passage through the rings lit up in a hot pulse. All around him Fedeles saw and felt spells turning and whirling like little whirlwinds. His hair and coat fluttered in the churning breeze.

Then the roof and walls of the temple seemed to melt away, offering Fedeles a clear view of the land below.

Spells scattered all across the dark city flared like campfires. The Shard of Heaven roiled with an inner golden radiance. Three bright blue shafts plunged down from the chapel, spearing through the seething gold forms trapped within the heart of the stone outcropping. By comparison the royal palace appeared as demure as the flame of a votive candle. Across the Gado River a scattering of chapels glowed faintly. But the sacred grove dominated the south side of the city like a bonfire lit against the night's darkness. A circle of immense gold branches shot up into the sky, all of them flickering and surging like forks of lightning. Fedeles found it marvelous and hypnotic to watch the way they lit up the tiny buildings and streets. He knew that he shouldn't have been able to pick out the frothy spray of the Shell Fountain, but somehow he could.

An enormous ring of shadows spread from the foot of the grove. Unlike the flat darkness of the night, these shadows seemed to gleam with the hidden depths of deep waters. Shards of color flashed briefly from within them. While the golden light danced into the heavens, the shadows curled and crept across the city like huge roots. They reached the edge of the river and a few coiled up around the supports of the Gado Bridge. Others wound to the city walls and even seemed to delve under.

The longer Fedeles gazed at the shadows, the more powerfully he felt the shadow curse within him flex against his restraint. It yearned to unite with them, to return to the source of its creation. To Fedeles's horror, he realized that the shadows of the sacred grove had begun to move as well. Two black ribbons crept farther along the length of the Gado Bridge. As if answering the shadow curse's longing, they quickened their pace, stretching over the river and then slithering up the empty streets. More shadows raced after them, like streams flowing into a river.

Slivers of color glinted through them and then, all at once, entire lengths of shadows burst apart and surged into the sky. A wild wind rose over Fedeles and the air filled with the sound of beating wings. Hundreds of glossy black crows blotted out everything as they filled the temple and circled over Fedeles.

The shadow inside him churned like an eel, lashing through his gut and struggling to climb up out of him. It hungered for release, to take possession of the power of the sacred grove.

I feel your gaze, child. Mean you to claim what I defend?

A woman's voice rose on the thunder of crows' wings and a strangely sweet perfume filled Fedeles's mouth as he drew in a breath. The crows shrieked and spread their talons as they descended.

The shadow curse rose like bile in the back of his throat. Fedeles struggled to contain it. But it was too strong. He felt it rising up from him, stretching out to grasp the crows and devour them. And all at once Fedeles remembered the shadow curse invading Captain Ciceron's corpse—he felt it ripping into his beloved friend Kiram's body—he choked and gagged as it burst from him to tear open his friend Victaro. He tasted the hot blood and felt Victaro's heart shudder in his hand. And still the shadow curse knifed into his flesh.

Fedeles couldn't stop it then. He couldn't stop it now.

In desperation he threw himself from the center of the temple.

Burning threads seared through his body. His arms jerked like they were caught in ropes and his legs tangled in invisible snares. He fell against the stone floor and rolled to his knees. Then he wrenched himself free from the rings of spells that had entwined him and staggered toward the open grounds. His shadow writhed and jerked, straining to drag him back into the center of the temple. Bahiim crows shrieked above him.

Fighting for every step, Fedeles lurched out of the temple's grip. Freed, he ran blindly across the grounds. A small hillock of buttercups snagged his foot and brought him down to his knees in the weeds and dirt. He rolled onto his back, expecting to feel talons tearing at him as his shadow dragged the birds from the sky.

Belatedly he realized that the crows and shadows of the sacred grove were nowhere to be seen now. An open sky of distant stars spread above him. Fedeles lay there, staring up at the flickering little constellations. A cool wind washed over him, turning his sweat clammy. Fedeles rolled up to his knees.

The temple stood silent and dark. Only the faint familiar spells that Fedeles knew remained, glowing through the grass and wildflowers. *Courage* and *Fearless* trotted over a cracked flagstone and stopped at Fedeles's side. He could hardly look at them, with declarations of bravery shining from the centers of their beings. They were so pure, utterly unspoiled by the corrupting rage and fear that saturated Fedeles's own being.

They were radiant creatures, like Javier.

Fedeles clenched his eyes closed at the thought of his valiant cousin. Had it been Javier here in his place he would have stood up, brushed himself off and charged back into the temple. No, he wouldn't have fled in the first place. He would have entered the temple and reached out to the sacred grove with certainty. He would have secured the holy place instead of enraging its guardians and nearly destroying them.

Fedeles hung his head.

He possessed neither Javier's self-confidence nor his unsullied soul. And the thought of returning to the temple again only filled him with a sick fear. What murderous horrors would he unleash if he allowed the shadow curse to spread and pollute the sacred grove? As much as he wanted to believe otherwise, deep down he knew that he couldn't muster the strength to restrain his shadow once it gripped a place of so much power. He could hardly control the monstrosity as it was now. If it grew stronger, Fedeles felt certain that it wouldn't simply defy his will, it would devour him completely.

He couldn't endure the pain and madness.

He yearned be the man Javier and Oasia and even Alizadeh seemed to believe him to be—capable, dependable and brave. But he wasn't any of those things. He was a corrupted, broken coward. He couldn't do what they wanted him to do.

He didn't look at *Fearless* or *Courage* as he regained his feet and stumbled down from the hill. He kept his head bowed, his eyes focused on the obscure, dark path before him. He felt the spells fading behind him, but didn't look back. Instead he wandered down the grassy hill as the first light of morning broke through the darkness at his back. By the time he reached the red gate of his home, songbirds were singing and the sky above him glowed with the colors of dawn. The spire of his household chapel gleamed and the white pebbles of the path before him glinted with dew and golden light.

It all seemed too beautiful and none of it should have been his.

The bountiful grounds and lovely mansion rightfully belonged to Javier. The fine weave of faint blue blessings strung across the buildings and hanging from the tree branches arose from Oasia's looms and were products of her labor. Fedeles had done nothing to deserve all this splendor and wealth; it had simply fallen to him, and now he feared he couldn't even keep it safe from himself.

He turned away from the great house and instead made his way to the familiar comfort of the stable. The warm air inside smelled of summer straw, horse droppings and the fragrant bouquets of rosemary and fleabane that the grooms had hung from the rafters. The two young grooms had already risen to begin feeding the horses. Fedeles exchanged passing greetings with them before working his way back to the largest of the stalls. Firaj lay sleeping with his big head nestled atop a mound of straw bedding. Despite his age, his black coat retained a glossy sheen and he seemed untroubled by the aches that so often kept other aged warhorses from their sleep. The gelding shifted slightly, sighed contentedly and then returned to snoring.

As he observed Firaj, a feeling of contentment came over Fedeles. Even his restless shadow calmed. Its sharp edges softened, and where it fell across the straw, it looked faint as a natural shadow. Slowly it stretched out to rest against the curve of Firaj's thick neck like a cat curling up to nap. Fedeles sank down against the wall of the stall and closed his eyes.

Soft whinnies and nickers of waking horses drifted to him, along with the morning songs of barn swallows. Sunlight crept into the stable, illuminating the painted floral designs carved all across the rafters. Knots of apple blossoms and sunflowers clustered above Fedeles. More grooms arrived. They greeted each other and exchanged jokes. The smell of fresh hay and fodder filled the air. Here, for the time being at least, a tranquil world flourished, and it required nothing from him.

His agitation at last drained away. He drifted on the edge of sleep.

Then Fedeles heard a page call for the duke. His voice sounded far away and not particularly concerned. A few moments passed. The familiar voice of a household guard also made an inquiry. One of the grooms replied that he'd not seen the duke.

Fedeles sighed and opened his eyes. He ought to go and see what fresh trouble awaited him. But the temptation to steal just a few more moments alone stilled him. Couldn't he have just a quarter of an hour in peace?

"My lord?"

Fedeles almost jumped at the intrusion, though Master Ariz's voice hardly rose above a whisper. The sword master leaned into the stall. Fedeles noted that despite his obvious effort to brush his short hair down flat against his skull, one tuft bristled up at the back of his head. As it so often did. Fedeles found the unruly lick of hair charming, though he supposed that it vexed a man as disciplined as Master Ariz.

"Come to finish our dance, Master Ariz?" Fedeles asked.

The faintest of smiles curved the sword master's lips, but he shook his head.

"Prince Jacinto calls for you."

"I suppose it's some emergency that I'm needed to address." Fedeles sounded exasperated even to himself. He probably struck Master Ariz as petulant. God knew, he probably was being petulant. A man as wealthy and indulged as himself should hardly fuss over the fact that from time to time he was expected to put some effort into maintaining his fortunate status.

"The matter is not so urgent that it couldn't wait a few moments." Master Ariz stepped quietly into the stall, drawing the door closed behind him. He crouched down at Fedeles's side.

Fedeles had to resist the urge to reach out and stroke that short spike of Master Ariz's hair. He felt certain that it would spring back up against his fingers.

"Does Jacinto bring me good tidings or bad?" Fedeles asked.

"Does it matter?" Master Ariz cocked his head in that way he did when considering something.

"No. Either way it's better to know than remain ignorant," Fedeles admitted. "It's only that I feel sorely in need of some good news just now. And I'm not certain of how much more calamity I can stand."

"Captain Ciceron was dear to you, I know. His passing . . . It's hard to lose someone so near your heart." Master Ariz lowered his gaze to the straw of the stable floor. "I'm sorry for your loss."

While his passive face gave away very little of his inner thoughts, it seemed to Fedeles that Master Ariz's movements always conveyed a great deal more. Just now the way he leaned in reminded Fedeles of Firaj—when the warhorse stood close to him, offering support without voicing a single word. Fedeles supposed the sword master wouldn't thank him for being compared to a horse, but to Fedeles's mind there was no creature of greater grace, candor and nobility. He felt grateful that Master Ariz didn't attempt to draw him into a conversation when all the turmoil he felt seemed too vast and volatile for words to capture.

The two of them sat quietly together.

Fedeles listened to the lively conversation of the grooms and the twitters of sparrows. His household, this stable, all the surrounding world seemed unchanged by Ciceron's absence, almost as if he'd never truly been part of Fedeles's life. He felt almost guilty that grief over Ciceron's death didn't overwhelm him—that he'd forgotten for a time that he should be mourning.

He glanced to Master Ariz and met his gaze. He wondered if the sword master would understand any of this? Would he think Fedeles hard-hearted for feeling mere melancholy in the face of death? Did he consider Fedeles an aberration for caring at all for the charming captain?

Fedeles studied the relaxed curve of Master Ariz's callused hands where they rested on his sword belt. He crouched in such an easy manner that it conveyed an immense calm, and yet Fedeles couldn't miss the coiled tension belying the swordsman's posture. Was he uneasy in Fedeles's company, or was readiness to spring into battle simply second nature for him?

Fedeles supposed that if he wanted to know Master Ariz better, then it fell to him to make the first overtures of sharing his own thoughts. Otherwise his interest could all too quickly come to resemble an employment interview.

"Ciceron and I weren't constant companions." Fedeles spoke before he could stop himself. "I enjoyed his company when he was with me. I believe he liked me as well . . . but what I'm most saddened by isn't the loss of what there was between us. It's the loss of what might have been—not just with me . . . but . . . but for all of us in Ciceron's life. None of us will ever have the pleasure of knowing the man he might have become."

Master Ariz nodded but didn't lift his head, and Fedeles felt like a clod for having burdened the other man with his woes. The last thing he wanted was to discourage the already laconic sword master from further conversation with him.

"It's a hard thing to lose a possibility. They are all we can imagine of our futures." Master Ariz lifted his gaze and Fedeles noticed for the first time how red his lashes and brows were. "But at the same time it's a hopeless venture to lament what never existed outside of imagining. There are too many things that will never come to pass."

Fedeles almost argued but then stopped himself. If anyone knew what it was to lose all the promise of his future, it was Master Ariz. From his careful response, Fedeles guessed that he hadn't spoken off the cuff, but instead shared a hard-won wisdom. Fedeles took a moment to consider Master Ariz's opinion.

What good came from conjuring the great romance that might have been, just for the sake of mourning it? It was both self-indulgent and self-pitying.

"I see your point," Fedeles admitted. He wondered what fantasies Master Ariz had once imagined for his own future. How painful had it been for him to abandon them all? What hopes did he allow himself now? Fedeles almost asked but then caught himself. If Ariz wanted to share his dreams, then he'd speak of them in his own time.

"So what is this morning's news?" Fedeles asked.

"I . . . I believe that Prince Jacinto wishes to inform you of Count Odalis's death. He passed away last night. They believe that his heart gave out." Master Ariz rarely betrayed anything of his personal feelings, but there was something about the way he hunched his shoulders as he spoke that made Fedeles wonder if the sword master hadn't known the hardened old count personally and felt sorrow in his demise.

"I don't know if that's good news or bad," Master Ariz added. "Prince Jacinto seems pleased."

Fedeles had not liked Odalis, and under other circumstances he might've welcomed this news. But Master Ariz's somber bearing suddenly reminded him that no death should be treated as something to celebrate. Odalis had numbered among Prince Sevanyo's opponents, but that didn't mean that there weren't people who would miss him and mourn him.

"Or perhaps it's not the count's demise that gives the prince joy, so much as power passing to the count's heir," Master Ariz added.

Odalis's young nephew, unlike his uncle, was a fervent supporter of Prince Sevanyo's. Fedeles nodded. It seemed like Master Ariz to immediately and accurately discern the political implications of the count's death. After all, the conflicts of dukes, bishops and princes had destroyed his entire family. If anyone understood how the private lives of nobles could have far-reaching effects, it would be him. In all likelihood, Master Ariz probably possessed a far more nuanced understanding of noble politics than Fedeles.

"You could be right," Fedeles said. "Jacinto isn't unfeeling by nature; sometimes his enthusiasm can make him a little tactless."

"He seems honest," Master Ariz replied. "I'd take an honest jackass over a tactful liar any day."

"Obviously." Fedeles smiled at the very forthright declaration. "Though one does hope that you have other options for companionship."

Again that faint smile lifted the corners of Master Ariz's lips.

"Very recently I did have the pleasure of claiming a rather charming dance partner." Master Ariz spoke so quietly that Fedeles almost missed the words. Then a rush of pleasure filled his chest like a fire lighting a hearth.

"Did you?"

Master Ariz nodded, then cocked his head. "Though it seems he's either a prodigy of dance or a little bit of a liar when it comes to his need for lessons."

Fedeles felt the hot flush of being called out coloring his cheeks, but at the same time Master Ariz retained his faint smile.

"A man can desire a dance lesson for reasons other than instruction," Fedeles replied.

"Would he perhaps like another then?" Master Ariz suggested. "For reasons other than instruction?"

"Very much so," Fedeles replied.

"I'll be free this afternoon." Master Ariz stood. "If you have the time then—"

"I'll make the time." Fedeles bounded to his feet and stepped close to Master Ariz. As he reached to open the stall door, he realized that an actual smile flashed across Master Ariz's face. The expression lent him a disarming warmth. Fedeles wanted very much to kiss his lips and see how much more expressive the sword master might become.

But then Jacinto's voice sounded from only a few feet away. "Ah! Fedeles! Didn't I say we'd find him in the stables?"

The mob of lesser nobles and courtiers surrounding Jacinto made assenting noises. As Jacinto led them nearer to Fedeles, Master Ariz's face lost all expression. He bowed his head and stepped back from the stall door into a long morning shadow. Neither Jacinto nor anyone in his company seemed to take notice of him.

"Until this afternoon, Master Ariz," Fedeles promised him. Then he strode out to meet Jacinto and face the rest of the day before him.

 ## CHAPTER TWENTY-FOUR

Narsi didn't think he would be able to sleep after Lord Vediya left him. Not the least because after that single passionate kiss, his entire body seemed to buzz with an awareness of Lord Vediya's proximity. A few times he half suspected that Lord Vediya also felt those thrills of arousal, as their hands brushed or when they bowed their heads together.

But even if they had only shared a conversation, Narsi would have been filled with a restless mix of excitement and fear. He'd originally called upon Lord Vediya with the only half-acknowledged desire to confess everything Father Timoteo had revealed to him about his father. Before he'd entered Lord Vediya's rooms, his personal secret had felt like an immense burden. And yet as soon as he'd fallen into conversation, he'd found himself drawn from his own troubles to matters far more urgent and dangerous.

Pondering magical brands, possible assassins and the reach of some unknown Cadeleonian witch had almost come as a relief to Narsi—an escape from thinking about himself. His own worry seemed small now, nearly insignificant. What did it really matter that his father had been Isandro Grunito? Narsi still planned to live his life as Haldiim physician, and Nestor Grunito would continue on as the heir to the earldom of Anacleto. Whereas uncovering the assassins held in thrall by of some kind of Cadeleonian witch was literally a matter of life and death.

Who could sleep with such matters on his mind?

More puzzling, was the question of who would want to sleep alone after that deep, hungry kiss. Lord Vediya, obviously. Though he'd not left Narsi without seeming to regret their parting.

Narsi sighed, then yawned.

He knew that he ought to try to sleep. He wasn't fully recovered yet and he'd be no use to himself or anyone else if he spent the entire night pacing and muttering over matters that he couldn't resolve. He changed into his nightshirt and dropped down on his bed. His hand ached and his eyes felt hot and dry.

The black cat padded in behind him and, after alighting on the bed, curled up beside his hip. Narsi stroked the cat's chin.

Then he snuffed his lamp and lay back. The scent of lavender drifted over him, assuring him that the maids had changed his bedding while he'd been up earlier in the day. He closed his eyes, but his thoughts still raced as he tried to envision a means of either catching Master Ariz out or proving his innocence.

"There has to be incontrovertible proof," he mumbled to the cat. It pressed its head against his fingers and Narsi scratched its chin and neck a little more. The exercise seemed to ease some of the pain in his joints.

If Lord Vediya planned to accuse Master Ariz of murder, then he would need evidence, otherwise the matter could all too easily descend into that most Cadeleonian of legal procedures: trial by combat. Narsi felt certain that Master Ariz would easily win such a contest. And maybe he would have a right to.

After all, Lord Vediya's feeling that he was an assassin wasn't exactly irrefutable proof. Nor did Master Ariz's mere capacity to move quickly and quietly prove that he used those skills to creep around murdering people. If it did, then the stealthy woman who curated the medical library in the Haldiim District of Anacleto was certainly a master assassin despite being well into her sixties.

So far the only real evidence implicating Master Ariz was the scar that marred his chest. But even that wasn't certain. Narsi couldn't be positive that the symbol Lady Hylanya had shown him exactly matched the scar Master Ariz bore. Considering how many other scars disfigured the man's body, it wouldn't have been surprising if a few of them intersected in something resembling a star.

First and foremost, Narsi decided, he had to establish that they were one and the same.

He wondered if, when he went to examine young Lord Sparanzo Quemanor, he could contrive to spill something—ink or a medicinal tonic—on Master Ariz's shirtfront, so that the sword master might remove it. The maneuver struck Narsi as decidedly awkward and also unlikely to accomplish his goal, since Master Ariz had already proven very reluctant to undress even to have an injury treated. More likely, he'd excuse himself and go change in his private rooms rather than strip in front of Narsi and the young lord Quemanor. Trailing Master Ariz to his private rooms was likely to rouse suspicion.

But there had to be something he could do. There had to be.

Before he realized it, Narsi's thoughts drifted into dreams.

When he woke, it was with a racing heart. His sleep had been filled with terrible scenarios of facing down two different men. Both shared Master Ariz's powerful form and dull expression. But where one man collapsed in relief at having been discovered, the other drew a long dagger and stalked toward Narsi, ready to kill to keep his secret.

Narsi sat there as his pounding heart slowed and the sensation of a blade punching through his chest faded away.

Still, his trepidation lingered. The night before, in Lord Vediya's company, the prospect of rooting out an assassin had seemed daring and made him feel like a hero in one of Lord Vediya's books. But sitting alone as cold morning light poured through his curtains, he recognized the true danger of the undertaking. He glanced down at his hands and took in the black scar left by the muerate that had very nearly killed him. For all the courageous feats Lord Vediya put to paper, there were doubtless hundreds of losses and tragedies that went unremarked upon.

Narsi had to be honest with himself. He wasn't in a storybook, and as much as he wanted to repay Lord Vediya's kindness, he simply wasn't prepared to throw his own life away just to please the man.

"Do I care about the truth enough to take the risk?" Narsi asked himself softly. He hadn't known Captain Ciceron or the guard Dommian, so their deaths didn't touch him personally or deeply. But the suffering attested to by Dommian's charm-book moved Narsi. The fact that others like him were at this very moment living in torture, that truly outraged Narsi. He didn't know how much he would be willing to do to stop so much torment, but he knew it had to be more than just sitting in bed feeling scared.

He threw back his blanket and stepped out of his bed. A disconcerting sensation shot up from beneath his right foot and he stumbled to the side. There at his bedside lay the stiff body of a dead garden snake.

The cat looked exceedingly pleased with itself. Then it leapt from Narsi's bed to the windowsill.

"Very nice. Thank you so much." Narsi picked up the snake.

His right hand felt nearly as stiff as the little corpse. He went to the window and tossed the dead snake out into the mulch below his new roses. As he petted the cat, his fingers regained more of their normal dexterity and the ache in his knuckles dulled. The black stain of the poison still stood out, but the surrounding flesh appeared far less swollen than it had last night. The cat seemed to appreciate Narsi's improved skill quite a bit, rolling and stretching beneath his fingers.

"You do seem to want to be kept, at least a little, don't you?" Narsi murmured to the cat. "Should I say that you are mine and name you Tariq? Or would that be too presumptuous of me?"

The cat nuzzled him for a few moments more, then it caught sight of a passing bird and bounded out the window. Narsi supposed he could take that response any way he liked.

If he didn't get himself murdered by Master Ariz, he decided that he'd look into having a fleabane collar made for the animal. He didn't know why, but the idea pleased him a great deal, and something of the happiness of it remained with him as he picked up Dommian's charm-book.

In the bright morning light he noticed a detail that had eluded him the night before. Inside the back cover there was a slit that ran parallel to the spine: a secret pocket cut into the thick leather. Narsi could just see the edges of pale silk-paper folded and hidden away inside. Using a pair of surgical tweezers Narsi carefully pulled the pages out. Neither the blue ink nor the delicate script matched Dommian's writing. These were letters, Narsi realized. They appeared faded by time and the writing struck Narsi as slightly awkward, as if penned very meticulously but by the unpracticed hand of a child.

Dearest D,

Thank you for telling me where he hid the books. I have read them and copied as many pages as I could. I think that you are right. He doesn't understand the importance of history. He only sees things that are of use to him. I will try to be wiser than that.

Yours truly, C

Narsi noted that several other pages contained similar messages. Thanks and notes about history books, as well as the locations of historic sites that Narsi had never heard of. Interspersed between these were mentions of finding an abandoned nest and raising one of the chicks, as well as the anxieties of attending dances in dresses that felt far too small, as well as anger at an older sister who was forever arguing with Father and making him angry at them all.

Narsi guessed that a noble daughter in the household where Dommian had previously worked must have come to think of the guard as a confidant. Clearly the two of them had shared a love of Cadeleonian history and mythology. One of the child's letters even made mention of the Summer Doe, noting that she alone of the Savior's warrior companions had survived the Battle of Heaven's Shard.

Is it possible that she stopped Our Savior's Waarihivu invocation from cleansing the world? Did she betray Our Savior? Or are we still awaiting the final battle of that war?

Narsi frowned at the questions as he remembered the voice in the Circle of Wisteria whispering in his ears. *A great battle begun in ages long past, but one that never truly ended.*

Was it just a chance turn of phrase, or could the two be in any way related? As he flipped through the remaining few letters, he found no further mentions of wars or battles, just the confessions of a child who adored raising songbirds and feared the strange man whom her father had chosen to be her husband.

Tonight I freed all of my larks. I wish I could fly away with them. I would build a nest outside your window and sing you to sleep every night.

Narsi wondered if the girl who'd written those words knew of Dommian's death. Would she mourn him, or had she forgotten him long ago? Narsi's attention drifted once again to the furious, defaced lines that Dommian had written himself. He picked out one legible section.

No use. Every tome I search says the same. Only death will break the brand. Damn him, damn him to the pits of the Black Hell.

A nearly incomprehensible string of obscenities followed and the script grew loose and inarticulate for two pages. The only words Narsi felt certain of read: *There must be another way to get free of him.* The desperation of those words filled Narsi with melancholy sympathy. If there had been a means other than death, Dommian would never find it now.

But perhaps others could. Lady Hylanya had said that a multitude of people lived under the thrall of this particular witch and that their numbers were growing. In its own way it could be considered a public health crisis. A plague of magic infecting more and more people every day.

The clear melody of the chapel bells rang out and Narsi realized that he needed to get moving if he was to have any breakfast before he kept his appointment with Master Ariz. He washed and dressed quickly, then slipped the charm-book into the pocket of his physician's coat before he hurried on his way.

Outside, light breezes blew through the trees and the warm air smelled of blooming flowers. Several guards acknowledged him with nods as he passed on his way to the chapel. Querra greeted him from across the kitchen garden. Narsi smiled at her and waved back. By the time he joined Father Timoteo and Berto for breakfast in the chapel garden, he felt almost as if he might fit into the household.

Though today both Father Timoteo and Berto looked glum. Narsi guessed that contemplating yet another funereal service in so short a span of days was bound to bring down their spirits.

When they inquired, Narsi reassured them that he felt much recovered. He made a little show a turning his spoon through the fingers of his bruised right hand, and that seemed to reassure and relax Father Timoteo. Berto, however, remained in his funk, absently stirring his porridge and contributing no more conversation than a few shrugs and one nod of his head while the rest of them discussed the upcoming masquerade celebrations. Father Timoteo offered a roll of his fine rag paper for the acolytes to cut their masks from. Remembering how few extravagances he and Berto had enjoyed as acolytes, Narsi dug out several coins and donated them to the acolytes for the purchase of beads and ribbons.

"Come into a fortune already, have you?" Berto scowled at his bowl.

"Well . . ." Narsi could hardly recount his adventure at the Green Door. "I've had a little run of good luck."

"As you always do," Berto replied. "I swear a cat couldn't land on its feet as often as you've managed to come out the better of any situation."

Narsi wasn't certain what inspired that from Berto or how to take it. He'd very nearly died two days ago. He didn't think surviving really qualified as coming out the better for the encounter. But before he could respond, Berto excused himself to return to organizing Father Timoteo's papers for publication.

"Poor Berto! I suspect that Mistress Delfia may be proving more difficult to woo than he expected," Father Timoteo commented.

"Oh. I see." Narsi's concern over his friend's surly temper faded. Romantic uncertainty seemed forever to wreak havoc upon Berto's heart. But if this was anything like the boyhood infatuations that Narsi remembered, then Berto's mood would brighten in a matter of a day.

"He can't help feeling a little jealous of your natural charm," Father Timoteo went on. "He doesn't mean anything by it."

"I know, I know." It had always been easier for Narsi to approach and chat with the women and girls around him. He supposed he had the advantage over Berto in that he didn't feel that he had as much to lose by their rejections. Whereas Berto's intensity could sometimes disconcert the very girl he most wanted to impress.

"Mistress Delfia hasn't rebuffed him outright, has she?" Narsi asked.

"Not at all. She simply declined his invitation for an evening stroll with him last night." Father Timoteo looked a little amused.

Hearing that, Narsi's concern for Berto disappeared and he noticed the sad contents of Father Timoteo's bowl. His meager serving of gruel wasn't enough to sustain a child. Narsi knew from experience that the father wouldn't take any of the sausages. He always left those for his acolytes.

"Berto always fears the worst. I have no idea why he's always so quick to assume women are only interested in men of extravagant wealth and noble titles." Father Timoteo lifted his spoon but then set it back on the table.

"I didn't get the impression that any affluent merchants or sly noblemen were vying for Mistress Delfia's hand." Narsi offered the cream pitcher to Father Timoteo.

"No, nothing of the sort." Father Timoteo hesitated a moment but then accepted the cream pitcher and poured a tot into his porridge. He still ate nothing. "I can't say that there aren't inconstant women in the world. There are just as many inconstant men, I'm certain. But Mistress Delfia has always struck me as unimpressed by frippery and flattery. I'm certain she had good reason for declining the invitation."

"As chance would have it, I happen to know exactly where she was last night and who she was with," Narsi said.

"Yes? You could reassure Berto then?" Father Timoteo's expression brightened.

"Even better. I could tell the news to you, so that you could inform him," Narsi replied. "But on one condition."

"What would that be?" Father Timoteo knew him well enough to look amused rather than suspicious, though one of the older acolytes eyed Narsi somewhat skeptically.

"You must eat all your porridge and one of those cream-poached eggs. Then I'll reveal all," Narsi pronounced in a tone of mock authority.

"Certainly the eggs would do a young man like yourself more good than me," Father Timoteo protested.

"You have my terms." Narsi crossed his arms over his chest. "Will you not pay my price to allay Berto's fears?"

Father Timoteo gave a soft laugh and took one of the eggs. But where another man would have gulped the thing down in a single bite, Father Timoteo ate slowly, almost falteringly, as if Narsi's request were a genuine challenge for him.

When Narsi had been a child he'd assumed Father Timoteo's asceticism typical of devout Cadeleonian men, but as he'd grown up he'd encountered many people of great faith, and none but those suffering penance for immense wrongdoing denied themselves and tortured their bodies as extremely as Father Timoteo. Narsi had begun to suspect that something more insidious than mere religious fervor fed the Holy Father's self-denial—though he'd never been able to imagine what crime Timoteo could have committed that he felt deserved such punishment. The Holy Father had been nothing but tolerant, kind and generous all the years that Narsi had known him. Most anyone who met him thought Father Timoteo was very nearly a saint.

But now Narsi remembered that agonized expression Father Timoteo had worn when he'd spoken of Narsi's father. Had guilt belied his grief? No—that couldn't be. Father Timoteo couldn't have played any part in his own brother's murder. Narsi felt almost ashamed of himself for even considering the possibility.

Finally the Holy Father swallowed the last of his egg.

"So where was Mistress Delfia?" Father Timoteo asked him and Narsi remembered their conversation.

"You can reassure Berto that she was with her brother," Narsi said. "The duchess had asked the two of them to sort through the belongings of the guard, Dommian. I happened upon them at their work while I was trying to find my way around the building. It didn't look like a small task, so I imagine that the two of them were working well past any decent hour for taking a stroll."

"Berto will be relieved to know as much." Father Timoteo smiled and then gently patted Narsi's hand. "Thank you."

"Happy to oblige," Narsi responded offhandedly, but it was no less true. He did hope that Berto cheered. Though contemplating Mistress Delfia reminded him of his fast-approaching meeting with her brother. He wished desperately that he knew even a little more of the man's nature.

"You wouldn't happen to know anything of Master Ariz, would you?" Narsi asked Father Timoteo.

The Holy Father looked surprised by the change of subject.

"I can't say too much about him. He doesn't often attend chapel nor does he make too much conversation at the master's table. I assume he's a naturally quiet kind of fellow. I'd like to think that perhaps his still waters run deep, though Berto says he's as dull as dishwater. Why do you ask?"

For an instant Narsi considered telling everything to Father Timoteo. But it struck him as too much of a betrayal of Lord Vediya's confidences. And he hardly wished to share his secrets with all the acolytes as well.

"I'm going to be looking in on Lord Sparanzo Quemanor while he's with the sword master, but the last two times I've encountered the man I couldn't find anything to talk with him about."

"Well"—Father Timoteo lowered his voice—"I can tell you that he and his sister come from the disgraced Plunado family. He would have been a nobleman up until ten years ago, when his entire family was stripped of their rank and possessions because of their cousin's treachery against Fedeles. Though none of that's likely to make for a cheery conversation. Perhaps the subject of dance would be one to explore. He's familiar with a good number of dances, but none of the Haldiim ones, as far as I've seen."

"Yes, that sounds good." Narsi nodded.

He'd been quite young at the time of the scandal that had destroyed the Plunado family, but he remembered all the rumors of the forbidden magic and vile torture that Fedeles Quemanor had endured at the hands of the family's heir.

"You wouldn't happen to know anything about . . ." Narsi trailed off as he realized how odd it would sound to bring up the subject of spells and thralls out of the blue.

"About?" Father Timoteo prompted, and Narsi decided that if he was going to seem a little odd, it might as well be with Father Timoteo.

"Well, when you alluded to Lord Quemanor's possession just now I wondered if the spells used against him weren't the same as those the Labaran witches are rumored to use to enchant men. Thralls, I think they're called."

"I don't believe it could have been," Timoteo responded. "As far as I could ascertain the Labaran thralls leave no mark upon the flesh. But when Lord Quemanor was possessed, a small symbol was burned into his skin. A tiny brand at the base of his back."

"Oh?" Narsi tried not to betray his interest. It wouldn't do for a Haldiim to appear too fascinated by a spell that once enslaved a Cadeleonian nobleman, particularly not in front of a gaggle of young acolytes who served in that nobleman's chapel. He knew from personal experience how quickly bored young men could generate conspiracies.

"Yes. It's actually a fascinating subject. Many people don't realize this, but in the oldest of holy texts there are a number of instructions for binding the wills of men and beasts in a manner much like the Labaran thralls. It's called a Brand of Obedience. I've seen two in my life. The scar left on Lord Quemanor, and the other was burned into the vellum of an ancient scroll. The vellum was said to have been made from the tanned skin of a retainer who served a northern bishop during the Mirogoth invasion. The symbol stood out quite clearly, an eight-pointed star inside a perfect circle."

Narsi just managed not to crow with glee as Father Timoteo described the symbol that Lady Hylanya had drawn—the very one he needed to know more about. Then it struck him that a holy man as learned as Father Timoteo was exactly the sort of person who would be familiar with such a profane and obscure Cadeleonian symbol.

Warming to his subject, Father Timoteo looked meaningfully at his six acolytes and went on. "The Brand of Obedience originated long, long ago, before Cadeleon was even a unified kingdom. Back then Our Savior traveled the lands, gathering followers to battle the demon kings who threatened to overrun our world. One of those who came to him was in fact a demon himself. To assure the demon's fidelity, the Savior branded the spell of obedience into the flesh over the demon's heart."

"Really?" The question came from the gap-toothed acolyte. "The Savior had a demon among his followers?"

"Oh yes." Father Timoteo grinned at the boy. "Not that most of the church fathers wish to admit as much these days. In fact the Savior was joined in his battles by a multitude of creatures and people whom we now blithely call heathens and monsters. Giants, Bahiim, witches and even Old Gods like the Summer Doe numbered among his companion warriors."

"Did he brand them all, then?" another of the acolytes inquired— this boy wore his bangs a little long, probably in an attempt to hide the large red birthmark that hung over his right brow.

"No, he only branded the demon. And according to the oldest accounts he only did so because the demon insisted on it, so as to prove his commitment to the Savior to the other warriors." Father Timoteo looked thoughtful and then added, "If I recall correctly, this all happened in the north, where the Gavado lands lie today. The Savior and his armies of allies built a stronghold there, then swept down into the south to fight a final battle here where our capital stands."

"The War of Heaven's Shard," the gap-toothed acolyte murmured.

"Yes, indeed." Father Timoteo gave the boy an approving smile. "The demon who served the Savior was called Meztli. So when you read a holy text recounting the war of Heaven's Shard and it describes how Meztli stood shielding the Savior with his own burning flesh as fires rained down upon them, remember that heroic act was performed by a demon. The Savior might have died then and there had he been too quick to judge Meztli by his appearance or his heritage."

Narsi frowned. He vaguely recalled the text of which the Holy Father spoke. He hadn't found it all that interesting as a boy. He certainly hadn't realized how radical of a conclusion might have been drawn from it. What he recalled of his readings were seemingly endless lists of those who died or were maimed, blinded or variously wounded in battle after battle. The sheer repetition of it all had rendered even glory and death a dull monotony.

Though now he wondered if he shouldn't go back and look the texts over again. Particularly if there was any further information to be found about this Brand of Obedience. As Narsi considered it, a distant memory of the story stirred.

"Wasn't it Meztli who taught the Savior the signs that protected him and his forces when they invoked the . . . ?" Narsi trailed off, unable to recall the name of the miracle that had turned the tide of the battle.

"Yes, yes! He forged the shields that protected Our Savior's armies," Father Timoteo supplied. "If it hadn't been for Meztli, the Savior and most of the greatest warriors would have perished when they invoked the Shroud of Stone. Even so, many died along with the enemy demon king and his army, either because they lost their shields in the battle or because they arrogantly refused to accept the wisdom of a creature whom they considered profane."

The young acolytes appeared impressed and Father Timoteo beamed at Narsi as if they'd planned this conversation in advance as an ethics lesson for the boys.

"I'm going to make my mask a demon," a very young boy proclaimed.

"You can't. This year it's to be beasts of the Great Hunt," the youth with the birthmark said, then he looked to Father Timoteo. "Tell him, father."

"I'm afraid Nillo is correct," Father Timoteo said. "But you know, there are many quite exotic creatures described in the *Book of Redemption*. Stallions born of lightning storms, sea serpents as large as ships and birds that burned as bright as shafts of sunshine. Divine creatures and Old Gods, as our Bahiim brethren called them."

The conversation naturally turned to which beasts sounded fiercest and how best to make masks that captured their visages. If it struck any of the boys as odd that the royal bishop would choose such a theme for the masquerade at a time when he so openly opposed Count Radulf— the champion of those ancient, wild creatures—none of them said so. Though two of them did wonder if they couldn't wear eagle masks or if they would be mistaken for Saint Trueno if they did. Hawks were safer, they all agreed.

Narsi listened absently, his thoughts still on Father Timoteo's mention of thralls.

"Is there a way to break the Brand of Obedience, do you recall?"

Narsi resisted the urge to whisper. Timoteo appeared a little surprised by the inquiry but then shook his head.

"Absolute obedience until death parts the soul from the flesh," Father Timoteo replied. "Even the oldest inscriptions describing it say as much."

Narsi nodded and remembered the notes he'd copied from Dommian's charm-book. Then another question occurred to him.

"But wouldn't that mean that Lord Quemanor—" Narsi began.

"Oh. No. Not at all. Lord Quemanor is absolutely free of all traces of the thrall that once possessed him. He is not at all corrupted," Father Timoteo clarified before Narsi could even complete his question. "The man who enthralled him died and that broke the bond between them."

"So, a person could be released if the person who enthralled them dies?" Narsi wondered if Dommian had known as much but been too oppressed to even consider doing away with the man who enslaved him or if he'd not realized that his own death hadn't been required.

"Yes. The death of either party ends their connection. But why do you ask?"

"Professional curiosity." Narsi shrugged. "Always thinking of conditions in terms of chronic or curable, even in the realms of the spirit."

Father Timoteo laughed and nodded. "You truly were born to be a physician."

"Speaking of my calling, I'd best move along if I'm to keep my appointment with Master Ariz. Thank you so much for the meal and good company." Narsi stood, and several of the acolytes as well as Father Timoteo wished him well as he took his leave of them.

Narsi strolled across the garden paths, basking in the warmth of the morning sun and absently noting the flocks of doves wheeling through the blue sky. A few red camellias peeked out at him from amidst dark green hedges, and Narsi exchanged morning greetings with several of the gardeners tending the plants' irrigation. Usto, the sunburned young man Narsi recalled from the previous day, shyly beckoned him over. Narsi gave the man a rinse of coinflower for the scratches a silverthorn had gouged across his forearms.

As they stood together, a party of very well-dressed Cadeleonians came around the hedge of camellias. A flutter of pleasure rose through Narsi when he recognized Lord Vediya sauntering between two resplendently dressed noblewomen. Three handmaids and two armed guards trailed them. One of the women laughed at something Lord Vediya said, while the other hid her flushed cheeks behind a silver lace fan. A moment later two brawny young men—nobles, from the look of their silk clothes—joined the party on their morning stroll.

The entire group wafted past Narsi and Usto without greeting or comment, though Narsi noted the way one of the women drew nearer Lord Vediya, as if she feared that it was only his presence that kept Narsi, or perhaps Usto, from lunging out and groping her. The noblemen following Lord Vediya both lifted their chins and puffed up their chests as they passed. Narsi wondered if they were attempting to intimidate him or just to approximate a little of Usto's broad musculature. One of the handmaids shook her head and offered the two of them a quick, tired smile. The guards appeared resigned and bored.

Narsi studied the group until they disappeared behind another wall of foliage. Lord Vediya didn't once glance back his way, and Narsi felt stupid for entertaining the childish fantasy that he might.

He turned his attention back to Usto before his mooning became obvious, only to realize that Usto was still gazing after the handmaid who'd offered the brief smile. His sunburned cheeks flushed even darker red when he noticed Narsi observing him.

"She seems very kind," Narsi stated.

Usto nodded. When Narsi left him, he was still peering along the pebble path, maybe in hopes of glimpsing the handmaid on her return.

Narsi entered the main house by a servant's door and made his way toward the fencing room. Compared to the sunny outdoors, the mansion corridors seemed gloomy and the air felt stagnant with the scent of woodsmoke. Diffused splashes of morning light reflected across the silver mirrors lining the hall and threw small halos of illumination across the wooden panels of the walls. Narsi passed a number of nobles and servants as he wound his way through the huge house. The nobles largely ignored him, while he and the majority of the staff exchanged passing nods.

Not bad considering that he only arrived here a few days ago. He felt certain that he stood a good chance of winning a few new friends in the coming months. At the same time he couldn't help but wonder how soon he could return to Cieloalta's tiny Haldiim District. He shook his head at himself and his own strange contradiction of wanting to belong to both worlds and at the same time never quite feeling satisfied with his place in either.

As he turned a corner he drew to a halt at the sight before him, and all his self-absorbed thoughts dissipated before his curiosity.

A stream of brilliant light poured through the narrow crack between two doors. A man peered into the illumination, the planes of his face burning to stark white. The rest of his body seemed to melt into the shadows, like some kind of apparition. He appeared fascinated by the view before him and failed to even take note of Narsi for several moments.

Fortunately the delay allowed Narsi to recognize the man and offer a proper bow when the duke did acknowledge him.

"Master Narsi." For an instant the duke appeared embarrassed to be caught out peeping, but then he straightened and his expression grew curious. "Here to see Master Ariz?"

Narsi had to resist the urge to respond with, *No I was hoping to peer at the man through the keyhole, but then I realized that you'd gotten here before me.*

"Indeed, Your Grace." Narsi paused as he assessed how best to manage the awkward situation. Pushing forward seemed like the wisest course. He wasn't at all certain of the duke's feeling about him treating his son. He decided to avoid that subject without resorting to lying. "I stitched an injury of his a few days ago and wanted to see how it's healing."

"His forearm." The duke nodded. "He said that you did very good work."

"I do try," Narsi responded, just to say something.

They both stood there for another moment. The duke blocked his way into the chamber and seemed unwilling to move. From beyond the doors Narsi picked out the sound of fast footsteps and then the clatter of wooden blades knocking together.

"Good. Well-blocked," Master Ariz's flat voice sounded. "But try to keep your left side behind the defensive line of your right arm. Like so."

The duke's eyes flicked from Narsi back to the scene he spied between the doors.

Didn't he trust Master Ariz with his son's lessons?

Maybe Lord Vediya had apprised the duke of his theory that Master Ariz was an enthralled assassin. Though if that was the case Narsi didn't know why the duke didn't simply enter the room and openly observe. His expression didn't strike Narsi as worried so much as fascinated. It made Narsi want to peer between the doors himself, if only to witness whatever sight so captivated the duke. He didn't know the duke well enough—and probably never would—to ask, much less lean in next to the duke to see for himself.

That left him standing, and waiting in awkward silence.

Narsi considered leaving the duke to his spying. There would be no point in Narsi slipping in during Sparanzo's lesson to examine his legs on the sly if the duke was standing here in the hall, watching everything.

Then the duke straightened and glanced farther down the dim hall. A group of well-dressed young Cadeleonian men hurried toward them. Several armed guards trailed them. Narsi recognized Prince Jacinto at the head of the group. He'd replaced his flamboyant silk rags with blue velvet attire, trimmed in gold. By comparison the duke's riding clothes appeared rather humble, though his raised head and imperious expression certainly weren't modest or meek.

"Fedeles, you must stop slinking off on your own!" Prince Jacinto declared.

"I was bored," the duke replied.

"You've a shorter attention span than your horse," Jacinto responded, but he sounded amused. He glanced to where Narsi stood and stopped short with a sudden, wide grin. "Master Narsi! Why, you are just the man I need."

"My physician is far too busy to spend his time in one of your plays," the duke responded. Which was rather high-handed, Narsi felt, particularly since he wasn't actually in the duke's employment, but Father Timoteo's.

"Don't be that way, Fedeles," Prince Jacinto replied. "Everyone knows you've no use for physicians, and my latest production requires someone to play an alluring Yuanese catamite."

To Narsi's surprise the prince winked at him. Several of the young men attending the prince eyed Narsi far less favorably, though the slim fellow with a cane at the rear of the group—Narsi recalled his name was Enevir—regarded him with an expression very like sympathy.

"The fact that Master Narsi is neither an actor nor Yuanese ought to give you a little pause," the duke replied, but he too smiled. He closed the distance between them and the entire party turned as the prince and the duke strode down the hall, pretending to argue over some absurd-sounding play.

Moments later Narsi stood alone in the hall. He considered knocking but couldn't resist leaning forward to see exactly what it was that had so enrapt the duke. On the other side of the crack between the doors Master Ariz stood, silently staring back at Narsi.

Despite himself, Narsi gave a shout and leapt back a step.

Master Ariz pushed the doors open and considered him with a disturbingly blank expression.

"You surprised me," Narsi said, as if that hadn't been abundantly obvious. Then a thought occurred to him—certainly the duke and Master Ariz hadn't been standing on opposite sides of the doors staring at one another, had they? Though it made for an amusing mental image. "How long were you standing there?"

"I heard Prince Jacinto's voice in the hallway and came to see if he meant to call on Sparanzo." Master Ariz stepped back, making way for Narsi to enter the fencing room.

The chamber blazed, sunlight pouring in through a multitude of windows and reflecting across even more mirrors. In the midst of all the light three dark-haired children stood. If Narsi hadn't known better he would have said that they were all siblings—the two boys could easily have passed for identical twins. The girl stood at the same height as the other two and gripped a small wooden sword in each of her hands.

Master Ariz closed the doors behind Narsi and then made a perfunctory introduction. The slim boy wearing a gold-threaded jerkin was Sparanzo, while the other two were Mistress Delfia's children, Celino and Marisol. Master Ariz's dull voice and blank expression betrayed only a trace of warmth as he spoke to the three of them.

"Master Narsi has come to examine all of us to ensure that we are all in our best health for Prince Sevanyo's coronation," Master Ariz stated.

Narsi hadn't expected to examine all of them, but noticing young Sparanzo's worried expression, he guessed that Master Ariz was right not to make the boy feel singled out. The excuse of further examinations also offered Narsi an opportunity to possibly look at the scar on Master Ariz's chest. So he nodded and opened up his physician's bag.

The girl, Marisol, stepped up to him directly and performed a curtsy. Narsi gave as much of an exam as he could without having the Cadeleonian girl remove any of her clothes. Her pulse beat strong and her breathing sounded clear. When he requested that she hop from one foot and then the other, she showed off a little, turning agile spins. Her arms and legs were surprisingly muscular for such a young child.

"You are in quite fine health, Mistress Marisol," Narsi informed her, and she grinned, displaying small pearly teeth.

Her brother followed her example and appeared just as toned and fit. After Narsi told him so, the boy cocked back his head and nodded, in a languid, confident manner that reminded Narsi of Lord Vediya. Sparanzo approached Narsi much more hesitantly. Young Celino actually caught his hand and drew him near.

"Don't worry," Celino told Sparanzo. "Mari and I are right here to defend you. And so is Uncle Ariz."

Sparanzo glanced back over his shoulder to Master Ariz. The fencing instructor produced a fractional smile—which Narsi thought had to be the first time he'd seen the man do so.

Just observing Sparanzo walk to him, Narsi noted the boy's limp, as well as his focused attempt to hide it. Even at his young age the child had obviously already absorbed the Cadeleonian ideal of physically powerful and perfect men. He seemed very aware that he did not quite measure up. His two strong, agile playmates likely made him all the more aware of his impediment.

"You're five years old?" Narsi asked.

"Six in a month." Sparanzo spoke very clearly and with a formality that seemed at odds with his youth. Narsi guessed that the boy mirrored the tone of either his mother or father when addressing a servant.

"Well, you're quite tall for your age," Narsi told him, hoping to reassure the boy.

Sparanzo nodded. His expression remained serious and disapproving. Still he allowed Narsi to examine him without voicing any objection—though the boy's entire body tensed when Narsi placed his hand on his left leg and felt the muscle of his calf.

"Does that hurt?" Narsi asked softly.

Sparanzo shook his head. Narsi considered him, attempting to tell if he was lying or simply afraid of having attention brought to his left leg. Narsi dropped his hands to the heel of the boy's shoe. Sparanzo remained tense. Narsi felt sympathy for the child, but he would do him no good by stopping his exam and pretending like nothing was wrong.

"Can you shift your weight onto your left foot and then back all the way over to the right for me?" Narsi asked.

Sparanzo nodded. As he shifted his weight, Narsi noticed that both Sparanzo's playmates did the same thing. He glanced to them to see if they were perhaps teasing the boy, but both of them appeared quite serious and focused on exactly emulating the slight wobble that marked Sparanzo's shift from his left foot to his right. They were both quite good at imitating the motion, which Narsi found truly strange.

Sparanzo repeated the movement and Narsi watched him closely. This time Narsi felt certain of the slight difference he detected in the length of the boy's legs.

"Very good," Narsi told him. "You're all done."

Relief showed plainly on the boy's face. He hurried to join his companions and Narsi rose and stepped back to Master Ariz's side.

"Now for your exam, Master Ariz."

"That's hardly necessary—" Master Ariz began.

"It doesn't hurt. And we'll be here with you, so don't worry." Sparanzo offered nearly the same assurance that Celino had given him.

"I really should have a look at your stitches," Narsi added.

Master Ariz didn't argue. He simply stood unmoving for several moments. Then he looked to the children and told them to perform some series of dance steps or fencing positions—Narsi was not familiar enough with either to know. The three of them set to work, taking turns lunging at one another and then springing back. Their reflections danced across the mirrors.

Master Ariz drew back to one of the weapon racks to remove his heavy coat and rest it across the rack. The pale fabric of his shirt showed the faint lines of dried sweat. The right sleeve displayed flecks of blood-stains. As Master Ariz rolled back his sleeve to expose his stitched forearm, Narsi noted both how well he used his left hand and the corded thick muscle of his arms. It suddenly occurred to him that breaking free of Master Ariz's grip—should he choose to grasp him—would not be easily done. The sword hanging from Master Ariz's belt seemed all at once glaring and ominous.

And yet the man himself remained bland in appearance and demeanor. He extended his right arm. Narsi studied the stitches and scowled at the bruised skin and red, inflamed scabs that mottled his neat, clean work.

"You would be wise to take better care of your arm while it's healing. If the wound festers, it could cost you your hand." Narsi quickly retrieved his remaining flask of coinflower distillate from his medical bag as well as a small washcloth. He cleaned the wound as gently as he could. Master Ariz gave no indication of pain as Narsi worked.

He leaned in toward Narsi and the smell of sweat rolled from him.

"What of Sparanzo?" Master Ariz asked.

"His right leg is a little shorter than his left," Narsi replied. "The matter is easily remedied by making the sole of his right shoe just that small bit thicker. The condition isn't uncommon and most children grow out of it."

"That's all?" Master Ariz asked.

"I believe so," Narsi replied. "Exact measurements of both his legs need to be taken, but I didn't want to embarrass him in front of his friends. Also, it might be more natural for his cordwainer to take the measurement, since he'll need to know the precise difference to make up in the shoe heels."

"Sensible," Master Ariz remarked. "I'll have my sister inform the duchess. She'll be relieved to know it's so simple a matter."

"Yes," Narsi agreed, but his thoughts were far from the subject of who should arrange for the boy's shoemaking. Instead he battled his own apprehension over broaching the subject of the brand Master Ariz bore. If he was going to do it, now would be the time. Or he could let the moment pass and simply withdraw to a safe distance from a man who might very well be a murderer.

Fear slithered through the pit of his belly, as he finished cleaning Master Ariz's arm. Lord Vediya had warned him against doing this, but he'd also been so delighted at the idea of knowing.

Narsi packed his medical supplies away. Then he straightened to his full height. He stood a good three inches taller than Master Ariz, though he suspected the Master Ariz outweighed him by a solid stone of hard muscle. Still, would he take the chance of attacking Narsi in front of the children? Narsi hoped not.

"You know when I first stitched your arm up I noticed a scar on your chest—"

At once Master Ariz's head came up. His gray gaze fixed upon Narsi's face, while his right hand dropped to his sword hilt. He said nothing and his expression remained blank as a mask. Narsi's throat felt dry and his heart raced, but he pressed on.

"I believe that it's a Brand of Obedience, and if so, then I'd like to help you break its control over—"

Master Ariz's left hand suddenly slammed into Narsi's throat, cutting off his words and nearly knocking him off his feet. Master Ariz's fingers clamped into the flesh of Narsi's neck. Narsi fought with both hands to break Master Ariz's grip, but his arm was like steel. Narsi gasped for air, and white specks floated before his eyes.

"Don't say another word." Master Ariz spoke so calmly that the children took no notice of them. His expression hardly altered, though beads of sweat had risen on his upper lip and his pupils flared wide: both signs of immense pain and intense distress, Narsi remembered from his medical schooling. He wondered if his own gaze was a mirror of Master Ariz's. His pulse seemed to pound through his entire body. Master Ariz's palm felt cold and damp against Narsi's skin. Tremors passed through his fingers as he very slightly loosened his choke hold.

"I do not wish to kill you, Master Narsi. But you've done a very foolish thing."

"Yes, I see that." Narsi started to draw back from the other man's grip, but Master Ariz shook his head.

"If you run, I will not be able to keep from giving chase. I will cut you down in an instant." Master Ariz whispered the words as if straining to push them from his mouth. "You must take my sword from me. Quickly." Master Ariz jerked his right hand back from his sword belt. His whole arm shook as he held it out from his side.

Narsi reached out and gripped the hilt of Master Ariz's sword and drew it. The weight of the weapon startled him.

"Now my dagger," Master Ariz directed him.

Had he not felt so terrified, Narsi thought he might have laughed at the strangeness of their interaction.

He quickly took Master Ariz's dagger from its sheath. Like the sword, it felt unwieldy in his hand. Despite the fact that he now held two deadly weapons against Master Ariz, Narsi didn't feel any more safe or certain of the situation. If anything, the sight of the naked blades worried him all the more. How easily could Master Ariz take one or both from him and run him through. Even if he could keep the blades, the weapon racks surrounding them brimmed with no end of swords, spears, maces and flails for Master Ariz to make use of. Narsi wasn't a swordsman and he doubted he had it in him to use any weapon against another person.

Narsi tried to calm himself and think, but it was hard to feel collected with Master Ariz's powerful fingers holding him in a strangling grip.

"Take your hand from my throat, will you?" Narsi attempted to maintain a light tone, for the sake of his own confidence. He didn't imagine that squealing or shouting would aid Master Ariz to remain collected, either.

"I'm trying to," Master Ariz ground out. They stood there in the strange tableau for what felt like eternity. Sweat poured down Master Ariz's face and soaked through the front of his white shirt. He sucked in air through clenched teeth, as if merely breathing was an agony for him, and still his expression betrayed nothing more than a slight frown.

Narsi watched him, feeling every quake and tremor of Master Ariz's struggle play across the delicate skin of his throat. Master Ariz's grip grew steadily tighter. The beginning of panic flitted through Narsi's chest as he struggled to draw in each breath.

"You must force me to free you," Master Ariz said at last. "Raise my sword to my chest. Make my flesh feel its bite."

Narsi hesitated for only a moment. He needed to breathe. He lifted the heavy sword.

Behind them the children laughed and bounded around each other. Out of the corner of his eyes, Narsi saw their shadows dance through long shafts of bright sunlight.

To Narsi's horror, Master Ariz stepped into the sword blade, and a brilliant red weal of blood welled up through the front of his shirt. Narsi almost pulled the sword back, but then he felt Master Ariz's grip on his neck ease slightly.

"Release me," Narsi rasped.

Master Ariz's hand jerked and shook as he dragged his clammy fingers back from Narsi's throat. Narsi gasped in a deep breath of air. A cold ache remained where Master Ariz had bruised the muscles of his neck.

Three loud bells rang from the distance of the chapel. Though it felt as though he'd stood here with Master Ariz for hours, Narsi realized that hardly any time had passed at all since he'd entered the fencing room. Now a knock sounded at the doors and the children stilled in their play. Narsi looked to them and found all three of them staring back at him.

"Very good, Master Narsi. But your sword arm is dropping slightly," Master Ariz said calmly, as if instructing him. Perhaps he was. Narsi lifted the sword a little.

Sparanzo and Celino both appeared to accept the idea of some impromptu fencing lesson, but Marisol looked slightly skeptical. She started toward them, her own small wooden sword gripped in her hand, but then the doors opened and two guardsmen leaned in to inform the children that they were expected back to attend the duchess.

"Off you go, then," Master Ariz replied. He glanced over his shoulder to the guardsmen. "Please tell my sister that I may be late. Master Narsi and I are in the midst of a lesson."

Narsi realized that if he was going to expose Master Ariz, then this had to be the moment, when there were at least two other armed men present. He met Master Ariz's gaze and took in his pallid, perspiring visage. The splotch of blood staining the front of his shirt continued to spread. The man looked half ruined, and Narsi knew that his rash decision was largely to blame for Master Ariz's suffering.

He'd taken an oath to do no harm, and yet his desire to please Lord Vediya had clearly led him to inflict agony upon Master Ariz. He couldn't lay Master Ariz bare now, in this moment of desperate suffering.

"It may be an hour or more, considering how much I still have to learn, I fear," Narsi announced. His voice sounded too loud and his attempted grin felt like a grimace.

Fortunately the guardsmen appeared largely disinterested in both himself and Master Ariz. They offered half bows to Sparanzo and struck up a pleasant conversation with the boy as they turned and led the children away. The doors fell closed. Relief washed through Narsi, only to be followed by anxiety.

What was he going to do with Master Ariz now?

"There's a length of rope hanging over the sword rack behind me and a stool beside that. It's well made enough to restrain me," Master Ariz told him. "Keep the sword to my chest and walk me back to it."

"You're bleeding and need—" Narsi began to object.

"It's nothing compared to what I will do to you if you relent." Master Ariz hardly raised his voice, but the certainty in his tone sent a rush of fear through Narsi. "Now drive me back to the rack!"

Narsi stepped forward. For a sickening instant he thought Master Ariz wouldn't budge. The tip of the sword sank deeper into his chest, then Master Ariz took a step backward and Narsi followed him. They moved together, almost like dance partners, except for the sword blade balanced between them and the blood that now streaked down to the waist of Master Ariz's shirt. They reached the rack in four steps.

Master Ariz caught the length of thick rope in his right hand. Then he went very still and Narsi realized that he'd once again descended into some immense internal struggle. He turned the rope through his hands and then leaned slightly into the sword point Narsi held between them. The sight sickened Narsi, but he didn't pull the blade back.

Master Ariz tied a slipknot and looped it around his left wrist. He jerked the rope tight and then looped another knot in the rope and slid his right hand through. Then he sank down to sit on the stool.

"You're going to have to do the rest yourself. I'll keep as still as I can for as long as I can, but you'd better move fast."

Narsi needed no further instruction. He caught up the free end of the rope and made very quick work of binding Master Ariz's hands and legs to the stool. The surgical knots he'd learned served him very well, though twice Master Ariz insisted that he pull the ropes tighter. And once he caught Narsi's hand in a crushing grip that required the pressure of a dagger to his back to allow him to loosen his hold.

By the end, Master Ariz hunched atop the stool with his hands bound to the front rungs and his legs tucked beneath the wooden seat and knotted to the back rungs. Splashes of his blood covered Narsi's hands and dribbled down the stool. But oddly, after tugging once against his bonds, Master Ariz seemed to relax. For the first time the tension drained from his muscles and he drooped like a cut flower.

"You're safe now, I think," Master Ariz said.

Narsi stepped back from him. He wondered if he shouldn't fetch Lord Vediya but then realized that the man could be anywhere by now. No. He'd been the one to start this and he was just going to have to see it through.

"Can you answer questions about . . . your condition?" Narsi asked.

"Not directly," Master Ariz replied.

Narsi considered that, then asked, "What about the person who branded you? Can you tell me about him?"

"N . . . Not . . . direct . . . ly," Master Ariz replied again, though this time he seemed to have trouble even forming the simple words.

"But you could tell me about something else? What you ate for breakfast, for example?"

"Yes." The relief sounded plainly despite Master Ariz's flat tone. "Four hard eggs and green porridge. Master Leadro—the music instructor—ate the last sweet bun before I got to the table. Mistress Ortez arrived after me and told him that he deserved his piles."

Narsi recalled Master Leadro's slim figure and his mention of suffering from hemorrhoids. He knew nothing of Mistress Ortez, but the conversation inclined him to think that there might be a roundabout way of getting information from Master Ariz.

"Did you know that Dommian was in a thrall?" Narsi asked.

Master Ariz went very still, then he nodded.

"Can you tell me what you know about *him*?"

"He'd been ordered by a man I know to kill Sparanzo, Celino and Marisol. I didn't realize until nearly too late, and then I stopped him."

"So you *can* defy this man who you both knew? At least indirectly," Narsi asked. That was hopeful.

"Not if I think of it as such," Master Ariz replied.

"How do you mean?"

"If I thought only of saving the children, then I could act," Master Ariz replied slowly, as if cautiously testing each of his words before he released them. "I could never focus on defying . . . that man and then act. The pain would destroy me."

"I see." Narsi wondered what contortions of thought Master Ariz performed even now to allow himself to have this conversation.

"Earlier you said something about . . ." Master Ariz paled and shook his head. Then he began again. "You wanted to break the condition that Dommian suffered from?"

"Yes!" Narsi followed his lead. "As I said last night, I'm quite interested in Dommian's history. I already know he carried a Brand of Obedience, which is an ancient blessing of a kind. It was first employed by the Savior, and I feel that there may well be a great deal of information concerning it in older Cadeleonian holy texts."

Master Ariz nodded. "My upperclassman at the Yillar Academy was exceptionally interested in those same texts. Just serving him as I did, I learned a few details. Though nothing that would have encouraged Dommian. The brand's power lasts until death."

"Yes. Father Timoteo told me the same thing this morning. However, he thought that the texts could be referring to the death of either party in the pact, not just the branded person."

"Truly?" Master Ariz asked and something like a smile tugged at his lips. Immediately, he tensed as if he'd stepped on a broken foot. The color drained from his face. He gasped as if struggling for breath. "I can't think about that."

"Don't then! We should talk about something else." Narsi groped for a new subject to ease Master Ariz's obvious pain. Then a thought occurred to him and he felt like an idiot for not considering it sooner.

"I can give you duera for your pain." Narsi started for his medical bag.

"It will make no difference," Ariz ground out. "I've tried. Talk to me. Distract me."

"I . . ." For a moment Narsi could think of no subjects other than the Brand of Obedience. Then he fell upon his favorite subject—the inspiration of countless conversations. "What are your favorite books?"

"I don't care for reading," Master Ariz replied through clenched teeth.

"Oh." That hardly gave Narsi much to work with. He tried again. "Perhaps you enjoy music more. I've heard that the new opera called *The Rogue's Folly* is quite entertaining."

"I've heard a few of the songs." Master Ariz regained a little color in his cheeks. His pupils remained flared, making his eyes look like black holes.

"Well, ah, Prince Jacinto is producing an opera—or perhaps it's a play." Narsi hadn't ever felt such urgency to maintain inane chatter. "He offered me a role just a few minutes ago."

"Oh?" Master Ariz's brows lifted fractionally. His lips didn't appear quite as bloodless as they had been.

"Yes. As a Yuanese catamite, if you can imagine that."

"You're rather tall to pass for a delicate boy of fifteen." Master Ariz gave a short cough that Narsi belatedly realized was a choked laugh.

"Obviously Prince Jacinto will need to construct a trench for me to stand in," Narsi added. "As I pose and swoon across the stage."

This time Master Ariz's laugh sounded somewhat natural, though still fleeting. Silence opened up between them. Narsi tried to think of something else to say. The weather? The upcoming masquerade? Dancing?

"My upperclassman at Yillar," Master Ariz said out of the blue. "He studied more than just a single holy text. He was fascinated with the Battle of the Shard of Heaven."

"Your upperclassman must have been an interesting fellow." Narsi felt almost certain that this upperclassman had to have been the one to brand Master Ariz.

"Our instructors described him as ambitious, and they didn't know the half of it. He means to . . ." Ariz trailed off, clenching his teeth. He lifted his gaze to the plasterwork decorating the ceiling as he drew in several slow breaths. "There have probably always been men who imagined themselves as embodiments of the Savior. As though God has anointed them to overthrow . . ." Master Ariz gnashed his mouth closed so hard that Narsi heard the clack of his teeth.

"Kingmakers, you mean?" Narsi supplied. "Like Evriso Tornesal, who restored the Sagradas to the throne?"

"Yes, exactly!" Master Ariz nodded. "We should discuss Evriso."

"I don't know much about him," Narsi responded, though in truth he considered himself quite familiar with the historical figure. "So please tell me all you can."

"Many people don't know that Evriso only restored the Sagrada rulership because he knew that he could control the younger of the Sagrada princes." Master Ariz spoke quickly, as if attempting to rush the words out before he could think on them too long. "He holds power over the king's grandson. His sister is the prize for the young prince's loyalty. Though I wouldn't wager on the prince lasting long on the throne, not after an heir is born. He—Evriso, I mean—will assassinate all other possible heirs so as to ensure his own eventual grip on both the throne and the title of royal bishop."

Narsi nodded. Little of what Master Ariz said described the historic actions of Evriso Tornesal. Except that he had placed his own brother-in-law on the throne. But the fact that Master Ariz had slipped into present tense made Narsi certain that they were discussing the man who held him in thrall.

"When do you think that Evriso . . . did these things?" Narsi asked.

"It was 1190." Master Ariz supplied the historical date correctly but then shook his head. "But if he were alive today, I know that he couldn't act until after the coronation. Otherwise the crown could be claimed by the current royal bishop as opposed to one of the new king's sons. Do you understand my meaning? Evriso needs the man he's chosen to be the only *surviving* heir. And he needs that man's only heir to be his own relation, to ensure that he can step in as regent when the child's father dies."

"But he couldn't hope to get away with such an open act of treason?"

"He'll ensure that his enemies are blamed for the murders. There's already talk of Labarans acting against the crown. You think that was an accident? It serves him to rouse anger against the Cadeleonian court. The Labarans and the Grunito family now have cause to oppose the crown. Lord Quemanor recently engaged in public argument with the royal bishop and the crown prince. With so much animosity from other directions, few would suspect—" Master Ariz shuddered and didn't seem able to go on speaking.

Narsi felt almost overwhelmed by the enormity of this plot and also at a loss as to who exactly the players were. He had no actual names— nor was Master Ariz likely to possess the capacity to tell him.

Just this conversation about a hypothetical plot had left Master Ariz bound, slumped and bleeding.

"If I free you—" Narsi began.

"Not yet. There's so much I have to tell you about . . . Evriso. He would be so much of a danger to this family if he were alive right now. And his youngest sister is up to something as well. She wants free of his control. We all do. But she has power and a plan."

"But you can't stay roped to a stool forever," Narsi objected. "So I need to know what you're likely to do when I untie you."

"You aren't the threat I first thought," Master Ariz replied. "At first I thought—I had hoped with all my heart that you'd discovered something in Dommian's book that . . . you knew a way to set *him* free. Were he alive now, Evriso would not have tolerated you freeing his assassins. He would have needed you dead. But you aren't a witch and you don't have a way to defeat his hold over m—men like Dommian."

Narsi didn't bring up the fact that he damn well intended to find a way to destroy the brand. Master Ariz needed to think of him as innocuous.

"On top of that, even if I learned anything," Narsi offered him, "who in the capital would take a half Haldiim like me seriously?"

"I take you seriously, Master Narsi. The first time I saw you, I knew that you could be the undoing of me. An omen of my death." Master Ariz met his gaze directly. "I still hope to God that someday you will be."

The last thing Narsi wanted was to destroy anyone—particularly someone who'd already suffered as much as Master Ariz.

"I wouldn't—"

"Don't worry. I realize now that you aren't a threat to the brand. Not yet," Master Ariz said. "You're safe from me. For today at least."

Before Narsi could reply, a soft knock sounded from the closed doors.

"Master Ariz, isn't it time for our dance lesson? I'd like to brush up on—" The duke broke off as he stepped into the fencing room. His pleased expression turned to shock as he took in the sight before him. And Narsi realized just how bad the scene had to appear.

Master Ariz tied up, sweat-soaked and bleeding, while he stood over the man with a dagger in his hand.

"This isn't—" Narsi began.

But already the duke's face contorted with rage. He strode forward fast and as he moved, a swath of pitch darkness rose from his shadow and surged toward Narsi like the immense, gaping maw of the Black Hell.

CHAPTER
TWENTY-FIVE

Atreau peered through the spy hole and leaned close to the wall to catch each of the words that passed between Narsi and Ariz.

Originally he'd meant to stop Narsi from approaching Master Ariz altogether, but the arrival of Suelita Estaban's siblings had delayed him. He'd played charming and ignorant when the relations had pressed him about the runaway girl's location. All the while he'd silently fumed at the stupidity of the situation.

If any one of these people who claimed to so adore Suelita had possessed a genuine insight into her character, they would have immediately known that Atreau could not have appealed to her as a lover—no man would have. She certainly wouldn't have entrusted her future to him and abandoned her entire family for his sake. But that realization would have required them to think of her as an independent person: a woman with desires, thoughts and plans far beyond the profitable alliance that her marriage to Ladislo Bayezar promised her ambitious father.

Not that Atreau had taken much of note of her himself before she'd run off with Sabella. She'd been a pretty girl, but not quite as attractive to him as her surly brother, who'd reminded him, just a little, of his long-gone classmate, Javier. He'd spoken with her perhaps twice in passing. Even so he'd immediately discerned that she dreaded Ladislo's courtship and fled him at every opportunity. When her brothers described her constant evasion of her suitor as a coy game, Atreau couldn't decide if they were deluding themselves or if they genuinely took signs of outright rejection from women as an invitation to more aggressive pursuit.

Ladislo, of all men, should have known better. He should have understood the horror of unwanted advances just as well as Atreau did. But then, Atreau recalled that Ladislo hadn't possessed a sympathetic nature even before Procopio had misused him at school. And abuse, in and of itself, hardly encouraged an outflowing of kindness and empathy. More often such hurt only taught victims how to beat those beneath them.

Atreau was reminded of the Labaran nursery rhyme that his mother had sung to him long, long ago.

A wronged man thrashed his bride,
So she whipped her dog's hide.
The bloody hound bit the wall,
And the house fell down upon them all.

Atreau had considered reciting it for Suelita's relatives but decided instead to respond to their demands and veiled threats by reciting a few stanzas from the latest play he'd penned to amuse Jacinto—and which the prince had built into the incomprehensible production that he was now intent upon staging.

"I'm an old and tired fox,
Too feeble now to catch a hen.
Chased by so many fiery cocks,
My crook'd tail must beckon men."

Suelita's married older sister had allowed herself to be amused, though the rest of the party less so. That in itself had turned uneasy, as the pretty young wife flirted playfully with him and her brothers began to seethe. All the while the middle sister worked her fan at the speed of a hummingbird's wing. When, at last, the eldest sister had asked him to take her to see Suelita, he'd replied with a rhyme.

"You ask pearls of a clam
Roses from a holly
Butter to make you jam
And a fool to stray from folly."

She'd studied him a moment, and he thought that perhaps she did understand more of the situation then she would admit. Her older brother, however, gave Atreau a murderous parting glance and made a passing threat to have him brought before the royal bishop on charges of abduction. The younger brother placed his hand on the hilt of his sword.

"We could settle this in a dueling ring," the young man declared.

Atreau considered the youth and recognized his stiff pose as that of a boy who'd performed decently in tournaments at school and now deemed himself a sword master. A more experienced duelist would never have issued such a challenge while standing so close that Atreau's belt knife would reach his heart before the swordsman could draw the full length of his own weapon. Any decent fencing instructor would've thrashed the youth for his mistake. Amusingly, his younger sister batted him in the back of his head with her fan.

"Don't brawl like street filth," she snapped, then she looked to Atreau. "You're stooping to his level."

Atreau stifled the urge to offer a rejoinder; it would only drag this idiotic exchange out all the longer. Both the brothers straightened into postures of almost comical dignity and the entire family took their leave. Their attendants trailed behind them and in a moment the whole party disappeared from sight.

Atreau raced back into the maze of camellias only to have the gardener he'd earlier noted standing with Narsi inform him that the physician had returned to the house. The chapel bells rang out the hour and Atreau cursed. Narsi would already be in the fencing rooms with Master Ariz by now. As he hurried along the pebble path to the mansion, Atreau considered his options and decided against making a scene by barging in on them. After all, he couldn't be certain that Narsi's life was endangered, nor should he assume that Narsi wouldn't be capable of gleaning any information from Master Ariz. At the same time he didn't want to simply leave Narsi to it and hope that an utterly inexperienced physician would prove himself a master of interrogation.

So he'd resorted to the hidden passages inside the mansion walls. Fortunately, he knew them all quite well, and the mirrors in the fencing rooms had been situated to offer a panoramic view. The first moment Atreau peered in he froze. Master Ariz held Narsi by the throat. Behind them, the children capered obliviously through shafts of bright sunlight.

Then, to Atreau's shock, Narsi reached out and drew Master Ariz's sword from its sheath and took his dagger as well. All the while Master Ariz maintained his tense stance and bizarrely dull expression, gripping Narsi's neck. But he clearly didn't mean to strangle Narsi, because Narsi said something and Master Ariz responded.

Atreau strained to hear the words the two whispered, but the laughter and squeals of the children drowned out much of the exchange. At last Master Ariz released Narsi, though not before Narsi had pushed the man's own sword into his chest and spilled a trail of his blood down the front of his shirt.

When Sparanzo's guards came and collected the children, Atreau readied to intercede and keep Narsi from being seized by the guards. But Master Ariz betrayed no alarm to the guards—perhaps he couldn't—nor did he display his bloodied shirtfront to them. They departed without appearing to take much note or interest in anything beyond their duty of escorting Fedeles's son back to his mother.

As Narsi backed Master Ariz nearer to where Atreau stood, he caught more of their conversation and it became clear that Master Ariz was doing all he could to assist Narsi to interrogate him—even going so far as to hold perfectly still and offer directions while Narsi bound him.

The ensuing attempt at communication verged upon comedy—though neither Narsi nor Master Ariz appeared the least bit amused, and what Master Ariz eventually revealed was nothing less than a plot of high treason on the part of Hierro Fueres. At least, that was what

Atreau deduced from the fencing instructor's convoluted and fantastical recounting of Evriso Tornesal's role in Cadeleonian history.

If he understood Master Ariz correctly, then Hierro meant to wed one of his sisters—most likely the newly and conveniently widowed Clara—to one of Sevanyo's sons. He would then place his new brother-in-law on the throne with the far-reaching goal of eventually seizing the crown through his sister's child. Seeing as Sevanyo's heir, Prince Xalvadar was already married and the next in line, Prince Gael, had been lost at sea, that left Jacinto as Clara's intended groom.

However it wasn't Jacinto whom Atreau's spies reported dining with members of the Fueres family. Only Remes had been seen keeping company with Hierro and Clara.

But Remes was destined for the celibate life of a royal bishop. He couldn't inherit—not unless his entire family was wiped out. There was precedent, but that had been long ago, before the Sagrada bloodline had blossomed into a veritable dynasty.

Atreau considered that for several moments. The entire royal family wiped out: every single man, women and child with royal blood. That would be nearly fifty assassinations to get through without anyone noticing a pattern in the deaths.

It was a mad scheme, almost ludicrous in its ambition, and yet Atreau could believe Hierro Fueres would embark on such a plot. Particularly after hearing Master Ariz's remark that the man believed himself chosen by God. The very fact that Hierro had been so arrogant as to allow a man like Master Ariz to know that he was enthralled betrayed the scope of Hierro's conceit and sadism.

In his place, Atreau would've been far more careful of how he handled such a skilled and determined swordsman. Even enthralled, Master Ariz had clearly managed to undermine Hierro Fueres's plots on two separate occasions. He was no mere pawn, but a very dangerous and strong-minded assassin. Had he been Atreau's to command, he would've been indulged and much more carefully manipulated. Certainly never allowed to suspect that his actions weren't his own will.

Briefly Atreau considered Master Ariz's bowed, bleeding figure. The man had no doubt endured his own hell. He clearly felt no loyalty to Hierro and wanted to defy him. Perhaps he could become a useful asset. As a loyal servant to Fedeles, Master Ariz could prove to be a truly effective weapon.

But the knowledge that Master Ariz had murdered Captain Ciceron nagged at Atreau. And considering the struggle required for him to admit the little he'd told Narsi, Atreau suspected that Master Ariz was too compromised and too broken to depend upon. Likely the best thing to be done was to kill the man quickly and free him from Hierro's grasp.

Atreau didn't like the thought, but he liked the idea of simply allowing Master Ariz to live and continue to serve Hierro Fueres even less. Pity wasn't reason enough to needlessly endanger Fedeles and his entire household, much less the entire extended royal family. It filled Atreau with an oily feeling of self-loathing to decide on Master Ariz's death while Narsi stood next to the man with an expression of pure compassion on his handsome face. And when Narsi spoke of finding a means to free Master Ariz, it didn't surprise Atreau at all. Of course he wanted to save the man. He was so young, so noble in his intentions.

And distractingly attractive. Atreau wanted to impress him. See him smile again. Even pretend to be the man who Narsi thought he was.

But now was hardly the time to allow himself to become sloppy.

Just as he'd reached that decision, Atreau noticed the door to the fencing room begin to swing open. An entirely different kind of alarm rushed through him as Fedeles stepped in. The tableau before Fedeles was undoubtedly horrifying, and Atreau knew exactly how it would appear to Fedeles and how Fedeles would respond.

Atreau flipped the latch that held the secret panel closed. He bounded out just as the horrific wave of darkness rose from Fedeles's shadow. It arched over Narsi like a serpent preparing to strike and Atreau threw himself forward. He plunged into a darkness deeper than a night sky and cold as winter. He felt a frigid razor's edge hiss across the back of his neck. He slammed into Narsi, wrapping his arms around him, and they both fell back to the floor. Narsi groaned and Atreau feared he'd moved too slowly, though the heat of life still blazed from his body and seemed to radiate into Atreau's chest. Atreau focused on that warmth as the cold darkness sank into him.

Behind them, Master Ariz shouted, sounding ragged and raw. Atreau didn't think he'd ever heard as much emotion arise from him before. "No! For the love of God, don't hurt him!"

All at once Fedeles released them from the icy darkness. Atreau found himself sprawled atop Narsi in a bright pool of sunlight. Narsi appeared completely stunned, but then he gave Atreau a dazed smile. Relief that Narsi lived washed over him, followed immediately by embarrassment at his own rash action.

One kiss, apparently, was all it took to undo years of self-preservation. But why not? He had already given Narsi his whole fortune once for less than that.

"Lord Vediya?" Narsi's eyes seemed to light with dazed wonder. "Where did you come from?"

"My mother's womb, if your modern medicine is to be believed." He rolled off Narsi at once and felt the back of his neck. The locks that had hung past his shoulders were shorn and now lay strewn across the floor. The collar of his jerkin and his shirt both opened in long slashes. But his fingers came back with only a tiny blotch of blood from the small scratch across the nape of his neck.

"Are you hurt?" Fedeles sounded almost frightened.

To Atreau's surprise, Fedeles didn't come to him, but instead rushed to Master Ariz. There was no mistaking the alarmed tenderness in his expression. Nor did Atreau miss the way Fedeles reached out to stroke Master Ariz's shoulder before he at once set to untying the man.

When had that happened? How had it happened? Master Ariz commanded all the allure of a lump of clay. And outside of Hierro Fueres himself, he had to number as one of the worst people for Fedeles to grow fond of. God's blood, but Fedeles had poor taste in his affections.

"Don't trouble yourself," Atreau called. "I'm fine, but thanks for your concern."

Fedeles glanced back at him and nodded, completely missing the sarcasm in Atreau's tone.

"Thank you for interceding, Atreau," Fedeles said. "Keep ahold of the physician, though. Until we know exactly who he's working for."

Narsi looked unsurprisingly alarmed, but to his credit he didn't immediately betray the fact that the two of them were in collusion.

"If Master Narsi has acted for anyone's benefit, it's yours, my lord." Master Ariz bowed his head as he addressed Fedeles. "You should not release me until you've heard what he has to tell you."

"What do you mean?" Fedeles stilled with his hands still gripping the knotted rope that restrained Master Ariz.

"If he tells you not to release him, you shouldn't." Atreau went to Fedeles's side. "I can explain everything, but you must leave Master Ariz be, for all our sakes."

"Thank you . . . Lord Vediya." Master Ariz's head hung low. The man's face revealed as much emotion as that of a corpse, but his posture radiated shame.

If Atreau had understood what he'd heard and seen of Master Ariz's confession, it would be important to keep the man from knowing explicitly how much he and Fedeles understood of his situation, if only to ensure that he wouldn't fight too hard when the time came to put him down. Though it would be good to see if they could pry a little more information from him first.

He beckoned Narsi to them. Narsi came but stopped next to Master Ariz and on the far side of Fedeles. Which was hardly a wonder considering that he'd nearly been killed by Fedeles's shadow, while Master Ariz had gone to pains to protect Narsi from himself. The entire situation was a mad wreck.

Likely Narsi was only minutes from packing his belongings and fleeing back to the safety and sanity of Anacleto. Atreau wouldn't have blamed him if he left now, but he hoped Narsi would hold out at least a short time more.

Fedeles glowered imperiously at Narsi but said nothing. He reminded Atreau of a stallion eyeing a groom whom he suspected of slipping medicine into his feed.

"Can you make certain those knots hold, while I and the duke have a little chat across the room?" Atreau asked Narsi.

"Yes, I will," Narsi replied, and Atreau had to admire how calm he remained.

He leaned in and added in a quick whisper, "You and Master Ariz should continue your conversation."

Then Atreau drew Fedeles across the room and out of earshot. Fedeles listened to what he said with an expression of rising alarm, but he didn't argue or even speak a single word until Atreau broached the necessity of disposing of Master Ariz.

"No," Fedeles stated flatly, as if the single word was any kind of reasonable argument.

"He's a danger to you, to your wife and to your son," Atreau told him. "He'll tell you as much himself."

"No," Fedeles repeated.

Atreau resisted the urge to bang his own head against one of the gleaming mirrors that surrounded them. A great part of what he adored about Fedeles was the man's staunch loyalty, but there was a point when steadfastness gave way to stupidity—muleheaded stupidity.

"I know that it isn't what any of us want—"

"You don't!" Fedeles snapped, then his voice softened. "You can't know, Atreau. You weren't the one they trapped in that hell and used. You don't know what it was like to endure that."

Atreau frowned. He hadn't reckoned on Fedeles's own years living under the control of a thrall affecting his sympathy for Master Ariz, but he realized that he should have.

"He isn't you." Atreau watched Fedeles's face closely. He was a man of powerful emotion and, like the horses he loved, much of his feeling showed in his large, dark eyes. Right now he was still in a kind of shock, still coming to terms with facts that he didn't want to believe. He resisted inevitable conclusions out of reflex, not reason. Atreau needed to appeal to his emotions, then.

"Master Ariz has been enthralled by Hierro for so long that he may not even be himself anymore." Atreau spoke calmly, trying to impress the reality of the situation upon Fedeles. "It has to have been more than a decade that he's lived as little more than an instrument of Hierro's ambitions. What can be left of him? What kindness would you do him by drawing out his suffering any longer?"

"By your own admission he still struggles against Hierro. He defied him only days ago." Fedeles gazed across the chamber to where Narsi crouched by Master Ariz's side. Atreau read the pain in Fedeles's face as well as the naked tenderness. "I know the hell he's living in. We have to help him—"

"He murdered Captain Ciceron. Stabbed him through the heart and took his head without a moment's hesitation," Atreau stated.

Fedeles gasped as if he'd been struck and turned to stare out the glass doors into the gardens beyond. Atreau briefly took in the potted yellow roses and rolling hillocks of thyme and moss roses. All very pretty, but nothing out there altered the situation in this fencing room.

"Hierro killed the captain." When Fedeles at last spoke, his voice was rough and his eyes shone with incipient tears. "Ariz was a tool he used, the same way that Scholar Donamillo used me to murder Victaro. The same way he would have used me to slay Javier if I hadn't been released from his thrall. The way he used me to cut Kiram's body into pieces even as he struggled to save my life and soul."

Two things became clear to Atreau at once: first, that he should have realized before now that the unknown person who murdered the groom Victaro years ago, when they had been at school, had been Fedeles. Of course it had been. He'd just avoided knowing it.

Second, he needed to make a clear distinction between Master Ariz's circumstances and those that Fedeles had endured. Though in truth there was little difference. Fedeles had simply been more fortunate and better connected than Master Ariz was. It wasn't fair to condemn one of them when the other had been saved, but life was not fair. And Atreau didn't possess the resources to pretend otherwise, not when it meant risking so many lives. But this, too, was a dangerous direction to allow the argument to go in.

"I stripped everything from Master Ariz and his family," Fedeles added. "All my anger at Genimo fell upon him . . ."

"You couldn't have known that he was enthralled at the time," Atreau said. "And that is still no reason to force him to go on like this. Neither you nor I can break the thrall he's under. He is suffering, and there's nothing we can do to stop that—"

"But Javier could." Fedeles's expression lit with hope.

Javier? Why not hold out hope that the Savior would descend from the heavens, if they were going to wish on distant stars? Frustration surged through Atreau. Javier had been exiled years ago. He courted execution if he returned to Cadeleon while the royal bishop still lived. Even Fedeles had to see that Master Ariz's freedom was not worth the risk of attempting to secret Javier back into the capital.

Or maybe he didn't. Could Fedeles be that smitten with Master Ariz? How could that even be possible? The man barely spoke a word, and the ones he did say were dull as the rest of him.

"What of Sparanzo's safety?" Atreau demanded. "Master Ariz may have thwarted Dommian's attempt, but you and I both know that Hierro isn't going to just give up because his first assassin failed."

Fedeles didn't have an answer to that, and Atreau felt certain that he'd won the argument. Then the doors opened and Atreau cursed his own shortsightedness in not thinking to lock them.

Mistress Delfia leaned in. Her face paled as she took in the scene before her. Then she disappeared back behind the doors and Atreau recognized Oasia's voice, issuing orders to her maids and guards. Oasia sent her maids and two of the guards to attend the children in the music room. The remaining two guards received orders to watch the doors and allow no one in while the duchess spoke with her husband.

Delfia cracked the door open again and Oasia followed her inside. Delfia locked the door behind them.

"What on earth is a Haldiim physician doing here?" Oasia demanded.

Both Master Ariz and Narsi looked up at the question, though Master Ariz simply nodded to his sister. Narsi, on the other hand, appeared alarmed to be suddenly called out. Likely he half expected the duchess to attack him in the same way Fedeles had.

"He's tending to Master Ariz," Atreau replied. "Apparently he suffers from a rather rare condition. Though I believe a number of your brother's other servants might have contracted it as well. You wouldn't happen to know anything of it, would you, my lady?"

Oasia met Atreau's gaze and then she pointedly turned her serene face to Fedeles. She pushed a thick curl of black hair back from her shoulder.

"I am aware of what my brother has done." Oasia addressed Fedeles as she glided to his side. "Despite that, Master Ariz has proved to be an indispensable source of information. He is extremely valuable to us."

Fedeles frowned but still allowed her to take his arm in hers. She drew him ever so slowly from Atreau's side, leaving it to Atreau to follow them back toward the stricken Mistress Delfia.

"You should have told me," Fedeles said. To Atreau he didn't sound angry enough by half. She'd allowed an enthralled assassin to live among them for years. Even after he'd murdered Captain Ciceron and the guard Dommian, Oasia had still sheltered Master Ariz.

"I feared that it would rouse unpleasant memories for you, my dearest," Oasia said quietly to Fedeles. She squeezed his fingers in her own.

Atreau wished that he could vomit on command, because that was the response Oasia's saccharine claim deserved.

"If you worried for me much more I'd live in complete ignorance," Fedeles told her, and Oasia had the gall to laugh.

"Oh, you have your own sources of information, husband mine. And you know I wouldn't have kept anything back that was worth knowing."

"Really?" Atreau asked. "Even your brother's plot to seize the throne?"

"Which one of his plots?" Oasia replied, and for just an instant her utter contempt showed as she looked at Atreau. Then her sneer vanished and she shifted her attention and gaze back to Fedeles. "He's plotted and schemed after the throne since he was a child. Presently, all I know of the current plan is that he's had Clara's husband killed so as to free her for marriage to either Jacinto or Remes."

"Remes. It has to be. Hierro's got no hold over Jacinto and a woman like Clara would hold no appeal for him—" Atreau began, only to be cut short.

"As far as you know," Oasia responded. "But you, Lord Vediya, have not been contending with my brother's machinations for as long as I have. What he may have allowed Master Ariz to hear and see may be only what he wants us to know."

Atreau scowled at the thought of that. If Hierro had fed lies to Master Ariz, then his plot could be altogether different. However, Master Ariz struck Atreau as a poor choice for the job. The man could hardly tell them anything, much less be depended upon to spread misinformation. And he was far more suitable and well positioned to act as an assassin.

"There's no need to school Atreau. We are none of us in collusion with Hierro," Fedeles chided her, but without much ire. He wiped his eyes with the cuff of his coat. "So, your brother had Count Odalis murdered?"

Oasia nodded. "His physician believes his demise was the result of an old man's heart attempting to keep pace with too young of a bride. But I know for a fact that he was smothered to death."

The three of them stopped only a stride away from Mistress Delfia, and all of them looked to Narsi and Master Ariz. Narsi had brought his physician's bag to the foot of the stool and seemed to be in the midst of inquiring after which drugs Master Ariz had already attempted to use to manage his pain.

"Smoke poppy?" Narsi inquired.

"I've given him that as well." Mistress Delfia moved a little closer to Narsi as she spoke. She knelt down and nodded at the bottle of milky fluid Narsi held up. "The pain doesn't relent until he's nearly unconscious. It's the same with white ruin, beer or wine. No relief until he's legless."

No surprise then that Dommian had been such a drunkard. Though Atreau did wonder how Master Ariz wasn't.

"So long as he can think, he can suffer," Master Ariz said, and Atreau noted that he was again speaking in the third person as if discussing the condition of some other man—Dommian, perhaps. "The spell binding him isn't a physical thing, but magical."

"That may be," Narsi replied. "But even magic must take effect through some physical process. From what you're describing, it sounds as if the spell causes pain by acting upon the brain and not the flesh of the body. There is no physical injury, but the mind responds as if there is. It's almost like the sensations experienced in a nightmare."

Mistress Delfia cocked her head, studying Narsi intently, as if she'd just noticed something astounding about him.

"Yes," Master Ariz said. "That's it exactly. A nightmare that can't be woken from."

"It might be a nightmare indeed . . . I wonder if, to some extent, y— er—Dommian was a kind of sleepwalker. If that truly is the case, it might explain certain things. For example, his inability to express spontaneous emotion and a certain imperviousness to physical pain."

"They say that if you die in a dream you will wake," Master Ariz mumbled. "I wonder where I will wake when I die?"

"In paradise, my darling. I promise you." Mistress Delfia reached out and embraced her brother. He bowed his head against her shoulder. The sight touched Atreau, made him think of how he'd embraced Spider the night before when he had wanted with all his heart to somehow make things right for his brother. It reminded him of how helpless he'd felt as well.

"I'm so tired, Delfia." Master Ariz's words were soft, but clear through the surrounding silence.

"I know. I know." Mistress Delfia stroked his back, as if she were soothing one of her children. "But it's over now. It can end here."

Master Ariz nodded.

Fedeles looked alarmed, but Oasia appeared as resigned as Master Ariz and his sister. Atreau decided to keep his mouth shut. He'd already made his argument to Fedeles. Let Oasia be the villain for once. Or better yet, let Master Ariz demand that he be killed himself. What could Fedeles say to that?

"Well, we're not just going to give up, obviously," Narsi stated.

Everyone, Atreau included, stared at him. Mistress Delfia wiped the tears from her cheeks. Even Master Ariz lifted his head in surprise.

"Whatever do you mean, Master Physician?" Oasia arched a delicate brow, but there was no anger in her voice. Her gaze had turned assessing and interested.

Narsi rose to his feet and again Atreau noted the young man's exceptional height and air of dignity.

"I've only just begun to diagnose how the spell that afflicted Dommian works, and as far as I can tell, only depressants have been employed so far in attempt to effect any improvement. But after just this brief interview I would think that what we are looking for is something more along the lines of a stimulant." Narsi turned his attention from both Oasia and Fedeles and returned to his crouch beside Master Ariz. "If the spell truly does work by shutting down certain regions of the mind, perhaps by compromising the subject's conscious will, then it's similar to a waking sleep. That means that there could be any number of ways to counteract it or even stop it. We must not give up hope before we've tried anything."

"The longer I remain, the greater of a threat I pose." Master Ariz hung his head. "Once he realizes that I've been exposed, he'll use me to do as much harm as possible."

A little sob escaped Mistress Delfia, but she quickly regained her composure. "I can do it quickly. So that he feels nothing," Mistress Delfia said.

Fedeles shook his head, but surprisingly, it was Oasia who spoke up.

"No, let us consider what the master physician has said before we rush to any rash decisions." She turned to Fedeles and held his gaze. Atreau felt certain that she read Fedeles as well as he had, perhaps better. She'd not escaped her brother and father's grasps by misjudging the men around her. She had to know that concealing Ariz's enthralled state had angered and offended Fedeles. He could see it in the narrow look Fedeles gave her now. She needed to regain his trust.

"Master Ariz is dear to us and has been a loyal servant for years. If there is a way to help him, we should take the time to attempt that." Oasia went on as if Fedeles was the one who needed convincing. "If he could be liberated, it would not only do him good, but he is in a position to do our enemies considerable harm."

Atreau clenched his jaw to stop himself from pointing out that unless Narsi pulled off some miracle in a day or so, Hierro Fueres could very well order him to murder them all. Was Oasia counting on him to argue for Master Ariz's death and thus earn Fedeles's ire? It would be like her—except that if there was one human being in all the world whom she seemed to truly love, it was her son. She wouldn't endanger Sparanzo, not even for Fedeles's sake.

"So what is it you propose that we do?" Atreau asked Oasia.

"We deliver Master Ariz to my sister, Clara," Oasia replied. "She sent word that she does not feel safe since her husband's passing."

Oddly, that comment inspired a snort from Master Ariz.

"Did you kill him as well?" Atreau demanded of Master Ariz.

Master Ariz met his gaze with a cold, dead stare. He gave a tired nod.

"Are there any murders in the city that you didn't commit?" Atreau could hardly credit it. If he had his count right, Master Ariz had killed three men in less than a week. And they were still willing to let him live.

"He had nothing to do with the priests who died at the south gate. Nor has he ever raised his hand against a holy sister." Mistress Delfia shot Atreau an accusing glower, which was rich, seeing as he wasn't the one who'd committed those crimes or even given Captain Ciceron leave to perpetrate them.

"We aren't any of us without guilt," Fedeles said.

Narsi started to open his mouth and then, meeting Atreau's gaze, seemed to think better of saying anything.

"My point is," Oasia went on, "that Clara hopes to use her tragedy as an excuse to be invited into our household. She wants to get closer to Sparanzo—"

"Absolutely not!" Fedeles stated and Oasia laughed.

"Those were my words exactly, darling," Oasia told him. "So I suggest that we beg off, due to our concerns over Dommian's murder taking place in our very household. Instead of having Clara come here, we send Master Ariz to offer her his protection. Then he will be near enough that he and Master Narsi can attempt their experiments, but Master Ariz will no longer be so intimate a part of our household that Hierro would have easy use of him."

Fedeles scowled, but Atreau had to admit that Oasia's plan wasn't a bad one—if they weren't going to simply execute Master Ariz. Moving him would at least get him away from Fedeles and Sparanzo. Though not anywhere as far as Atreau would have liked.

"We couldn't ensure his safety if he is sent to the Odalis household," Fedeles objected. "We could just as easily send him to safety in Rauma or Anacleto, where Hierro would not look for him."

"He could not spy for us if he were sent away to Rauma," Oasia replied. "And I do not think it would be good for him if Hierro realizes that we have discovered his secret. He would torture you just to vent his frustration, wouldn't he, Master Ariz?"

Master Ariz shrugged. But his sister nodded.

"And we would also be depriving him of Master Narsi's care," Delfia stated, then she looked to Narsi. "Do you truly believe that your Haldiim teachings can defeat a holy Cadeleonian spell?"

"Well, I'm not thinking in terms of Haldiim or Cadeleonian, so much as in terms of where the mystical and the physical interact." Narsi stood again and gifted Mistress Delfia with a warm, supremely confident smile. "From everything I've read, in Haldiim texts, Cadeleonian holy books and even Lord Vediya's writing about the Labaran War, it seems obvious that no matter what the origin of a spell, or blessing or curse, it has to manifest through some physical means to be effective. Even the Old Gods had to take on physical form to engage in their battles. They might have started out as elemental spirits, but to actually attack the demon lords, they had to be channeled into living bodies. Isn't that right, Lord Vediya?" Narsi glanced to Atreau and Atreau couldn't help but smile back.

Narsi really had memorized his books. Not just the obscene sections. Everything.

"That is quite true," Atreau said.

"Right. So no matter what its origin, the spell on Dommian and all the others under Hierro's control has to be physically embodied and has to take effect through physical processes that a physician might be capable of affecting."

Atreau could see the line of Narsi's reasoning but wasn't certain that he was right. What physical process was it exactly that allowed Count Radulf to turn into a dog, or his sister Hylanya to float in the air for days on end? On the other hand, Narsi had been able to wake her when no one else could, and by only using a medicine.

Delfia appeared uncertain, and neither Fedeles or Oasia looked particularly convinced. Narsi sighed.

"You're all allowing the idea of magic to confuse you. But try to recognize that this condition, like so many others, is merely a case of cause and effect. Then you will realize that if I can localize the physical areas affected, I may well be able to interrupt the processes at that level. The cause, whether it be a magical or natural disorder, doesn't matter if I can disrupt its expression into physical flesh."

Atreau thought that if nothing else had betrayed him as a Haldiim, his belief in his own reasoning—even in the face of a duke and duchess's disbelief—would have given him away at once.

"From what I've learned, I'm going to begin with the premise that my patient simply suffers from something very like a disorder of his sleep. And there is absolutely no reason for me to assume that I can do nothing before I've tried anything. That would be utterly defeatist, foolish and an affront to both my intellect and my duty as a physician."

In the ringing silence that followed Narsi's oration, Atreau felt a change in the atmosphere of the room and in the faces of the people in it—like the first rays of light illuminating the sparkling world after a calamitous thunderstorm. He was inspiring, no doubt, but they still had a practical problem.

"But your *patient* can't return here for his treatments, and I don't think it would be wise to send you into Clara Odalis's lair. You two will need to meet somewhere away from both households . . . ," Atreau said, pondering where would be best.

"It isn't unusual for me to travel to the south side of the river to practice against the swordsmen at the Red Stallion," Master Ariz offered. For the first time he looked Fedeles in the eye, which caused Fedeles to give him a teary smile.

"Only a few streets down from the Candioro Theater, where Jacinto is staging his play." Atreau ignored their weird flirtation in the hope no one else would notice.

Sabella would be at the theater as well, which would help insure Narsi's safety. If anyone could be a match for an assassin, it would be another assassin.

"That's perfect!" Narsi beamed. "Prince Jacinto just offered me a role. I'm not sure he was serious, but I could at least claim that I thought he was and show up to meet Master—er, my patient—once. We could find another meeting place—"

"No. The theater will be the best," Atreau decided before either Master Ariz or Narsi could place themselves in a location beyond his control.

"Jacinto will be delighted to have you in his production. I'll make certain there's a role for you."

"I should warn you that I'm not a very good actor," Narsi admitted. "Also I can't sing to save my life."

"You certainly can give a lecture though," Fedeles commented.

"I'll tailor the role to your skills," Atreau assured Narsi. "A Yuanese court astronomer, perhaps? The bright robes would suit your height and dark complexion, and the role wouldn't require more of you than to stand in the background looking enigmatic and wise beyond your years—which sums up your demeanor most of the time anyway, so, no stretch of acting ability there."

"Could it work?" Mistress Delfia addressed the question only to her brother.

"I don't . . . maybe. Maybe it could," Master Ariz said. "It's not the spell that Master Narsi is trying to destroy. He's just helping me with my sleep . . ."

Mistress Delfia nodded and added, "You do sleep very poorly many nights."

"That's right," Narsi put in. "I'm not a Bahiim, or priest or witch. I'm simply a physician who can only treat your health. Nothing else."

Master Ariz nodded slowly, seemingly to himself.

"And speaking of your health," Narsi went on, "I really do feel that we need to remove these ropes so that I can clean the cut in your chest."

Master Ariz tensed but didn't argue as Narsi and Mistress Delfia began to loosen the ropes binding him. Atreau dropped his hand to his belt knife as casually as he could, while Oasia made an odd gesture of her hands, which reminded Atreau of the motions he'd seen so many Labaran witches perform as they readied for magical combat. Standing between the two of them, Fedeles looked on with the same strained expression he'd worn when his favorite horse had fallen ill and needed nursing through two full nights.

Master Ariz kept control of himself as the ropes fell away. He straightened and rose from the stool quickly, despite the fact that his hands and feet had to be numb. When Narsi attempted to open his shirt to clean his injury, Master Ariz waved him aside.

"It's a scratch. Nearly scabbed closed already." Master Ariz's words conveyed no emotion, but Atreau guessed from the way he moved that he was embarrassed. Clearly he was not accustomed to being the center of much attention. He gathered up the rope, coiled it and returned it to the weapons rack. Task completed, he stood beside the rack like a stuffed dummy.

"I'll send my condolences to Clara along with a letter of introduction for you to deliver to her, Master Ariz. I believe we could have you on your way before the first bell of night," Oasia said.

Mistress Delfia withdrew to Oasia's side and reassumed the posture of a modest lady's maid.

An odd quiet filled the room and Atreau realized that all of them were waiting for Fedeles to say or do anything.

"I should pack my things—" Master Ariz began at last.

"That can wait," Fedeles cut him off. He looked to Oasia and then to Atreau. Frustration and hurt showed in his expression, but all he said was, "I would have a little time alone with Master Ariz."

Atreau wasn't convinced of how wise an idea that might be, but he didn't have it in him to engage in another pointless argument with Fedeles just now. So he turned to Narsi.

"It seems that we had best go and secure that role for you from Jacinto."

Narsi simply nodded and followed him out through the garden doors. After they'd reached the cover of the camellia hedges, Narsi stopped.

"Something the matter?" Atreau asked.

"No, just . . ." Narsi offered him a wry smile. "It's one thing to read about these sort of things in one of your books, but to actually undertake them . . ."

His face looked suddenly grim and exhausted.

Atreau pulled him into his arms, thinking that he would comfort the young man. But the moment that he felt Narsi's arms wrap around him, he realized that he was the one who needed reassurance. He wanted to feel the warmth of Narsi's body and the rhythm of his breath and to know with physical certainty that Narsi was alive and well.

Voices rose from the other side of the hedge and Atreau stepped back, releasing Narsi. But he continued to study him.

He was so young, and so out of his depth here. He'd been poisoned, confronted an assassin, and—though he'd not known it—he'd come only inches from a horrific death at Fedeles's hands. All because he felt obligated to repay Atreau for an act of kindness that had been inspired by far more alcohol than altruism.

"If you've had enough, say so now." Atreau found himself half hoping that Narsi would back out. As much as he wanted the young man's skill and company, he realized that he truly did not wish to see Narsi killed. Not even for Fedeles's and Prince Sevanyo's sakes. "If you go now, you'll be outside the city gates and on your way to Anacleto before Fedeles or anyone else realizes you've gone. You have nothing to gain by becoming involved in this game of noblemen. You shouldn't let yourself be used just because misfortune brought you within our proximity."

Narsi considered him with a long, appraising look. Atreau had no idea what he saw or thought, but the doubt in his expression resolved.

"This isn't only a nobleman's game," Narsi said. "Our nation will be at risk if this madman succeeds in murdering the royal family. If he puts the blame on Labarans, we'll be at war. If he scapegoats the Haldiim, then we're likely to see another age of purges of our people—my people. I can't just allow that to happen. I can't run away from any of this."

Atreau feared he was right.

Narsi glanced down at his own bruised, scarred hands, and when he lifted his gaze up at Atreau, he seemed slightly embarrassed but not at all frightened anymore.

"I know that coming to the capital to meet you and make myself part of your adventures was something of a childish undertaking. But that doesn't change the fact that I'm here and you are going to need all the help that you can get."

Atreau shook his head, but he couldn't offer an argument.

"Anyway." Narsi smiled. "If I fled now, who would you cast in Prince Jacinto's play?"

 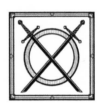

Chapter
Twenty-Six

Ariz waited in silence while Lord Quemanor stared out the windows. His muscles seemed tensed like a runner at the starting line of a race, just awaiting the signal to burst forward. But no signal sounded and he remained suspended on the edge of taking action.

"I had no idea," Lord Quemanor said at last. He still didn't turn to face Ariz. "All this time I've been such an ass, imagining that I was the only one who could know what it had been like, how terrible it was, and all along you were suffering. You even tried to speak of it on Crown Hill when you brought up Elezar. But I heard none of it. I was only trying to . . ." His voice failed briefly. "How could I not see it? You are still suffering, and I've only added to your hardship. Stripped you of your title and noble rights. I'm as bad as the rest of them."

Ariz realized that he had to do something other than stand there mute as a sack of filthy laundry. It felt so unnatural to act of his own volition without being ordered or driven by desperation. But he closed the distance between himself and Lord Quemanor and placed his hand on the other man's back. The leather of his green jerkin felt warm and supple beneath Ariz's fingers.

"You are not to blame," Ariz assured him. "I've been happier here in your house than I ever expected to be. Your home has been a respite for my body and spirit. For that alone, I owe you all my thanks."

"All I've done for you is indulge myself in your company, Master Ariz." Lord Quemanor finally turned to face him. "You are a splendid companion, truly. There are so many courtiers who do nothing but boast and spout empty flattery. But you are always so calm and . . ." He trailed off, his expression collapsing beneath his misery. He hid his face in his hands. "But that isn't even who you really are, is it? It's just been convenient for me to assume that you're a quiet, reserved man, but that's not you any more than I was a gibbering idiot when Donamillo and Genimo had enthralled me . . ."

Ariz hadn't expected that, but then, it followed. Of all the people around him, only Lord Quemanor possessed the experience and empathy to truly understand what it was that Ariz endured.

"I've never been outspoken." Ariz carefully drew Lord Quemanor's hands away so that he could see his dark wet lashes. "But I used to smile and I laughed a lot when I was very young. I don't know if I still would now, even if I could."

"Do you enjoy fencing, or is that . . ."

"Yes. I loved to fence and to dance." Briefly Ariz felt a little of the old delight rise in him. It had been so long since he'd allowed himself to actually remember who he'd been before Hierro. He'd possessed such dreams and foolish fantasies back then. But now, what was he? Ariz shook his head but forced himself to keep talking to Lord Quemanor. "That was what caught *his* attention about me right away. I could match him in the dueling rings despite the fact that I was younger and smaller."

"I remembered you from the Autumn Tournament, you know." The duke smoothed the shoulder of Ariz's ruined shirt.

"Did you?" Ariz felt oddly flattered and embarrassed. He'd been such a graceless clod during the tournament—though he'd scored better than any other first-year student from the Yillar or Sagrada Academies.

"I remembered you as well," Ariz admitted.

"I was hard to overlook, running around shouting the names of horses and grinning like a lunatic." An embarrassed flush colored Lord Quemanor's tanned face.

Ariz hesitated to respond. Unless he was offering instruction, he wasn't accustomed to saying more than a few words. But he wanted to speak and he wanted to be as honest as he could be. And this might be his last chance.

If Master Narsi's treatment failed to cure him, Ariz knew that he would be killed. He simply represented too much of a threat. And unlike Lord Quemanor, neither Oasia nor Atreau was so compassionate that either of them would allow Ariz to live simply for pity's sake. That was, if Ariz couldn't manage to do the job himself.

This could be the last time they would ever meet.

"Genimo and Hierro exchanged letters. They'd known each other from childhood and shared an interest in old stories of spells and curses," Ariz said. "I read several of their exchanges on the sly. I was still hoping that I could find a way free other than slitting my own wrists . . ."

Lord Quemanor nodded. Ariz had seen the other man's scars and knew that he understood perfectly, though the sympathy in his expression made Ariz uneasy. He didn't want to seem like a hapless creature.

"In any case, I learned about you from the letters," Ariz went on. "Genimo was trying to convince Hierro that using a mechanical engine could be more effective than relying on power to pass down along bloodlines . . . something about it requiring too much inbreeding."

Lord Quemanor gave a bitter smile and Ariz belatedly recalled the rumors of incest that surrounded his conception. In truth he didn't resemble the rest of the Quemanor family much—certainly not as remarkably as he resembled the Tornesal and Gavado descendants of the royal Sagrada bloodline.

"I had thought that if I could just speak with you, we could somehow . . ." Ariz didn't really know what he'd believed they would have done, and now he wondered if it hadn't just been desperate isolation that had spurred him to want to reach out to the one other soul who might have understood him. "But with your family all surrounding you, I couldn't ever get any words out. I couldn't even tell them what I knew about what had been done to you."

"Well, I couldn't manage to either, so you're in fine company on that count." To Ariz's surprise, Lord Quemanor offered him a smile. "I don't want you to go. Especially now. I don't want to send you away to endure this alone."

His concern touched Ariz, but it also made him all the more certain that he had to leave this house. He didn't think he could stand it if Hierro succeeded in using him against the Quemanor family.

Without warning, Lord Quemanor threw his arms around Ariz and embraced him. For a moment Ariz felt too stunned by the gesture to respond, but then he lifted his arms and returned the embrace. They held each other, too hard and too long. Lord Quemanor's strength astounded Ariz, as did the warmth of him. His body felt so good. Ariz's whole being roused at every point of contact, as if Lord Quemanor's mere touch eroded the effect of Hierro's brand.

A thrill passed through Ariz when Lord Quemanor bowed his head and his lips brushed the curve of Ariz's ear.

Then Ariz noticed a motion outside the window. A hen burst from the bushes and a scullery girl came pelting after it. He pushed gently against Lord Quemanor, who released him at once, looking flushed and handsome and sorrowful—like one of those paintings of Our Holy Savior gazing down on all of humanity. More than anything Ariz wanted to lift the melancholy from him and make him happy.

"I'll be fine. Enduring is what I do best." Ariz attempted to sound jovial, but as always his voice betrayed him, lending him the flat tone of some kind of sullen dullard.

"No." Lord Quemanor shook his head. "Dancing is what you do best. Better than anyone I've ever seen."

Ariz gladly accepted the compliment.

"Then, would you care to have one last dance?"

"I would love to dance with you." Lord Quemanor offered his hand. "But it will not be the last time. I promise you, Master Ariz. I will find a way to free you. I will not give up."

Ariz nodded but held out little hope that anyone could save him. To think on that possibility—to believe anyone else could actually help him, much less save him—would only rouse agony from his brand and murderous fury. Instead, as he closed the shutters and plunged the room into twilight, he reverted to his practiced state of fatalism. He accepted a future consigned to Hierro's will, while drawing out the consolation of the present as long as he could.

Right now he could enjoy the pleasure of dancing. They spun and circled, linked hands, turned and released each other again and again. Lord Quemanor's grace delighted Ariz. His broad smile lifted Ariz's spirit. His shadow washed over Ariz and for a little time it felt almost as if the brand could have fallen away from his flesh.

In that moment he dared say more than he would have at any other time.

"You may not wish to know this," Ariz murmured. "But I believe that you possess an immense magical potential. If you didn't then Hierro would've moved against you directly. He would have tried to seize control of you, as Genimo did. But something kept him at bay. I think that was the shadow that you seem to hate so much."

Lord Quemanor's carefree expression tightened into displeasure, but Ariz went on. Lord Quemanor had to know this. He needed to understand that he not only possessed great power, but that his practice of restraining his might would not serve him against Hierro. Ariz had sparred with them both and he knew that the only way to defeat Hierro was a relentless attack. He all too readily exploited moments of hesitation and mercy in his opponents.

"Your shadow does not seem to me to be Genimo's or Scholar Donamillo's creation. They are dead and the shadow is yours alone."

Lord Quemanor stilled and pulled his hands away.

"I know you do not want to hear this, but it's true," Ariz said. "I was afraid to tell you before, but now I don't want to leave you without letting you know."

"I appreciate your honesty, but you are mistaken."

"You don't appreciate my honesty," Ariz replied. "But I'm not mistaken. I've stood in your shadow and allowed your presence to protect me from the worst of Hierro's will more times than I can count."

"You have?" Lord Quemanor frowned down at the darkness pooling around both their feet.

"Yes," Ariz assured him. "You've given me respite without even knowing that you were doing it. I should have told you, but I would have had to admit so many other things that I couldn't. But now . . . you may need every advantage you can claim in the coming weeks and months."

Lord Quemanor's expression remained troubled, but he didn't argue.

The chapel bells rang out the passage of yet another hour and Ariz realized that he couldn't linger here, pretending that he could remain forever in Lord Quemanor's company. His mental trick of stretching the present out as long as possible to avoid the fatalism of his future only ever lasted a short while. He had to pack his things and say his goodbyes to his nieces.

"I should go," Ariz said. "Before they come for me."

"I wish . . . ," Lord Quemanor began but he didn't say more.

Probably for the best, Ariz thought. Under other circumstances they might have found something in each other, been something to each other, but Ariz knew he could only do Lord Quemanor harm as he was now. Best for neither of them to think on what might have been but could never be. That was a course in misery that Ariz had already taken and felt no need to repeat.

"Keep safe, my lord," Ariz told him. "It has been an honor to know you. I pray that I have done you some good in preparing you for your enemies."

Lord Quemanor stared at him silently. As Ariz started toward the garden doors, Lord Quemanor reached out and caught his hand. He pulled Ariz into his arms and Ariz went to him. Ariz hoped only to enjoy another brief embrace, but instead Lord Quemanor kissed his lips. When he opened his mouth in surprise, Lord Quemanor leaned into him. The heat of his body pressed into Ariz and seemed to flush from his chest down to his thighs.

Ariz couldn't remember ever having been kissed and he felt overwhelmed with pleasure. Lord Quemanor's mouth and tongue felt hot, soft and full of longing. Ariz returned as much passion as he could, though he knew himself to be artless and unpracticed. He'd wanted this so badly for so long. It felt like a miracle to have it at last.

Lord Quemanor caressed the curve of his back. A thrill traced the passage of his strong hands as he ran his fingers below the line of Ariz's sword belt. The dull ache of Ariz's brand fell away as he pressed into the duke's wonderous touch. The pain in his stitched arm and bloodied chest evaporated like dew in sunlight. Sparks of pleasure surged through his numb flesh, waking a golden heat. For the first time in more than a decade, he felt entirely free of hurt and flushed with desire.

A loud knock sounded at the door and Ariz recognized Enevir Helio's voice calling for the Duke of Rauma. Lord Quemanor held Ariz even more tightly, but Ariz drew away. Lord Quemanor's shadow clung to him and as he stepped back, he noticed that his sensation of recovery hadn't been pure romantic fantasy. The cut in his arm was now a stitched scar. No blood rose from the gash in his chest either.

"Fedeles!" Prince Jacinto now raised his voice. "Atreau has had the most wonderful idea and I'm afraid that I am truly going to steal your physician away."

"You have to go." Ariz forced the words out. "As must I."

He turned away before Jacinto and his courtiers poured through the doors. Before any of them noticed him, Ariz slipped out the garden doors. As he left Lord Quemanor, he felt alive with longing and heartbreak.

But he did feel alive.

∽∽∽

Ariz knew that he couldn't ride into Clara's household with a smile on his lips and his heart full of the revelations that he'd managed to entrust to her enemies. But the comfort of Lord Quemanor's shadow seemed to cling to him, like a cooling balm spread over a burn. Even that small respite from the pain of his brand infused him with flutters of excitement and joy. He felt his mouth tugging into another smile and forced himself to frown.

He had to stop thinking of Lord Quemanor's embrace and the pleasure of his kiss.

He couldn't afford to expose any hint of the sense of promise whirling through him like a summer storm. Happiness of any kind could give him away and hope, in particular, had always been a quality that Hierro quashed.

So Ariz focused on objects far removed from himself. The ostentatious grandeur of the Odalis house afforded no end of distraction. Anything that could have been gilded was: turret spires, garden statues, even the entry doors. He half expected the tawny, feral-looking cat prowling across the grounds to glint in the light.

Inside the mansion the blaze of gold continued. In addition, the walls and ceilings were encrusted with amethyst tiles and pearl-studded mirrors. The floor spilled out in a game-board pattern of amber and mauve marble. A haze of funerary perfume drifted through the still air.

Painted silk screens created a catacomb of the entry rooms and gigantic lapis lazuli vases overflowing with perfumed peacock feathers abounded. The marble staircase appeared to drip with carved floral work. On his way up to present himself to the newly widowed countess, he passed a group of footmen laden down with gray silk swags and ribbons. They shrouded the plump nymphs carved into the railings. He supposed that their sedate additions to the gaudy chaos of the house were intended to indicate a house in mourning, but they made little impact upon the vibrant property that Lord Odalis left behind.

The wing of the house where Clara held sway was markedly more sedate. No flowers, shells or stuffed curiosities occupied any of the little sideboard tables or sconces. Instead religious portraits and even a number of framed relics held pride of place. A smell of dry bones replaced the clouds of floral perfumes and bracing animal musks.

Uneasiness tingled down Ariz's spine like a droplet of ice water. He stopped as he sensed something like a phantom voice whispering from the back of his mind. The ruddy footman who'd led Ariz up the stairs and into Clara's wing looked back at him questioningly.

"Lord Hierro Fueres . . . is he here?" Ariz just managed to make the statement sound like a question.

"Yes. Didn't I mention that her ladyship's brother has come to offer his condolences for her loss?"

"No." The word came out flat and uninterested, despite Ariz's alarm.

The footman, too, appeared somewhat anxious.

"He didn't seem to be in a good mood," the footman whispered. "Not at all."

Ariz recognized all that went unspoken. He didn't resent the footman for turning back down the stairs after merely directing him the rest of the way to Clara's drawing room. Ariz had lived long enough as a servant that he understood the pretty footman's need to avoid catching a man like Hierro's interest. Moreover, he didn't expect to be waited upon when he was fully capable of presenting himself and the letter he carried from Oasia.

He passed framed paintings of ancient ossuaries as well as mounted penitents' paddles, studded with sharp-edged holy stars. As he turned down the corridor he sighted a group of four lady's maids hunched together outside the tall gold door that opened to Clara's drawing room. All four wore tellingly dull expressions, particularly considering how much agitation and fear their postures conveyed.

They too bore Hierro's brand, then.

Ariz couldn't think of any other reason that they would leave Clara alone with Hierro. Not when their distress at what could be happening behind the door was so obvious in the way they took turns trying to grip the doorknob to open it and then jerked their hands back with gasps of pain. The youngest lady's maid looked no older than thirteen. Tears dribbled down her slack pale face.

As Ariz drew near them, all four of the lady's maids looked at him. He read their alarm clearly and now, hearing the low fury of Hierro's voice through the door, he realized that they were all terrified for Clara. Whatever her failings might have been, she'd clearly won the affections of these women.

"I bring news from Oasia Quemanor, Duchess of Rauma, for her sister, Lady—"

"Please do go in, good sir." The tallest of the maids stepped aside to allow him past. Ariz felt the brand flare painfully through his chest as he reached for the door. But then a fluttering shadow of the relief he'd experienced in Lord Quemanor's arms seemed to rise in him like a shield. Ariz gripped the knob, shoved the door wide and charged into the drawing room.

Hierro and Clara stood before the crushed bodies of two little songbirds. The cage that had housed them lay near a blue divan. Clara gasped, her face darkening to a terrible violet as she stared over Hierro's shoulder to Ariz. Hierro seemed to take no notice of Ariz. He looked utterly enrapt, leaning over his sister, strangling her.

Ariz didn't think, he simply allowed his momentum to carry him into Hierro. He rammed his right leg into Hierro's knee, but then the brand gushed up like a geyser of agony searing through his entire body.

Ariz moaned in pain and his shaking body collapsed on top of Hierro. All three of them fell together.

Ariz shook against the polished floor, unable to even pull himself upright.

But Clara scrambled to her feet first, gagging and gasping. The front of her gray bodice had been slashed open by a knife that left a fine track of blood. But it was the pale scar tissue just below Clara's breasts that caught Ariz's attention. A brand—one so old that it had faded and lay flat, but still recognizable to his eye. She crossed her arms over her chest as she bolted back behind the divan. Ariz had suffered more than a decade of Hierro's control, but Clara, he realized, must have endured his cruelty even longer.

Horror and sympathy rose through Ariz. Then the pain of Hierro's black boot slamming into his ribs eclipsed all thought. A whimper escaped Ariz's throat. Hierro's gold spurs jingled like bells as he punted Ariz again.

"How dare you lay a hand on me!" Hierro sneered down at Ariz. He drove his boot in again and the stab of pain that shot through his kidneys joined the vast waves crashing through his whole body. Agonized tears welled up in Ariz's eyes as he struggled to reclaim that brief shade of respite that Lord Quemanor had imparted to him.

If he could just get up . . . or barring that, at least summon the self-control to catch Hierro's boot and jerk the man off his feet. But Ariz could hardly draw in a breath now.

Hierro smiled at him as he landed another brutal kick. Ariz remembered Hierro kicking a hunting dog to death in this very same way years before.

It couldn't end like this. Not when he'd finally found a spark of hope to make him want to survive.

"I—"Ariz struggled for anything that could save him. "Your back was to me. I didn't know—" Ariz couldn't finish the sentence in a lie. Instead he simply cut himself off short as Hierro's boot punched into him again.

"Please, Hierro," Clara rasped. "Please stop!"

Surprisingly, that did still Hierro. He turned to regard his sister with an exasperated expression. "God's tits, do you ever cease your incessant begging?"

Clara bowed her head, perhaps in shame or obedience. Though Ariz remembered doing the same thing to save himself from having to look at Hierro and feel the agony roused by murderous hatred of his handsome face.

"Please," Clara whispered again. "He didn't know it was you. How could he have raised a hand against you if he had? He was only defending your sister."

Hierro made a disgusted noise but stepped away from Ariz. He tossed himself down into the blue velvet divan and swept his hand through his hair, smoothing it back. For a moment none of the three of them moved. Hierro lounged, while Clara stood looking bedraggled and beaten. Ariz sucked in a breath. His ribs felt like knives scraping his lungs, but he had to breathe—he had to keep himself alive. He lifted his gaze to the painted ceiling, attempting to think of nothing but the blue sky and spills of holy gold stars above him.

"Close the door!" Hierro shouted and one of the lady's maids immediately obeyed him.

Out of the corner of his eye Ariz noticed Clara back away to a card table. She plucked a white lace shawl from the back of a chair and wrapped it around her. Hierro leaned forward in his chair.

"So, why are you here, Ariz?" he demanded.

Ariz closed his eyes. The afterimage of gold stars shone violet behind his lids.

"I was sent with a letter." Ariz managed to get control of his left arm well enough to draw Oasia's letter from his coat. "For Lady Odalis."

Hierro snatched the letter from Ariz's hand. He cracked the jade-green wax seal and then read the missive. Anger began to fill his face again and Clara retreated behind the card table.

"Your idiotic obsession with saving that limping brat hasn't just cost me one agent but two!" Hierro glowered at Clara. Then he crooked his finger and beckoned her to him. The color drained from her face as she staggered toward him.

Ariz managed to roll onto his side. He wondered if he could make himself catch hold of Hierro's leg, if the other man started after Clara again. Hierro didn't even bother to glance down at him. His attention locked on his sister as she dragged her feet steadily toward him.

"It seems that Oasia doesn't want you living under her roof. What a surprise! And on top of that she's decided to send this"—Hierro nudged Ariz with the toe of his boot—"to stay with you."

"That's good. It would have been foolish to use Ariz to assassinate Fedeles Quemanor." Clara gripped the arm of the divan as if attempting to use it to anchor herself from drifting nearer to her brother. "Since he came directly from your service, it would cast suspicion back on you—"

"Are you trying to claim to have arranged this for my good?" Hierro gave a cold laugh. "After so many husbands, I would have thought that you'd be a better liar than that."

"I can't lie to *you*, Hierro." Clara very obviously released her grip on the divan and stepped up to Hierro's side. "I truly do believe that it would have been shortsighted to use Ariz directly against Fedeles Quemanor, when he could be exploited to far greater effect."

Hierro curled his hands around Clara's throat but didn't close his grip. He studied Clara's pallid face. Ariz wondered if his own expression was as curious as Hierro's.

"All right," Hierro said at last. "You've got my attention. But your explanation had better be damn good, my dear."

"It's no secret that you hate Fedeles, so if he's assassinated by a man who can be traced back to your service, then that will cast suspicion on you and everyone who supports you." Clara spoke in a hoarse whisper and Ariz wondered just how close Hierro had come to actually killing her. "But if Ariz were to kill Fedeles Quemanor's enemy, then his actions would obviously be attributed to the Duke of Rauma, not you or Prince Remes."

Hierro's mouth twitched, but then a thoughtful expression spread across his face. He tapped his fingers across the red welts that marked his sister's neck.

"Use him to murder the royal bishop, you mean?" Hierro asked.

"He is a threat to Remes's claim to the throne," Clara said. She dropped her gaze to Hierro's feet, but Ariz noticed the slightest smile flicker across her lips. "Or there is . . . Papa."

Hierro raised his brows as if surprised by his own admiration of Clara.

"A death in our own family would remove suspicion from you," Clara went on in the same sad soft tone. "And at the same time Papa's demise would provide you with complete control of the Gavado armies. You will require them to suppress those nobles who don't accept Remes immediately."

Ariz stared at Clara, feeling nearly as awed as he was horrified by her cleverness.

"Oh, Clara, you're so frail and pious. Sometimes even I forget what a heartless little bitch you truly are." Hierro laughed with genuine warmth. Then he glanced down to Ariz. "And you. You don't breathe a single word of this to anyone. Not one word. Understood?"

Ariz nodded as if he was convulsing and he bit down on his tongue to keep from letting any admission of what he'd already confessed slip out of his mouth. Fortunately, Hierro quickly returned his attention to Clara.

"I do like your plot, but it still leaves us with the problem of how to be rid of Fedeles and Oasia and their brat."

"Once the duke and duchess are implicated in the assassinations, the entire nation will turn against them," Clara responded. "Their lawful arrests and executions will return our nation to peace and legitimize the rightful ruler of Cadeleon."

Hierro nodded but then commented, "I notice that you failed to mention the crippled whelp."

A shudder, almost like a suppressed sob, shook through Clara. She clasped her hands together as if in prayer as she lifted her head to gaze up at Hierro.

"He is innocent. Completely innocent," Clara whispered. "You must spare him."

"There is nothing I *must* do," Hierro replied. "Only what I will or won't."

"Please—" Clara began, but Hierro silenced her with a quick slap across her cheek.

"Don't ruin my mood," he chided her. "I happen to be feeling generous and willing to indulge you in something, but not that. So ask for something else before you begin to annoy me."

Clara sagged but then straightened again. "Then will you move against that Haldiim abomination, as I asked?"

"Captain Yago has already done away with the Bahiim in charge of their little park," Hierro replied.

"Her body may be dead, but the sacred grove still blazes in my mind." Clara caught Hierro's hand between hers. "And there's a chance that your enemy on Crown Hill could seize the grove. You remember the letter, don't you?"

"Of course I remember the letter." Hierro sighed in the theatric manner of the much put-upon hero of a romantic comedy. Or at least, as if he found all of this somehow funny. "And yes, I remember the royal bishop's rants about Meztli's scarlet shields rising from Crown Hill to save us all if the Labaran attack on the Hallowed Kings continues. Those were just two of the reasons why I wanted Fedeles and Oasia removed immediately. If you recall."

"Do you really believe that your assassins armed with mere blades could have killed either of them?" Clara offered Ariz an apologetic glance. "As skilled a swordsman as he is, not even Ariz would have been a match for Oasia, not inside her own home. The instant he moved against her, Oasia would have torn him apart."

Ariz knew Clara was right. In fact, the idea had been a kind of comfort to him on some occasions.

"And Fedeles Quemanor's shadow is not a thing that can be laid low with a common blade," Clara said. "Remes already lost two assassins attempting that very same thing. Those poor men were slaughtered like lambs. Had I not intervened as I did, Ariz would have remained in that house and died for nothing."

"Oh please," Hierro cut her off. "You could hardly have known that Oasia would send him to you."

Ariz wasn't so certain and the realization filled him with an icy dread. Had Clara asked to stay with Oasia knowing that she would be refused and that Ariz would be sent to her instead? Did she understand her sister so very perfectly? Or did she possess some other means of manipulating events around her? She'd known Dommian's name and character well enough that Ariz had suspected him of being her informant. But there could be someone else.

"If Oasia and Fedeles are to be completely destroyed," Clara went on, "then they must first be stripped of their power. Only when they are helpless and friendless can we be assured of killing them. And only then can their deaths serve a greater purpose."

"No doubt. But there's not much sport to be enjoyed in such a plan," Hierro commented.

"We aren't trying to win a game. This is a holy war," Clara replied.

Hierro laughed.

"When you're chosen by God, the two are the same thing, darling." Hierro pulled his hand free of Clara's fingers. "But just for your sake I'll go and see if I can't stir up the Haldiim District—"

"You have to destroy their grove."

"I don't *have* to do anything," Hierro snapped.

Clara bowed her head and this time Ariz glimpsed the fury that she hid in the shadows of her loose hair.

"It isn't just in Anacleto that the Haldiim are spreading. They may seem like nothing with their quaint trees and ill-kept grounds, but those little parks of theirs harbor dangerous power. Ancient power that could ruin everything. They will corrupt all that is true and holy just as a cancer consumes a body—"

"Fedeles Quemanor is no Bahiim and he's no more welcome in their grove than I am. You should have seen the show last night. He ran away from Crown Hill crying after one paddling from that dead crone in the grove. A second violation might well kill him." Hierro gave a laugh but then cocked his head and considered Clara. "I suppose I might have a use for the grove after all."

"You will destroy it?" Clara asked.

"Of course. Eventually," Hierro replied. "Though there's more than one way to destroy something. You of all people should know that."

He stepped over Ariz and, tossing the door open, he left them. In his wake the lady's maids crept back into the drawing room. Clara knelt and gently touched each of the dead songbirds as if offering them last rites. Then she moved to Ariz's side and offered him a tired smile.

"Never fear, Ariz. Hierro's games will be his undoing in the end." She wiped the beads of cold sweat from his brow. "And your death, when it comes, will be glorious."

CHAPTER
TWENTY-SEVEN

Having listened inattentively to the descriptions of Jacinto's new theatrical masterpiece, Fedeles gave his blessing for Jacinto to abscond with Atreau and Master Narsi. Then he hastened to his wife's wing of the mansion. He left his guards behind in the hall before he strode into Oasia's study.

Inside he found his son playing cards with Mistress Delfia's twins. A soft rosy glow lit Sparanzo's winsome face as the ruby necklace he wore lit in response to Fedeles's seething shadow. The necklace resembled one Hylanya had worn, except that these stones were smaller and seemed to Fedeles as if age and the elements had weathered them down to a kind of purity. When he'd touched them they radiated safety and strength. The locket at the center of the necklace was so sedate that Fedeles found himself overlooking it, even when he attempted to make a study of its worn surface. His gaze seemed to slide off it.

He didn't feel entirely comfortable with Oasia's decision to make Sparanzo wear the string of blessings that Clara had sent. At the same time he could hardly argue with the fact that the necklace bore only protective signs and that there was no one whom he would rather have protected.

Both Sparanzo and Celino betrayed the fact that they perceived the blessings flaring to life when they looked to the shining stones. Marisol on the other hand turned her head immediately to where Fedeles stood. The color drained from her face as she glanced to Fedeles's shadow. She straightened as if she thought she might have to fight him off.

"I'm sorry." Shame tempered Fedeles's frustration. He spoke softly and smiled, though he suspected that neither action reassured the children while a writhing monstrosity still spilled out from around his feet. "I didn't mean to startle you."

"I'm not scared, Papa." Sparanzo gave him a guileless smile and then lowered his gaze to Fedeles's shadow. "Are you scared?"

"No. I'm a little agitated. We have so much to do before the coronation and I need to talk with your mother about a great number of matters."

Sparanzo nodded, but his attention already returned to his cards. Celino and Marisol also lifted up their cards, but the twins continued to watch him attentively as he strode past them to the large oak table where Oasia and a dozen of her lady companions worked in a circle at their lace looms.

Mistress Delfia did not sit at the table but stood near a window, with her back to the rest of them. Fedeles guessed that she had watched her brother as he carried his belongings to the stables and readied his mount for their departure. For an instant he wanted to go to her and offer some comfort—try to assure her that he would do all he could to save Ariz. But how presumptuous would that be? He who had stripped her, her children and her brother of everything now offering up the hollow consolation of words? Worst of all, he knew that such talk wouldn't represent any real power he currently possessed to free Ariz. He simply wanted to be able to offer assurances to assuage his own guilt.

But it was truth, not comfort, that brought him here, he reminded himself.

He turned his attention back to the table where Oasia sat surrounded by her ladies and great cascades of fine lace. On the loom before Oasia, countless silk threads hung on tiny wooden bobbins and spread out from intricate, half-finished designs of pale ivy and stallions. The threads of Oasia's loom glinted with faint sparks of blue light. To Fedeles's eye the spells cast an entirely different pattern over the delicate silk.

More blue sparks lit from her fingers as she twisted three bobbins of silk threads into a fine braid and then wove them into a larger pattern of lace. A multitude of her blessings gleamed across the silk. Eventually the lace would adorn the shirts that Sparanzo, Celino and Marisol would wear for Sevanyo's coronation.

Oasia glanced up to him and then down to the restless shadow curling around his feet. Fedeles wished to God that he could control the damned thing at least enough to stop its constant thrashing.

"I think that my darling husband would like a word alone with me, my dear friends," Oasia announced.

In a matter of moments her ladies-in-waiting and her handmaids joined Fedeles's guards in the hallway. Delfia left last, leading her two children and Sparanzo away with promises of a game of Rabbit's Run in the ballroom.

"But can't Uncle Ariz join us?" Marisol asked.

"No, my dear. He must go and look after Sparanzo's aunt Clara."

Sparanzo offered some objection, but Fedeles couldn't make it all out as the heavy door fell closed.

"Come and sit down." Oasia patted the seat next to her own.

Fedeles almost refused. Frustration and anger smoldered through him, making him want to stand over her and shout. But not only was that impulse petty and bullying, it lay at odds with his greater need to hear the truth. Grudgingly, he sat.

Briefly he studied the large circle of finished lacework that covered the center of the table. Outwardly it resembled a simple map of the city. To Fedeles's eyes it blazed like an alchemist's blue fire. At the heart of the silk map rose a shining miniature of the very house they now stood in. Beyond that the rest of the city spread out in a haze of cerulean light. Several sectors—the Haldiim District, the Savior's Chapel and the Shard of Heaven in particular—were represented by their dark absences, but between the Royal Palace and the Quemanor household, Oasia's wards formed a resplendent tapestry of protection. For all the hundreds of guards and captains who imagined themselves as Prince Sevanyo's protectors, none rivaled Oasia in her silent defense of the kingdom. Not even Fedeles knew exactly how many magical attacks she had thwarted, nor how much of her distant expression and serene manner arose from how very much of her soul she stretched out to shelter the city.

Looking at the wards, it was hard to remain angry. But then Fedeles remembered what he came here for.

"Would you care for a little of the tisane Delfia has brewed?" Oasia asked.

Fedeles shook his head.

"A honey biscuit?"

"How long did you know?" Fedeles demanded.

Oasia's serene expression tightened only fractionally.

"About Ariz?" she asked.

Fedeles nodded, not quite trusting his voice not to betray his hurt.

"I suspected the very first time I laid eyes on the boy trailing my brother around the grounds of our family house. I tried to warn him and his sister not to be taken in by Hierro's allure, but they were just children and I was not so safe myself that I could do much more than that." Oasia lifted one of the wooden bobbins, but her expression was distant and she set it back down. "I knew Hierro had enthralled Ariz for a certainty after I took Delfia and her children in. She told me what had happened to her brother and begged me to help him."

"And did you try to free him?"

"Of course I did," Oasia replied. "But the spell Hierro used to bind Ariz is both powerful and deep-rooted. I couldn't pull the brand from his flesh without ripping him apart. And though it might have been a mercy, I didn't wish to kill Ariz. I am a little fond of him, you know."

Fedeles guessed that she must be, otherwise he doubted that she would have allowed him anywhere near Sparanzo.

"But you didn't tell me. Why?" Fedeles demanded.

"Do you think that Atreau tells you everything he knows?" Oasia replied. "Do you think that Ciceron did?"

"No, but neither of them are my wife," Fedeles snapped.

A faint, fond smile curved Oasia's lips.

"Indeed they are not. I'm the only one who has entwined my entire future and fortune with yours, for better or for worse," Oasia agreed. "Atreau is free to run off and hide in whatever bed pleases him. Don't think he won't abandon us to save his own skin, just as he left Miro to die in that squalid little room of his. But I've made my place here with you. My fate and Sparanzo's are tied to yours."

"And yet you kept this from me." Fedeles met her gaze. "How could you?"

"Setting aside the fact that it was not my secret to divulge to you?" Oasia drew in a deep breath, as if preparing to scold him, but then her expression softened. "At first I kept it a secret because it is my nature to keep secrets. And I knew that once you were aware of the truth, you would not be able to keep your knowledge from Ariz. You would be overwhelmed with the need to console him. You would assure him that you would do everything to free him—"

"What is so wrong with that?"

"Only that Ariz would not be able to keep himself from revealing all your promises to Hierro. And the instant my brother realized that you knew about Ariz's condition—that you felt guilty for his suffering—then he would turn Ariz against you."

Fedeles scowled.

"If you had told me all of it, I wouldn't have approached Ariz."

A short laugh escaped Oasia.

"You are many wonderful things, Fedeles, but you are neither a talented liar nor a skilled actor. As soon as you knew, it would have shown."

Oasia sighed. "And in the years since Ariz joined our household, it's begun to matter to me a great deal that the truth could hurt you . . . and him. Look what it's done to you both today."

Fedeles couldn't argue with that. "Still, there's the principle of the matter. You should have been honest with me."

"I was not dishonest," Oasia countered.

"You kept the truth from me."

"Yes. But what good has revealing the truth accomplished? Has it brought you happiness? Or saved Ariz, or relieved Delfia? It's only endangered us all." Oasia shook her head. "Sometimes knowledge may do as much harm as ignorance. Life isn't so simple that any of us can always make the correct decisions. I did what I felt was best for us all."

Fedeles frowned at the vast tapestry of fine silken threads. The pattern of lace appeared so pretty and perfect that it seemed almost unimaginable that it arose from such a chaos of tangled, scattered lines.

"At least now I understand what he's going through."

"Are you happier for that?" Oasia asked. "Do you imagine that Ariz is? Or that he would have wanted you to think of him as a tortured puppet? He may seem unassuming and humble, but he is still a man. He possesses enough pride to want you to see him as more than Hierro's pawn."

"I know that he's more than a pawn." Fedeles felt his anger ebbing, his shadow settled into a sullen pool. "I kissed him."

"And?"

"He liked it. He likes me, I think." Fedeles sat quietly for a few moments while Oasia brushed at a corner of her lacework. A spark seemed to snap at her but she crushed it out with the tip of her finger. Then she turned her attention back to Fedeles.

"Is something else troubling you?" Oasia asked.

"He thinks that I might be able to challenge Hierro if I can master this thing." Fedeles kicked the toe of his boot into his shadow.

"It is not a thing," Oasia said, as she had so many times before. "It is part of your spirit. Just as this"—she opened her hands and a sphere of luminous blue mist briefly rose over her palms—"this is part of mine."

"Your witchflame, Lady Hylanya called it," Fedeles said. The young woman had caused an uproar at court with her candor, but Fedeles had found her company informative and refreshing.

"It is the light of a strong soul, that was what my mother said." Oasia ran her hand over a silk thread. "Hers was vibrant as a star."

"My grandmother used to get embarrassed and hush me whenever I mentioned the green lights that danced around her. But it was beautiful and radiant when she prayed in chapel." Fedeles supposed that she would have been mortified if she'd lived to see him playing at magic up on Crown Hill. She'd strongly disapproved of the way Javier had flouted the church and made a show of his Hell-branded soul.

Oasia nodded from her halo of clear blue light. Again she crushed out a few wayward indigo sparks. They seemed concentrated on the south side of the city, not far from the Theater District. Oasia made a motion as if waving aside smoke, then leaned back in her chair.

"Master Ariz could be correct. You may well possess the power to free him. Or at least the potential to challenge Hierro."

Fedeles contemplated his shadow. Could he unleash it against Hierro? If he did, could he ever reclaim control of it?

"If this thing is my soul, then what does that say about me?" Fedeles murmured. "It's such a corrupted thing—"

"Your spirit is marked by the hardship you've endured. You carry a deep scar from that time, no question, but that doesn't mean you are corrupted." Oasia placed her hand on his. Her skin felt soft and warm against his cold fingers. "Hierro's soul shines the brightest blue I have ever seen, but I promise you that is no indication of his purity. He may seem beautiful, but inside he's a monstrosity. The world is not so simple that good hearts always beat beneath handsome flesh."

Fedeles knew she was right, but it wasn't just the appearance of his shadow that seemed malevolent. It all too easily lashed out in violence.

"In a just world our beauty would be judged by our actions, not our faces." Oasia studied her lace map of the city, but then shrugged.

"Atreau wrote much the same thing in a poem of his, you know," Fedeles commented. He felt relieved to be able to turn the subject from himself.

Oasia scowled at the mention of Atreau.

"About me, no doubt," Oasia said.

"He didn't mention you by name," Fedeles assured her.

"The man does know how to leave out just the right detail. I noticed his memoirs omit the months he spent fucking my husband as well as the night he left him to die," Oasia responded. "He so loves to cast himself as the hapless lad at the mercy of a cruel world, doesn't he?"

Fedeles considered the thought. "A long time ago I think that might have been the case, but he's changed. He's grown." Fedeles wished that Oasia and Atreau could overcome some of their animosity. Both of them possessed good hearts and quick minds—even if their personal histories had led them to do harm; they were both becoming different people. Better people.

"I'm pretty certain that he's not outgrown his penchant for fucking married men and seducing lonely wives," Oasia responded, but she sounded more distracted than angry. She ran a hand over her lacework, smoothing it out. Then she returned her attention to Fedeles. "If you aren't careful, my dear, you know he's bound to come sniffing around your bedroom door sooner or later."

Fedeles laughed at the idea of that. "If Atreau makes an appearance in my bedroom you can be assured it would be to steal my bedding for the comfort of some needy waif who's won his sympathy. Or perhaps a pair of barmaids."

"A strapping soldier, more likely," Oasia replied flatly.

"You don't truly believe that, do you?" Fedeles had always imagined Atreau's affair with Oasia's first husband as an anomaly—a single curious coupling in a vast catalogue of female partners. Atreau had certainly never made an advance toward any of the men in Fedeles's household.

"Have you *read* the passages from his first memoir describing Elezar Grunito?" Oasia raised her brows.

"I . . . I've not read the entire thing in detail, no," Fedeles confessed. In truth he'd hardly skimmed the books, though he often mentioned them, just to gauge other people's reactions. "Those days embarrass me. I wasn't myself . . ." Fedeles trailed off. He didn't need to tell Oasia what a mess he'd been. But then he realized something and grinned. "But *you* really have read it?"

"I have. Mistress Delfia—or perhaps it was Ariz—one of them owned a copy." Oasia frowned as Fedeles continued to grin at her. "Anyway, Delfia and several of my handmaids took turns reading passages aloud while we worked at the looms."

"And did you enjoy it?" Fedeles asked.

"I found it . . . informative." Oasia again placed her hand on her lace loom. She regarded Fedeles with a thoughtful expression.

"Do tell," Fedeles prompted.

"There was one passage that has been nagging at me for months. I think I just realized why it bothered me." Oasia drummed her fingers over her loom.

"Let me guess. It involved his adventures in a brothel?" Fedeles rarely got the opportunity to tease Oasia even a little.

"Of course it did. You'd think from Atreau's telling that the Sagrada Academy held classes inside the Golden Rod and taught you boys nothing but chatting up tarts." She gave a short laugh, but then her frown again returned. "But this section of his memoir bothered me for a different reason. It's early in the book. Two of the girls employed at the brothel share gossip about the Yillar students with Atreau and they mention Hierro by name. A few passages after that they talk about how dark his . . . private areas looked when compared to Genimo Plunado's."

Fedeles could see why Oasia's expression had turned queasy at the mention of her brother's genitals, but he didn't see how this information could be useful.

"That implies that Genimo and Hierro were enjoying the girls' services together," Oasia went on. "And that led me to suspect that not only did Genimo remain in contact with Hierro after they went away to school, but that they could have colluded throughout the time that you were under Genimo's control."

Fedeles felt a sick drop in his stomach, but he nodded.

"Master Ariz did say that Genimo and Hierro exchanged letters about . . . my condition." Fedeles hated to think of all the intimate details Genimo had likely betrayed. "But if Hierro attempts to use the letters to expose anything of my private affairs, not only can I claim that I was not under my own control at that time, but I might be able to charge him with conspiracy. I don't think he'd dare to make the letters public."

"No, he wouldn't," Oasia agreed. "But what has begun to worry me is that Hierro could be in possession of some or all the plans for the mechanical cures that were used to suppress your soul and house the shadow curse within your body. If he could unleash another shadow curse, he could wipe out the entire Sagrada bloodline just as the Tornesals were destroyed."

The horror of that thought rooted Fedeles in place for a moment.

Scholar Donamillo had successfully murdered dozens of men and women without anyone ever suspecting him of any wrongdoing. He hadn't needed assassins or agents willing to tip poison into wineglasses. He'd simply employed ancient magic and modern mechanisms. One by one members of the Tornesal family went mad and died in agony. Fedeles's mother had numbered among those killed.

Fedeles had destroyed every remnant of those vile mechanisms, and until just now, he'd felt secure in the knowledge that they were gone forever. He'd not considered that Genimo might have shared his designs with his childhood companion, Hierro Fueres. Fedeles's pulse quickened with anxiety. His shadow rippled.

But no mechanical plan alone, no matter how detailed, could recreate the devices that had entrapped him, Fedeles reminded himself. Merely constructing a machine hadn't been enough to create a shadow curse. That had required Master Donamillo's secret knowledge of Haldiim curses and Bahiim magic.

"Hierro would need to find a recent curse, like the Old Rage, and wake it," Fedeles said as much to himself as Oasia. "He would have to carve away the wards used to pacify it . . ."

The only place such curses rested were sacred groves where Bahiim trapped them and slowly dissipated their malevolence. He thought suddenly of Javier's missive, urging him to protect the Circle of Wisteria. The full ramification of his failure last night spread through him like a clammy nausea.

If Hierro seized the grove, he would have exactly what he needed to wipe out the entire Sagrada family—and anyone else who opposed him—at his leisure.

Fedeles felt the blood draining from his face. Oasia didn't seem to notice—or if she did, she likely attributed Fedeles's response to his memories of the years he'd spent as prisoner.

"Hierro may be charming, but I don't think any Bahiim would simply allow him to enter one of their sacred places and begin tampering with wards." She shook her head. "He's not so skilled an actor that he could maintain a pleasant demeanor long enough to convince anyone that he wanted to convert, either." Oasia relaxed a little. "So perhaps my fear is unfounded . . . I'm sorry that I brought it up."

"It's all right. You should never feel that you can't talk to me, even if the subject rouses an unpleasant memory or two."

Fedeles desperately wanted her to be right about Hierro's inability to access a sacred grove. But the death of the last Bahiim who had protected the Circle of Wisteria gnawed at him. Her spirit still guarded the place, but how much longer could she last? If Hierro truly wished to awaken a curse, certainly he would already have made a play to seize the sacred grove.

Fedeles calmed a little.

"Due to recent events I've also read through Atreau's second memoir, *Five Hundred Nights in the Court of the Scarlet Wolf*." Oasia sounded eager to change the subject of conversation and Fedeles felt happy to oblige.

"Oh yes?" Fedeles asked. "Where did you manage to find a copy?"

"I *borrowed* the volume from your private library." Oasia offered him an apologetic smile.

That thought washed away Fedeles's previous anxiety in a wave of mortification. Several of the books locked away in his personal cabinets were indisputably pornographic; one all but burst with robust illustrations.

"I didn't lay a finger on anything else in your collection," Oasia added quickly. "Anyway, my point is that Atreau describes one of the sister-physicians disrobing before their frenzied intercourse. He mentions her wearing a necklace very like the one Clara sent to protect Sparanzo. The sister-physician tells Atreau that it was a gift from another lover, who claimed to be the descendant of an Old God." Oasia held up her forefinger. "Later he mentions the grimma—whom we know numbered among the Old Gods who battled the demon kings. He describes the Sumar grimma in particular wearing great cascades of jeweled necklaces like armor. The spells housed within them act like *shields*. Later still, he describes Lady Hylanya wearing a necklace that the young count refers to as her *ruby shield*."

"The ruby shield that the royal bishop has been searching for?" Fedeles wondered.

"Pieces of one, at least." Oasia nodded. "I've received a letter from a friend in the Gavado convent. And she relayed some very interesting information concerning the oldest texts kept there. The very first ruby shields aren't associated with Labaran witches. Apparently for a hundred years or so the term was reserved for the blessings that Meztli forged."

"Meztli from the holy books?" Fedeles asked. The figure from holy lore was associated with one thing: a war against a demon king, and not just any demon king, but the very one who was said to have been defeated at the Shard of Heaven.

"Exactly," Oasia said. "If I'm right, then Clara, the royal bishop and possibly even Lady Hylanya have been searching for relics required to survive a battle against a demon lord."

His earlier conversation with Oasia at the palace fountains came back to him.

"Are they simply fearful that the Hallowed Kings will fail, or . . ." Fedeles couldn't bring himself to say the rest aloud. Oasia nodded grimly.

"The most likely reason that they've become suddenly so obsessed with the relics is that one or all of them are plotting to undo the Hallowed Kings' protection of our nation," Oasia said.

"But not even Hierro would be so idiotic as to purposefully release a demon lord. It would destroy everything that he covets and ruin . . ." Fedeles paused midthought. "Though Nugalo . . ."

"He *has* grown more and more erratic these last six years." Oasia nodded. "With Count Radulf gaining power all across Labara and the Haldiim faith spreading through the south, he might actually feel justified in bring damnation down upon all of us who have lived in contempt of his holy decrees. Clara would likely welcome the idea as well."

Fedeles could all too easily imagine Nugalo embracing such reasoning. Though he didn't think it would be the royal bishop's first choice. He wasn't so removed from worldly ambition as that.

"Nugalo's plan may not be to actually release a demon lord. He might just want the power to do so. With that kind of threat hanging over the kingdom, Sevanyo wouldn't dare to defy him, not even after he's crowned king."

Oasia nodded, then ran her hands almost anxiously over her silk threads.

"Whatever his motivation or his final plan," Oasia said after a moment, "it seems clear to me that these relics both he and Clara are after play a central role."

"At least we know that they're still searching so they can't have found them yet," Fedeles said.

Oasia released a weary sigh, then raised her gaze to Fedeles again.

"Considering how little we know and how few agents we have in our enemies' houses, maybe it's a blessing that Master Ariz has gone to join Clara."

Fedeles wanted to offer some argument, but the truth was that they did need to know more. They needed informants placed nearer to Hierro and Clara. He just didn't want that agent to be Master Ariz.

Oasia suddenly sat upright. Fedeles looked to her but then saw the circle of intense indigo flames burst up from Oasia's silk map. He leapt to his feet but had nothing to do. Oasia gasped like the breath had been knocked from her. The indigo flames gushed up over the narrow silk pattern of the river and spilled out into the Theater District. Oasia lunged forward and slammed her hands down across the lace. The indigo fire wavered and fell back, but it didn't die out.

"Hierro. He's moving against the south of the city," Oasia whispered. She didn't look away from the lace map. "I don't have enough wards there to stop him."

Already the indigo fire circled around her fingers and smoke began to rise from the silk threads of the map.

"He wants the Circle of Wisteria," Fedeles realized, and he knew what he had to do. "I have to reach Crown Hill—"

"Go," Oasia ground out. "I'll hold him back as long as I can."

രുരുരു

Fedeles swung down from Firaj's back and raced across the overgrown grounds for the temple. Spells lit up as his feet hammered across the flagstones. *Courage* and *Fearless* gushed up beside him like geysers of fire. They fell in behind him.

He took the temple steps in a bound.

Before him, the four rings of gossamer wards blazed like a wall of fire, but this time Fedeles didn't hesitate. He threw himself into their burning threads, hardly feeling how they seared into his skin.

He had to redeem his earlier failure. He had to stop Hierro—that was all that mattered.

The moment he reached the center of the temple, the carved stone, wildflowers and even Firaj were washed from his sight by a surrounding sphere of shining gold light.

"The Circle of Wisteria!" Fedeles shouted, and like the night before, all the miles of the city appeared to surge past him, carrying him across the Gado Bridge. Before him the sacred grove's luminous trees reached up into the heavens. The light of their branches hurled out long black shadows. A sea of indigo flames circled them.

Flat black crows broke from the shadows and threw themselves into the indigo flames, smothering a few before being consumed.

Fedeles heard the birds cry in pain and he felt Hierro's sadistic pleasure radiating from the indigo fire like waves of heat. Farther back, a wall of Oasia's lacelike cerulean spells blocked Hierro's flames from reaching north beyond the Gado Bridge.

But only a few smoldering crows opposed his attack on the Circle of Wisteria.

For a fleeting moment uncertainty gripped Fedeles. He had no idea of how to fight Hierro; he knew so little about crafting spells or weaving tapestries of wards. But he couldn't just allow this to happen.

Timoteo had been right, inaction could be as damning as a misstep. Ariz's insistence that he could fight Hierro rang through his mind.

Fedeles reached out to the shadows of the Circle of Wisteria with his own darkness. At once he felt a jolt pass through him and shake him like hitting a wall running.

Mean you to claim what I defend?

As it had the night before, a woman's voice rose and the air surrounding Fedeles filled with a sweet perfume. But now the voice was hardly a whisper and Fedeles could taste the tang of blood along with the fragrance of flowers. Even beyond death this Bahiim guardian fought to defend the sacred grove. She would fight him just as she now battled Hierro. To her he was just another invader.

And all at once Fedeles understood where he'd erred the night before, why it had all felt so wrong and sickening to him.

"No," Fedeles said. "I wish to take nothing from you, only to give you my strength and beg you to use it to defend the Circle of Wisteria." Despite how greatly it terrified him, Fedeles released his grip on his restless shadow. He allowed it to flow into the dark roots of the sacred grove and feed them. The golden glow of the trees flared and Fedeles felt as if their light drew him into their branches.

Bless you, child. We will fight as one. And as thousands.

Fedeles nodded his assent, though the motion felt clumsy and numb. His senses seemed far from the husk of his corporeal body. He launched into the air, taking in the city from hundreds of eyes. He spread his wings, catching the wind and soaring. Tongues of indigo fire leapt up after him and he ripped them apart with his gleaming talons. Shredded threads of spells hissed and screeched as they unraveled. At the same time he felt his feathers catching light, felt his skin blistering as he burned in agony.

Pain scorched up his spine and smoke filled his lungs. He cried out as he burned. But even as one of his bodies plummeted, another surged with power. Living strength flooded his muscles and set his heart pounding. He burst from the shadows of the sacred grove, increasing his numbers by the hundreds. He filled the blue sky like a storm cloud as again and again he savaged Hierro's fires.

Inch by inch the indigo conflagration fell back, seething with frustration.

Fedeles fought on, though now not even Hierro's flames seemed to warm him. He felt distantly aware that his body lay sprawled across the stone floor of the abandoned temple. He pushed the image from his thoughts. So long as Hierro's flames still shone, he had to keep fighting.

He'd endured years of agony inside the cage of Donamillo's mechanical cures. A few hours burning alive was nothing. Not when he could end Hierro Fueres, here and now. He could free Ariz, he could save Sevanyo, protect Oasia and make Javier proud of him.

His wings caught fire, he burned and fell from the sky. He died and arose again. On cold stones far away his earthly body gasped and convulsed. Blood filled his nostrils and blisters rose across his hands and feet. None of that mattered, because at last he had found a way to fight for the people he cared for. And he was winning.

Hierro's indigo flames cringed before him. Then they receded, fleeing back to the shimmering violet fortress of the Savior's Chapel.

The coward was hiding behind the prayers of pious clergy and devout common folk, masking his radiant avarice behind the glow of holy devotions. Frustrated anger surged through Fedeles. He would tear it all down, rip away every blessing and ward, until he found Hierro.

No, child. He will draw you into his trap there. The woman's voice was gentle but firm. *We've done enough today. The sacred grove is safe.*

Fedeles felt himself flung back across the Gado Bridge, over sprawling gardens and fields of wildflowers. Then he plunged down into a husk of shivering cold flesh.

Cracks of blue sky peered through the eaves above him. Pale beams of sunlight filtered down, but otherwise the temple was strangely dark. The scarlet spells that had always lit the ancient walls were gone. Fedeles drew in a breath of the cold, damp air. He tasted his own blood and coughed. His chest ached, his hands and feet felt blistered and he couldn't seem to unclench his fingers from the tight fists they'd curled into.

He closed his eyes and focused on another slow inhalation.

When he opened his eyes he saw that *Fearless* and *Courage* knelt next to him. Three other gold spells lay across his body, shielding him and warming him. The darkness filling the temple slowly coalesced into a black silhouette a few feet to his right. Yellow eyes opened from the depths of the darkness and a crow rose up from the flagstones. It ruffled its glossy black feathers and hopped to Fedeles's side.

It nudged Fedeles's aching right hand with its beak. His fingers uncurled like flower petals opening. Fedeles stared at the shining red stones lying in his palm. The blessings that had hung through the temple glowed from the hearts of a dozen rubies. Fedeles concentrated on his left hand, and after a moment the feeling returned to his fingers. He opened his fist to find the remaining spells encased in the scarlet stones in his left hand.

At his side *Courage* fluttered and *Fearless* flickered. Then both of them unwound into long gold threads. *Fearless* curled into Fedeles's left hand, while *Courage* threaded through the stones in his right hand.

Fedeles stared at them for a moment, then slowly—only half believing his own eyes—he brought his hands together. At once *Courage* and *Fearless* wove together into a thick gold cord. Between them all of the spells of the entire temple glittered from within ruby bodies.

The chain of spells seemed to vibrate with excitement and power. Just holding it made Fedeles's battered hands throb.

Meztli's shields arise once more.

"This should be yours," Fedeles whispered.

The crow bumped Fedeles's hand away and shook its head.

Crown Hill has chosen you, child. The burden of its power is yours to shoulder. The curve of the crow's beak lent it the appearance of gazing at him with a sly smile. *You will need it for the war to come.*

The story continues
in volume 2.

Glossary of People, Places & Terms

A

Alizadeh—Bahiim mystic, uncle (by marriage) to Kiram.

Anacleto—Port city in the south of Cadeleon. Center of Haldiim culture and power.

Ariz Plunado—Sword and dance instructor in the Quemanor household, formerly Hierro Fueres's underclassman.

Atreau Inerio Vediya—Fourth son of Baron Nifayo, author. Attended the Sagrada Academy, member of the Hellions there as well as Nestor Grunito's upperclassman.

B

Batteo Ciceron—Captain of south gate guards.

Bahiim—Holy order of religious practice adhered to by members of the Haldiim, Irabiim peoples as well as a segment of the Labaran frogwife population.

Berto Rene—Religious scholar and Narsi's childhood friend. Serves Father Timoteo.

Bhadia Rid-Itf—Bahiim mystic who fought alongside the Savior. She is said to have taken on the form of a mare, with which she carried the Savior and the Shroud of Stone into the heart of the demon armies.

C

Candioro Theater—Theater and troupe supported by Jacinto Sagrada.

Celina (Celino) Plunado—Ariz Plunado's niece, though she maintains the pretense of being a boy. She is the elder twin daughter of Delfia Plunado and Hierro Fueres.

Cieloalta—Capital of Cadeleon.

Clara Odalis—Second daughter and youngest child of the Duke of Gavado, currently married to Count Zacarrio Odalis.

Cocuyo Helio—Twin brother of Enevir; currently in Prince Jacinto's entourage. Former Sagrada Academy student.

Crown Hill—a.k.a. Wadi Tel: "Guardian Hill" in Haldiim. Defenders' stronghold during Our Savior's battle against the demon lords.

D

Delfia Plunado—Ariz's sister and maid to Oasia Quemanor.

Donamillo Urracon—Scholar of Natural Law at Sagrada Academy. Used Fedeles Quemanor's body to house a Haldiim curse before taking possession of Fedeles entirely. Defeated by Kiram Kir-Zaki.

Dommian—Guard in the Quemanor household.

Dorio—Footman in the Quemanor household.

Duera—Painkiller and sedative derived from a common flower.

E

Elenna Ortez—Nineteen-year-old lady-in-waiting to Oasia Quemanor; also her cousin.

Elezar Grunito—Third son of the Earl and Lady Grunito of Anacleto. Member of the Hellions when he attended Sagrada Academy. Current lover and champion of Count Radulf.

Enevir Helio—Twin brother of Cocuyo Helio, member of Jacinto's entourage. Strong ties to Irabiim clans. Uses a cane. (Leg shattered during a horse race his third year at Sagrada Academy.)

Esfir Kir-Naham—Pharmacist; Querra's daughter and Mother Arezoo Kir-Naham's niece.

Espirdro—Atreau's third brother. Goes by the nickname of Spider. Currently owns the majority of the Fat Goose Tavern.

F

Faro Numes— Minister of the Royal Navy.

Fedeles Quemanor—Cousin to Javier Tornesal and Prince Sevanyo; Duke of Rauma.

Firaj—Fedeles's black gelding; formerly belonged to Kiram Kir-Zaki.

G

Gael Sagrada—Prince Sevanyo's third son. (Royal commander of the navy; lost at sea.)

Genimo Plunado—Dead; betrayed Fedeles. His crimes against Fedeles caused the Plunado family to be stripped of lands, wealth and titles.

H

Hadie Plunado—Ariz's mother, dead of illness complicated by starvation.

Hallowed Kings— A rotation of three souls who maintain the wards that protect the Shard of Heaven. Historically they have been Sagrada kings. The current three kings are: **Gachello** (born in 1191, crowned in 1229, died in 1255), **Yusto** (born in 1205, crowned in 1255, died in 1275) and **Leozar** (born in 1255, crowned in 1275, died in 1305).

Hellions—Band of outstanding and audacious students at the Sagrada Academy. Most infamous members of the group were Javier Tornesol, Elezar Grunito, Atreau Vediya and Kiram Kir-Zaki.

Heram—"Shunned one" in Haldiim. The state of having been formally shunned by society.

Hierro Fueres—Heir to the dukedom of Gavado.

Hilthorn Radulf (Skellan)—Ruler of Radulf County in Labara; powerful witch. Battled and destroyed a demon lord.

Hylanya Radulf—Younger sister of Count Radulf; also a powerful witch.

I

Inissa—Artist. Mistress to Prince Jacinto; was once Atreau's lover; now involved with Spider.

Irsea—Last Bahiim ancient who guarded the Circle of Wisteria. Murdered, but her spirit remains in the bodies of her familiars. Her murder remains unsolved.

Isandro Grunito—Dead; firstborn heir to the Earldom of Anacleto.

J

Jacinto Sagrada—Prince, poet, deadbeat. Fourth son of Sevanyo Sagrada. Atreau Vediya's former upperclassman and friend.

Javier Tornesal—Bahiim and guardian of a sacred shajdi. Former Duke of Rauma, Javier converted to the Bahiim religion (as Alizadeh's student) and was declared a heretic and excommunicated. He fled into exile with his lover, Kiram Kir-Zaki. He currently serves Count Radulf as his astrologer. He is Fedeles Quemanor's cousin, though many believe that the two are in fact half brothers (Javier's father having engaged in an affair with his own sister to father Fedeles).

Juleo Sagrada—Current king of Cadeleon. Born in 1275, crowned in 1305, very unwell.

K

Kaweh—Bitter but stimulating drink popular among the underclasses of Haldiim and picked up by Cadeleonian intellectuals.

Kili—Hylanya Radulf's champion.

Kiram Kir-Zaki—Haldiim genius from very wealthy and respected family of candymakers. Fled into exile with Javier but now is master mechanist in Count Radulf's court.

L

Labara—Protectorate nation of Cadeleon. Divided into four counties. Radulf County, the largest and most northerly, has recently broken away from Cadeleon to become fully independent. Famous for roses, witchcraft and their great love of butter.

Ladislo Bayezar—Nobleman. Attended Sagrada Academy. Former underclassman to Procopio Nolasar.

Leadro—Music instructor in the Quemanor household.

Lliro Vediya—Atreau's eldest brother; attached to the ministry of the navy. Heir to barony.

Lord Wonena—Supporter of the royal bishop. In conflict with Fedeles over upkeep of shared roadways.

M

Marisol Plunado—Ariz's niece and younger twin daughter of Delfia Plunado and Hierro Fueres.

Meztli—Mythical demon enthralled by the Brand of Obedience by Our Savior. Meztli harnessed the power of Crown Hill to forge his ruby shields.

Meztli's shield—A huge ward that protected Our Savior's forces during the Battle of the Shard of Heaven.

Miro Reollos—Oasia's first husband; lover of Atreau, killed by Elezar after attacking Atreau in a jealous rage.

Morisio Cavada—Atreau's school friend, from a merchant family. Scientifically minded, sails on the *Red Witch*.

Moteado—Ariz's old dappled stallion.

Mother Arezoo Kir-Naham—Owns a pharmacy in the Haldiim district of Cieloalta and is an Honored Mother (though she has no biological children). Aunt of Esfir; friend and sister-in-law to Querra Kir-Naham.

Muerate—Extremely deadly poison, leaves a black scar on the very few people who recover from its effects.

N

Narsi Hilario Lif-Tahm—Master physician in the Quemanor household, attached to Holy Father Timoteo.

Nillo—Acolyte serving Father Timoteo in the Quemanor household.

Nube—Atreau's gray stallion.

Nugalo Sagrada—Royal bishop, second-born prince of the realm.

Nunes Yago—Captain in the royal bishop's guard in the capital.

O

Oasia Quemanor—Wife of Fedeles, widow of Lord Reollos, eldest daughter of Duke of Gavado.

Old Roots—a.k.a. Old Routes. The tunnels dug by Haldiim as hiding places and means of escape from the city during the first purge, three hundred years ago. Most have collapsed, but some are still used by smugglers and black marketeers.

Ollivar Falario—Elezar's former underclassman; playwright and member of Prince Jacinto's entourage.

P

Paulino Fueres—Duke of Gavado.

Pepylla Dacio—Operator of the Green Door, loyal to Jacinto.

Peraloro River—River that divides the capital and runs east to the sea.

Procopio Nolasar—Courtier to Jacinto.

Posco—Holy Father who performed and sanctified Narsi's parents' marriage.

Q

Querra Kir-Naham—Cadeleonian convert to the Bahiim religion, widowed. In charge of kitchen gardens in the Quemanor household. Mother of Esfir.

R

Rafie Kir-Zaki—Haldiim physician and Narsi's mentor. Married to Alizadeh Lif-Moussu.

Red Stallion—Sword house where illegal and legal duels are held for cash prizes. Members are infamous for their brutality and immorality, but the public duels always draw huge crowds.

Remes—Royal bishop's heir and Sevanyo Sagrada's second son. Infatuated with Clara Odalis.

Rinza—Riquo's sister. Spindly knife market informant, employed by Atreau.

Riossa Grunito— Painter. Wife of Nestor Grunito, daughter of a city judge.

Riquo—Rinza's brother. Thief employed by Atreau.

S

Sabella Calies—Swordswoman. Friend to Atreau. Her uncle owns the Red Stallion sword house and she makes much of her living there, when she isn't being hired out as an assassin. Famous in Anacleto; romanticized versions of her biography have been made into a number of books and stage plays there.

Sacred Groves—Bahiim holy places comprised of rings of ancient trees or other plant life. These include Circle of Wisteria, Circle of Crooked Pine, Circle of Red Oak, Circle of the Willow Grove, and Circle of Long Kelp.

Sahalia Kir-Khu—Haldiim physician who attended Narsi's birth. She later relocated to the Salt Islands at Father Timoteo's prompting.

Salt Islands—Chain of volcanic islands south of Cadeleon. Famous for the Butterfly Temple and also hot springs.

Savior (the/Our)—Born Tormen Cadeleon. Warrior chief and mystic who battled the second invasion of demon lords alongside a coalition of other powerful warlords, witches, Bahiim, Old Gods and mystics. He sacrificed himself and four chosen followers in his final assault against the demons at the Peraloro River, where the spell he unleashed—the **Shroud of Stone**—resulted in the Shard of Heaven being formed. With the defeat of the demons and Cadeleon's death, a cult sprang up. They eventually grew into the Cadeleonian Holy Church.

Sevanyo Sagrada—Crown prince, born 1297.

Skellan—see "Hilthorn Radulf."

Sparanzo—Son of Fedeles and Oasia.

Suelita Estaban—Cryptographer, mathematician, Sabella's lover.

T

Tariq—Black cat that shares Narsi's rooms (name means "whisper" in Haldiim).

Timoteo—Holy Father, older brother of Elezar and Nestor Grunito.

Trueno—One of four Sagrada siblings who joined the Savior's army. He became the Savior's personal guard and was one of the four chosen for the assault against the demon lords' army. He is said to have been transformed into a giant eagle, and as such shielded the Savior from above and cleared his path to the heart of the army. Trueno's nephew became the first recognized king of the nation of Cadeleon.

U

Usane—Kingdom to the west of Cadeleon. Known for metalwork and closely guarded glassmaking techniques.

Usto—Gardener in the Quemanor household.

V

Victaro Irdad—Groom at Sagrada Academy, killed under mysterious circumstances.

Villo—Parrot belonging to Oasia Quemanor.

W

Waarihivu—Mythic sect of realm-traversing sorcerers at war with demons; used the Black Fire to destroy whole worlds. Most members of the sect were hunted down and killed or converted by the Bahiim.
Wadi Lif-Tahm—Narsi's mother; died when he was twenty-one. Lived as *heram* ("shunned one") until her mother died when Narsi was ten. Returned to the Haldiim community when he was twelve, though many elders refused to recognize her.

X

Xalvadar Sagrada—Prince Sevanyo's heir.
Xavan—Sailor; sometimes-informant for Atreau.

Y

Yah-muur—An Old God, known as the Fawn Goddess, also the Summer Doe. Said to take on a new body and shed her old horns every time she is slain. She was one of the four chosen to unleash the Shroud of Stone against the armies of the demon lords.
Yara Nur-Aud—Haldiim actress and part-time agent for Atreau.

Z

Zacarrio Odalis—Count. Elderly husband to Clara. Supporter of the royal bishop.

Also by Ginn Hale

Wicked Gentlemen
The Long Past and Other Stories
Maze-Born Trouble

The Cadeleonian Series
Lord of the White Hell Book One
Lord of the White Hell Book Two
Champion of the Scarlet Wolf Book One
Champion of the Scarlet Wolf Book Two

The Rifter Series (print)
The Shattered Gates
The Holy Road
His Sacred Bones

Novellas & Short Stories
Feral Machines—Tangle
Things Unseen and Deadly—Irregulars
Swift and the Black Dog—Charmed and Dangerous
Counterfeit Viscount—Devil Take Me
Shy Hunter—Queer Wolf
Blood Beneath the Throne—Icarus Magazine
Seed Stitch Solution—Once Upon A Fact
Treasured Island—Scourges of the Seas of Time (and Space)

The Rifter Series (ebook)
The Shattered Gates
Servants of the Crossed Arrows
Black Blades
Witches' Blood
The Holy Road
Broken Fortress
Enemies and Shadows
The Silent City
The Iron Temple
His Holy Bones

About the Author

Ginn Hale lives with her lovely wife in the Pacific Northwest. She spends the many cloudy days observing plants and fungi. She whiles away the rainy evenings writing fantasy and science-fiction featuring LGBTQ protagonists. Her first novel, *Wicked Gentlemen*, won the Spectrum Award for best novel. She is also a Lambda Literary Award finalist and Rainbow Award winner.

Her most recent publications include the *Lord of the White Hell*, *Champion of the Scarlet Wolf* and *The Rifter Trilogy*: *The Shattered Gates*, *The Holy Road*, *His Sacred Bones*.

She can be reached through her website: www.ginnhale.com as well as on Facebook and Twitter. Her Instagram account, however, is largely a collection of botanical photos...so, be warned.

Content Warning

Characters in this book encounter and fight against racism, sexism, homophobia, transphobia and ableism. When I have dramatized these conflicts, I've done my best not to make the scenes over-long or graphic. I've tried to avoid real-world insults and slurs, which may be triggering.

Several protagonists are survivors of sexual assault. However there are no scenes depicting sexual assault in the book. Passing reference is made by characters to abuse in their childhoods, however no scenes are dramatized. There is reference to a stillborn child.

Characters in the book deal with depression and thoughts of self-harm. Suicide is not depicted nor is it romanticized.

The violence that is depicted is largely in keeping with a fantasy adventure. There are sword fights and assassinations. Bloodshed, injuries and deaths are dramatized but I have shied away from gratuitous gore.

Above all, I've done my best to write a fun, inclusive story that I hope you enjoy.

—Ginn